The
CANDLEMAKER

THE
Kinkades

The
CANDLEMAKER

BESTSELLING AUTHOR
DR. REBECCA SHARP

LN
♡P

The Candlemaker
Paperback Edition
Copyright © 2025 by Dr. Rebecca Sharp

Love N. Books Press
An Imprint of Wolfpack Publishing
1707 E. Diana Street
Tampa, FL 33610

www.lovenbookspress.com

This book is a work of fiction. References to historical events, real people, or real places are used fictitiously. Any similarity to real persons, living or dead, is purely coincidental and not intended by the author.

All brand names and product names used in this book are trademarks, registered trademarks, or trade names of their respective holders. Wolfpack Publishing is not associated with any product or vendor in this book.

Cover design by Okay Creations LLC
Internal graphics design by Rachel Chaya Design
Edited by My Brother's Editor

The Candlemaker was originally self-published in 2024 by Dr. Rebecca Sharp.

Paperback ISBN 979-8-89567-161-0
Ebook ISBN 979-8-89567-160-3
LCCN 2025946488

The
CANDLEMAKER

CHAPTER I
CHANDLER

"Another one fell through?" I pulled off my blue-light blockers and stared at my VP, Tom Morgan.

At his grim expression, I let the glasses drop onto my desk, and I pinched the bridge of my nose, the familiar pound in my temples coming into focus. *Damn headaches.* I'd worked late into the night for as long as I could remember, but only in the last few years did my head start to pound by eight o'clock. I wasn't going to cut back my hours. Not a chance. So, I'd settled on the glasses to help with all the screen time, but I was starting to suspect even they weren't going to cut it for much longer.

"Afraid so." Tom grimaced and crossed his arms. "They didn't give a reason either, except to say they were no longer interested."

Just like the last five.

I was still getting used to his bald-and-beard look since he started shaving his receding hairline, but honestly, it took at least ten years off his sixty-eight. I wished it took off ten years from his impending retirement because I wasn't sure what the hell I was going to do when he retired from Collins Realty and Acquisitions. He'd been my right-hand man from the beginning. Older. Wiser. His name belonged on the front of the building just as much as mine, but he'd never allow it. Never wanted it. Never wanted anything but my success. So I refused to think about how I'd manage all of this when the man who'd been with me through everything left.

"What the hell is going on up there?" I muttered quietly, my jaw clenching. This deal—this *should've been a piece of cake* sale—was turning into a shitshow.

Nine months ago, I'd inherited an old, long-closed, former inn in the small town of Friendship, Maine, from my father. And I wanted nothing to do with it. *Not the inn nor the man who'd abandoned my mother.* So, I did what I did best. I slapped a for sale sign on it.

Collins Realty handled forty percent of the commercial real estate sales in Manhattan and almost sixty percent of commercial deals in Boston. The sale of some nondescript, historic inn in some seaside tourist town in Maine should've been a breeze. Instead, each of the five prospective buyers had fallen through with no clear reason why.

I'd never had so many prospective buyers evaporate so suddenly before, and it was starting to piss me off. I wanted nothing to do with my father—nothing to do with anything he decided to leave me—including this damn inn.

"It's like he's still fucking with me. Even in death," I growled. "Like he knows I'm going to destroy what he left behind."

My father was also in the real estate business up until a few years ago. His company, GC Holdings, had been strong while he'd been at the helm, but after he got sick and stepped down, things started to flounder, and I saw my opportunity. Over the last three years, I'd carefully begun acquiring properties I knew my half brother, Mark, was bidding on. I had more capital. More resources. It got easier and easier to pluck investments right out from under them, and GC Holdings started to flounder. And in a few weeks, it would more than flounder. It would sink.

"Or it's just not our usual inventory," Tom offered instead.

He wasn't wrong. Collins Realty dealt in billion-dollar buildings. High rises. Condos. Hotels. Not in ramshackle inns.

"There's still one offer on the table—"

"No," I clipped. "The Kinkade offer is too low."

"Maybe they'd up it if you talked—"

"And it's too messy," I cut him off, and it earned me the kind of chiding stare only Tom could dole out to the CEO. "Sorry," I muttered.

When my *dear* old dad passed, the deed to this inn was given to my younger half brother, Mark—the oldest child from his current marriage. A legal oversight because I'd done my damnedest to distance myself from Geoff Collins. However, a closer inspection of Geoff's will indicated the inn was supposed to go to his oldest son—not from his current marriage. Not from any marriage. Oldest son, period. Which was technically me. *In name fucking only.*

But in the lag time between Mark thinking the inn belonged to him and realizing it was willed to me, Mark sold it to a local family in Friendship. Kinkade. I couldn't even remember the guy's first name. So, there was a whole legal shit show because the property was never Mark's to sell. Anyway, once Collins Realty listed it for sale again, Kinkade made a second offer. I admired the perseverance, but the offer was too low, and the whole thing was too fucking muddled to sell it back to them.

"All right." Tom sighed, knowing when he'd hit that stone wall of stubbornness in me. "I'll drive up next week and see—"

"No." I sat back in my chair, glancing out the windows lining my corner office for the first time all day. Below, Copley Square was lit up for the night, a crowd of people all dressed to the nines collected under the red awning at the Fairmont hotel across the street. A wedding, it looked like. *How much of my life have I spent watching other people live outside my window?*

I shook off the thought and added my signature to the document I'd been reviewing when Tom came in and sent it off, sealing my acquisition of a multi-unit property in Boston that would've promised salvation for GC Holdings. But in my hands, it spelled their ruin.

I looked up at Tom and declared, "I'll go. I just signed the paperwork for the Stocker building. I need you to finish up the acquisition."

I'd tried to give Tom this office when we opened our New England headquarters, but he wouldn't even consider it. Something about how if I didn't have windows, I'd never get any sun. At that point, I knew any attempt to argue would only result in a conversation we'd had countless times before, and one I didn't want to have again. I respected the hell out of Tom

Morgan, but only my business was his business, not my lack of work-life balance or personal life.

"Are you sure?"

"Yeah," I interrupted, my jaw clenching. "I'll stop and visit Mom."

That instantly appeased him because he visited her more than I did. Another tenuous conversation we'd had multiple times.

"She'll be happy to see you."

For all the wrong reasons. A sharp pain pinched my chest, making me clear my throat. "Yeah."

Mom and Tom were the only two people I really cared about and the only two people who cared about me. Well, it was more like one of them these days...

"And you're sure about the Stocker deal?"

I narrowed my eyes on him. "Why wouldn't I be?"

He stared at me for a long moment, finally accepting that I was going to make him spell it out. "Because it will mean the end of GC Holdings."

My jaw twitched. "That's the whole point."

"Is it?"

I ignored his deeper intonation. "GC Holdings will go under, and I'll buy what's left of it for more than anyone else, but still at much less than what it's worth now." *And the last of my father's legacy would be gone.*

Tom cleared his throat. "And the fact that GC is based in New York?"

"We have an office there. It will expand," I said nonchalantly. "I'll move there for a few years until everything is incorporated."

"A few years..." He trailed off and shook his head, his distress obvious.

Mom was up here, living in Maine. My visits to her

were already too infrequent for Tom's liking, and New York would only give me another excuse to stay away.

He let out a deep exhale. "I hope this is really what you want, Chandler."

"It is." I dared him to question me again.

Instead, he gave me a sad smile and a nod, and somehow, that managed to feel even worse. It was times like these, when our conversations strayed from business, that I really saw his age and the toll this job took. And his worry about what it was taking from me.

"You should go home. It's late," I said gruffly and rubbed along the side of my jaw.

"And what about you?"

I had a good thirty years on him, not to mention the stamina, the drive, and the buried resentment to keep me going.

"I'm fine."

"Did you even eat dinner?"

I didn't even know what time it was. I sure as hell hadn't stopped when it was time to eat.

"I'm fine, Tom," I said firmly and glanced at the door.

"I promised her I'd look out for you," he reminded me with a low, resolute voice.

My jaw locked tight. That was back when Mom was here—physically and mentally—and saw the work-obsessed path I'd been heading down. She was the only one who had the pull to get me to step back and take a break. And she hadn't been able to do that in five years since the dementia set in. Now, she hardly remembered who I was. Which, ironically, was preferable to the alternative—*when she thought I was my father*.

That was why my visits had become less frequent.

Nothing like wanting to see one of the few people I loved only for her to mistake me for the singular man I hated.

"Good night, Tom."

"Do you want me to arrange transportation—"

"No." I shook my head. "I'll drive."

His chin dipped, and he gave me one last look—the kind that spoke volumes—before letting himself out.

I swiped open my iPad and typed in the address of the inn, watching the pin drop on the coastal stretch of Friendship. It was a prime location—an ideal spot for an inn or any business, really. My eyes narrowed. There was a business name tagged at the spot. *The Lamplight Inn.* I grunted. This Kinkade fellow must've claimed his business before the property reverted back to me. Another tap brought up the image of the business—an artist's rendering of the inn—and refocused the map, with several other businesses highlighted nearby.

The Maine Squeeze.

The Friendship Lighthouse.

The Kinkade Gallery.

Maine Stems.

The Candle Cabin.

How fucking quaint. My jaw tightened, and I closed the screen. If there was one thing I'd learned in this industry, it was that there was no coincidence when buyers repeatedly walked away from a deal. Something questionable was going on in the not-so-quaint seaside town of Friendship—something that was scaring away every chance I had to remove all ties to my fuck-up of a father. And I was going to find out what.

"Tell Scott the deal was fifteen million. He knew that walking into the building, and I'm sure as hell not going to let him try to talk me down from it now," I barked to my assistant, Ashley, her call filtering through the speakers in my car. "If he's not interested at the agreed price, there are a dozen other developers who will be."

"Will do, Mr. Collins."

"Thanks." My voice rasped a little just before we hung up, and I made a mental note to message Tom to buy Ashley's lunch today for my boorish behavior.

I hadn't slept more than a few hours last night—all of them on the couch in my office. That wasn't an uncommon occurrence. I'd usually head down to the gym in the basement, work out, shower, and then just change into one of the dozen spare suits I kept in my closet there for this exact reason. Except that what I was doing today *was* uncommon.

So, it wasn't the minimal sleep or the lack of caffeine that sent my attitude squarely to the center of being an asshole. It was this. Having to deal with this fucking inn and whatever the hell ties it had to my father.

I flipped my blinker and made a hard turn onto Maine Street. "Jesus—" Before I hardly hit the brake, my Tesla jolted to a halt, alarms blaring to alert me to the person in the crosswalk.

I hadn't hit her, but for some reason, my hands

tightened harder on the steering wheel rather than relaxed when I met her surprised stare. Not met. My windows were tinted so she couldn't see me, but damn, could I see her.

It was breezy outside because it blew strands of her honey-blonde hair in front of her face, and they caught on a pair of the fullest lips I'd ever seen. Almost too full, I would say, if they weren't balanced out by her big brown eyes.

Damn.

I didn't have time for this, I chided myself, pressing back in my seat and waving her on like she was wasting my time.

I drove on, slightly slower now, down the central street in Friendship, the sides of it rimmed by seaside shops that would make the picture-perfect postcard. Mom loved it up here. Kennebunkport. Ogunquit. She loved the slow coasts where it wasn't too hot or too crowded. It was the reason I'd moved her to Edgewood Estate when it became clear she couldn't live on her own.

The private, expensive assisted-living facility was about an hour inland from here. When I'd picked it, I thought it would make for easy day trips out to the beaches and lighthouses she loved.

That was before the dementia got so bad that she rarely remembered who I was.

Again, the Tesla slowed on its own when I got too close to a pickup truck moseying through town.

"Seriously?" I muttered under my breath, trying to peek around the side of the vehicle. "Not all of us have nowhere to be."

The GPS dot ticked painfully closer to my destination. I was surprised the car even registered a speed rather than a picture of a snail on the screen. Letting out a drawn exhale, I glanced in the rearview mirror, wondering if the woman I'd almost hit was catching up to me.

What the hell did that matter?

The corner of my eye caught on a bright orange sign. *The Maine Squeeze.* But it was the coffee menu stuck to the window that caught my attention. I was already in a shit mood. If I was going to find out what the hell was going on with this property, I shouldn't do it without caffeine in my system.

I swung into a spot right out front, and the thought struck me that I couldn't remember the last time I'd parked on the street—parked, period. I rarely drove myself in Boston. Even for short distances, I used a driver so I could take calls and work on my laptop in the back seat. There was too much to do. And it was easier to not think about what I was missing if I never looked.

Shutting off the car, I flipped down my visor, ran my fingers through my hair, and saw what I imagined the woman from the road seeing—*an out-of-town asshole.*

"Dammit," I grunted and tugged my tie loose and pulled it through my collar. Tossing it onto the passenger seat, I unbuttoned my collar and then reached for the cuffs of my sleeves, rolling them to my elbows.

I should've already thought this through. Appearance—perception—was everything. Walking into town as the callous real estate investor who was going to sell some historic landmark to the highest bidder wasn't going to make me any friends—not that I wanted friends, but enemies wouldn't share information. And information was what I needed.

I got out of the car, and it locked itself behind me.

The bell above the entry into the Maine Squeeze toned off-key as I entered, alerting the barista behind the counter to my presence.

The charming smile that graced my face was staged, just like the rest of me. Like the buildings I sold, I knew how to look and what to say to get people to buy into me—*into the person I wanted them to see.*

"Welcome to the Maine Squeeze," the barista said cheerfully over her shoulder. She was in the middle of cleaning the espresso machine. "We'll be right with you."

We—

"Hi. Welcome," another woman said as she appeared from the back, a bag of cups in her arms. When she looked up, I did a double-take, my keys falling from my hand onto the floor.

It was the woman from the crosswalk. Except it wasn't.

Her hair was styled differently—braided down either side of her head—and she had big glasses on, and her clothes were now a Maine Squeeze uniform, but it was her. *It had to be her, right?*

I swiped up my keys, and when I straightened, she regarded me with a pleasant, ignorant smile.

Tinted windows, I reminded myself.

"Welcome to the Maine Squeeze. What can I get for you?"

My eyes flicked to her nametag. Lou.

"Iced Americano."

"Small or large?" Her smile was constant.

"Large."

She plucked a cup from the stack and noted my order in marker. "Name?"

"Col—Chandler."

Her brows perked up, and I knew the reason.

"Like from *Friends*," I grumbled, learning long ago it was easier to get the association out from the start and move on. Though it was easiest to avoid the conversation all altogether by introducing myself as Mr. Collins.

Unfortunately, that didn't fit with this version of myself. Or my goal to conceal who I was from these people.

"Yes, right," she said and nodded, almost like Mr. Bing hadn't been her first thought. "I love that show."

So did my mother.

"A classic," I offered as she passed the cup to her counterpart at the espresso machine.

"Did you guys just open for the day?" I wondered casually.

I didn't check the schedule on the door because the sign said open, but that was the only way to explain how she was crossing the street only a few minutes ago.

"Oh no," she gushed. "We've been here since five this morning, but you're a little early for the regular crowd."

Since five—

"Anything else? We've got some amazing blueberry muffins this morning."

"I...sure," I fumbled and pinched the bridge of my nose when she went to grab the pastry.

What the hell was this place? The Twilight Zone?

She—Lou—was the woman in the road. I knew she was. I hadn't looked at a woman and had it affect me like that in...a long time. But if she had been here since five...

The bell clanged again, the flat sound interrupting my thoughts.

And my reality shifted again—which was far too many fucking times before eight a.m. and coffee.

The woman from the crosswalk—windswept waves, flushed cheeks, and loose blue pants—breezed into the coffee shop, the whole atmosphere altering with her presence.

There were two of them.

My exhale barreled out of my chest.

I wasn't going crazy. They were twins. One in the crosswalk and one in the coffee shop.

"Hey, sis," Lou called to the woman I'd almost hit. "I have your usual on the counter."

"Great. I need it this morning after—" She broke off when she saw me. There was a blip of uncertainty—of questionable recognition—before it disappeared, and she smiled wide like her sister.

"Hi, I'm Frankie." She strode right up to me and extended a tiny but brash hand, her head tipped almost all the way back to meet my eyes. "You must be new to Friendship."

"Frankie—" her sister started.

"Just visiting," I replied and took her hand. Warm, soft, small...and firm. Damn, this woman reeked of small but mighty.

"For friends, family, or work?" she probed without a filter.

"Family," I replied easily and then took my coffee and muffin from her twin sister's hand.

"Oh, you got a blueberry muffin. Those are Lou's

favorite," she said, her eyes twinkling in a way that was less like stars and more like the fuse on a stick of dynamite.

"Makes sense she recommended it then."

"Wow." The way her mouth moved over that word was fucking sinful—and not what I should be thinking about right now. "She must really like you to offer up one of her favorites."

Lou blushed, then stammered, and then channeled her focus into wiping off the counter no one had dirtied. Meanwhile, her twin sauntered over to the register and picked up her drink like she owned the damn place.

The two of them were night and day. Lou, the serenity of the moon, and her—Frankie—the bright flash of the sun. Or maybe more like the violent explosion of a star.

"How long are you in town for, Mr...."

"Just a few days." I took a bite of the muffin and addressed Lou so I could avoid sharing my name—or anything else about me. "This is amazing," I told her. "Thank you."

She avoided my eyes. "You're welcome."

"Are you familiar with Friendship at all? My sister has some other great recommendations for places around town, don't you, Lou?" the bold one hinted and then wrapped her lips around the straw of her coffee.

I gritted my teeth, feeling my dick start to thicken. Jesus Christ, maybe there was some brand of insanity infused into the air.

"Yes. Well, a few, but—"

"A few?" She tsked. "My sister is too humble. She knows everything there is to know about things to do and sights to see in Friendship. She wants to go into hospitality, so just ignore her protests. She'd love nothing more than to be your local guide."

"Frankie," Lou hissed, and it was only because my head swiveled a half-second too slowly that I caught the quick wink from the outspoken twin.

I might be a workaholic and a social hermit, but I knew when I was being set up.

But...if Lou knew everything there was to know about this town, maybe she had an idea why the hell no one was buying my goddamn inn.

I gave Lou my best charming smile. "Well, if you have the time, I'd love a private tour." Thank God for muscle memory, though I was sure some dust fell from the corners of my mouth with how infrequently it tipped up like this.

Lou's blush deepened, and it was adorable. Beautiful, even. But for some reason, all I wondered was if her sister blushed the same. *No,* was my instinct. It would take much more to bring color to Frankie's cheeks, and the idea of that challenge was one I couldn't get tangled up in.

"Of course," Lou stammered and returned a hesitant smile.

"She's off tomorrow," Frankie said, a coy grin teasing her full lips around her straw.

"Is there anything else you need, Frankie?" Lou stared at her sister, and neither of us missed the edge in her tone.

"Nope." The *p* popped out of those full lips. "I left candles for you and Kit, if you could bring them to the gallery for him when you go later." She looked at me and explained, "I have a candle shop a few blocks down if you need any souvenir ideas. Lou can show you where it is tomorrow."

"Bye, Frankie." Lou's eyes flicked to the door.

"Talk to you later." She bit into her lip to control her smile, and damn, the sight was intoxicating. I barely managed to drag my eyes from her lips when she tipped her head toward me. "Pleasure meeting you."

She didn't even care that she didn't know my name.

And I shouldn't care that she didn't care.

But for some damn reason, I did.

CHAPTER 2
FRANKIE

"Morning, Bea," I called over the familiar bell.

"All ready for you." The newest barista at the Maine Squeeze dumped a scoop of ice into my coffee. Like Lou, she had big glasses resting on her nose and her dark-brown hair braided back along either side of her head.

"Wow, Lou trained you well." The compliment brought a huge smile to her face.

It was more than training. My twin sister was a model of dedication and loyalty and compassion and care and everything. Lou is a model for everything. Meanwhile, I tended to be nothing but trouble.

It was fine. I'd long embraced stereotypical Frankie. The brash prankster. Unwavering matchmaker. Outspoken firecracker. I'd strengthened her. Nourished her. Loved her. *Not that I had much of a choice.* When you're a twin—an identical twin—the tendency for comparison is weighted, and even the smallest differences in personality become exaggerated just to differ-entiate you.

Case-in-point. My cousin, Nox, would tease us when we were younger that Lou and I were *double, double, toil, and trouble*. The Kinkade twins, hard-working Elouise and jokester Francesca.

Bea snapped the lid on my coffee and handed it to me. "Tourists are great, but regulars are our main squeeze," she said with a wink.

I chuckled. "Sounds like Lou."

There was nothing exaggerated about my sister, though. She was soft-spoken, honest to a fault, kind, and the perfect role model for Bea, which is why I was happy to see it was more than barista training that Bea was learning from her.

I took a big sip of the iced coffee and sighed. "Perfect."

"Thanks." She beamed. "Busy day?"

"So busy," I gushed and handed her my credit card. "I'm finishing up a huge order for Maine Stems. I created a seaside scent to go with their 'beach blooms' summer bouquet sale."

"Oh, I didn't know that. I just ordered one of those for my mom. She'll be so excited to get one of your candles with it." She rang up my drink and handed my card back to me.

"It was a last-minute thing, but it's hard to say no to family."

Main Stems was a flower delivery startup founded by my cousin, Max Hamilton—Nox's older brother—about seven years ago. It didn't take long for his idea to blow up. Forgot an anniversary? A birthday? Main Stems delivered a custom bouquet within two hours.

Need to celebrate a new promotion? Send mourning flowers? Seasonal or custom bouquets delivered on demand. It was like Amazon, but for flowers. And now Max was expanding his business into events. It was great for him—and good for me—because what went better with flowers than a handcrafted candle?

"Speaking of"—I tipped forward on the counter—"that guy from yesterday…" The one who was far too handsome and far too presumptuous to invade my dreams like he had last night. Especially when he was perfect for Lou.

Fitted gray pants. Crisp white shirt. Expertly *coiffed* dark hair. Sure, he might've unbuttoned his collar and rolled up his sleeves, but even those rolls were perfect. As though even his relaxation had rules.

Which was why I'd tried to set him up with my sister. He was clearly a big-city workaholic, and though Friendship was a small town, Lou worked all the time—three jobs while she saved up for her dream—and hardly left any time for herself to relax. Obviously, they could be each other's distractions. Even if only for a few days.

It was a perfect plan.

As perfect as his firm lips and square-cut jaw and the fit of his shirt to his muscular shoulders. I shivered at the memory. Not what I should be thinking about. *Again.* But even I wasn't spared from my own troublemaking thoughts, which went immediately to his deep, coal-black stare as soon as my eyes shut to take another sip of my coffee. The intensity. The energy. His stare was as subtle and as potent as smoke—appropriate for a man whose body was pure fire.

Bea blushed and blurted out. "He was so hot."

A *workahottie* I'd dubbed him since I hadn't wasted any precious time yesterday learning his name. I didn't need his name—didn't want it. He was for Lou.

"Yeah," I agreed and took another big gulp of my drink, hearing the embarrassing way my voice turned husky.

We get it, Frankie, he's hot. Like you've never seen a hot guy before.

Not one who looked at me the way he did.

Not true.

Fine. Not one whose look made me feel...made me ache...the way his did.

"Bea." I cleared my throat and the internal dialogue from my mind. "Do you know if Lou—"

The bell above the door clanged like shots fired.

"Frankie."

I spun and whipped a smile to my face. *Speaking of my twin.* "Hey! What are you doing here? It's your day off." *And you're supposed to be giving Mr. Workahottie a tour.*

"Can you give us a minute, Bea?" Lou looked past my shoulder at the other girl, who read her tone like I did. *It wasn't a question.*

"Sure," Bea chirped and disappeared.

"What's up?" I asked casually like I couldn't tell she was upset with me.

Lou shrugged her bag higher on her shoulder and strode over to me. "I shouldn't be here. I should be prepping for Kit's next show, but instead, I'm having to give out a *tour* of Friendship."

A sound of glee burst from my lips—one that

deflated quickly when it was pierced by the daggers in her eyes.

"A tour of Friendship to the man who upped the town's hotness level by a factor of ten," I countered, but she didn't budge. "Seriously, Lou?"

"*Seriously?*" She gaped. "Just because everything is a *joke* to you doesn't mean that's what the rest of us want—or want to be a part of."

I flinched, feeling an unexpected pain in the center of my chest. Lou never got angry. Annoyed? Sometimes. Frustrated? Rarely. But angry? Never. And to say something like that...

"Wow, Lou."

Remorse instantly washed over her features, and she pulled me in for a bear hug. "I'm so sorry, Frankie. I didn't mean—"

"It's okay," I interrupted and hugged her back, feeling the slight tremor that went through her. "Why are you really upset?" I asked softly, able to read her like she did me. *Better than anyone.* And there had to be something wounding my sister to the core for her to lash out at me like that.

"There's another offer on the inn." The hollowness to her voice was like a knife to my gut.

Three jobs. A seven-day work week. No time to relax. It was all for the old Lamplight Inn. Her dream. And the way that dream had been yo-yo'd in and out of my sister's grasp was the very definition of cruel.

To believe our family had purchased it only for some insane legal snafu to take it away and put it in the hands of one *Mr. Collins*—a man who had more wealth and properties and business than was easily fathomable, yet couldn't bring himself to sell an old, dead inn for *a little* less profit to the one person who would put her heart and soul into bringing it back to life.

There weren't many people I harbored ill will toward, but the CEO of the Collins Corporation was one of the few. If I ever met the cold-hearted capitalist, I wouldn't shake his hand, I would strangle him. *And no, that wasn't a joke.*

Lou deserved for things to come easy—to work out perfectly. Instead, it was my business that came together in the blink of an eye and flourished with every passing year. All the while my perfect sister toiled and toiled and toiled...and fate chose to smile on trouble.

"It'll be okay, Lou."

"It's a cash offer. Ten percent above mine," she said softly. We had a childhood friend, Adele, who worked for the law firm representing the current owner of the inn. She passed along any information she received about potential buyers, wanting Lou to know what she was up against.

But it wasn't exactly how we used the information.

"It doesn't matter." I set my coffee on the counter and gripped her shoulders, giving her a little shake to look at me. Watery amber eyes met mine. "I'll handle it," I promised her.

Natural comparisons existed between twins, but this was the reason I exaggerated my personality. I didn't want my sister to fade into the background. Something she would easily and probably happily do if no one stopped her.

My earliest memories were of Lou secluding herself to play alone in our room. Meanwhile, I was the one knocking on the door, asking the proverbial, *do you want to build a snowman?* Time and trial and error proved that the only thing that brought her out of her shell was her desire to protect me. If I wanted to be loud, she'd speak up to temper me. If I wanted to do something reckless, she'd come along to try and stop me.

So, my extroverted nature became outspoken and eccentric because it was the only way to engage her. Because my sister was too good of a person for the world to not know her.

"Not this time. Adele said the buyer—Mr. Fairfax—wants to demolish the inn and build condos..." Lou shook her head and then shook off my hold, quickly wiping all traces of tears away.

I stilled. First, because what the hell was it with the world that everyone just wanted to tear down everything that was old? Did no one want to preserve anything anymore? Did no one feel pride and satisfaction in taking what was tattered and forgotten and building it back up? Giving it a fresh purpose?

And second, because I now realized why she was so upset. Not because the offer was so much higher than hers, but because this Mr. Fairfax had no interest in the inn...and therefore wouldn't care if it was haunted.

Yes, the old Lamplight Inn was haunted. At least, that was what every local in Friendship would tell any outsider who was asking.

It wasn't a lie...but neither was it the whole truth.

"I'll look into it." I kept my voice calm, knowing if overthinking were an Olympic sport, Lou would take the gold.

"Frankie, he won't care—"

"You don't know what he will care about," I interrupted, shooting her a hard stare. "So let me do what I do best."

"Meddle?" she grumbled, but there was a hint of a smile on her lips.

"Yup." I swiped my coffee from the counter and took a drink.

The town of Friendship was family. They'd known my mother, Ailene, my grandmother, Gigi, and my uncle, George, since they'd moved here. Supported Mom when she opened Stonebar Farms as a single mom of two teen boys and infant twins. They'd watched us grow, and we grew with them.

And there was not a single person in town who wanted the old inn—an iconic staple on Maine Street— to be sold to anyone other than my sister.

Which is why they would swear until the cows came home that the inn was haunted. And it was.

By me.

"Crap, he's here." Lou straightened her spine and rolled her shoulders back. "Do I look okay? Ugh, I'm—"

"You look perfect," I said and picked up my coffee. "I know your mind has a million things weighing on it, but maybe an afternoon stroll around town with a hot stranger could be a good thing?" My voice lifted, begging her to agree.

"He's not for me, Frankie." She was annoyingly certain.

"You gave him one of your favorite muffins—"

"*Because it's my job,*" she insisted with a half-laugh.

Fair. "Well, you only just met him. You should give him a chance because you can't know—"

"If I can't know, then why can't he be for you?"

"Me?" I rocked back. The notion shouldn't have the

power to make the ground tilt under my feet, but it did. The idea that his stare made me hot and achy was for a reason. That his smile and those firm lips were meant to be mine—no. *Absolutely not. Mr. Workahottie wasn't for me.* "No, he's way too gorgeous and clearly too much of a good guy," I said cheekily, trying to bring a smile to her face before she walked out of here. "Obviously, whoever is meant for me is going to be one-thousand-percent bad to the bone and wrong for me because that's how I roll."

Lou sighed and headed for the door, pausing just before she walked out. "So, then his name means nothing?"

I frowned and felt my brow furrow. "What do you mean?"

She blinked, and a dust of color rose in her cheeks. "Frankie...his name is Chandler."

WHAT WAS IN A NAME? NOTHING. HIS NAME meant nothing. It was just a name like any other. No reason to dwell on it. And more reason than ever to not dream of him. Not how soft his hair might feel. Not how his lips might taste. And definitely not how hard his muscles were.

"Oww—" I hissed and doubled over, clutching the knee that I'd just rammed into the corner of my desk.

Biting back a curse, I limped around and grabbed the first pen in sight from the clear jam jar on my desk that had served as a pen holder for the last three years.

Instantly, my eyes focused on the worn label sticking out of the glass. The edges curled slightly, but the blue ink in the center hadn't faded in the slightest.

Chandler.

Gigi's squiggly handwriting had never looked so clear. *So accusatory*.

"Frankie?"

Shit. I fumbled the pen in my fingers, managing to catch it before it fell as my head snapped up, meeting my oldest brother Jamie's curious stare as he brushed a strand of red hair back from his forehead.

"Yeah?" I croaked and straightened.

"You okay?"

"Yeah." I gave him a pained smile. "Just banged my knee on the desk." *Not false*.

"Should I add bumpers to it?" Jamie teased with a chuckle.

He'd made the desk for me almost two years ago now. Jamie was an expert carpenter and craftsman and had his own business making custom furniture in one of the old, restored barns on Mom's property.

I stuck my tongue out at him and then said, "The last boxes of candles for Max are in the back room." I pointed over my shoulder to where a curtain covered the doorway into my workspace.

This cabin—the Candle Cabin—was my sanctuary. I'd bought it four years ago with the earnings from selling my candles at the Stonebar Farms store. Mom would've let me sell there forever, and I still sold candles there, but I wanted my own space. I might be a lot of things—many of them lighthearted and playful—but not when it came to my business. Not when it came to my candles.

Jamie hesitated, and I was sure he was going to ask something else, but then he strode to the back room, the curtain whooshing behind him and giving me a moment alone.

The front part of the building housed my shop, open for a few hours in the afternoon most days to customers, and the back was my workshop. I spent my morning hours there in peace and solitude, testing and sampling new scents as well as making candles for any larger orders. *Like this*.

"Is Max okay?" I called to him.

Max was supposed to be the one stopping by to pick up the second batch of five hundred candles today, not Jamie.

While I waited for his answer, I caught sight of the offending label again. Gritting my teeth, I reached for the jar and plucked the slip out of it, yanked open the bottom drawer of my desk where I shoved all the things I didn't want to think about, dropped it inside, and closed the drawer tight.

I heard my brother grunt and the box shuffle, and then he appeared through the curtain, all of him tense as he strode through my store with the last box of candles that easily weighed about sixty pounds.

A few seconds later, he came back inside, his arms banded over his chest. "Yeah, Max is fine. He said something was going on with his friend, so he asked me to bring these up."

"Have you talked to Lou?" he called, and then I heard his grunt and the shuffling of the box.

"This morning. Why?" I asked cautiously when he returned and rested the box on my desk.

"Kit told me there was another offer on the table."

I stilled and then nodded, choosing my next words carefully because if there was anyone who would realize when one of my *plans was* afoot, it was Jamie Kinkade.

Jamie went beyond older brother material. My and Lou's dad left Mom when he learned she was pregnant and that he wasn't going to get any of the Stonebar fortune, and from the moment he walked away, Jamie had stepped up. He'd been a teenager when we were born, so it was hard to say that he had even really been an older brother—or technically a half brother—even though that was what he was.

Jamie had raised us. Start to finish. The strength of our moral compass. The steadiness of our character. Mom...Mom was incredible. But Jamie...he was both brother and father. Guardian and friend. Between him and Mom—who they called *CI-Ailene* for a reason—there was no secret that went uncovered.

Well, except for the one time I'd listed Jamie's cottage on a vacation rental website without him realizing it. I was desperate to find someone for him—to find some happiness for him. *And a little reprieve from his overbearing concern for me.* Thankfully, that worked out better than I could've ever imagined. The woman, Violet, who'd rented his cabin was now his wife.

"Yeah, she mentioned that." I kept my eyes focused on the sheet of notepaper I'd been doodling on, trying to perfect a scent that had eluded me for weeks.

"Someone who wants to tear it down."

"Mm-hmm," I hummed, my heart rate starting to pick up.

"Frankie..."

"Jamie..." I returned his drawn-out tone.

He came right up to the desk and lowered his voice. "Don't think I don't know where the rumors around town are coming from."

"Rumors?" I stared at him blankly. "You know I'm not one for gossip."

"Francesca."

Full name meant full trouble.

"What?" I didn't blink. Didn't flinch.

"Rumors are one thing, but trespassing is a crime."

"It absolutely is, and I would never say it wasn't," I said staunchly.

Jamie's nostrils flared. I swore I was the only person in his life who gave those things a workout.

"Why are we talking about trespassing?" And how did my brother seem to know what I might need to do before I'd even decided on a plan?

"In case someone got an idea in their head to make those rumors about the inn seem a little more real."

"And how could someone make a *ghost* seem real?" I chuckled like the band around my chest wasn't tightening.

"I'm serious, Frankie." His frown deepened. "It's one thing when it's us, but these people...Christ, I can't believe I'm having to say this, but please, promise me you won't trespass on the inn's property."

My mouth opened and shut once, and then he started to growl.

Good grief.

"I promise I won't ghost anyone," I said, even as my inner five-year-old crossed one ankle over the other like I could believe that made it okay to tell a lie.

Jamie let out an audible exhale, shaking his head as though he knew I was going to find some way around it

—some *other* way to get what I wanted. When this was all over—when Lou finally had her inn—he'd see that the ends justified my means.

"He's coming to town, Frankie."

"Who? The buyer?" I would've assumed he was already here by now, which is why I didn't have a lot of time.

"No. Collins."

I stilled.

"You don't get that many zeros attached to your net worth without having an equal number of capable brain cells. And for someone who built an empire selling property, he's going to recognize pretty quickly that something is off," Jamie warned with a low voice.

I shifted my weight and muttered, "I make candles, Jamie. Not control the spiritual realm."

"The only thing worse for Lou than losing the inn will be if something happens to you in the process."

Wrong, I wanted to shout, but Jamie was as stubborn as the sea was deep. Lou had wandered for so long —been unsure of what she wanted to do with her life for *so* long. And when she finally found her passion— thinking that she was going to manage the Lamplight Inn—it changed everything. I saw it. *I felt it.* Call it intuition. Call it instinct. Hell, call it *a twin thing.* But my sister needed this, and I would happily incur a little risk to make it happen.

I stood unmoving as his heavy footsteps carried him out of my store, but it wasn't until the door shut that I allowed my shoulders to drop and my chest to exhale.

"Crap," I muttered and pinched the bridge of my nose.

I needed cinnamon.

I blew through the curtain barrier and went to the far corner where I mixed and tested oils for new fragrances. I opened the glass cabinet on top of the counter, pulling out vial after vial of various scents and feeling a little like the sea witch in The *Little Mermaid* as I picked and plucked without even needing to read the tags.

Uncapping the bottle of cinnamon oil, I dabbed some on my wrist and then rubbed it on my temples. *Focus.* Cinnamon helps with concentration, and I was going to need it in spades if I was going to come up with a foolproof plan to put Lou back in the running.

This whole *haunted* thing started—as most of my plans do—as a joke. After months of legal shenanigans, we got word the inn was going to be listed again for sale. By then, we knew a little more about its rightful owner, the billionaire Mr. Collins. Real estate mogul. Ruthless. A classic cold-hearted capitalist. And Lou felt... hopeless.

She'd never be able to compete with the kinds of offers Collins would get from his circle of investors. Word on the street was his commercial properties were offered privately to a select group of his associates first before they went on the market. Whether that was true or not, the inn made it onto the market, and Lou about had a panic attack.

So, I did what I always do. I promised my sister I'd fix it, and when she said there was nothing I could do, I told her if it came down to it, I would personally haunt the old rundown building to make sure no one wanted to buy it.

Well, it came down to it.

Honestly, it didn't take much—hadn't taken much.

The first couple of buyers who'd come up to see the property...all I'd had to do was plant a few well-placed rumors about betrayal and death of Revolutionary War spies to send them running.

The last two had been more hands-on. There'd been a pretend séance as they'd arrived to look at the building. Some sneaking around to bang windows, and a few yards of fishing line to make doors slam shut. In my opinion, it was all very amateur, but somehow, it worked.

But this time...if this Mr. Fairfax wanted to tear the building down, who knew if he'd even want to take a look at the property?

If he did, well, I'd just received my first official Jamie warning.

Trespassing was illegal.

I understood that, *but* the inn was abandoned. Was it really trespassing if no one lived in or cared about the property? How many times had he and Kit snuck into the inn on a dare back when they were in school?

But if he didn't want to see the building, then I'd have to find some way to talk to him myself—convince him about the ghosts.

Or there was the alternative. Confront Mr. Collins.

My heart tripped. I wasn't usually the one to back down from a challenge or confrontation. I'd been the spokesperson for myself and my sister for our entire lives. I would say something if someone in our class was teasing or bullying Lou for being quiet. I would be the one to call if we needed to make reservations for dinner or a spa day. And I would be the one to stand up to our brothers—mostly Jamie—if they were being too over-bearing.

But to go toe-to-toe with the man standing between Lou and her dream. My stomach tightened. *What if I didn't make it better? What if I couldn't fix it?*

There was no going back once Collins knew who I was.

The wood chime at the entrance to my store dinged at the arrival of a customer, and I jumped in surprise. *Crap.* My eyes darted to the vial I'd just tipped onto the counter. *Cinnamon everywhere. Double crap.* I righted the glass as I slid off the stool and called, "Coming!"

Whoever it was didn't respond. Most likely a new customer, since if it were family or someone from Friendship, they would've yelled back to me.

I grabbed a fistful of paper towels, piling them over the oil spill, and quickly mopped it up. There was no saving my hands though. They were covered in the scent, and it would take days to completely wash or wear away.

Oh well. Good thing my cinnamon candle was one of my bestsellers.

Rolling my shoulders back, I tied up all my frustrating thoughts with a wide, welcoming smile, pulled the curtain to the side, and stepped into the front of my store and into full-blown customer service mode.

"Welcome to the Candle Cabin. I'm—"

"Frankie."

No.

Shit.

Why was he here?

CHAPTER 3
FRANKIE

"Chandler." I blinked several times to confirm that he was really standing here. In my candle shop.

My eyes traveled up his height. *Was he this tall yesterday?* Today, he'd made an effort to dress more relaxed in dark jeans and a white linen button-down, the sleeves rolled up his forearms—*his very nice, very veiny forearms*—again.

"What are you doing here?" I blurted out in the most ungracious way.

Wow, Frankie. Smooth.

"Sorry." I shook my head and tucked my arms across my chest. "I thought Lou was giving you a tour today." She was giving him a tour, and somehow, he'd ended up here. *If she'd done that on purpose...*I inhaled deeply.

"She did, but I didn't want to monopolize her whole day," he said, his mouth tipping on one side as he stopped and examined the main display I had set up on a round table just inside the door; it featured a few extras of the seaside scent I'd crafted for Max.

"You definitely could have. She works too much." My weak laugh cracked when he picked up one of those seaside-scented candles, his hand big enough to almost completely wrap around the jar.

Good grief.

His eyes flicked to mine. "I managed to secure dinner with her, so I figured I'd quit while I was ahead."

Dinner. They were going to dinner.

I should be thrilled—elated that she'd agreed to spend more time with him. This was exactly what I was hoping for. So then why didn't it feel like what I wanted?

"Oh, good. I'm sure she recommended a great place, too."

"Brazos," he replied.

"Mmm. They have the best steaks." Brazos Steakhouse was a newer establishment in between Friendship and Stonebar Harbor—and by newer, I meant it opened about fifteen years ago. But that was how it went around here—almost every business had been open for generations, passed down through families.

"That's what she said." He looked back at the candle and then glanced around my store. The walls were stacked with shelves Jamie had built for me, and they were all filled with my candles. Scents of every variety and strength, and they changed all the time. That was my favorite part about the Candle Cabin— every week the candles I made changed.

New mixes. New scents. There was always something different to find here, from one day to the next.

"Your sister said you make all of these yourself."

"I do." My chin lifted, and my chest swelled with pride. I'd come a long way from making candles in Mom's basement.

"Very impressive," he said huskily, and the sound lit a flame right in the center of me.

No.

Absolutely no.

"So, what sights in our lovely town did my sister take you to see?" I redirected the conversation back to Lou like she was the lighthouse in the middle of whatever revolt of nature was happening inside me.

It was a single compliment. Genuine. Not over the top. Not attached to strings. And still, it made something flutter in my chest that should definitely not be fluttering.

"She showed me the beach first."

"Of course." My eyes darted around, searching for anything to focus on except the way Chandler moved lazily around the room. Even compared to Jamie, who was one of the biggest men I'd ever met, this man's presence invaded the space the way my brother's never had. I cleared my throat. "The morning is one of the best times to go. Not too crowded."

"There was no one there. It was..."

"*Peaceful*," I offered, and he finished at the same time.

His dark eyes caught mine, and I quickly turned away, busying myself with arranging the candles on the nearest display, making sure all the labels were facing forward.

"She pointed out the lighthouse from there. Mentioned your brother lives in it..."

I didn't trust myself to say anything this time,

instead only allowing my head to bob while I shuffled the candles around.

"We walked some path along the coastline for a little while and then wove back to the street a different way."

"Lou is the expert on Friendship. She knows all the best and most of the secret spots around town." And that was why that inn needed to be hers. She loved sharing every inch of this town with anyone who came through—loved making people feel like they were at home here.

"Most of the secret spots?" I hadn't appreciated how nice his brows were until now—until one lifted in my direction, and I made a concerted effort to avoid it.

"What else did you see?" Something tiptoed over my cheeks—almost imperceptible and warm—*was I blushing?*

"We stopped at the bakery for some blueberry muffins. The chocolate shop. Passed by your brother's art gallery and finished at the Stonebar Farms store," he said and picked up another candle—my new honey-orange scent—and uncapped the lid.

"Sounds like you got all the highlights." I wasn't blushing. I didn't blush. I didn't get embarrassed because why would I? I loved myself more than I cared what anyone else thought, and I had no problem making mistakes and laughing at myself for them.

There were enough things in life to take seriously.

"It sure felt like it," he said, bringing the candle to his nose. His eyes closed, and his expression softened, and even though I'd only known this man for the equivalent of maybe an hour—if I was being generous—it was striking to see his face relaxed. Like even here, on a little vacation, he still couldn't let loose.

"Damn, that smells good."

My face split with a smile for an instant before I reeled it back. I'd heard the phrase hundreds of times before. There was no reason for my face to react like it was the first.

"Thanks," I murmured. "It's a honey-orange scent made with honey from my cousin's bee farm. She's really into beekeeping."

His eyes found mine over the edge as he took another whiff, and I swore I felt the rush of his breath as though it was directly on my skin rather than across the room.

And then I dropped the lid to the candle in my hands. *Get a grip, Francesca.* I crouched to pick it up, willing my traitorous body to calm down before I got into trouble. I knew trouble—*I was trouble*—but never like this. Never in a way that affected me the way that being attracted to him did.

"Well, I'm glad you enjoyed your morning with Lou—"

"There was one place she didn't tell me much about," he interrupted with a low voice, clearly intent on whatever he wanted to say.

My heart tripped, and I let out a weak laugh. "Not much to tell about a candle store."

"Actually, it was the big building in the center of town. An old inn."

My cheeks were on fire. *So much for being able to deny the blush.* What would make me think he was talking about my shop? I mentally pulled my foot out of my mouth and exhaled.

"The Lamplight Inn," I confirmed and started to ramble, as though it would erase the moment when I'd assumed he was talking about me. "It was a landmark in town for decades—even before my family was here—but it's been abandoned for a little while now, unfortunately."

"Abandoned? Do you know who owns it?"

"Someone who's got too much money to care about an old inn that needs some TLC," I answered without filtering the sentiment or the snark from my tone.

His head tipped, dark eyes swirling. "He sounds like a jerk."

"I haven't met him, so I can neither confirm nor deny," I quipped with a tight smile. "But I can safely say he has no idea what the inn means to this town or the people in it."

"Oh? How's that?" That perfect brow arched once more, and it pierced the fog of frustration that led me a little blindly into this conversation.

I shouldn't be talking about this. Chandler was a stranger—a visitor—and that meant he needed to hear the same story anyone else who came into town did.

"Well, for starters, the inn is haunted."

The energy in the room—and *the energy around him*—changed. Sharpened. His eyes narrowed suspiciously at me. Nothing surprising considering what I'd just said. It was usually disbelief I faced first, but by now, I had my story pretty much down pat.

"Haunted?" His voice, formerly the perfect blend of strength and steadiness, faltered.

"Yup." The p popped before I could stop it. "Legend has it several of George Washington's spies used the inn as a meeting point before venturing down to Boston and even further on to New York," I said blithely as I returned to the display at the front of my shop, arranging the candles like they needed arranging. "They even say that Paul Revere stayed here before his infamous ride."

The thread of my story frayed as he moved toward me. "Spies?"

I swallowed over the lump in my throat, fighting to keep the fabric of my tale unblemished by uncertainty.

"Informants, really, who passed information to the Culper Ring," I barreled on, fishing for the facts I'd preserved from that one spy show Nox convinced us to watch a few years ago. "They relayed information about the counterfeit Continental currency plot as well as evidence of Benedict Arnold's betrayal."

"Hmm...the wolf in sheep's clothing." He folded his arms over his chest, and I couldn't tell which part of him it made look larger—his shoulders that stretched the seams of his shirt or his arms that appeared to have grown more muscle.

What I could tell was that he was closer—too close. *When had he gotten so close?*

"Yes." I nodded uncontrollably. "Unfortunately, several of them were caught right here in Friendship— at the Lamplight Inn—by a particularly vile British soldier, Captain Simcoe, and were killed."

"Simcoe?"

You know, I probably should've double-checked to make sure he was a real character.

"They say while the inn was still running, the ghosts took comfort in the gossip of the guests," I contin-ued, ignoring his question and hoping he didn't decide to fact check it later. "But since it closed, they've done nothing but haunt the grounds."

"Interesting..." And he sounded far too interested. Great. The last thing I needed was some gorgeous ghostbuster gallivanting around the inn that I was fake haunting.

"You said you're visiting family near here?" I veered sharply onto a different topic and grabbed a candle from the display. "If they don't live right by the ocean, I'd recommend this for a host gift." I shoved the beach-scented candle awkwardly toward his face without shame. "It's been so popular for summer—"

"Wait," he ordered, and I froze. His dark eyes weren't so dark anymore, but they were sparkling with bright bits of electric light. "What's that smell?"

Could he smell it through the lid? That would be impressive.

"It's a limited-edition seaside scent I made for my other cousin—" I broke off when a very large—very warm—hand clasped around my wrist. Shackled it, really, since his fingers locked easily around the entire thing.

"No," he rasped. "This." He pulled my wrist up to his face and took a deep breath.

Oh god. My inhale tangled deep in my chest, inextricably knotting itself to the inside of my lungs.

"It's..." His rough voice trailed off into a groan that moved over me like hot coals, charring heat wherever it touched. His eyes roamed my skin, his thumb brushing over the small scar at the base of my palm where I'd burned myself with hot wax a few years ago.

My lips parted, losing all thought and sense between them. A little more bend to my fingers or a slight sway of his head and his mouth would touch my skin. Those perfect lips and bright teeth. I wondered what it would feel like if he decided to bite my finger. Or my palm. I wondered if the heat of him would burn me, too.

The idea of him making a mess of my skin sent heat pooling between my legs. But that was nothing compared to the thought that came after. A man like Chandler didn't leave things a mess. He struggled to unbutton his shirt and roll his sleeves. *No*, whatever mess he made with his teeth, he'd surely clean up with his tongue.

Jesus, Francesca, you're losing your mind.

One touch and I was tangled in a web I'd neither made nor saw coming, and I was as surely trapped in the moment as if the whole of me were held down in chains.

But it was all because of the sight of him.

The slight crease of his brow. The hard knot at the corner of his jaw. Like he hungered for something he couldn't understand or deny. Something too feral for his immaculately refined life.

I knew the power of smell. The way a scent could transport someone...or transform them. The way it coaxed and comforted, lingered and lured...scent was the most effective spy. It snuck into the brain under the cover of aroma but had tied to it all the details to encode a memory or a moment for eternity.

Like this one.

Though every second that passed and every press of his touch went beyond encoded to something that felt like it had been carved straight into my bones.

"Chandler..."

His eyes flung open, and there was no mistaking the anger that flared in them or the way he abruptly released me.

"That scent. What is it?" His demand cut through the warm fog blanketing my body.

"Cinnamon," I said quickly, linking my hands in front of me. "I was working with it in the back..." *And now, I was afraid I'd never be able to work with it again.*

Not after this.

"Right." He cleared his throat and took a step back, his eyes darting for the nearest exit. "I should get going."

"Yeah," I agreed lamely, losing the mental capacity to fabricate some acceptable explanation for why he had to go.

"I'll just take—" He lifted the candle I'd handed to him. "This."

"Of course." I jerked my chin in a nod and beelined for my desk, tapping furiously on the iPad stationed there to ring him up. "Anything else I can get you?"

I did not get embarrassed, I had to remind myself as I replayed the question I'd just asked over again in my mind, confirming with perfect clarity the huskiness in my voice.

"That's it." His tone was hard.

"Great." I tapped on the screen, hoping I selected the right option before I flipped it toward him to pay. "Well, I hope you enjoy your date—*dinner*—with Lou tonight."

"Thank you." He tapped his card to pay and then shoved it back into his pocket.

"Do you want me to wrap—"

"No. It's fine." He tucked it under his arm and stepped back.

"Okay, well, thank you." I clung to my smile like it was a life raft in the middle of a sea of awkwardness. "Enjoy dinner with my sister."

While I spend the rest of the night fantasizing about how you smelled my wrist.

"I will," he said, and his tight smile didn't reach his eyes.

I shouldn't have watched his ass as he left, but at this point, what the hell? No surprise that it looked just as good as the rest of him.

"Dammit, Gigi," I muttered, cursing my grandmother and her stupid premonitions.

Chandler. She'd written that name—*word*—on a label five years ago, and I'd proudly shown it off as proof that my new business was meant to be.

A chandler was a candlemaker, after all.

By chance, I caught sight of the receipt still hanging out of the machine. *Crap.* I ripped it off and rushed toward the door.

I could give it to him another time—or give it to Lou. But I didn't want either of those things. I just wanted to see him again for another minute—wanted to feel that heat again for just a few more seconds.

But he was gone. My shoulders slumped as I scanned up and down the street, no sign of Chandler in either direction.

I couldn't say what drove me—couldn't pinpoint what invisible force it was that brought my gaze down to the paper in my hand. Maybe it was fate. She certainly seemed to be enjoying the tangled trap she'd set for me.

But tangled wasn't enough. Apparently, she wanted that trap to be torturous.

My heartbeat slowed—slogged against my chest like it pumped through quicksand as my focus narrowed on the bottom of the receipt. To the bold, sharp strokes of his signature along the dotted line.

And then lower.

To the printed name of the card owner below that line.

Chandler Collins.

Jamie's voice echoed distantly in my mind. *"He's in town, Frankie."*

Mr. Collins.

My inhale felt like a hot blade burying itself in the center of my chest.

Chandler was the owner of the inn. He was the man who was trying to sell it to people who didn't care about its history and didn't want anything to do with my sister's offer.

He was the cold-hearted capitalist trying to destroy Lou's dream.

And I was the one who'd blindly pushed her into the lion's den.

I had to fix this.

Fate was a troublemaker...but so was I.

CHAPTER 4
CHANDLER

Haunted.

The word echoed with every ring of the call.

"Hey, Chandler," Tom answered. "How's it going up there?"

"Haunted." For all the years I'd been involved in this business, this was one conversation I'd never had to have.

"Excuse me? Are you on your way to Edgewood? The service out there can be spotty. I could've sworn you said—"

"Haunted," I repeated and forced out an exhale. "Apparently, the inn is haunted."

"Well. That's certainly...interesting."

My grip tightened on the wheel, midday sunlight splattering through the shroud of aged trees onto the drive, shadows hanging like ghosts from their branches.

"None of the buyers said anything about it? No one when you were up here mentioned—"

"Of course not. I can employ a certain amount of

discretion when I tell you things, but I wouldn't have held something like that back," he said firmly. "No one ever even hinted that the reason they were no longer interested was...paranormal."

"Dammit," I muttered.

I sped down the long, tree-shaded lane toward the Edgewood Estate. Nestled in the woods and pitted against the peaceful placidity of the thoughtfully named South Pond, the old colonial mansion had been transformed into an assisted-living home. One that cost an arm, a leg, a firstborn, and an entire bitcoin to reside at—*a price I would happily pay ten times over for my mom*.

Laura Collins had been the mom everyone wanted. Thoughtful. Caring. Kind. She'd bent over backward when I was younger, doing more than she needed to— more than seemed humanly possible—to make up for a mistake that hadn't been hers. She didn't want me to feel any kind of deficit, having only one parent in my life, and I never did. *Only anger at the man who'd put her in that position in the first place*.

"Chandler, now, I'm not going to make claims about spirits or the afterlife, but that inn isn't haunted. I stayed there when it was open. There was never any mention of ghosts." Tom sounded—for lack of a better word—flabbergasted, and that was a considerable feat for a man who retained an admirable degree of control over himself.

"I know it's not haunted, Tom," I grunted. Not a fucking chance.

I'd been there. Stood in front of it today. The massive stone facade. Generous paned windows. Wrought-iron sconces and lamps. For a second, I'd stepped back into colonial times, in awe of the character of the building that couldn't be dulled even after decades of disuse. It might be old. Run down. But it sure as shit wasn't haunted.

"Who did you hear this from?"

My body hummed tightly. *A coy candlemaker*.

"A local shop owner."

"Well, they have to be mistaken." I could practically hear him shake his head and then scratch the back of his nape, perplexed.

"I'm going to look into it," I said, full well knowing I was going to do more than just look. There was something in her eyes—something when she'd told me about Revolutionary War ghosts—that I couldn't quite put my finger on. And it was something that—for lack of a better word—*haunted* me. "I just needed to know if you'd heard anything along the same lines—"

"No. Not a word."

"Right." I breathed out and let off the gas as I approached the last corner of the drive. "I'm almost at Edgewood and will probably lose you."

"All right, I'll see if I can dig up anything." He sighed. "Just try to forget about it while you're with her, Chandler. The stress...she can sense it."

"Yeah," I croaked and then mumbled a goodbye.

Around the bend, the large, whitewashed building came into sight. The striking columns of the two-story porticoed front porch towered over a line of wooden rocking chairs that stretched from one end to the other. *Those chairs were new*. I wondered if Mom liked them.

If the owners hadn't turned this place into an elder-care facility, they could've easily transformed it into a luxury bed-and-breakfast. *That was my suggestion when I'd sold it to Chip and Dianne.* But before the ink was even dry on the papers, Chip started showing signs of early-onset Alzheimer's, so Dianne changed all their plans. Instead, they'd decided to restore the manor to be a place for them to still enjoy, but one that could also accommodate Chip's deteriorating health.

In many ways, it had the same B&B atmosphere they were originally looking to create but with more permanent guests.

Like Mom.

I'd called Dianne the day Mom looked me in the eyes, smiled, and called me Geoff. I'd corrected her no less than a dozen times that night over dinner, and each time, she'd remember for a few minutes, and then by the next course, I'd be my father again.

Never. A low noise rumbled from deep in my chest. *I'd never become like my father.* Never give myself the chance. Marriage. Children. Fatherhood. It was all off the table for me. The only thing I was interested in building was a business and a better legacy.

I slowed and turned into the small parking lot for guests, all the spots marked *Reserved.*

From the lot, there was a wide path that led down to the pond, a favorite of Chip's and many of the other residents here. According to Tom, Mom thought it was okay. *Probably because it wasn't the beach.* But Tom would know. He came up here every other weekend to visit her...and then discreetly gave me any updates when I would see him.

He wasn't judging me. He understood—*knew* how hard it was for me to come up here. I had a million work-related excuses at the ready to explain why I put off visiting Mom, and I was happy to fall on the sword of appearing an asshole if it meant avoiding the truth. There wasn't anything more painful than having the one person I loved see me, talk to me, *want me to be* the only person I hated.

And it wasn't her fucking fault. Wasn't her fault her brain confused me with Geoff Collins or that my genetics helped the association by giving me his notoriously good looks.

I turned into one of the parking spots out front and shut off the engine. Reaching for the keys set on the center console, the candle I'd unceremoniously dropped in the passenger seat caught my eye.

"It's a limited-edition beach scent."

Air hissed through my lips as I grabbed the candle and secured the lid. I should smell it first—make sure it was halfway decent before giving it to Mom as a present. But if I did that, I'd lose the scent of her.

Cinnamon. A little bit of sweet, a lot of spice, and wholly intoxicating.

It was honeyed but with a punch—the kind that didn't hold back when it hit you, didn't try to bury itself under other aromas, but said *you're either going to like all of me, or you're not.*

It was bold. *Unyielding.* And if that wasn't the whole goddamn vibe of Francesca Kinkade, I didn't know what was.

Hell, it wasn't just her. "Unyielding" should be their family motto, given the way her sister kept trying to buy my inn. *Learning Lou stood for Elouise, not Louis, was a fun lesson yesterday morning.* All this time, I'd pictured Louis Kinkade as some heavyset country bumpkin trying to swindle himself a deal. *What were the fucking chances the first people*

I'd met in town were the very family I wanted to avoid?

A piece of frustration broke off deep in my chest and erupted as a groan. At least they were still unaware of who I was. *For now.*

I shoved myself out of the seat of the car and strode toward the building. Mom would like the candle. Frankie wouldn't be in business if she didn't make candles that smelled good.

The pastel blue front door swung open, Edgewood's longest-serving employee on the other side of it to greet me with a smile.

"Morning, Cathy."

"Mr. Collins. It's so good to see you." She pulled me in for a hug like she always did. I could be a beggar, a billionaire, or the Prince of Sheba, and Cathy would still greet me like family. *One of the many reasons I'd pay any price for Mom to stay here—because they treated her like family, too.*

"I know it's been a little bit," I admitted. No beating around the bush here.

"You're very busy." She patted my back gently and gave me a sympathetic look. "And it's hard."

My throat tightened. I wasn't sure hard was the right word to describe how it felt to face a loved one with dementia. I wasn't sure there was a right word.

"Not an excuse, Cathy." I was a decisive businessman. It was how I started my business. Ran my business. Made my business what it was. The rest of the industry and the tabloids could call me cold. Ruthless. But all I did was keep my emotions out of my decisions. I saw a situation for what it was—good and bad. And I didn't spare myself that assessment either.

There were many ways I was a good son, but for this, for avoiding her, I was an ass.

The inside of the old estate was cozy rather than clinical. Sure, there were doctors and nurses on staff, but it never looked like it.

"They finished the screened-in porch since the last time you were here, Mr. Collins." She pointed as we walked through the main room, the large windows that overlooked the pond on the far side now revealed a closed-in area with large couches and tables where I could see some of the residents playing games.

"Chip loves chess," I murmured, recalling Dianne telling me about the porch a few years ago as part of her future plans.

"Miss Laura enjoys the porch," Cathy said over her shoulder.

"What about those rocking chairs out front?"

Her smile grew. "She loves those on a nice day like today."

Perfect. I firmed my lips and nodded. "How is she today?"

Her smile held, but her eyes changed. And not for the better. "Quiet," she answered, and then gathered some enthusiasm in her tone. "But she'll be happy to see you, Mr. Collins. Very happy."

Me? Or my asshole father?

I followed Cathy up to the second floor, listening to her give me all the updates to the estate since I'd been there last. *Had it really been almost four months?* Guilt filled each step down the hall to Mom's room. Her suite was all the way at the end, giving her windows on two sides of her room with views of the forest and lake.

I hadn't just sold this estate to Chip and Dianne. I'd

invested in it, too. The new porch this year. The restored fireplace in the common area last year. The community garden the year before. The French chef before that.

I'd paid for it all—and I'd pay for more if it made Mom's time here better. Happier. *Fuller*.

Because if she couldn't remember the past, all she had was now.

"Let me know if you need anything." Cindy patted my shoulder again, leaving me at Mom's door.

I drew a deep breath, holding the candle a little tighter as I knocked.

"Mom?" I paused. "It's me. Chandler." My jaws clamped together, locking my breath tight in my chest.

The door swung open, Mom's wide smile greeting me. "Oh, Chandler. It's so good to see you, honey."

Relief swamped me. *She remembered*. It was a good day.

I bent down to hug her, thinking that she had to have gotten a little shorter in the last four months. *And skinnier*. Her loose, pale purple blouse hid her thinning frame, and I felt the blade of her shoulder against my hand. "Good to see you, too, Mom." I held her close and breathed deep, able to pretend for a second that this was how it always was.

"Well, come in."

Even her hand felt more fragile as she took mine and guided me through the door into a room covered in lilac and butterflies. Mom loved butterflies. Every bare wall held at least one frame containing either a butterfly photo, piece of artwork, or preserved butterfly specimen —*the monarch was her favorite*. The spacious sitting area housed two loveseats on one side with a small table between them, usually covered with photographs, but it was empty today. I looked at the cabinet along the wall and found the photographs stacked on top of it, and my brow creased. *Were they being cleaned? Did she want them changed?* I'd have to ask Cathy.

On the right side of the room were two doors, one to a powder room, the other to Mom's bedroom and bath.

Mom ushered me to one of the couches. "So, come sit and tell me, how are you? How is school going?"

School.

I stilled, feeling the lightness in my chest deflate. *She thought I was visiting from college.*

I forced myself to swallow and smile. "I'm good, Mom. Keeping busy." I never knew what to do in these situations. Did I try to correct her, knowing it would be futile? Or was it worse to go along with something that wasn't the truth? "How are you doing? What's new with you?"

"Oh, I'm wonderful, honey. The company here is excellent, and the food is superb." Well, at least I'd done something right. "I always tell Cathy that I'd live here forever if I could." Her eyes twinkled as she laughed, completely unaware that she was living here forever.

"I'm happy to hear that," I said, my voice lowering.

Mom picked up her glass of water, taking a sip, and then walked over to the mirror on the wall, adjusting one of her white curls so it sat just right.

"Have you seen him lately?"

I stilled. "Who? Tom?"

She looked over her shoulders and chuckled. "Tom?" Her head shook. "No, Geoff, I'm talking about Chandler."

It was like a bucket of ice water over my head every

time. Even now—after years of experiencing the muddiness of her memory—it was still like a wound ripped open.

I knew I looked like him. One didn't have to see too many photos to see the resemblance. Hell, maybe I even sounded like him, though I was far less certain about that. But what I didn't get was why would her mind *want* to picture him? Why would her memory choose to put her back in those few good years they had together?

All questions I'd never get answers to.

"I brought you a present," I offered—a plea to return to the gift and the present moment. That was the only place I could visit with her now.

"Oh, a candle." She clasped her hands and came back to the couch. "I do love a good candle."

I fished a lighter from my pocket, popped off the lid, and carefully lit the wick. "It's a beach scent." I extended the jar for her to smell, the first hints of salt and sea grass hitting my nostrils.

Her smile didn't waver as she leaned forward, her serene expression telling me she was still adrift between the past and present. And then she closed her eyes and took a deep breath.

"Oh my." Her eyes fluttered back open, her head tipping to one side.

Shit.

I wasn't thinking. Was this a bad idea? Had I just made it worse?

"This smells wonderful, Chandler." Her voice sounded stronger. Like instead of floating, it was tethered to solid ground.

"Mom?" My voice cracked. She was calling me Chandler again.

"This was such a thoughtful gift. You know how much I love the ocean."

It was the first thing I'd thought earlier when Lou had led the way onto the beach—a beach that looked vaguely familiar to me. How many vacations had we spent on the coast of Maine? Mom loved the shore, but not the tropical, suffocating sunshine shore. She loved the rocky coastline and rough waves. Her favorite thing to do was get ice cream after dinner and find some rocky perch or another to sit on and eat it while we watched the rumbling tide.

I gritted my teeth, emotion threatening to split my chest and flay open my skin. "I do."

She didn't like the beach at its best. She loved the ocean at its most honest. Sometimes calm. Many times stormy. But beautiful all the same.

"Remember that one time Tom and I took you to the beach in Friendship? You could've only been maybe five."

My jaw went slack. "In Friendship?"

She nodded and took another deep breath close to the candle. "We walked along the beach and collected seashells."

I stilled, vaguely recalling the memory.

"There's a lighthouse there, and you wanted to go all the way over to explore..."

"But it's impossible," I murmured, recalling the exact spot I'd been standing this morning when Lou pointed out the Friendship Lighthouse, sharing it was where her brother, Kit, lived and worked both as the lighthouse keeper and as an artist.

"You remember?" The irony that she was asking that question wasn't lost on me.

"I was there this morning."

"You were?" Her brows lifted.

"Stood on the beach. Saw the lighthouse. Walked along Maine Street and got the lay of the land." From the Maine Squeeze all the way down to the inn, Lou had pointed out businesses old and new along the way, including her brother's art gallery that she managed— *the Kinkade Gallery*.

I blinked, and Frankie's stormy gaze stared back at me, reminding me of the tangle of our conversation. Her, trying to focus the conversation on my time with her sister. And me, trying to learn why the hell Lou wouldn't share much about the inn—*and no, it couldn't be because she knew who I was. She would've been pleading her case rather than giving me a tour of the town if that were the situation.*

"Oh really?" One of Mom's brows arched the way it did when I was a kid, and she knew I was in trouble—or about to be. "And what interest does Collins Realty have in a small seaside town? Last I checked, there were no skyscrapers there, honey, only sandcastles."

I wasn't sure I could reply, her lucidity left me speechless. I couldn't remember the last time she'd been so with it. Sure, there were moments here and there. A split-second answer before it was gone. But not this. Not the makings of a conversation. To be fair, I wasn't exactly around her enough to make the claim that these moments were rare in general—they were just rare when she was around me.

My throat tightened. What I wouldn't give to not have this moment unravel. All my money. All my properties. *I'd give it all...*

"Come on." She patted my knee, drawing me out of

my thoughts. "I know you weren't in Friendship for vacation. Heaven forbid, Chandler Collins *doesn't* work a day in his life..."

"Mom." I let out a pained chuckle and managed to give her a guilty smile. Damn, if seeing her—having her like this—wasn't the most bittersweet fucking experience of my life. *And it was all because of that candle— because of Frankie fucking Kinkade.* I cleared my throat and told her, "There's an inn..."

"The Lamplight Inn?" she asked with a small gasp and then gushed, "Oh, I love it there." Her eyes swung around the room as she let out a soft sigh. "Or I did. It closed quite some time ago..." When I nodded, she continued. "Are you selling it or buying it?"

Well, she clearly had no idea my father had owned it—or willed it to me. And I wasn't about to bring it or him up. "Selling."

"Oh." Her face fell.

"I'm up to take a look. It's not under contract yet."

"Well, tell Tom to only bring you buyers who want to preserve the place," she declared, and I swore I was having déjà vu. How many times had she put her own stamp on my business dealings? Not a lot of them, but always ones that had history or character or meaning. Mom always took a stand for those.

"It's absolutely charming and quite a landmark for the town, so be sure you sell to whoever is going to preserve that."

Which was definitely not John Fairfax. The condo king.

"Noted," I said with a tight voice, my knuckles turning white where they held my knee. Fuck if that wasn't going to make this deal more painful to close.

"It reminds me a little of this place, actually," she said, her voice softening as her gaze strayed around her room. "Warm and welcoming." She looked back at me and then waved her hand over the candle, wafting more of the scent toward her at the same time as it made the flame go out. "A place that can make you feel at home."

The significance of her words wasn't lost on me. The Edgewood Estate wasn't her home—not the one she'd give the designation—but the place and the people were enough to give her the same kind of comfort. It wasn't what I wanted for her, but what I wanted wasn't possible. So, this was all I could do.

I took her hand in mine, giving her small fingers a gentle squeeze. "And it's close to the beach," I added with a small smile. "Maybe we could go over there one day."

She smiled back, blinked, and then broke me. "What beach, Geoff?"

CHAPTER 5
FRANKIE

"I 'm sorry." Story of my life.

"You're...sure?" Lou's stricken voice made me wince.

I sat on the couch next to my sister, watching as her throat bobbed and then her whole head followed suit, but it was her eyes that gave her away. Her vacant stare saw nothing but iterations of the truth...of what would happen next...of how this was the end.

"Yeah."

I took deep breaths in and out, biting into my cheek while I waited for my twin to say something. Twenty-seven years of knowing her meant anything I said right now would go in one ear and out the other. Lou needed time to process while I dove straight into plans.

"He told me he worked in real estate, but I didn't ask...never thought...I can't go," she declared solemnly. "I'll text him—"

"Absolutely not." I took her hand and squeezed. "You have to go Lou. First off, he doesn't know that I know, and now you know, that he's Chandler Collins—"

"Do you hear yourself?" A broken laugh escaped her. "You sound like a rerun of a *Friends* episode."

"Listen to me," I ordered her and took a deep breath. "This is your chance."

Her eyes bugged wide.

"You have the advantage," I pressed on, standing as I spoke. "You know who he is—"

"And he knows who I am! I told him about Mom and Jamie and Kit—" She broke off when I bent in front of her, meeting her nose to nose.

"And he still asked you to dinner." I lifted a brow, daring her to disagree.

Lou creased her brow, and I pulled back. Sometimes it was a little disconcerting staring into your own face. Like a mirror, except the reflection moved on its own will.

"I can't—"

"You absolutely can. You can find out why he's here. Why he asked you to dinner. And more importantly—most importantly—you can show him who you are."

I was shocked and then in disbelief and then angry that the man could, in one breath, refuse to sell my sister the inn of her dreams and, in the next, ask her to dinner. I shouldn't have been surprised. He was a heartless businessman. *Who bought a beach candle for his mom.* I shook off the silly reminder. That didn't matter. Chandler Collins was enemy number one, and whatever he was thinking, I wasn't going to let him hurt my sister.

"What?" Lou's jaw fell dangerously close to landing on the floor.

"This is your chance to give him some insight into

you—the woman who wants to buy his inn." I started to pace, otherwise I'd be tempted to shake my sister into understanding. "You have an opportunity none of the other buyers have—to show Mr. Inconspicuous Collins why you are the best owner for the inn. Why you want it. Why you care. What it would mean to this town to have it restored to its former glory." I kept going even though her eyes were getting wider by the syllable. "You can tell him how lost you were until we were going to restore the inn. Share all the plans you've come up with—"

"No." Her head swung side to side. "I can't do that."

"You can." I stepped in front of her again and sank to my knees, taking her hands in mine. "Only you can show him how much this means to you…and how heartless he would have to be to sell it to some stranger."

The last strains of my breath left my lungs, and I waited for her to agree.

"I can't do it," she declared, and then bolted for the powder room, slamming the door behind her.

"Shit." I shoved off the floor and went to the door, knocking gently. "Come on, Lou. It'll be okay." My plea was met with silence. If there was one secret Lou was good at keeping, it was when she was in pain. Her tears. Her hurt. She bottled it inside and tried not to bother anyone with it.

I let out a deep exhale, my head tipped to rest on the door. "All you have to do is be yourself." It wasn't hard—it wasn't like I was telling her to do anything different than she would've already…*except maybe frame a conversation or two to her advantage.*

"I'm sorry, Frankie," Lou's soft, unsteady voice eked

under the door. "I just don't feel right...knowing who he is."

"Don't feel right being yourself? Telling him the truth about your dreams?" I rested my forehead on the wood, grateful Lou and I were alone at the house. Mom and Gigi had gone out for the afternoon to help my younger cousin, Harper, assemble her beehives. After countless hobbies over the last few years, she'd fallen in love with beekeeping and had sectioned off a corner of Stonebar Farm's property to use for her hives.

"I can't do that and pretend to not know who he is."

Maybe I shouldn't have told her. Maybe I should've tried to figure it out on my own—*no*. No, this was Lou's baby. Lou's dream. I wouldn't do anything without her knowing. And honestly, I didn't trust myself around the far too handsome Mr. Collins. Not the way he made my body sizzle and spark like an electric current with no ground. The feeling was...unnerving. My body was only reckless on my command...*not in his presence.*

And that was all aside from the fact he knew who I was—who Lou was—and still hadn't revealed himself. It was dubious. Sinister, even. He already had the upper hand. Why would he hide who he was? Maybe from Lou. I could *maybe* see that. *Girl takes you on a "tour" date, and you realize you've been crushing her business dreams for months...awkward.* But then to come to my shop...

No, there was something off about Chandler Collins, and it was more than the haywire heat he struck in my body.

"I think you could, Lou. I think you could pretend if your life—your dream—depended on it."

There was a long pause, and I swore I heard her

breathing from right on the other side of the door. Thinking. Considering. And something panged in my chest. I knew my sister better than anyone. She was my other half. The yin to my yang. The calm to my storm. She *could* do this to fight for her dream...but just because she could do it, didn't mean she should.

I knew the toll this deception would take on her— even if it was a slight lie. A white lie. A lie of omission. Even if it was justified. *And even if it was only an omission that mirrored his own.*

My breath went out of me, taking with it all the will I had to push her. She was right. *She* shouldn't do this.

Don't do it.

Don'tdoitdon'tdoitdon'tdoit.

"Fine. I'll go."

The door swung open, but I was already halfway up the stairs, my determined stride carrying me quickly through the house.

"What do you mean you'll go?" She chased after me.

"I mean, I'll go to dinner and face him," I said over my shoulder as I pushed into her room. "I'll tell him what the inn means to you. Everything—all the plans you've laid out and how hard you've worked to save for the project."

"You don't have to—"

"You know I do," I insisted, stopping in front of her closet. "You know someone has to shake some sense into this guy."

"Frankie—"

"Do you really want to see the inn torn down for condos?" I demanded, watching the question crumble the last of her protest.

"Fine." Her mouth thinned—frowned in a way I was familiar with. It was her "for the record" frown, the one that came out when she begrudgingly agreed to whatever plan of mine she inherently disagreed with.

"Good." I spun and threw open her closet doors just as my sister grabbed my arm.

"What are you doing?" Her gaze slid to her clothes.

I swallowed hard and then forced a wide smile onto my face. "Changing, and then you're going to braid my hair." As her eyes widened, I dipped my chin and said softly, "I'm going as you, Lou."

"Frankie..." Lou folded her arms, the timid titan in her returning.

"I can't go as myself. How does it look that he invited you to dinner and your twin shows up? That kind of bait-and-switch definitely won't help your case. And to tell him the truth—that we know who he is, and I'm there to convince him on your behalf—that's even worse."

She chewed on her bottom lip. "But you hate the idea of..."

I stiffened for a second. "I know," I said and gave her a brave smile. "But I'll do it for you."

I hated pretending. *No, not quite.* I hated the idea of pretending to be my twin. How many movies, how many stories, hell, how many times had my sister and I been asked if we ever traded places? Until today, the answer was a firm no.

"Now, pick out your most 'Lou' outfit and help me get ready." I pulled her in front of me to sort through her clothes. My taste in clothes ran toward the rainbow, while meanwhile, Lou lived calmly in a sea of neutral and beige.

"Okay." She reached forward, instantly picking tan linen pants, a white blouse, and a long white blazer and handing them to me.

"One Lou Kinkade coming right up." I smiled and began to strip.

For all my tricks and jokes and shenanigans, I'd never asked Lou to switch places. I was happy to be outspoken, brave, playful, and a little wild at my best. I was also happy to be immature, compulsive, and reckless at my worst. I was happy to be me. Good and bad. Right and wrong. Imperfect in many ways. And no matter what I wanted to accomplish, I never wanted to be anyone else. Let alone the one person in this world who looked exactly like me.

I was me. Take it or leave it.

But tonight...tonight I'd be Lou. Just this once. Because she deserved this. Her dream. Her happiness. And if all that took was a little flirting with Chandler Collins, I'd suffer through it.

"Ow." I winced, my hand crashing into Lou's spare set of glasses for the third time in fifteen minutes and jamming them into the bridge of my nose.

"Careful," she chided, pulling my old VW Bug up to the curb to drop me off.

"I'm fine." Huffing, I pushed the glasses onto my head and rubbed the corner of my eye where it itched, letting the glasses flop back down when I was done.

Then I ran my hands along the braids in my hair.

The collar of the blazer. The linen lying comfortably and loosely on my thighs. *Breathe, Frankie.*

I wasn't nervous. I shouldn't be nervous. *I was never nervous.* But what other reason could there be for my thumping pulse and flushed cheeks? I had to be nervous, had to be afraid to mess this up for Lou. The alternative was the whole haywire sensation starting even *before* I saw him. And that was out of the question.

"All right, I'll text you when I'm done," I said just as she stopped at the curb in front of the steakhouse, the low-lit sconces and carved topiaries setting the stage for the kind of fancy to expect inside.

"Okay, Frankie—"

"Be careful, I know." I smiled at my sister—or at least, I think I did. Even just the slight prescription of her glasses made everything foggy.

It was one of our many differences, but only one of the few physical ones. Lou had contacts and said I could just pretend to be wearing those...but she never wore her contacts. This wasn't only about convincing Chandler that I was Lou. It was anyone else from town who might be at the restaurant that I also had to worry about.

I took the two small steps up to the entrance carefully and then turned. Lou still hadn't driven away, so I shooed her with my hand and then waited. I wasn't going inside until she was gone.

She hesitated a beat, then caved with a small wave and drove off.

All right, time to enact the next phase of this plan. WWLD. What Would Lou Do?

I opened the door and stepped inside, inhaling deep as soon as I was firmly planted inside Brazos. Everyone agreed that scent stimulated appetite, but I would argue it did far more than that. Scent set the scene whether there was food or not. It was the way salt and brine could take you right to the edge of the waves with your toes in the sand. It was the lingering pinch of cedar embers and smoke that drew you up to a crackling campfire. It was only aroma that had the immense, invisible power to paint a picture of where you were or where you wanted to be.

And here, there was cedar wood. Bergamot. A hint of pepper—*no*. I flung my eyes wide open. Lou wouldn't be smelling the room to get a sense of the restaurant. She'd be scanning it. Cataloging her surroundings for who was there—who was new and who she knew. So, I wrinkled the last hint of thyme from my nostrils and set my eyes farther into the space.

The shadowed atmosphere was tempting. Sultry, even. Pools of light peppered the space, centering around each of the round tables, some secluded by booths along the perimeters, others, larger and in the center, on display for everyone who walked by. I couldn't remember the last time I'd been here. The dark wood, midnight tablecloths, and rich bronze sconces were all new. But in spite of the updated interior, I instantly picked out the roots that tied this place to Friendship. A portrait of the original owners. The farm. Several large seascapes spaced along the walls.

I looked back to the hostess stand, instantly recognizing the blonde at the podium. Charlie Moore. My body tipped forward, about to take a step, and then I caught myself. Lou wouldn't approach the podium. She'd either send me, or she'd wait until the hostess noticed her and called her forward.

Linking my hands in front of me, I stayed put, lowering my gaze to the floor and imagining roots growing around my feet, securing myself from the urge to take charge.

"Hi, Lou. You can come up," Charlie called.

My head snapped up, the room wobbling through Lou's glasses for a second. Only when Charlie addressed me did I step forward. "Hi, Charlotte." Lou never called her Charlie, only Charlotte. "I'm here to meet a...friend." Lou would've faltered on the word, but so did I. "I'm not sure exactly what name it is under, but it's for two people at seven—"

"It's under Chandler," a deep voice spilled from behind me, the edge of his name lifting on the quirk of his smile.

CHAPTER 6
FRANKIE

Like a match to a wick, his voice lit a flame of goose bumps along my spine. I forced myself not to shiver. Not to tremble against the controlled, combustible heat of him as he came to stand beside me. I watched the color of Charlie's cheeks deepen even in the dim lighting. Of course, they did. How handsome he is was probably the only thing his money couldn't buy.

I had to turn. Had to greet him. I took a deep breath. *Sandalwood.* He smelled of sandalwood. *And a hint of clove.* I shoved the breath out and started to face him—but hesitantly. Lou would be nervous. Uncertain. My shoulder brushed into him, my jacket dampening the sparks. And then I was staring at his broad chest.

"Good evening, Lou."

He was a liar. A liar and a dream killer.

I lifted my gaze and smiled. "Hi."

Thank God for Lou's glasses. They were like looking through a low-dose funhouse mirror, distorting his dark eyes, softening his square jaw, and obscuring the rest of his deceptive handsomeness that I'd loathe to admit threw me off guard.

His head tipped, those molten eyes sinking deeper into mine for an instant before they swept over me, and I let mine return the gesture. *Sizing up my opponent*.

Navy suit and white shirt, all tailored to perfection. He had one hand in his pocket and the top button at his collar undone, as though refined ruthlessness was his own style.

"I can take you to your table." Charlie's voice interrupted what could've only been a few seconds.

"After you." Chandler stepped to the side, extending an arm to let me proceed first. *Like the gentleman he wasn't*. As I moved past him, I felt the slight prick of heat low on my back. His fingers, I realized too late, were ever so gently guiding me forward. Even through my layers, the touch felt like the lure of a low flame, begging me to move closer, aching for me to let it burn hotter.

No.

My shoulders rolled back, and I walked a little faster, out of his reach, as Charlie led us to the back corner of the steakhouse, the round table suddenly seeming more like a fighting ring. I sank down into one side of the booth and Chandler went to the other. The casual flick of his wrist to unbutton his jacket as he sat did *not* make my cheeks warm. Absolutely not. It was just hotter back here.

And to prove it, I slid my arms out of my jacket.

Before we had a chance to say anything, our waiter, Marty, introduced himself and offered us water. Chandler took the opportunity to order a bottle of red wine, the name and year meaning nothing to me but clearly something to him—that he pulled the vintage right off the top of his head like a rabbit from a hat.

"Thank you for joining me for dinner," he said as soon as we were alone. "I don't get company for meals too often."

"Oh?" I choked out, not for a single second believing his words. This man had brokered half of Boston and had been given a face Narcissus would be jealous of. There was no chance he ate alone regularly.

Why was he trying to hide who he was?

Before I got another answer—another lie—Marty returned with water and the bottle of wine that he presented to Chandler and then poured him a taste. The exchange would've almost seemed a little ridiculous if I wasn't caught off guard by the way Chandler sniffed the wine first, his eyes shutting and his jaw tensing as the aroma hit him. He looked the same as when he'd smelled my candles—as though it were one of the few, rare times he gave himself a moment to just breathe.

I guessed breathing just wasn't lucrative enough for Mr. Collins to do it regularly.

I blinked, and Marty had filled both of our glasses. Taking the opportunity to follow his lead, I let a little piece of Frankie slip out as I brought the glass to my nose, swirled the wine, and inhaled.

Rich, but fruity. *Was that black cherry?* I could make something similar...

I opened my eyes, instantly snagging them with Chandler's and feeling my cheeks flush.

"I have a few specials for tonight." Marty linked his hands behind his back and rattled off descriptions of their dry-aged cowboy-cut steak and a salmon special.

Lou would've picked the fish. She was the surf to my turf.

"Are we ready to order?"

I smiled, the word *salmon* on the tip of my tongue.

"After you," Chandler murmured, and his voice put a chink in my charade.

"I'll have the filet." I shoved my menu back in Marty's direction and reached for my wine. As Chandler ordered, I smelled the deep red again and took a sip, sneaking a glance at him over the rim of my glass.

What was his game? His plan? Why invite Lou to dinner if he knew who she was—and what she wanted from him?

"What do you think?" he asked, and I stared, my mind suddenly blank. "Of the wine." He nodded his chin toward my glass.

"Oh, it's good," I rushed to assure him, locking my gaze on my glass as I returned it to the table. "Very good." I slid my tongue over my lips to get the last of the taste, and I swore I heard a low noise from his side of the table, but when I looked, he was adjusting his napkin on his lap.

"This is a nice spot. A nice ambiance."

Even though most of the tables were filled, the hum of the conversation was quiet, making it easy to ignore— to forget—there was anyone else in the room except us.

"Yeah," I agreed, and then latched onto the opportunity. "Pete and Carole did a really nice job with the renovation."

"You know the owners?"

"Of course." I started to smile wide but quickly curtailed it with a sip of wine. Lou's glasses were already making me feel tipsy, but it was the only sure way to not look too long at him. Every time our eyes connected, I felt a spark, and I knew enough about fire to know that too many sparks led to a flame. "Charlotte, the girl who seated us, is their niece. Their daughter, Jenny, works as a waitress here, and her husband is in the kitchen."

"Oh?" He seemed genuinely surprised—as though the only kind of mom-and-pop restaurant was a hole-in-the-wall tavern or tacky diner.

I pointed across the room to the painting on the wall near the hostess stand. "That's Carole's great-great-grandparents. The way she tells it, her great-great-grandmother was the daughter of a farmer, and her great-great-grandfather was the son of a butcher, and that was how they met."

"Over a love of red meat."

I nodded, a small smile bursting on my lips that I couldn't stop. *This is why I didn't pretend to be Lou.* "That painting is of their original farm, a few miles outside town. And that one there is of their first restaurant before it burned down." One by one, I walked him through the artwork on the walls. What came off as fine art to the unknowing eye of a stranger was really a history—a legacy nailed to the very walls. "And there is one of the first paintings of the Friendship Lighthouse. Unsigned, but legend has it that it was painted by John Trumbull."

"Wow," he said in a low tone, his gaze rising and sinking from one painting to another, staring like it was more than the paintings he saw.

Because it was more.

"Friendship might look like just one more of those iconic coastal towns dotting the shore, but there's a lot of history here. Community. Family," I went on quietly, adding, "Memories."

He listened and continued to look around, the expression on his face shifting to something I couldn't immediately decipher. Was it sadness? *No, not quite.* I bit into my bottom lip. Was it hope? *No, it wasn't that either.* Regret? *That didn't even make sense—not for the man trying to sell out and sell off a piece of this community to a condo developer.*

"And it's something that all of us who live here try... and fight...to preserve."

As soon as I said the word "fight," his gaze snapped back to mine. I reached for my wine glass—a dangerous crutch in this game—but I didn't have a choice. When his smoked whiskey eyes settled on me, it was as though he saw right behind the mask. Except there was no mask. It was my face. My sister's face. *We were identical.*

Chandler cleared his throat. "Your sister mentioned this place had a history, but I had no idea."

I stilled. *Me.* He was talking about me. *Was it because he realized who I was?* No, that couldn't be it. He'd known us for a collective couple of hours. There was no possible way for him to think I was...me. In the back of my mind, the little voice in my head said that if Lou and I had attempted switches like this before, I wouldn't be so nervous about this now.

And I definitely should move on. Change topics. I shouldn't probe—I shouldn't risk.

Don'tdoit. Don'tdoit.

"You talked to Frankie?" This wasn't what I was here to discuss—*I* wasn't supposed to be part of this night at all. But Lou would be curious—she would do anything to avoid talking about herself.

Marty returned then with our meals, the table suddenly filled with perfectly cooked steak, asparagus, and three different kinds of potato sides. I couldn't help it as I closed my eyes and took a deep breath, every scent stitching this scene to my memory. And then Marty asked if I'd like my wine glass refilled, and I answered yes before I could think better of it. *I'd already had a full glass on a mostly empty stomach.*

As soon as he left, I cut into my steak, fearing the conversation he'd interrupted wouldn't pick up again. It was probably better that way—

"I stopped by her candle store yesterday to pick up a gift."

My heart thudded, and it was a miracle I didn't choke on my food.

"Oh? What did you think?" *Lou would ask. Lou would care,* I continued to tell myself...and held every ounce of my breath, waiting for his answer.

"Very impressive." His nod of appreciation—admiration—was genuine.

I exhaled, unable to stop my smile from pulling higher on my cheeks as though it were lifted by the butterflies in my stomach. Chandler Collins, billionaire broker extraordinaire, was impressed by my candle shop. Warmth oozed through me like it stemmed from my very bones, heating my cheeks, my chest, and then lower—*no, that had to be the wine.*

"Thank you"—*shit, that had to be the wine, too*—"for her," I stammered with a quick smile. "She's worked really hard...since she was sixteen...to bring her candle-making business to life."

"Wow. Sixteen? She must really love it to sacrifice for a business so young." His head tipped, a lock of dark-brown hair breaking from its mold ever so slightly and trespassing onto his forehead. "Seems like entrepreneurship runs in your family's genes."

I inhaled swiftly, catching on the hook. This was my chance—the perfect opportunity to segue into the conversation I came here, as a pretender, to have. This was *not* my opportunity to tell him about my candles or my business or the fact that I wanted to create something that smelled like cedarwood, thyme, and a hint of dark cherry like the steakhouse and the wine. No, this wasn't my opportunity at all, no matter how much I wanted to bask in the heat of his compliments.

I'd never been one for praise. I worked hard. I was certainly proud of what I'd accomplished. But even after all the years of running my business, I still felt a surprising awkwardness when people complimented me. Saying they liked my candles or that the scents were different. Of course, I enjoyed that. But praise for my business—it was like they were trying to fan an already strongly-burning flame. At least, that was how it usually felt. This time, though, his words were like small bursts of accelerant tossed on my inner fire.

But I didn't want his praise, I reminded myself. *I wanted his inn.*

"My mom. My brothers. My sister. My cousin...I hope it runs in the genes for me, too..."

"Oh?" One of his brows lifted, belying the fact he already knew.

Hooked.

"I want to run an inn," I began softly, my brief smile

wistful. "The Lamplight Inn...where we ended our walk yesterday."

"The one that's rundown?"

Oh, you think you're good, Mr. Collins, you have no idea.

"Yeah." I took another sip of my wine. "For a long time, I thought I was the only one in the family who didn't get the entrepreneurship gene, but then my sister-in-law was going to take over the inn, and it...it was like a match. The idea...the purpose ignited inside me, and planning how to restore it became the only thing I could think about."

"So, you'd try to restore it?" He swirled the wine in his glass and scrutinized me.

You can do this—you have to do this. For Lou.

"Oh, absolutely," I gushed. "The center of Friendship—the center of its history—is that inn." For long minutes, I stitched together for him Lou's plans for the inn like they were the fabric of my own dreams. What would stay. What would change. What would be better. "It would be so incredible to have that focal point and piece of the past be returned to the town. How many inns can boast registers showing Paul Revere and John Adams and George Washington all stayed there?"

"Really?" He dug into the last of his food.

"It was the only visit George Washington ever made to Maine, and it was for a fishing trip." Lou loved that part of the story, and "twin thing" or not, I felt her enthusiasm for the tale bubble through me. "There's so much history at the inn...so much that's been forgotten as it's fallen into disrepair. Don't you think something that has seen so much, something that has lived a life of its own, deserves to have those memories be honored? Brought back to life? Shared with everyone so they can appreciate and love them?"

I fought for Lou's dream because it had been my own—to remember something or someone or someplace exactly as it had been, staking it to memory with the tines of scent.

Somewhere in the restaurant, a champagne bottle opened, and the sound popped the bubble of my thoughts. I quickly looked at Chandler and found him staring at me, something tumultuous in his gaze. Everything else about him might have been crafted to look relaxed—in control—but the pulse of his jaw and the storm of his stare made me think I'd said something wrong. Something that pained him. *Angered him.*

"Chandler?"

Instantly, the emotion was gone. Dissolved from his face like it had been doused in acid.

He blinked and flashed a tight smile. "Unfortunately, sometimes, those memories are no longer memories but simply ghosts," he declared and then gave a slight flick of his wrist, calling Marty to the table to ask for the check. My brow creased, wondering what had wounded him—*that* was what he'd looked like. Wounded.

Who would be upset about preserving history? Or revisiting cherished or important memories? I shouldn't care—he certainly didn't. But I did wonder. What could wound a man who had every defense that life and privilege could possibly give?

Marty rushed off, and Chandler reclaimed the conversation before I could reel in my thoughts.

"Speaking of ghosts...your sister mentioned the inn was haunted."

Crap.

My throat bobbed. "Many people do believe that to be the case."

"Do you?"

I opened my mouth and then snapped it shut again. Lou was too practical to believe in ghosts, but that didn't matter right now. *What was that saying? In for a penny...*

"I haven't personally experienced any of the sightings, but I believe those who have. Thankfully, from what I've heard, it doesn't sound like the spirits have any harmful intent."

"And what if opening it back up makes them angry?"

"Oh, it won't," I blurted out a little too confidently as his eyes narrowed. "I think they're just a little frustrated that their home has been left to decay for so long." I tacked on a soft smile and laughed at the end like the message wasn't clear. *The sooner I—Lou—took control of the inn, the hauntings would stop.*

Marty returned with the check and discreetly took Chandler's card.

"Thank you for dinner," I said. Better to steer clear of the ghost conversation. "It was delicious."

His tipped smile made my stomach do something I'd also later attribute to the wine. "Thank you for the company. And the conversation."

Heat prickled in my cheeks.

Perfect.

I couldn't hold back my smile as we strolled out of the restaurant. Whether it was the glasses or the glasses of wine, I took the two small steps outside too quickly and turned my ankle on the landing.

"Shit—" Air whooshed from my chest as I collided with something hard—something I knew instantly was *not* the ground. It was far too warm and far too...alive.

"Are you okay?"

I tipped my head back, my balance steadying on the twin dark points of his eyes. They were so close. So intense. But my mistake wasn't looking at him or touching him, it was breathing him in. It was breathing in his spiced sandalwood musk and the dark cherry wine lingering on his breath. Letting it fill my nostrils and infuse straight into my veins. Like his own brand of adrenaline, it made my heart skip and pound and my body ache and ache...and ache.

No...

"Yes," I murmured, my fingers curling into the lapel of his jacket, and took another breath.

He was...*intoxicating*. My lungs craved the scent of him more than oxygen, my head growing light as it sacrificed air in exchange for him. With every breath, I expected him to pull away. I'd told him I was okay. Steady. He could let me go.

But he didn't.

If anything, his hands on my waist grew tighter. His body swayed closer. His head dipped lower.

My eyes didn't dip into the depths of his, they dove. Deep beneath his collected veneer and calm aloof. Deep until I reached the source of his heat—and the source of my own.

"Chandler..." What should've been a plea to end this instead left my lips in desperation for more.

Scent was the precursor to taste. It prepared our

mouths for what was to come, our tongues for what to expect. I'd understood the relationship between those senses for a long time and experienced it for far longer, but this was the first time scent had ever prepared my mouth for the taste of a kiss.

But the taste of him was about the only thing I was prepared for, as his mouth claimed mine with a heavy groan.

Restraint was the difference between the warmth of a candle and the blaze of a wildfire. And this kiss lacked all of it. Chandler hauled me against him, his lips crushing—bruising in their hunger. Maybe I shouldn't have liked it—the way everything about this blaze signaled instant havoc and destruction—but I more than liked it. I craved more.

This kiss was trouble, and I craved it all.

My arms wound around his neck, my mouth opening to let the warm velvet of his tongue spear deep and tangle with mine. I felt his deep rumble of desire against my chest, my nipples pebbling painfully at the sensation. I'd never felt like this before. This instant, ravenous want. I bowed closer to ease the ache, but it wasn't enough.

He sucked on my tongue. I bit into his lip. He growled and wrapped one hand around my braids, tugging my head back and giving him deeper access to my mouth.

The kiss consumed me. Every lick. Every stroke. He was the fire, and I was the candle, my entire body melting under the heat of his flame. Dissolving. Disintegrating for a man who thought I was my twin sister. Reality, like a cold, heavy stone, plummeted into my stomach.

I don't know what would've happened if we'd been left like that—how far or how hot the blaze would've burned. I do know it would've been destructive. It already was.

The door to the restaurant opened, and with it came the boisterous laugh of a woman with her friends.

"Shit," Chandler muttered and practically shoved me away from him.

Shit was right.

I wiped my mouth like I could wipe the kiss from my memory. Unfortunately, I already knew how impossible that would be. Of course, the best kiss of my life would be with the one man that family and loyalty dictated that I detest.

Dammit, Frankie.

What had I done? I straightened my jacket, then folded my arms and clasped my hands in front of me. I fidgeted, the electric heat building inside me suddenly having nowhere to go. *Crap. Crap. Crap.* The women looked between us and giggled as they walked by. The whole time, I bit into my tongue, leashing the wild thing until it was just the two of us again.

"I'm so sorry, Mr. Collins, that was—"

No.

I stopped. My gaze snapped to his. Chandler stilled.

And then our lies crumbled.

His expression hardened. "You know who I am?"

My jaw dropped, my tongue suddenly dead weight in my mouth. "I do." *Think, Frankie. Come up with a story—an explanation.* "Were you ever going to tell me the truth? Or were you just going to continue to lead me on, believing you were a gentleman?"

Or just go straight for the jugular.

His eyebrows rose, the barb well-aimed.

"I was," he began slowly, the sparks in his eyes making me think I should be running for cover. "I was just waiting to see how long you were going to lead me on...believing you were your sister."

My jaw dropped, and I swayed. *No. How*—I swallowed the lump in my throat. The only way through this now was to keep on going.

"How did you know?"

He let out a bitter laugh, the question also a confirmation. "The scar on your wrist."

My gaze dropped to my hand like I didn't know exactly where the hot wax had left a permanent mark on the inside of my wrist. But the fact that he'd noticed it in my shop—that tiny thing when I'd handed him the ocean candle—*dammit*. Gritting my teeth, my head snapped back up, sending my vision swimming again.

I yanked off Lou's glasses and shoved them in my pocket. No reason to keep them on now.

"What can I say, Mr. Collins? I had to look out for my sister." I folded my arms.

"You think I came here to hurt her?" His incredulous look would've been comical—even cute—if I wasn't so determined to hate him.

"I think you already are—holding her dream hostage and then pretending to swoop in here like some prince—"

"First off, no one swooped. I stopped in for a cup of coffee, and if I remember correctly, *you* were the one who insisted she give me a tour of town without getting my full name—"

"And when you learned *her* full name, you didn't

think that was the appropriate time to tell her that you were the man standing in the way of her dreams?"

"Do you think it was?" He threw his arms out. "I don't know your sister that well, but I don't take her for the type to enjoy confrontation." *Unlike you* went unsaid but not unheard.

I opened my mouth and then snapped it shut. He was right about that. Lou would've...not taken to the news very well in the moment.

"So, you just invited her to dinner instead?" I volleyed back, taking a step toward him. I didn't care if he was a good foot taller than me, a solid billion richer, or an entire empire more powerful—I wasn't going to back down. Not when it felt like so much was at stake.

"I invited her to dinner because I enjoyed learning about the town from her, and I wanted to learn more—"

"About the town or the inn or her?"

"All of it," he answered, answering my interrogation without even a single crack in his demeanor.

"Why?"

"Because I have a property here I want to sell. It's called market research," he quipped, and I glared at him.

"And here I thought hiding your real identity was called catfishing."

"Is it, *Frankie*?"

Touché.

"If you knew it was me the whole time, why didn't you say something?"

"Because I wondered why you'd come instead of Lou...and why you were trying to hide it from me."

But then it hit me...the whole time, he'd known it was me. At the end...minutes ago...he knew.

"And the reason you kissed me?"

His eyes darkened, the spark in them signaling the hunger that had been there before.

"A momentary lapse in judgment."

The weight of a thousand butterflies fell in my stomach, feeling like nothing and everything at the same time.

"Maybe we should just consider this whole night a lapse in judgment."

His lips twitched. "I think that's a good idea."

I breathed just a fraction easier. As long as it meant he wouldn't hold this against Lou, I would get over his coldness...and his kiss.

"So, you'll still consider Lou's offer?"

His exhale was acerbic. "You're a business owner, Miss Kinkade. You should understand the importance of making smart business decisions," he answered, adjusting the sleeve of his jacket.

I pursed my lips, ignoring the twinge of soreness that reminded me of our kiss. "I know that all the good business decisions in the world don't make you a good person."

His head snapped up, his gaze fuming. "Your sister's offer isn't the most attractive. It's nothing personal."

Nothing personal. From the man who'd just devoured me on the sidewalk.

I moved closer, keeping just enough room between us so his scent didn't overpower my senses again.

"I think you're overestimating your own attractive-ness," I quipped. *Take that, Mr. Not-Personal.*

"Oh?" He stepped toward me, and I gritted my teeth when his spiced warmth hit my nose, fueling the ache that still lingered low in my stomach. "And how's that, Miss Kinkade?"

"Very few people want to buy a haunted property, Mr. Collins. But you're welcome to do your own... market research." My smile pulled tight. "My sister's offer will still be on the table when you're done."

I left him standing on the sidewalk, deciding to walk all the way down to the Maine Squeeze before calling Lou to come and get me. I needed distance. I needed to cool off.

I needed to make a mental note of all the mistakes I'd made tonight that I could never make again.

First, pretending to be my twin sister. Second, kissing the stranger who held her future in his grasp. And third...*wishing it would happen again.*

CHAPTER 7

CHANDLER

"*Very few people want to buy a haunted property, Mr. Collins. But you're welcome to do your own market research.*"

"Chandler?"

I tensed, brought back to reality by Mom's voice. I shouldn't be thinking about Frankie or the goddamn inn —*or that kiss*. But Christ, that woman infected me. Frankie Kinkade was pure fire. Bright. Bold. Hot. Tempting. She made it so damn easy to draw close, so damn warm and inviting and sweet, and then holy hell, did she deliver a burn.

"I'm sorry, what did you say?" I sighed and smiled apologetically, my gaze flicking to the candle that had sparked my distraction.

After the other night, I didn't want to believe that the ocean scent could work miracles, but sure enough, Mom's fog when I first arrived evaporated as the flame stretched its tethers through the air and anchored her mind to the present.

"I asked what you thought of my newest friend."

She pointed to the far wall, a preserved monarch butterfly hanging on display in the small square case.

"Very nice." My smile was quick, my own mind too unmoored to focus for very long. "Where did you get it?"

She blinked like it was a silly thing for me to ask. "Tom brought it, sweetheart." She motioned to the other butterfly frames and artwork on the wall. "He brought me all of them. You know that."

"Oh," I rumbled. *Did I know that? Had she told me that?* I knew Tom visited her often, but I didn't realize he brought her gifts.

"What's going on?" Mom patted my knee. "Your mind seems...away."

I let out a quick breath. I knew I should brush it off. Say it was just work and talk about something else. But who the hell else was I going to share this with—this thing that twisted and knotted in my chest? *This woman.*

"Ghosts."

"Oh." She sat back and then chuckled. "Well, that would be very distracting. Real ghosts?"

I grunted. "Apparently."

I'd spent all week making my rounds through town. Visiting the local shops and businesses and meeting the generations of locals who'd lived in Friendship their entire lives. At every turn, I was met with one singular agreement. *Absolutely, the old inn was haunted.*

No doubt. No uncertainty. It was only the twinkle in their eyes that betrayed them. Truth never came with a twinkle.

Some said it was Revolutionary War ghosts. Some claimed it was Paul Revere himself. Others, ghosts from the Prohibition era. Everyone built a good story around the foundation Frankie had planted, but I was convinced that what they were creating was nothing more than a house of cards.

"Friendly ones, I hope?"

"Fake ones are more like it," I said low.

My sister's offer will still be on the table when you're done.

It wasn't a promise. It was a...foreshadowing. Like she knew she had the upper hand. I saw it in the glint of her eyes the same way she'd looked in the restaurant when she thought I believed she was Lou. Identical or not, I'd never not know her. *No, let me rephrase.* Identical or not, parts of me would never not know her.

Lou Kinkade was like a cool ocean breeze, calm and reassuring, but Frankie was a damn sun flare. They could both be standing in front of me, covered head to toe in potato sacks, and I'd still always know—only be drawn to the warmth of one.

"Fake?" Mom laughed. "You're going to have to explain more than that, Chandler."

"The people of Friendship believe—want everyone to believe—that old inn is haunted."

"No, it can't be. Can it?"

I didn't want to get into this, but I couldn't help myself. The smile on Mom's face. The twinkle in her eyes. She was interested. Engaged. *Present.* And it was only a matter of time before I ran out of these moments with her.

"I don't think so. Ghosts aren't real, but they are a convenient ally for someone who doesn't want me to sell the inn," I grumbled and let out a long breath.

Maybe I should just let the Kinkades have it. What

the hell did it matter to me? I never wanted it in the first place, and it wasn't like my business or career needed this sale. The inn was a blip in the billions. I'd come up here out of curiosity, and I sure as hell had more important business to handle back in Boston, but after meeting her...after realizing what was going on...

I told myself I was staying on principle—acting on sound business practices. But goddammit, the truth was I couldn't stop thinking about her and that kiss and wondering when the last time was when I felt something so strongly that I couldn't resist it. Because that was exactly what happened.

The feel of her pressed to me. The part of her pink lips. The hungry haze in her eyes. And that kiss—I'd gone from businessman to beast in the span of a heartbeat. God, I'd wanted to devour her right then and there on the sidewalk. And I would've if she hadn't stopped me.

"They don't want you to sell it?" Mom reeled me back to the moment. "Why not? It would be so wonderful to have it up and running again."

My tongue felt like it sat in a pool of acid. I wasn't sure what made me the bigger asshole—wanting to sell it to someone who planned to tear it down or lying to her about it. I let a long exhale pass my lips. It was business, and I didn't want to argue with her or upset her. I didn't know...I was afraid I'd lose her if I did.

"I think they want to dictate *who* I sell it to."

"So, they all decided to believe it was haunted?"

"One of them," I croaked, my gaze locking on the damn candle. "One of them decided it should be haunted and enlisted all the rest."

"Oh my..." She trailed off, and I looked at her,

watching a smile appear. "In all my years...what a drastic, clever idea."

Dammit. Hot air blew from my lips. Even Mom was admiring my adversary now.

"Not clever. Frustrating."

"And you don't like their buyer's offer?"

My jaw clenched tight. I liked Lou Kinkade. I liked her ideas. Her plans. I liked how she knew her town and her market, and I admired that she'd delved so deeply into this project that even her twin sister could rattle off her dreams as though they were her own.

But *like* had nothing to do with business.

"It's not the best one." The best one was from a man I was meeting with this afternoon at the property to light a fire under this deal. I couldn't remember the last time I'd personally met with a buyer for any property of mine. I'd never needed to. Until Frankie Kinkade had become a thorn in my business—one only I could pluck out.

"But is it the right one?"

I stilled. "They're the same thing."

I hated the way her shoulders slumped a little and the light in her eyes dimmed. I hated feeling like I'd somehow let her down. But she understood—I knew she did. She'd worked by my side in this business for too many years to not know.

"Did you know monarchs migrate almost three thousand miles every fall?"

I stared at the preserved butterfly in the frame, forcing myself to accept I'd lost her focus. Every time, it was like being dunked in a bucket of ice water. Sudden. Frigid. Painful. And it took me several seconds to adjust.

"No, I didn't."

"New little butterflies emerge from their chrysalis in the northern states, ready to take this long, strenuous journey all the way down to Mexico. And they know the way. Without question, without anything to lead or guide them, they know the right path to take." She traced the edge of the frame with her fingers and then surprised me by reaching for my hand. "I know you'll take the right path, Chandler. You were born knowing the right thing to do."

I inhaled sharply. *She was still with me.* My throat tightened, but I managed to say, "I don't know about that, but I'll figure out how to handle this. I always do," I assured her.

The right thing to do would be to forget about that damn kiss—a kiss that was far more *haunting* to me than this cocked-up story about ghosts at the inn. The right thing to do would be what I came here to do—sell the inn to the person who presented the best offer and then leave. Anything else was a waste of time...or worse.

"Then you can add ghostbuster to your resume."

I breathed out a laugh, watching Mom lean toward the candle. "This candle is really just wonderful, Chandler. Where did you say you got it again?"

From the woman I can't get off my mind.

"The Candle Cabin. It's a store in Friendship." One more dilemma I faced...I needed more of these damn candles.

If the beach scent was what kept Mom in the present, I needed to buy a storehouse of them. And that meant returning to enemy territory.

Not that I cared about enemies or confrontation. I'd dealt with my fair share over the years. But her...to face her again was different. Especially since I'd faced her every night since our dinner in the depths of my dreams. I faced her gold-flecked eyes, hooded, as they looked up at me. Her soft-spun hair and the way it curled like a vine around my fingers. And that mouth— the fire it breathed, the sweetness it housed.

Air hissed through my lips. It had been months, maybe, since I'd been with a woman. Clearly a mistake because I was dreaming about that damn kiss and everything else I'd wanted to do to her and waking up every damn morning hard as stone.

"It's so wonderful." She moved closer and took another breath. "We should get one for your room. You always love being at the shore."

The cold wave crashed over me once more. *My room?* How old did she imagine I was now?

"That would be nice," I murmured.

"Oh, good." She patted my knee. "Now, help me hang this frame, Geoff, before you run off again."

Another crack echoed from inside my chest. Her words were easy—ignorant of how painfully true they'd come to be.

I picked up the candle and blew out the flame. It gave me a couple of clear moments, but it wasn't a miracle. It couldn't fix what was happening inside her brain. It could only let me forget for a little bit that I was slowly losing her.

"Come on," I muttered, tapping my fingers on the steering wheel and staring at the flower delivery truck in front of me blocking the street.

Maine Stems. Catchy.

I'd been stuck behind it—*parked* behind it for ten minutes—and ten minutes was a long time when nothing had been loaded onto or unloaded from it. What the hell were they doing? Growing the damn flowers from seed?

Back in Boston, I would've been honking by now. Or my driver would've been. But here, to honk at someone was the equivalent of a hit-and-run. Now that Frankie had outed me, I wasn't a fan-favorite in the community who consistently lied to my face about my own property. I didn't want to deal with...whatever they'd do next if I started blasting my horn at local business delivery trucks that were holding up traffic.

I should've just walked. Everyone walked around here. Home. Shops. Shore. Especially this time of year and this close to the center of town. But I didn't want to be from around here. I wanted to keep my distance from this town and this inn and her.

My phone buzzed. A reminder for my meeting with Mr. Fairfax that was starting...*now*. I glanced at the clock, frustration staining my attitude. *Dammit.* I opened up a message to him and let him know I was trying to find parking and that I'd be there in a few minutes.

Almost as soon as the message was sent, the tall delivery driver appeared and rounded the back of the truck. He looked about my age, and as he reached for the door, he looked at me, tipped his head, and smiled as if to thank me for my patience.

"Yeah, yeah." I gave a halfhearted wave. Just before he climbed into the truck, I swore his smile looked more like a grin.

Jesus. I was starting to imagine everyone in this damn town was in one pocket or another of Frankie Kinkade's.

The truck rumbled back to life, and we finally started to move.

I scanned the side of the road for street parking, but everything was blocked up as I approached the inn. The truck made it a little hard to see too far in front of me, so I slowed, opening up some distance so I could see if Mr. Fairfax was there yet. A purple Maserati appeared like a shiny, sore thumb on the side of the road. *Yeah, he was here.*

Sure enough, Fairfax stuck out just as much as his damn car did. No one—not even a visitor to town—would be caught wearing a beige suit with a deep purple hat. But that was Cornelius Fairfax. Eccentric, obnoxiously skeptical, and painfully superstitious.

The man once refused to buy a piece of waterfront property simply because there were red tulips growing in one of the window planters. There was still debate over whether it was the color red, the tulips, or both that caused it.

I didn't like doing business with him because the man had no trust in anyone. And while there might be many finer points to my reputation, untrustworthy wasn't one of them. But when it came to this inn, beggars couldn't be choosers. Fairfax wanted a central location with good views for a condo complex, and the property of the inn delivered.

I was about to stop and put my hazards on—since

that seemed to be the norm around here—and let Fairfax know I'd be right there, but as I got closer, I saw he was already talking to someone. Great. Hopefully, his assistant—

I squinted. *Not great.*

Fairfax was talking to Frankie. *What the hell?*

My jaw started to pound with how hard I clenched it. They looked in deep conversation, and if there was one thing I'd learned about Frankie Kinkade, it was that deep was dangerous. And that became more apparent as my car crawled closer. Fairfax had his back to me, so I couldn't see his face, but Frankie...she was animated. Cheeks flushed, arms moving. She motioned to the inn and then down at the sidewalk. *Why the hell were her candles all over the sidewalk?*

And why was she talking to Fairfax about it?

After that, I couldn't find a parking spot fast enough. Anger thumped like a war drum in my head as I stalked down the street toward them. From this angle, I could tell Frankie was doing all the talking because I could see Fairfax now, his face shaded by his hat but his mouth firm and unmoving.

He wouldn't give a shit about ghosts. At the end of the day, he was here for the land, not the building. Frankie was going to realize really quick that this wasn't small-town business she was meddling in. I appreciated her tenacity and the authenticity of her sister's offer, but feelings were never a good barometer for business. Hell, feelings were never a good barometer for anything.

The beat in my head grew louder the closer I got, and I didn't wait for a break in their conversation before I stepped in.

"Fairfax. Good to finally meet you." I extended my hand, half-blocking Frankie from his view. "Chandler Collins, CEO of Collins Realty. So sorry to keep you waiting." Cornelius was flustered for a second before he quickly switched gears and returned my handshake. The whole time, Frankie's glare bored a hole in my back. *Good.* Maybe that would clue her in to the hollowness inside my chest.

"Pleasure," Fairfax replied gruffly, and then cleared his throat. "This young lady here has been sharing some...details about the property with me."

"Well, I'm glad Miss Kinkade could entertain you with her local lore while I parked," I drawled casually and extended my arm toward the main gate. "Why don't I show you around and give you all the facts myself—"

"Is this property haunted, Collins?"

Goddammit.

"No—"

"Yes—"

I whipped my head around and glared at Frankie, anger and attraction sizzling through me like ungrounded electricity.

"No, it's not," I bit out, my eyes still locked on her, daring her to contradict me.

And she did.

"I'm sorry, Mr. Collins"—her sweet voice was as saccharine as raw honey—"I know you've just arrived in town and aren't familiar with the area or much of its heritage"—*touché*—"but I promise you, the old Lamplight Inn is most assuredly haunted. Feel free to ask *anyone* who lives around here." Her eyes never broke from mine, the golden flecks in them tap dancing over my irritation. She knew I'd asked around —knew I would ask around. And now she rubbed it in my face that I'd walked right into the net she'd planted for me.

If I wasn't so damn annoyed and inconvenienced by her gall, it would be one more thing on a quickly growing list of the reasons I was attracted to her. A list I'd retitled *Reasons to Avoid Frankie Kinkade*.

"Miss Kinkade, even if ghosts do exist, I can assure you, it's no concern of Mr. Fairfax. It's the property we're here to look at. Your ghosts will rest in peace once the building is rubble," I bit out, losing another layer of restraint. So, what if she knew the buyer I wanted to sell to not only offered more but planned on destroying the historic inn?

Business was business.

Frankie's jaw went slack, her full lips separating just enough to make me want to slide my tongue back inside them. My tongue...and other parts of me. *Fuck*.

I forced my lips into a cold smirk. "Isn't that right, Fairfax?"

"Oh, no," Frankie interjected before he could answer. "Ghosts don't just disappear when the building goes. They haunt the land, and they'll probably be even angrier that you've destroyed their home." Her eyes flicked from me to Fairfax, and whatever she saw must've made her realize she was losing her foothold because she pressed her hand to her chest and then reached for my arm with her other. Heat blasted through my veins. Heat and hunger. "But what I'd be more worried about is the cemetery underneath the inn."

"Cemetery?" *Jesus Christ*. My hand slowly curled

at my side. This was the kind of shit that only happened in small towns. Rumors and secrets and...*shenanigans*.

I turned my head and met her stare, and she didn't flinch. When my fist balled tight, it flexed my arm underneath her fingers, and I heard the small catch of her breath before she dropped her hold.

My nostrils flared. *You're playing with fire.*

Playing with fire is my job. Her gaze seemed to respond a second before she actually did respond. "There's a Native American burial ground that colonial settlers built over—according to legend." *Or according to Frankie's imagination.*

"Collins, if I tear this thing down and end up with zoning and historical society and preservation society hoopla because of a damn burial ground—"

"There is no burial ground underneath the inn," I snapped. Later, I'd regret losing my cool and wonder what the hell it was about her particular brand of impertinence that got so far underneath my skin.

"I wouldn't be so sure about that, Mr. Collins." Frankie stepped to the side, holding her smile and batting her not-so-damn innocent lashes. "But as I told Mr. Fairfax, when I heard the inn was for sale, I wanted to help in any way I could. Of course, there was no way for you to know about the ghost problem." She put her hand on my arm, heat branding my skin again. "So, I've been performing séances here every week to help appease the spirits."

Are you fucking kidding?

When her eyes widened, I realized the rumble around us wasn't traffic on the street but the growl erupting from my chest. Gritting my teeth, I tugged my arm away.

"Look, Fairfax, I can assure you—"

"I'm going to need more than assurances here, Collins," he blustered, reaching and adjusting the seat of his hat. "No burial ground. No ghosts. Or no deal. I'm not going to pay a premium for this property only to have all my investment go six feet under."

"Absolutely. I will provide you with documentation of the historical uses of this land, as well as radiographic scans to prove there are no bodies underneath the ground."

"And the ghosts, Mr. Collins?" Frankie probed sweetly, her almond eyes waiting for mine to land as my head whipped back to her.

I didn't know what was more unbelievable right now—that I was having a legitimate conversation about ghosts or that I still wanted—*with an insane amount of lust*—the woman who had been single-handedly derailing a dozen multi-million-dollar deals.

My glare was so fixed on her that I jerked back in surprise when something broke through my line of sight. I blinked and turned and found the culprit—*a butterfly*. By the time I saw it, it was far enough away that I couldn't tell if it was like the one in Mom's frame, but at that point, it didn't matter. A butterfly had appeared at this exact moment, and all I could think about was what she'd said.

"You'll know the right thing to do."

"Do you have physical proof they exist?" I demanded quietly.

"Proof? Of ghosts?" Her laugh was like individual rays of sunshine. Something that made me want to close my eyes and bask in its warmth...if only she wasn't my adversary. "Oh." She stopped suddenly, pressing her hand to those damn lips. "Oh, I thought you were joking." The corners of her mouth turned up, and so help me, all I wanted to do was kiss the damn coyness from her face. "I don't know that I can provide proof, Mr. Collins. It's just common knowledge when you live here, but if you'd like, I can continue my séances—"

"You know what?" I interrupted her, a wide smile breaking over my face. *The first clue that I'd lost my fucking mind.* "I have a solution." I faced my counterpart, almost completely cutting Frankie out of the conversation. "I will prove to you the property isn't haunted, Fairfax. Personally."

The other man folded his arms, his beady eyes narrowing. "How?"

I straightened and made sure my expression didn't falter. "I will stay here—sleep inside the inn for an entire week to assure you it's not haunted."

Frankie's gasp was the first taste of my victory, but I didn't stop to savor it. She wouldn't give up that easily.

"But how can you be sure you don't encounter them? That you're...accurately recording your experience?" She blurted out. "Mr. Fairfax should be absolutely certain you've done your due diligence."

"Which is why, Miss Kinkade, you're going to stay here with me." The words were out before I could stop them. A gauntlet of sorts tossed into this ring.

The look on her face couldn't have made me smile any wider. The shock in her eyes. The flare of her nostrils. She thought she'd have the upper hand because there was nothing she wasn't willing to do for her story. Well, there was nothing I wasn't willing to do for this sale.

This was the right thing. Fairfax was the right

choice. He had to be. Not this woman with her sparkling eyes, her smile made of sunshine, and her kiss made of sin.

"Clearly, as the resident expert on the paranormal state of the inn, who better to confirm my findings? I'm happy to take any other suggestions, but as you've already spoken to Mr. Fairfax at length about this, I'm sure he'd be more comfortable if you were there, too."

Her mouth opened, then shut, and then slipped open again.

"Yes, Miss Kinkade. Since you seem to have the knowledge and the tools"—he motioned to the candles littering the sidewalk—"for this kind of thing. I'd prefer you both ascertain the truth to these rumors."

I lifted an eyebrow, daring her to find some excuse otherwise.

Frankie slid her tongue out over her full mouth, reminding me that its demands had matched my own. Damn, that kiss had been unexpected. Both because it happened and because of how it happened—like a match to a goddamn gallon of gasoline. I watched her pink lips close as she swallowed, and it hit me what I'd done.

Fuck.

Fucking fuck.

"Okay, Mr. Collins," she agreed, her voice less smooth, her cheeks even pinker. "I'll happily stay at the inn with you this coming week—"

"Tonight." Not a chance in hell I was going to give her a single day to boobytrap the damn place like she'd boobytrapped the collective memory of this whole town. "We start tonight."

Her throat bobbed. "Tonight then," she agreed, her

smile nowhere near as confident as before. *Then again, neither was mine.*

"Good," Fairfax grumbled. "I'll look for your report at the end of the week before I can even consider moving forward with an official offer."

He tipped his head and departed down the street, leaving Frankie and me rooted in front of the inn.

"Looks like we'll get to the bottom of these ghosts after all, Miss Kinkade." My gaze roamed her face. "I appreciate your assistance."

In the span of seconds, her fiery perseverance had restored its provocation. "I'm happy to help, but as I told you the other night, Mr. Collins, in the end, my sister's offer is going to be the only one left standing."

I was willing to do anything for a sale—including sleeping in an abandoned inn. I wasn't afraid of ghosts —especially not ones that didn't exist. But there were worse things than ghosts that could haunt me, namely the woman I'd just signed up to spend the next six nights with.

Frankie Kinkade was like the apple—both trouble and temptation—and if I wasn't careful, if I didn't keep a strict distance, one more taste of her would destroy my whole world.

CHAPTER 8
FRANKIE

"I'm sorry. You're doing what?" Lou gripped the edge of the desk like she was about to topple over.

Unfortunately, there weren't really any seats in my brother Kit's art gallery, so I didn't have much choice but to let my sister know about this latest development while she was standing.

"I'm going to be staying at the inn all week to prove that it's haunted," I repeated casually, like staying in an abandoned building with a stranger was an everyday occurrence.

Her eyes blinked slowly several times, looking wider behind her round frames, before her thoughts finally slowed enough for a response to catch on her tongue.

"Why?"

"I told you, to prove it's—"

"Why do you need to prove it, Frankie?" she demanded, and I knew she was really upset. She never interrupted or demanded. "You said the rumors would be enough—that getting the whole town involved in your plan would work."

I had said that. I'd been wrong.

The damn man had talked to everyone and their brother—well, not my brothers—but everyone else, and still, Bea had overheard him on the phone at the Maine Squeeze a few days ago, instructing one of his minions to set up a private tour between him and the buyer for this afternoon. He was trying to circumvent any interaction with anyone who could sway this mystery man, Fairfax, to walk away from the property.

"Well, that was before."

"Before what?" She uncapped her water bottle and took a good swig.

"Before today."

Her bottle slammed onto the counter. "What happened today?"

"Collins set up a meeting with this other offer at the inn." I refused to say his name. *Chandler*. Chandler was the man I'd kissed. The one whose scent made my heart flutter and whose kiss turned my bones to mush. Collins was the jerk who only cared about a good deal.

"You didn't..."

"I had to do something, Lou." I waved a hand at her in frustration and then shoved it into the bag of gummy lobsters I'd been snacking on.

Her knuckles turned white. "What did you do?"

I chewed slowly and then swallowed with a shrug. "Brought a few candles over to the inn."

"You trespassed—"

"No, of course not." I smiled. At least I could ease her mind about that. "I just set them up on the sidewalk and told the buyer I was performing a séance."

Lou whimpered and let her head drop into her hands. "He's never going to take my offer, Frankie. Not after you—"

I grabbed her wrists and yanked them down, forcing her to look at me. "He was never going to take your offer, Lou. Not with all your careful and conscientious dreams. Not with all your kindness and pleas. Not with all the history of what that inn means to this town." I took a deep breath and let it out slowly along with the rest of the cold, hard truth. "Chandler Collins doesn't care that you're the right person for the property. All he cares about is who is going to pay him the most money."

"No," my good-hearted sister protested. There was no one in the world who could believe in the good in a person like Elouise Kinkade.

"Yes." My throat tightened, fighting down the words I knew were coming. I swore I wasn't going to tell her this part—swore there would be no need. But as I stared into her hope-drenched eyes, I knew she'd never be convinced of the lengths I'd gone to if I didn't. "Lou, the other offer...he's going to tear down the inn."

Her jaw dropped, and she made a sound like I'd just stabbed her in the chest. "No—"

"He doesn't want to save it. He wants to build condos."

Twin tears ran down her cheeks, and the heartbreak on her face only strengthened my resolve. *Screw you, Chandler Collins. You don't want this inn, and you certainly don't need the money.*

"That's why I told him I was doing a séance." *And that there is a gravesite underneath the building.* "It's more than the offer now, Lou. It's the building, this history, our town."

She didn't move for long moments, stilled by the shock of the news, but finally—thankfully—her chin lowered in a nod. She understood.

"I'm sorry." I clasped her hands tight, releasing one when she went to wipe her cheek.

"So why do you have to stay there?" she asked quietly.

I straightened. "Well, they still didn't believe me."

"So, you offered to stay there?"

My lips parted, but the answer got stuck on the tip of my tongue.

"Frankie..."

"Collins said he was going to sleep at the inn to prove there weren't any ghosts," I blurted out, watching her eyes really grow wide this time. "I said that his... assessment couldn't be trusted."

"So, you offered to go instead?" She gaped, and I wished it were the truth.

"Not exactly. He dared me."

"What?"

"Chandler—*Collins*. He said that since I was the expert, I would have to stay, too." I shrugged and popped another gummy lobster into my mouth.

This time, I thought for sure Lou was going to lose it. That I was going to have to leap across the counter and hold her up to keep from collapsing. But maybe I needed to start giving my twin a little more credit. She was shocked. Of course. But she didn't waver.

"You're staying in an abandoned inn with a stranger?" she asked in a choked whisper.

"It's not like the building isn't sound." Before the whole musical chairs of ownership debacle, Mom, Lou, and Jamie's wife, Violet, had a construction company come in and assess and then repair the foundation structure of the building. They'd just finished the repairs when we learned the inn wasn't really ours.

"Frankie..."

"And he's not a stranger." *Not the way I'd kissed him.* But Lou didn't need to know about that. Not when telling her meant having to explain why I hated that I wanted it to happen again.

"*Frankie.*" Her shoulders slumped, and creases worried her brow. "It's too much. This is too much. You don't have to—"

"Lou, I'm not going to let Collins swoop in and throw away centuries of history and a decent offer just to prove he's a ruthless businessman." Nor was I going to let butterflies from one kiss turn me soft on a man.

Sure, there were good men out there, my two brothers and two cousins were proof enough of that. And I knew life-changing love did exist. Again, my brothers' relationships evidenced it. It wasn't that I didn't think there could be someone out there for me to love or to love me, I just didn't want to. Not after what my father had done to Mom. Used her. Abandoned her. And after everything, she'd risen back up. Stronger. More successful.

But I wanted that from the start. Which was why I focused solely on my business and matchmaking for everyone else in my life. Because then, no one looked too closely at why the only flames I let into my life were the ones I created for myself.

"But it's his property."

I jammed my finger down on the counter. "And this is my town," I said with a little more force than intended. "I'm sorry. I know you're worried, but I didn't have a choice, Lou. I know you think I did, but I didn't. And one day, I promise you, you're going to end up in a situation where you only have a split second to decide how life—your future—is going to play out. There won't be time to sit and think, to worry or rationalize. There will only be a single second to either go after what you want regardless of what you have to risk...or to let the dream go."

She chewed on her bottom lip, silent for a moment. "Well, I hope that day is far, far away for me."

"Me too."

Whenever it came, I knew my sister would act— would fight—no matter how strongly she thought she'd cower right now.

Lou tugged the bag of gummies across the counter and plucked one out for herself. "So, Chandler is staying there to prove it's not haunted, and you're going to be there to show him it is."

I wish she'd call him Collins, too.

"Yup."

"How are you going to prove it's haunted when it's not?"

I frowned. That was the least of my problems right now. "I'll figure something out."

I had another six hours before I had to be back at the inn. *Nine p.m. sharp.* Maybe I could call Nox again. My cousin had been happy to borrow his brother's truck and lend me a blockade earlier when I told him I needed traffic held up on Maine Street. It wasn't like it affected anyone other than the tourists passing through. *And Chandler on his way to the meeting.*

"You're sure you going to be okay there...alone with him?"

My heart stumbled, and air knotted in my lungs. I knew this question was coming from the start, and still, I faltered on the answer. *No, I wasn't sure...but* not in the way she meant. I'd agreed to six nights with Chandler Collins. Six nights alone with the man whose kiss made me want things that I'd decided not to have an interest in long ago.

"I'll be fine—"

"Lou?"

Crap. We both turned toward our brother's raspy voice, the bell at the front of the gallery chiming his arrival.

"I've got another—" Kit stopped short when he saw me. "Frankie." His dark brows furrowed as they looked between Lou and me. "What's going on?"

"Nothing," I answered. Lou would never be convincing with the lie. "Just stopped in to say hi on my way back to my shop." It was the truth. *More or less.* "But I should get going." I looked back at Lou and smiled. "I'll talk to you later." What I was really saying was, *please don't say anything to Kit.*

Kit would be upset and protective. He'd tell Jamie. Jamie would be furious and tyrannical. I'd never make it back to the inn tonight. Lou would lose her dream of the inn. *And I would lose my chance to kiss Chandler Collins one more time.*

It wasn't the right thought to have, but it made sense. If I was going to kiss anyone—*want to kiss anyone* —Chandler was the perfect person.

Who safer to kiss than the man who was my enemy?

If stillness had a scent, it would've been the only one in the cool air wrapping around the inn. There were only a handful of people out on the sidewalk this late, one or two lingering glances spared in my direction. I smiled back like it was completely normal for someone to be standing on the sidewalk in lounge clothes, a camping backpack, and a pillow hugged to her chest.

A girl had to have her pillow.

Thankfully, my family had been otherwise occupied when I stopped back at Mom's house to grab some of the camping gear tucked away in the basement. I hadn't camped in a while, but I figured I wouldn't need more than a sleeping bag, blanket, and pillow. Standing out there, though, I wondered if I should've brought two blankets.

"Come on..." I muttered and checked my phone. I was early on purpose. I wasn't going to give the clever Mr. Collins any excuse to doubt my commitment to my cause.

With a sigh, I tipped my head back, staring up at the stars that pricked pinpoint holes in the fabric of the night sky. Another breath of stillness sent a shiver tumbling down my spine. Six nights. Six nights at the inn. With Chandler. For Lou.

Unless he was bluffing. It was nine o'clock. *If he was going to stand me up—*

"Frankie."

I spun and shivered—not from the cold this time. "Chandler." I lifted my chin and leashed my smile to a minimum, but even there it faltered as my gaze swept over him.

Jeans. T-shirt. Zip-up jacket. My mouth parted. This was the first time I'd seen him without buttons. No button-up shirt. No unbuttoned shirt sleeves. No single-button suit jacket. He almost looked...relaxed. And it was like seeing Superman without his cape. *Chandler's no hero,* I reminded myself. So maybe it was more like seeing the devil without his horns.

He stepped closer, my pillow thankfully disguising the sudden hitch in my breath when his chest was close enough to brush my arms if either of us breathed too deep. Sandalwood and cloves sank their seductive claws into my chest. Maybe I should make a Chandler candle. Not to remember his scent—never that—but to desensitize myself to the instant ache it seemed to create.

"I see you're prepared." His stare prickled my skin, dotting it like the night sky with thousands of pinpoints of heat.

Me? "Of course." I clutched my pillow tighter. "I'm always ready."

I was about to ask if he'd changed his mind—ignoring the unexpected twinge and deflation of my chest at the thought—when he turned to the gate. *That was why he stood so close.* With a gulp, I stepped back so he could fit the key into the lock.

"I'm sure," he muttered under his breath as he stepped through and held the gate open for me.

It wasn't until I walked through and glanced over my shoulder that it struck me that he *wasn't* prepared. He had no...stuff. No bag. No clothes. *No pillow.*

The urge to ask made it to the tip of my tongue before I clamped my jaw shut and swallowed it back down. If he planned on sleeping in his clothes on the old hardwood floor, that was his problem. I was going to be as snug as a bug.

I followed his lead to the front door, my eyes darting around as he unlocked what looked like a shiny new dead bolt installed on the door. I bit back my smile. As long as he hadn't replaced the faulty latch on the back window in the kitchen, he could install whatever locks on the doors he wanted.

"Should I knock before we go in? I wouldn't want to upset any of the ghosts," he taunted.

"You don't believe there are ghosts, so why should you care about upsetting them?" I countered sweetly. "Unless you're worried that I'm right, and it is haunted."

His eyes flashed, and then he swung the door wide. *No knock then.*

Again, he held the door open for me, tension rippling through his body like it pained him to be a gentleman. *Good, it pained me too.*

I stopped just inside, the shadows painting a familiar picture of the wide entrance hall, the staircase tucked on the left that led up to the second floor, the long living room on the right. Walking straight down the hall led to the dining room and then the kitchen at the back of the house. I closed my eyes, a different scent filling my lungs—a scent of history that only dust and must and all the boarded-up secrets of the inn could create.

"Sensing the spirits?" His deep voice interrupted

my thoughts. My eyes flung open just as the door closed and engulfed us in darkness.

I heard my sharp inhale as I scrambled for my phone and the flashlight on it, but then fresh light spilled through the space.

Chandler's heavy footfalls carried him in front of me, the floor creaking like it was waking up to the notion of having the weight of guests traipsing over it once more. The light ebbed and flowed from a camping lantern held by his side, its warm glow oozing around him like he was the flame himself.

"I never claimed to sense spirits, Mr. Collins. Only that they were here."

He made a low noise and headed for the living room. *Crap.* I was hoping he'd pick one of the rooms upstairs. It would make sneaking in and out of the kitchen window a little easier.

I hadn't exactly figured out a plan on how I was going to effectively haunt the inn. Between preparing to tell Lou what was happening while concealing it from our brothers, figuring out what I needed from Mom's house to stay here, and avoiding all thoughts of entire nights alone with Chandler Collins, I hadn't made it to the ghost part of this plan yet.

That was for tomorrow. There had to be YouTube videos on how to do this. *How to Haunt* 101 or *Ghosting for Dummies.*

"Frankie."

I stopped, having taken a few steps toward the staircase.

"Where are you going?"

"To find a room upstairs if you're taking the living room—"

"You're not staying upstairs."

And who are you who gets to tell me where I am or am not? I swallowed down my bluster of pride. He was the obstacle I had to appease if there was any chance of my sister getting this inn.

"Okay." I forced a smile. "I'll stay in the dining—"

"We're both sleeping in the living room."

Both of us? In the same room? In the stillness of massive space, I swore he could hear the sound of my heart plummeting into my stomach because I certainly could.

It wasn't even my plan that was the first worry that came to my mind. It wasn't how exponentially more difficult it would be for me to sneak around and do whatever it was going to take to haunt this place. All of that should've been my first thought, but it wasn't. It wasn't even the second or third thought. All of those rungs were taken up by the idea of spending six nights not just in the same inn, but in the *same room* as the man I really wanted to kiss again.

"I don't think that's necessary," I stammered.

"Miss Kinkade"—*we were back to formalities*—"if you think I'm going to let you hole yourself off in a secluded corner of this building where you can concoct God knows what to try and prove it's haunted, then you must think I'm an idiot," he drawled with a casual smile.

I stilled. Obviously, he didn't believe it was haunted, but for him to think—to know—the lengths I'd go to and call me out on it within minutes of the first night of this charade...if that was how he wanted to play this, fine.

Challenge accepted.

My fingers curled into my pillow like it was a shield of steel as I approached him. "And if I think you just want me in the living room so you can try and kiss me again?"

His smile fell, deflated by the sharp pulse of frustration in his jaw. My victory was short-lived, the barb, double-sided.

"Don't worry, Miss Kinkade. I never mix business with pleasure." He motioned to the doorway, the lantern light treading over the threshold.

Liar. He knew who I was at dinner when he'd kissed me. He knew and kissed me anyway. A small voice inside my head reminded me, *You knew and kissed him back.*

Dammit.

"Oh?" I feigned innocence and moved right in front of him, letting my eyes swing lazily down and back up his body. "Well then, I'm so sorry."

His brow furrowed. Up close, in the harsh light from the lantern, he somehow managed to look more handsome. The way the shadows cut sharpened the ridge of his brow. The straight line of his nose. The edge of his tensed jaw.

"Sorry for what?"

My smile widened. "If you don't mix business with pleasure, and you're always doing business, then... well..." I let my eyes lower down to his waist, the harsh shadows of the lantern making it impossible to see anything except the point I was making. "Muscles atrophy when they don't get used."

CHAPTER 9
FRANKIE

Whatever upper hand I'd gained by taunting him disappeared the moment I stepped into the vacant living room. At least, it had been vacant the last time I'd been inside the inn.

While I'd spent the hours between accepting this deal and now worrying about my family and worrying about being alone with Chandler, he'd clearly spent the afternoon here.

I stared at the massive air mattress inflated in the center of the room, crowned by the stately brick fireplace behind it. It was stacked with blankets and pillows that made me shiver just thinking about how warm it would be underneath them all right now.

Against the wall was a huge case of bottled water, two more battery-operated lanterns, and two flashlights.

My nostrils flared. I'd met him outside thinking I was the one prepared...that this billionaire boor had no idea what he'd signed himself up for when he'd suggested—almost recklessly, it seemed in the moment

—to camp out here for a week. *It was what he'd wanted me to think.*

"Everything okay?" he asked, not bothering to hide the smile on his face.

"Yep." I popped the word from my mouth, volleying a smile back at him.

"I'm going to the dining room to change. I'll be right back," he warned, grabbing a small duffel I only just noticed tucked against the wall.

"Thanks for the warning," I said low, catching the sounds of a soft chuckle trailing behind him from the room.

It took a second to realize he'd left the lantern for me. *How was he going to see?* Not my problem. I grabbed the handle and marched toward the other side of the room, firmly staking my gaze on the spot where I was going to put my sleeping bag so it couldn't wander toward the shuffling shadows in the dining room where Chandler was changing.

I took another sweep of all the comforts and supplies he'd brought. I guess it was too much to hope a man as wealthy as him wouldn't be able to rough it for a few nights.

My heavy sigh echoed in the empty room. He must've opened some windows earlier, too, because the musk wasn't as thick in here as it was in the hall.

Sliding my bag from my shoulders, I set it down along with the lantern and went to the windows. The glass was so grimy I could barely make out the street-lamps through it, but to imagine them clean and sparkling, a candle lit in each one, welcoming weary travelers inside...my chest tightened. *This had to work.*

I returned to my bag, deciding that putting my

sleeping bag on the side of the air mattress closest to the door was my best bet. I would've loved to lay it out right inside the entryway, but that would've been far too obvious that I was setting myself up to make a break for it once the midnight hours hit.

Even still, I was going to have to enlist Nox again for whatever I came up with. It was the only way to be able to deny any culpability on my part.

I bent to unzip my backpack, tucking my pillow under my arm because I refused to set it on the ground —or worse, the air mattress. Opening the zipper wasn't an issue, but pulling out the sleeping bag was a problem; it was packed so tightly inside, I couldn't...

"Come on—"

"Let me." The low rumble of his voice surprised me —right before my pillow was unceremoniously tugged out from my arm and freeing both my hands.

God, his chivalry was annoying. Why couldn't he make it easy to hate him? Or at least easier to not want to kiss him?

"It's going to get colder overnight. You should put your sleeping bag in front of the fireplace."

My head jerked up from my bag, putting my eyes directly in line with his waist and the muscle I diagnosed as atrophied. *Breaking news... It was not atrophied.* Not according to Dr. Gray Sweatpants.

Crap.

I quickly straightened all the way, my eyes snapping to his. Hopefully, he saw the red in my cheeks as a sign of frustration and not anything more.

"There's no fire in the fireplace," I said on instinct. *Always my first mistake.*

"There will be when I'm done helping you."

Of course, there would. Somehow, I managed to antagonize the only billionaire Boy Scout in existence.

Taking my bag from the floor, I marched to the other side of the air mattress and yanked my sleeping bag from its pack, something small flying out and landing on the floor at Chandler's feet with a thud. Our hands collided as we reached for it at the same time. Maybe I was the only one who felt the heat because I pulled back while he picked up the bottle.

"Fireball?" He arched an eyebrow.

I laughed and shook my head. "That probably belongs to Nox—my cousin." I carefully swiped the nip from his fingers. "Fireball is his favorite fireside drink." And he'd probably shoved it in this bag the last time he'd gone camping with my brothers.

"And here I thought you were going to tell me it was a necessary ingredient to summon the ghosts."

I pretended to examine the amber liquid. "I'm sure it could summon some ghosts," I drawled, catching his gaze over the top of the cap. "But probably not the ones we're looking for."

"You're looking for," he corrected, and my smile went flat.

"The ones that are here." I shoved the tiny bottle into my pocket and went back to unrolling my sleeping bag.

It was almost comical how flat and uncomfortable it looked compared to the plush air mattress inflated next to it. *Almost.*

"Thank you." I plucked my pillow out of his hold and set it on the sleeping bag.

While I continued to arrange my things, Chandler made good on his word and unwrapped one of those slow-burning logs. There was a stack of them tucked next to the hearth, mostly in shadow.

"Has the chimney been cleaned?" I asked, hearing him place it in the fireplace, followed by the unmistakable clicks of a lighter.

"A few months ago." *When he was given ownership of the property.* "I also had them come and double-check it today."

"You thought of everything."

"He who fails to plan, plans to fail."

I stilled, the husk in his voice catching my attention and driving a shiver along my spine. It sounded like something Jamie would say—would've said to us growing up. I glanced over my shoulder, taken for a moment by the sight of Chandler crouched only a few feet away, his gaze locked on the small but growing flame.

I couldn't look away. He appeared so...unguarded. Like the moment I realized his full name, this was like I was seeing the whole of him for the first time.

"Who gave you that nugget of wisdom? Dear old dad?" A faint laugh pushed through my lips. I had an image in my mind—a small Chandler bouncing on his father's knee, the older man waving a wad of cash, chiding, *he who fails to plan...* "I'd say he failed to plan when it came to this inn." It was the ambiguity of the will that gave my family the inn and then took it away again.

"No," Chandler clipped out and stabbed the log with the end of the lighter like it had insulted him. "My father was a selfish, careless prick who failed at nothing so spectacularly as being a father." The words were harsh and direct and so cold, they might as well have been carved from ice.

Crap. I hadn't meant to upset him. Not like this. I knew what it was like to have a poor excuse for a father, but I just assumed because Chandler had been given the inn, well, whatever I assumed about their relationship, I'd been wrong. And while I wouldn't feel bad taking a jab at his atrophied penis, I did feel guilty about this.

"I'm sorry." I turned and sat on my sleeping bag, pulling my knees to my chest.

The light bounced off the pulse of his jaw. "I'm going out back to piss." He rose abruptly, grabbed the lantern, and stalked out of the room.

Smooth, Frankie.

I let out a small groan and rested my chin on my knees, watching the flames dance in the shelter of the hearth.

I didn't know why I said that—no, I did.

I wanted him to be a stereotype. To be easily hated for what he was doing with this inn and how it affected my sister. And part of me did dislike him for that—*strongly*—but another part of me warmed to him like a flame to a wick, wanting to melt away all his layers until I found the man underneath.

I didn't hear him return until the groan of the air mattress announced his weight.

"Any séances you want to perform before we go to bed?" he drawled, almost as though our last exchange hadn't occurred.

"Not tonight." I turned to slide into my sleeping bag, and my breath caught almost as sharply as the light hooked on the muscles of his back—*his bare back*.

Frozen in place, one foot under the blanket in my sleeping bag, I watched his long fingers crawl the fabric of his shirt higher up his back until the seam was in his grip and then lift it completely over his head.

My mouth parted, drinking in the sight. He was gorgeous. Perfectly bronzed and made of muscle. Why did *this* have to be the one stereotypical thing about him?

I should've turned over and gone to sleep—or pretended to. He clearly didn't want to continue the conversation about his father, and I shouldn't want to either. I shouldn't want to know more about him. I shouldn't want to know what had happened, how it shaped him. I shouldn't want it for all the same reasons I shouldn't want to kiss him—*because it only spelled trouble*.

But trouble was who I was.

"My father was a selfish, careless, gold digger," I offered to the silence.

Several long seconds passed, and I didn't realize I was holding my breath for his reply until the low tenor of his voice reached out and unlocked the air from my lungs.

"My father left when I was six. Left my mom with nothing. Moved away. Started over—started a whole new family while we struggled to make ends meet." Every statement was like a bullet from a gun, putting lethal holes in the character of the man that Chandler could hardly even refer to as his father.

My throat was tight as I went to swallow. I understood his anger. His bitterness. I understood because it had been my own.

"That's why you want to sell the inn," I said softly, seeing more of him as a layer of his persona melted away.

Again, silence chewed through minutes, until I thought for sure he wasn't going to respond. This conversation was beyond business. It was beyond the inn, beyond ghosts, beyond taunting and flirting. *It was beyond dangerous.*

"He never should've left it to me," he said like it had been a dagger in his back.

"I've only been a Kinkade for nine years," I confessed in return. "My father met my mom and got her pregnant with Lou and me not long after they started dating. He wanted to marry her, but when she insisted on a prenup to protect her business, he left her —left us."

"I'm sorry." His apology sounded like mine—more understanding than sympathy.

"When Lou and I turned eighteen, we changed our name to Kinkade. For Mom and our oldest brother— half brother—Jamie, who was more like a pseudo-father. Him and my uncle George." I let out a deep breath. "That was the last—the only tie—we had to him, and it felt good to let it go."

There was a rustle on top of the mattress, but I didn't dare look.

"I'm working on escaping all the ties to mine." The huskiness of his voice was different this time. Raw, not from anger but from pain.

"Oh?"

Was he talking about the inn? Because that would be easy to escape if he'd just take a little less and accept Lou's offer.

"My father was also in real estate," he revealed like he needed to get this off his chest, even if it was to me.

"I'm slowly reducing his business to nothing, and then I'm going to buy it. And dismantle it."

"You mean..."

"Remove all traces of it—of his legacy," he declared solemnly. "And then I'll be free of him."

Even though I wanted to say that didn't sound like freedom but more like simple revenge, I held back. It wasn't my place...and I shouldn't even think about caring what path his life was headed down after he left Friendship.

"So then, where did your advice come from?" I wondered instead.

Again, the fire crackled into the conversation for a few breaths as though it was the only thing going to respond to me. I worried my lower lip until I couldn't resist the urge to glance in his direction. Not that it helped. I couldn't see much except for his arm that must've been folded on top of his chest. It rose and fell with the deep movement of his breath.

"My business partner, Tom...he's been a family friend for a long time."

"He sounds like a smart man." I could hear that he cared for this man—that they were close by the emotion in his voice even if he tried to downplay it.

Chandler grunted. "He also doesn't believe in ghosts."

I sucked in a breath. "Chandler—"

"Good night, Frankie," he doused the conversation, and I didn't need to look to know that the grunts and grumbles of the air mattress were from him giving me his back.

"Good night," I murmured and turned toward the fire, welcoming its warmth so I could pretend the heat I felt had nothing to do with the man sleeping on the bed next to me.

But even that was impossible because the first deep breath I took was filled with him—more musk and sandalwood than clove. *He'd held my pillow*...and he'd let me think the small chivalry was the worst thing about it. Now, there was no escaping him. Not tonight. All because I'd failed to plan.

Tomorrow, I'd do better, I swore as my eyes closed and the scent of him wrapped its fingers around my fantasies and held onto them tight.

Tomorrow, I'd come up with a plan. To haunt the inn. To forget our kiss. To keep my distance. Because in six days, Chandler Collins was going to walk out of my life in one of two ways—me hating him or him hating me. And in neither of those cases was it safe for me to feel anything other than strictly professional toward him.

His perfect muscles and small chivalries and wounded soul were none of my business.

CHAPTER 10
CHANDLER

"*Ow,*" her soft voice muttered from the floor beside me.

I stifled a chuckle, listening to her muffled grumbles from the floor next to my bed. I couldn't remember the last time I'd slept on an air mattress—probably at least two and a half decades ago at a friend's house in middle school—but it wasn't too bad. Definitely better than a sleeping bag on the floor, that was for sure.

I turned my head, careful not to move anything else, so I could watch her stand. As she rose, I caught her subtle scent of cinnamon again, its prickly sweetness making my lungs burn. *Or maybe it was the way the soft morning light caught the gold in her hair as it fell down her back.*

Frankie started to gather her things with quiet franticness, and my jaw clenched. I'd never had a woman so desperate to leave the morning after. Sure, this was different. I'd never spent a night like this with a woman.

But whatever the circumstances, I'd also never woken up wanting her to stay...*like I did now*.

"Good morning."

Frankie gasped and spun, her hand slapping to her chest and drawing my focus to the swift rise and fall of her breasts. *Fuck.* The whoosh of my exhale carried my smile with it. She had on a white tee, Maine Squeeze written on it in that blocky seventies-style font. It would've been cute if it didn't show her tight little nipples peaked against the thin fabric. And in this light, I swore I could see their color. *Fucking cinnamon.*

I'd heard her take off her sweatshirt overnight. I'd heard the cadence of her breath between the crackling of the fire. I'd heard the swish of her sleeping bag every goddamn time she shifted or turned. I'd heard because —contrary to her little jab—my cock wasn't atrophied. It was aggravated. Angry to be feet from the woman I fantasized about with no relief in sight—let alone sleep.

I sat up, letting the blankets pool at my waist and hiding the way my cock thickened. She frowned, scanning my chest. *She was either getting a good look at my bare torso or my morning wood*—I made the presumptuous decision she'd prefer my chest.

"How'd you sleep?"

Her eyes snapped back to my face, pink clouding the faint smatter of freckles on her nose. They must only come out in the sun.

I thought I'd been clever—cleverer than her—when I'd suggested this damn charade. But every second since the words came out of my mouth had only proved I'd been nothing but a fool. I should've blustered—dared Fairfax to take the deal or make his superstitions public.

Being the man I usually was—cold, confident, uncaring —would've sealed the deal in minutes.

But that would've ended...*this*...with her.

"Great." She smiled and folded her arms, unable to fully mask her wince. There was no way she wasn't stiff after a night basically on the floor. "How about you?"

"Ghost-free," I replied, watching her smile turn into that damn adorable frown.

"Maybe." She shrugged, and my dick twitched at the way it moved her breasts. *God, it was so fucking inconvenient the way I wanted her.* "There are still five more nights." She pulled on her sweatshirt, and I bit into my tongue when her raised arms teased a glimpse of the skin of her stomach.

I lowered my chin. "True."

"Okay, well." She bent forward and grabbed her bag. "I guess I'll see you tonight."

She didn't even wait for a reply before bolting from the inn, and I smiled when I saw the murky outline of her shape flee down the front path. She was going to see me a lot sooner than tonight, and I was going to enjoy the look on her face when she realized it.

But for right now, I was going to get back to my hotel room, into a cold shower, and fuck my hand as fast as humanly possible.

"FRANKIE, WHEN DID YOU START MAKING THESE orange honey ones? They are divine!"

The almost-shouted compliment was the first thing

I heard when I walked into the Candle Cabin almost an hour later, and the old woman it came from was impossible to miss. Anyone with bright orange hair was hard to miss, but when it was a cloudlike perm attached to a woman who had to be in her eighties? Impossible.

The old woman was small—I wouldn't say frail because I got the sense if I did, she'd take the cane that was tucked underneath her arm, clearly giving her no support, and whack me with it. She stood at one of the displays, smelling the same scent several times with a smile on her face.

Whoever she was, Frankie must know her because she didn't reply, and there was no way she couldn't have heard the woman yell. And there was no way the little orange-haired old lady was going to take silence for an answer—or at least, there hadn't been a way until she saw me.

"Well, hello there. Welcome." Eyes wide under her thick glasses, a smile beaming a familiar path to her wrinkles, and the cane still hooked under her arm, she strolled right up to me. "Welcome to the Candle Cabin, Mr...."

I smiled back. "No mister, just Chandler."

"Chan..." Her wide eyes filled the frames of her glasses, and her jaw dropped.

I froze, afraid I'd given the woman a heart attack. *Did she know who I was? Had Frankie told her?* I pushed the thought aside. There was no way. Then, just as quickly as her expression morphed into shock, warm excitement bloomed back into her face.

"Welcome, Chandler, it's so good to finally meet you."

Finally? She took hold of my arm and led me deeper into the store.

"You can call me Gigi. Everyone does. So, what brings you to Friendship, Chandler?"

Okay, so she didn't know me...

"In town for some business." I let her guide me farther into the store, my eyes flicking to the doorway to the back where I could hear the first strains of muffled voices.

"Oh, just business? I hope you'll take some time for yourself to relax and enjoy everything our little town has to offer."

Like ghosts and a gorgeous candlemaker...

"I'll certainly try."

"Well, I'm so glad you've stopped here. The Candle Cabin is my granddaughter Francesca's shop. She's just in the back now, but I'll introduce you in just a minute when she comes out."

Granddaughter. Of course. Instantly, I knew where Frankie's wildness had come from.

"This is quite a shop—quite a selection." Using my free hand, I picked up a candle from the display in front of me. Instantly, Frankie's sweet spice hit my nostrils. *Cinnamon.* Instantly my body turned hard. *Again.*

Shit. I swallowed a groan. I wasn't sure it was possible to get high on the smell of cinnamon, but damn, I felt willing to try if it eased the want humming through my veins.

"Oh yes. Francesca is very talented. She makes all these candles by hand, and all of the scents are ones she designs herself. For example"—she pulled me to a different shelf, but I couldn't put down the cinnamon candle—"this one is one of her bestsellers." She plucked the bold, dark blue candle for me to smell. *Blueberry Buzz*. I took a whiff, and it was exactly that—sweet and tart. "Her mom and I run Stonebar Farms. Our Maine blueberry jam is our best-selling product. When Frankie was sixteen, she decided she wanted to make a candle to match the jam."

"Sixteen?" My brows rose.

"Oh, yes." Her head bobbed, and her smile widened. "Said she wanted people to take one breath of her candle's scent and instantly need to taste the jam."

My jaw clamped tight, the jar in my hand taunting that it was that way for all her candles—one scent of the cinnamon, and all I wanted was another taste of Frankie's lips.

"Her whole business started from that one candle." Pride gushed from the soft tremor of her voice. "When Francesca knows what she wants, there's no stopping her."

"Sounds like an impressive woman," I murmured.

"Oh, yes," she said again in a way that was suddenly characteristic of her. "Impressive and independent. A very fierce combination."

Fierce. That was certainly one word for her.

"Chandler."

I turned and instantly found Frankie's eyes, warm and molten and crackling with life—and irritation. "Frankie."

I loved surprising Frankie Kinkade. There was just no other way to describe it. Maybe it was because of the way her breath hitched or the way her mouth parted into this perfect "O"—an image that reinforced the fantasies that made me wake up this hard—but mostly... mostly it was because I had a feeling Frankie was rarely ever surprised. I had a feeling that she was the one always responsible for the surprises. And for some reason, I enjoyed far too damn much the idea that I did something for her that no one else did.

Then I noticed the man behind her.

He was tall. Built. Blond hair. My eyes narrowed, realizing where I'd seen him before. He was the driver of the flower delivery van I'd been stuck behind yesterday. The one who'd smiled and waved at me like he knew something I didn't. And the way he stood so close to Frankie...I had a feeling I knew who he was. *Her boyfriend*.

A feeling I'd never felt before whipped through me. Something dark and ominous and a gray green like the sky before a storm. *Did he know she'd spent last night at the inn with me?* The first question cracked through me. *Did he know we'd kissed that first night when she'd pretended to be her twin?* The second question hit a second later with a loud boom.

"What are you doing here?"

"Oh...oh..." I heard Gigi's soft confusion quickly turn to understanding. "You know each other. I didn't realize, Frankie—"

"Your grandmother—"

"Gigi."

"Gigi was just telling me about the humble beginnings of your shop," I said smoothly, unable to stop my eyes from flicking to the man who stood by her side. I walked toward them, and the boyfriend didn't even flinch. *Idiot*. I'd be putting myself squarely between Frankie and any other man if she were mine—*fuck*. "Hi, I'm Chandler." I extended my hand like I hadn't envisioned its grip around his throat like I was some sort of brute rather than a businessman.

"I'm—"

"Nox Hamilton," Frankie interjected and stepped forward, preventing him from shaking my hand. "My cousin."

Cousin. The relief I felt was fucking ridiculous. Insane and ridiculous and unfuckingcalled for.

"Frankie, how could you not tell me about Chandler?" A head of bright orange appeared next to me.

My forehead pulled tight, watching as Frankie glared at Gigi. If any look could threaten to cut off someone's tongue, it was that one.

"Because Chandler—"

"Is here to buy more of the same candle I did the other day," I finished, holding her stare firmly like I could leash the truth with a look.

I watched her weigh her options, and her decision to agree with me and not reveal I was the owner of the inn told me everything I needed to know. *She hadn't told her family about our little bargain.*

"Of course." She tipped her chin and then looked at her cousin. "Thanks for stopping by. I'll talk to you later."

He didn't say anything back, just gave her a nod and then gave me that same damn smile from the street the other day. I didn't like that smile.

"Tell Mom I'll see her later, okay, Gigi?"

"Oh, I'm going to tell her." Big, perceptive eyes swung between her granddaughter and me. *Shit.*

"Gigi..."

"Chandler." The old woman beamed at me. "It was a pleasure to meet you."

"You—"

"If you're going to be staying in town for a few more days, I know my daughter, Ailene, Frankie's mom, would love to meet you and have you over for dinner. Would Wednesday work?"

Frankie didn't bother to hide her groan of displeasure. It almost would've been insulting if the pink in her cheeks didn't tell a different story.

"I'll see if I can rearrange my schedule," I promised, shaking her bony but firm grip in mine.

Nox and Gigi headed for the door, her loud whispers making it back to me.

"It was Chandler."

"I know, Gigi—oww."

Gigi swatted the younger man. "*Chandler.*"

I was missing something about the whole exchange, but it was the least of my concerns when I faced Frankie again, her expression making me feel like I was about to be missing my head.

"What?" I smiled at her.

Her eyes flicked around the store. "Not here," she huffed, grabbed my arm, and pulled me to the back room with her.

CHAPTER 11
CHANDLER

"What are you doing here?"

Here, in the privacy of her workshop, I let my eyes roam the way they'd wanted to out there in front of her family. In front of everyone. She had on bright red pants with flowers stitched all over them and a white tee, over top of which she was wearing a smock that was dotted with wax like a melting Jackson Pollock.

"I told you. I want more of the candles I bought the other day. The beach..."

"Beach Bum."

"Yeah." I folded my arms.

"How many?"

"Whatever you have left."

Her eyes turned into slits. "Why?"

"Do you interrogate all your customers?" I chuckled.

"Only the ones who lie to me from the start," she quipped and strode to the back of the room, returning after a few seconds of shuffling and grumbling with a box of candles that she set on the counter next to me. "This is all I have."

"And I'll take this one." I set the cinnamon candle on top. At least the reminder of her would be invisible to everyone but me.

"If you think buying up a bunch of my candles is going to soften me up so I back down from our arrangement, you're—"

"Not trying to soften you up." Though the words conjured up a whole damn different image in my head. A soft Frankie. Soft and naked and mine—

"What then? Bribe me?" She shook her head. "I don't want your money or your support, Mr. Collins."

My jaw pulsed, and without thinking better of it, I ventured into the shallow end of the truth. "My mom likes this candle," I said, and she stopped and turned. "Your...Gigi said that you hand make all the candles, so I wanted to make sure I got whatever was left of this batch."

"Oh." Pink obscured the freckles on her cheeks again. "Your mom liked it?"

I shouldn't have said anything.

"She loves the beach." I still shouldn't be saying anything. And so, I did what I always do, I made it about business. "What do I owe you?"

Frankie stiffened and quipped, "An inn."

"Cute."

Our eyes collided at the word, sparks threatening to melt every bit of wax she had stored in here.

"Just take them. They were leftover anyway," she murmured and returned to a line of beakers on the counter, flanked by vials with droppers in them.

"Is this how you make your scents?" I wondered... and wandered closer.

"Yes, and it's all proprietary, so you can go now."

I fought a smile. "I have no intention nor desire to steal your recipes and make candles."

"No?" She tipped her head over her shoulder, her eyes piercing mine. "I thought you liked stealing other people's dreams right out from under them."

Touché.

"I'm not stealing anything from your sister, Frankie. That's just business." I stood beside her, my voice lower.

"And so is this, so if you don't mind..." Her focus returned to her work—or at least that was what she wanted me to believe.

"I'm not leaving."

"Why not? Don't you have *business*?"

I rested my hip on the counter, watching her eyes lower for a second down to my waist, and goddamn if it didn't feel like the hard hold of her stare had wrapped tightly around my cock. *Jesus.*

"I do. And it's right here."

Her full lips parted and then tightened into a line. "What are you talking about? I'm not your business."

"You are when you're the one blocking my deal with your whole haunted inn fable."

"Not a fable, just fact."

"Then it shouldn't be a problem for me to hang out here and make sure you don't do anything extreme."

"Like suggesting we sleep in an abandoned inn to prove it's not haunted?"

God, that mouth of hers. Fire oozed under my skin. The things I wanted to do to her smart mouth...*the things I wanted to let her smart mouth do to me.* Not smart. Not smart at all.

"Like setting up and faking ghost activity to ensure you win the deal."

The dropper in her fingers tumbled onto the counter, splattering several drops of scented oil over the top.

"Really? Is that what you think?" she said flatly, but I swore the color in her cheeks deepened.

"You set up a sidewalk séance."

"That was different." She wiped the drops of oil so vigorously, she looked about to rub a hole in the counter. "You're the one who suggested we sleep there. Not me."

"True, but..."

"But what?" Now, she faced me, hips cocked on one side and arms folded.

"You're not one to back down from an opportunity when it presents itself," I said and stepped closer, watching the hitch of her breath.

"Who would?" She notched her chin higher. It was meant in defiance, but all it did was put her mouth—her fucking delicious, damaging mouth—in line with mine.

"Someone who recognizes when they're playing with fire."

Her eyes lowered to my mouth, the color in them shifting from bronze to molten amber. The kind that fossilized every fleck of desire in them. "Lucky for me, that's all I do."

I should look away—step away. I was way beyond all the lines I should've stayed behind—way beyond any semblance of business being here.

My gaze left the depths of hers to roam her face.

Freckles dusted her nose and cheeks, hidden by the pink of her blush—a shade of rose that was darkened and then echoed in the full swells of her lips. *Fierce and so fucking kissable.*

My head lowered, drawn to her—to the scent of her. Cinnamon. Sweet but subtly sharp, luring you in with honeyed warmth, and only when you went to move away did you realize the hooks left in you made it impossible to smell anything without a hint of it. *Impossible to do anything without thinking of her.*

And that was a problem.

"So, you're going to booby trap the inn?" I asked and took a step back, the distance like a hit to my gut as it stole all the oxygen from my lungs.

"And how would I do that?" She scoffed and spun back to her mixing station on the counter.

My eyes locked on the open bottle of scented oil, and I reached for it without thinking, needing something to chase the scent of her away.

"What—"

"Is that...cherry?"

I caught the slight widening of her eyes, a burst of admiration warming her expression for a split second before she shielded it. This woman...she didn't admire my billions or my business or my looks, but she admired that I could identify a damn scent.

"Black cherry."

"Right," I murmured, taking one more breath before she plucked it from my fingers.

"Look, I have work to do, but if you insist on staying—"

"I do."

"Then you're going to work, too," she said, flashing

me a breezy smile before pulling out a box from underneath the counter and shoving it against my chest. "Follow me."

I got lost in the sway of her hips, unable to focus on what I was carrying or where, until she spun, and my eyes snapped back to hers.

"That"—she nodded to the box—"goes in here." She lifted the lid off a giant silver container on the counter. It had a spout almost like a drink dispenser and was plugged into the wall.

"All right." I set the box down and opened the top. It was filled to the brim with thin white flakes.

"Four-six-four soy wax." She reached in and let a handful of flakes flutter from her fingertips before dumping them into the metal container. "This is what melts it together, and then"—she reached across the counter for a thermometer—"we'll pour it out when it's about one-eight-five."

"So, my job is to dump wax into a pot?"

"And monitor the temperature." Her smile was too close to a smirk for my liking. "I don't want to give you anything too strenuous or dangerous."

"Dangerous?"

"You could burn yourself."

"Maybe I like wax play."

She choked on whatever flippant remark she was going to make next, and it was worth whatever line I'd crossed with the comment—to see her lose her cool for a second. To see behind the bravado.

The thermometer clattered from her fingers, which she quickly slapped into silence with her palm.

"Well." She cleared her throat. "I don't have another apron, so the only thing you're *playing* with is your very nice, very expensive clothes," she warned as though it would make me change my mind.

My smile widened. "Good thing I can afford to buy new ones." I set the box on the counter, enjoying her soft mutter of frustration as she went back to her scent-making.

"So. Sixteen years old?" I picked the scooper out of the box and took one full scoop over to the giant melter.

"I see Gigi was quite chatty this morning."

"I can't imagine her not being chatty," I admitted, carefully adding another dose of wax to the melter, watching the flakes start to disappear into one another.

"She's a force to be reckoned with."

"She says the same about you." The wax landed with a flurry in the pot. "So why candles?"

"Do you have something against candles? Or just historic and community preservation?"

I laughed. I couldn't fucking help it and couldn't fucking explain it. If I were back in Boston, in my office, and someone said that to me, I'd be that much more determined to do whatever the hell I wanted to do, consequences be damned. I wouldn't laugh. I wouldn't *enjoy* being criticized. But for some reason, even her critiques were like cinnamon. Barbed but sweet.

"I have nothing against either." I stirred the thick wax, adding another scoop of flakes just as the last had almost finished melting.

"It's because he sold it to us, isn't it?" she asked quietly and straightened.

I felt her eyes on me, but I didn't turn—didn't move.

"It's because I have a better offer. That's all." And it had nothing to do with the fact that the Kinkades were who my half brother had chosen to sell to when he thought the inn was willed to him. Nothing to do with the fact that I wanted to distance myself from everything involving Geoff Collins, his children, and their decisions.

"Excuse me."

I tensed, realizing she was right beside me, but instead of moving away from the counter, I only turned, thinking she just wanted to check the temperature of the wax. She did, but that wasn't all she came over for.

Her shoulder brushed my chest when she dipped the thermometer in the wax and swirled it for a second before taking a reading.

"If it's too hot when I add the fragrance oil, some of it will evaporate, but if it's too cold, it won't bind well," she explained softly. "You can keep adding." She wiped the thermometer tip off and moved in front of me again.

It wasn't the process that was fascinating—I mean, it was. But what had a hold of my attention was her. The way she moved, both with precision and without thought. I watched, mesmerized, as she slid a digital scale from where it was propped against the wall, pressing some of the buttons before she placed a small beaker on top and began to measure out some of the scented oil she'd been mixing.

"How do you know how much to use?"

"The rule of thumb is six to ten percent of the volume of wax you're using is how much fragrance to add." She plucked the beaker off the scale, now filled with the murky red liquid.

Again, her shoulder brushed against my chest because I didn't move out of her determined path fast enough. *Maybe I didn't want to.*

"Gigi was the one who bought me a candle-making

kit for my thirteenth birthday. It was just something fun at first. Something I'd do here and there with Lou. With my friends." She tipped her head, assessing the level of the wax and then dunking the thermometer once more before murmuring, "Perfect."

She moved like a candle nymph. Flitting around me as trays of empty glass jars appeared and then three metal pitchers, one larger than the other two. The entire time, it was arms to shoulders. Chest to arms. I brushed against her so many times, it was a damn miracle the wax hadn't evaporated from the heat.

"I need you to wipe out all the jars for me. Sometimes there are smudges on the inside." She handed me a towel, and one of my eyebrows lifted. "Please."

I palmed the base of one jar, wiped the inside, and replaced it on the tray. The task was mindless, which let my mind wander right back to where it wanted to be. *Her*.

"What happened at sixteen?" I asked again as she held the larger metal container under the spigot of the wax melter and opened the valve and let a rush of burning wax fill the container.

"The way Gigi tells it, or the truth?"

My heart thudded. What I wouldn't do for even a sliver of the truth from her...

"Both."

"When I was sixteen, I wanted to make some extra money, so I started playing around with blueberry-scented candles, knowing I could sell them at my mom's store along with her jam. I wanted to be a part of the business, but I wanted to do it my own way."

No surprise there, I thought. "That's Gigi's version."

She hesitated. "Yeah."

I stilled. "And the truth?"

She stopped the wax from pouring out and brought the metal container over to the scale. I stood silently—impatiently—as she set an empty pitcher on the scale and began to measure out wax from the container she'd just filled into it. Her concentration on the task was disproportionate to its simplicity. She wasn't weighing the wax as much as she was weighing the decision to tell me the real story or not.

"When I was sixteen, my brother Kit came home from the hospital for the second time," she began slowly, and with just one sentence, the story veered from anything I'd been thinking. "The first time was what brought him home from the war. The second time was after the marathon bombing."

Damn. I forced the air through my lips, the weight of her story pressurizing my chest. I couldn't imagine what that was like—I didn't even feel like I had the right to. But I couldn't stop myself from imagining her. Sixteen. Both of her older brothers clearly had filled the void that her deadbeat father had left. And then to almost lose one of them. Twice.

"I'm sorry," I said, wishing there was some sum of money I could pay to make those words feel like they actually solved something.

"It was hard for him—hard for all of us." She moved the pitcher off the scale once it weighed the correct amount, and then did the same with the second pitcher. "Gigi started dying her hair. My cousins and I started pulling silly pranks on each other—anything to try and lighten the mood. And Kit...he pretended well enough during the day, but at night..."

I finished wiping all the jars clean when Frankie

grabbed the thermometer again and checked the temperature of each pitcher. The whole time, I didn't say anything—I didn't want to say anything because I wanted her to finish, and the silence felt like one more challenge between us. To sense who would be the first to break it.

"Perfect," she murmured, and then grabbed the smaller beaker of her fragrance. "I like to add it when it's just under one-eighty-five."

She poured the fragrance into the hot wax, tipping forward and taking a deep breath. She wrinkled her nose, and you would've thought the way my dick hardened, she'd decided to strip right in front of me, but no, I was turned on—aching—from a damn nose twitch.

Her eyes fluttered open, staring at the wax, but I could tell she wasn't seeing it. She wasn't seeing anything except the continuation of her story.

"The nightmares got so bad, he stopped sleeping in his room because he knew he kept waking us. So, Kit moved to the couch. It helped us sleep better, but not him." She robotically repeated the process with the second pitcher, using a container of fragrance that was already mixed. "One day, I decided to make candles—blueberry candles to mimic the scent of Mom's jam to sell in her store. Anyway, I lit the candle, *forgot* I lit the candle until around midnight, and I ran downstairs to douse it, and that was when I saw him. Kit was asleep on the couch. He was sleeping soundly."

Damn. Before I could say anything, she plucked something from the shelf below, and she handed it to me with the instructions, "Now, we stir."

"Chopsticks?" I took a pair and followed her lead,

dunking them into the second pitcher and stirring while she did the other.

"I order a lot of takeout while I'm working, so I have a lot of extra sticks," she explained, pausing for a few long seconds before she finished her story. "Of course, I thought that night was a fluke...that it was just a random, peaceful night of sleep. So, I tested it out every night for the next two weeks, and every night I lit that candle, Kit slept...soundly."

"Wow," I rumbled, not knowing what else to say. *What the hell else did you say?* At sixteen, I'd been preoccupied with two things—girls and how I was going to make so much money that Mom never had to worry again, so much money that my father would know my name and regret walking away from someone who'd achieved so much.

At sixteen, she'd started a business to save her brother's life. Not literally, but damn if it wasn't fucking close. And this whole time, I'd looked at her candles—her store—as some quaint little hobby that only a tiny town with a huge tourist population could turn into a business.

"At first, I wanted to understand it—how it helped him. So, I looked online and read all these articles and papers on the psychology of smell." She took another sample of the scented wax. "Compared to our other senses, smell can trigger an immediate emotional response, along with a memory."

I stilled, Mom's face flashing in my mind the instant she breathed in that beach candle—the instant she came back to me. It was the whole reason I was here—to make that last.

"Scents that evoke a personal memory can trigger slower, deeper breathing. A reduction in stress."

I cleared my throat and willed my focus to stay on her and her story. "So, the blueberries brought him back..."

"We'd all grown up making that blueberry jam together with Mom and Gigi. Mom joked that she made so much jam while she was pregnant with us that there might be blueberries rather than blood running through our veins." Frankie sighed. "Kit moved out not long after that, but when he left, he asked me to keep making him candles."

My jaw pulsed as I watched her tongue swipe over her lips and her lashes flutter against her cheeks. She didn't have to be staring straight at me for me to see the way her eyes glistened.

"And that's when you started your business."

Her head bobbed. "Everyone always thinks the candle's light is the only way out of the darkness, but it's not. You don't always need a light to be able to find peace." A shadow of a smile teased her lips, and holy hell, I was never going to look at a candle the same way.

My jaw clenched, and I managed only an "I see," my mind consumed with thoughts of Mom—of telling Frankie what that damn beach candle had done for her.

"I can prove it," she declared softly, taking my silence as doubt when it was nothing short of pure, humbling admiration.

Frankie lifted her chopsticks from the pitcher and stuck them right under my nose, leaving me no choice but to breathe in the final result. I'd expected the black cherry and had a good guess at the other scents she'd incorporated. I hadn't expected the memory—the scene. *The restaurant.*

"The steakhouse."

Her wide smile made my chest pound. "Black cherry. Rosemary. Peppercorn. Cedarwood."

I inhaled again, but it was more than the memory of the restaurant that assaulted me this time. It was those seconds seared into my mind of that kiss, and when my eyes opened and met hers, I knew she was thinking the same.

The wine. The ambiance. The attraction. *The lies.* That night, we'd been people who didn't have to be enemies.

"Frankie..." My voice was hoarse.

Her hand wavered, and I grabbed her wrist. The scent didn't matter anymore, but I didn't want her to pull away. She shivered, goose bumps rising to the call of heat on her skin.

This woman was fire. Bold. Bright. Burning with life and determination. And all I wanted was to make her melt for me.

I left my chopsticks sitting in the wax and reached for her neck. Just the catch of her breath made my dick even harder in my pants. Maybe it was the scent of her —maybe later I'd blame the damn cinnamon for making me think...making me want something I'd never otherwise consider. *What fucking asshole would do this? What asshole would kiss the woman whose sister was trying to do business with him?* It blurred so many goddamn lines—opened up so many avenues for legal and ethical impropriety...but for the first time, I just couldn't fucking care.

Not when her lashes fluttered shut, her cheeks

dusting with a deeper shade of pink. Not when her lips parted—lips that had both criticized and cursed me all within the last hour. *She was fire, and I was Icarus, who flew too close to her flame.*

I growled and brushed my mouth to hers, softly at first like I was diffusing a bomb, one wrong move and this whole place would go up in smoke. But soft—slow —wasn't in Frankie's wheelhouse. Not when it came to what she wanted. *Not according to her grandmother.*

Once Frankie knows what she wants, she'll do anything to have it.

And she wanted this kiss.

Her mouth surged up to mine, her small frame tipping into me when she went up on her tiptoes and demanded something deeper.

This time, the sound I made was feral as I hauled her to me. I wasn't mixing business with pleasure. I was fucking obliterating it for one more taste of her. My arm locked around her back, holding her almost aggressively to my front, where there was no mistaking the way she affected me. We could banter and bicker—hell, she could legitimately hate me, but that wouldn't change this.

The wick might hate the flame, but that wouldn't alter how it would burn.

My thumb slid underneath her chin, tilting her head back, but it was her tongue that searched out the seam of my lips first. Fearless. Fierce. I gave her what she wanted—at this point, I was sure I'd give her anything as long as she kept moaning the way she was.

I tangled my tongue with her silky one, the sweet bite of cinnamon setting off a chain reaction in me I was powerless to stop. It made me weak. Ravenous.

Desperate for more. My hand slid to her ass, and that was when she started to move—gently rocking against the ridge of my cock. Stars erupted in my brain.

"*Fuck,*" I hissed into the warmth of her mouth and spun her against the counter. Too forcefully because the whole thing jostled and rattled, something tipped over with a crash, and instantly, Frankie pulled back.

Panting, our eyes locked. Her fists curled into my shirt. My hand bracketed around her neck. Our hips wedged together like the heat between us could evaporate our clothes. This was wrong. All wrong. But neither of us wanted to move—to burst the bubble where it felt so right.

"The wax." Her voice was firm but fragile like an eggshell as she slid out of my hold, leaving my hands gripping the edge of the counter for support.

Her attention returned to the long-forgotten pitchers on the counter, while meanwhile, my concern was solely focused on whether or not I was going to be able to walk—*move*—with how fucking hard I was.

Taking deep, painful breaths, I looked at her as she checked the temperatures in the pitchers. Her shoulders slumped with relief at the reading, so everything must still be okay. *As long as she didn't check my temperature, it would be.* My blood felt like it was fucking boiling.

"We have to pour the wax before it cools," she instructed, her tone brittle with false bravado as she tried to conceal the effects of our kiss. "There's a bag of wicks under the counter. I need you to stick one to the inside of each jar, and then I'll pour the wax in."

My jaw locked. *She wasn't asking me to leave.* After what just happened, she had every right to. Hell, after what just happened, I should want to—I should be desperate for a second to cool down and become rational again. Logical. Emotionless.

But I didn't want that. I didn't want distance or relief. I wanted the torture of remaining in her presence for a little longer. So, I did exactly what I was told and wondered how the hell I was going to spend another night alone with the woman who set my body on fire, let alone another five more after it.

CHAPTER 12
FRANKIE

I was going to kill him.

The inn's living room was unrecognizable, which was saying a lot considering it was empty until last night. But what was there—all the things Chandler had brought and the few things I'd left—was in disarray.

The air mattress was propped against the wall. Water bottles were laid out in a pentagram on the floor —in the center of them, our three pillows were stacked on top of one another. There was another pentagram streaked on the wall above the fireplace with the ashes from last night's flame. The sheets from his bed were draped over the windows. And the snacks...

Dammit, Nox.

To be fair, I'd begged him to do this—not *this*, but something. Something haunt-y. And I would've gone into greater detail if Chandler hadn't shown up at my store and put a swift end to the meeting I'd called and begged my cousin for as soon as I'd left the inn this morning.

"I guess the ghosts aren't happy we're here," I murmured, banding my arms over my chest as I watched Chandler stalk around the room.

Fury shouldn't look so handsome on a man.

Yes, my cousin had taken my request—my plea—into his own hands, but for the look on Chandler's face right now, it was worth it. I bit my lip to keep from smiling. Chandler's head whipped around, the muscle in his jaw ticking as though to count every silenced curse. He didn't understand—couldn't fathom that he might be wrong about the ghosts.

Chandler stopped in front of one of the windows, glared at me, and then yanked down one of the sheets covering the glass, the fabric fluttering around him like a fireless flame.

"There are no such things as ghosts," he said through locked teeth, balling the sheet in his hands.

"Then what happened here?" I extended my arms, moving farther into the room. "Because you've babysat me all day." At that, his stare flicked angrily to me. "So I couldn't have done this."

The muscle in his jaw twitched because he couldn't argue the facts. He'd spent the entire day by my side. First, at the Candle Cabin, then we'd grabbed dinner to-go from Beach Dogs, a gourmet hot dog shop a few doors down from the Maine Squeeze. There were better options—better restaurants—that I was sure a man like Chandler would've preferred, but the less we were seen together in public, the better. I didn't want anyone getting any wrong ideas. Especially Gigi. But I'd deal with my grandmother and her silly premonition later.

"There are no such things as ghosts," he repeated,

grabbing the air mattress with one hand, the muscles in his forearm putting on a show as they flexed and pulled taut to drag the bed back flat on the floor.

His sleeves had been rolled up all day, and I'd be lying if I said it wasn't a sexy silver lining of having the man help me make candles. I tried not to look. To keep my distance—and my anger at him. But it was hard when he was unexpectedly genuine. Even harder when my body responded to him like a wildfire. Every time I got close, thinking I could douse the feeling, more of me was pulled into the burn.

First, our conversation earlier. How many times have I shared the origins of my candle-making? Countless. How many times have I shared the truth about what that candle did for Kit? Next to none.

And then, that kiss. *A mistake.* Which was why I'd spent the rest of the day interacting with cool civility toward him. Never mind how my lips were still charred from the embrace and my body scorched with ache.

It was a mistake, and one I was happy to pretend never happened.

"I'm going to check the doors," he declared, snatching a lantern—miraculously one of the few things Nox had left untouched in its original spot.

Chandler flipped the switch to turn the lantern on, mid-stride toward the door, and nothing. No light came out. *Off. On. Nothing.*

Not untouched.

"What the..." He popped open the bottom, the cavity where the battery should've been was obvious even in the quickly fading daylight. He was nothing if not thorough—both of them, Nox and Chandler—

because Chandler checked inside the lantern, too, and found the bulb missing. "Seriously?"

"Don't look at me." I huffed and set my bag on the floor. I rifled through it for a lighter and one of my Cinnamon Swirl candles I'd packed earlier, planning to light it anyway just to clear out a little must from the air.

"I'll run to the store and get—"

My laugh made him stop talking. "It's ten o'clock in Friendship, Mr. Collins. We don't have Starbucks, let alone stores open past nine," I informed him as the wick on the candle smoldered to life, cinnamon light spilling into the room. "Here." I passed him the candle, pretending my fingers didn't respond just like the wick when they brushed his.

A grunt was the only gratitude I received as he stalked out of the room.

"Check the windows, too!" I called after him, confident he wouldn't find the broken latch on the one in the kitchen. It looked like it was locked, and the wood frame was so swollen with age and elements that it felt locked on first tug, requiring several good hefts before the seal gave way and opened. *At least, that was how I'd explained it to Nox in the short minutes I'd spoken with him earlier.*

Lifting a second candle from my bag, I lit the wick before I even checked the rest of the lanterns by the wall. *Nox was definitely thorough.*

To the tune of Chandler's heavy, determined footfalls, I began to deconstruct Nox's masterpiece. Placing the candle in the center of the room, I collected the pentagram of water bottles and lined them up along the wall, removed the remaining blankets from the windows, returned the air mattress to where it was this morning, and somehow found myself re-making his bed.

I shouldn't have. I should've left it for him because this was blurring an already-blurred line. But I felt a tiny bit bad. *For the guy who only cares about selling this place to the highest bidder? Come on, Frankie.*

I dropped his pillows in the center—like not putting those in place negated the effort I'd put into restoring the rest of it.

Clutching my own pillow to my chest, I looked for my sleeping bag. *The one thing I hadn't seen yet.* I walked the perimeter of the room, but there weren't many places for it to hide. Picking up the candle, I checked the hall next. The creaky closet. The empty dining room. My head whipped side to side, my steps more frantic as I searched the crevasses of the first floor before I returned to the stairs, somehow bypassing Chandler entirely in my path.

I looked up at the second floor. *Come on, Nox.* My cousin wasn't thrilled about my request. The pausing traffic for my faux séance was one thing, but this...he was skeptical. *And that was without knowing that I was staying at the inn, too.* I could claim I hadn't had the chance to tell him that part yet, but even if Chandler hadn't shown up at my shop earlier, I hadn't planned on telling him.

I claimed I needed plausible deniability, but if Nox had done all this, he would've found my sleeping bag and realized the truth. *Maybe that was why my sleeping bag was the only thing hidden in Timbuktu...if it was hiding at all.*

I took the steps two at a time, my heart thudding heavily when I reached the second floor.

There were no ghosts, but the second floor was still creepy as hell. Dark hallway. All the doors shut.

You're the one who invented the ghosts, remember? my inner trouble reminded me.

Gritting my teeth, I went to the first door and flung it open. Dust. Dirty windows. No sleeping bag. It was the same with the second room across the hall. The third. The fourth. The fifth. If he took it with him because he realized I was sleeping here too...*no, he wouldn't*. The last door stuck in the jam, requiring a little shoulder grease to shove it open.

Empty. "Dammit—"

"What is it?"

I spun with a gasp, my foot catching on the uneven floorboard that stopped the door from opening smoothly. As quickly as it sent me toppling backward, I was yanked forward into Chandler's arms—against his chest.

Heat burst through my skin, sinking its teeth deep into my chest and stomach and...lower. *Dammit.* I squeezed my eyes shut. *Why was this happening? Why did I want him like this? Why couldn't it be anyone else but him?*

My heart raced like I'd run a marathon. I should step back. Move away. *Run.* But I needed a second. Air dumped only the scent of him into my lungs, overtaking everything else like a Trojan Horse let loose in my chest.

"Frankie..." His chest rumbled under my fingertips, and I tilted my head up, following the trail of bronzed skin that started at the unbuttoned collar of his shirt, up the thick cords of his neck, along the pulse of his jaw to his full, firm lips, and finally to the dark embers of his stare.

"What are you doing?" I choked out like he was the one at fault when I was the one still clutching his shirt.

"Looking for you." Dark eyes searched mine. "What are you doing?"

My lips parted. "Looking for my sleeping bag."

His big body tensed, sending a warm shiver through my own. We both considered the consequences—*that there was now only one bed between us.*

I stepped back, quickly but carefully this time.

"Did you find it?" he rumbled and moved around me to double-check the room. Or at least pretend like he was—just like I pretended not to see his hand move to his waist and his stance widen as he adjusted his hard-on.

"No. It's nowhere."

"Let's check downstairs again." He grunted and led the way back down the hall.

"Was everything still locked up?"

I caught a shadow of displeasure cross his face before he moved ahead of me down the staircase, and my stomach did a small victory flip. "Yeah. Everything was still locked."

At least part of my plan was working. Back in the living room, I picked up a water bottle and cracked it open, watching him scour the nooks and crannies once more.

"I don't see it."

"Well, at least you know now this definitely wasn't me," I grumbled and gulped down a mouthful of water.

He set the candle he was holding on the floor and then rose up, his head tipping as he regarded me slowly. "Unless you're trying to get out of staying here."

My eyes went wide, and I almost choked on my drink. Maybe that was what Nox was hoping for all along. If he was...he didn't know me as well as he thought he did. *Or maybe he just didn't know how I felt about Chandler*.

"And give you the opportunity to claim I'm responsible for the ghosts?" I scoffed and shook my head. "I'm not going anywhere. I still have my pillow, and the floor is just fine—"

"You can take the mattress."

"No." I shook my head. *Absolutely not*. "I'll be fine on the floor. I have my pillow. A blanket. And the fire will be warm—"

"The firewood is gone, too."

I was going to murder my cousin. First degree. Premeditated. I was going to wrap his body in my sleeping bag and burn it on top of all the firewood he'd taken.

For a second, I wondered if this was how my brother felt when I'd listed his cottage for rent in a desperate attempt to get him to meet a woman, but then I shoved the thought aside because my pranks were for other people. They weren't supposed to be self-inflicted.

"I guess they want to freeze us out," I said, burying my frustration.

"Take the bed, Frankie." He grabbed my pillow and tossed it on the mattress. The soft sound of its landing was like an invitation for me to join it.

I rolled my lip through my teeth, the temptation to sleep comfortably too strong to protest right away. But I wasn't a damsel, and I definitely didn't want to add this to the already too long list of chivalries he'd achieved against my will.

And that left only one option.

My head snapped in his direction and met his gaze.

"Fine, but you're taking the bed, too," I declared. "I'm not going to let you get a bad back from sleeping on the floor and use it as an excuse to get out of this challenge without accepting the ghosts are real."

It was quite possible that a ghost appearing in that moment would've been less shocking to him than the words that had come out of my mouth.

It took him a beat before his jaw worked up enough control to force the words out.

"You're suggesting we...share the bed?"

"Are you afraid I'll come for you in your sleep?" The words tumbled from my lips, thinking they were cloaked in flippant finery when what they really were was naked and suggestive.

Chandler's nostrils flared, his stare dragging over me like hot coals on my skin, and my nipples hardened to the point of pain. *How did this keep happening?*

"It's not a big deal." I fumbled forward, trying to sound as nonchalant as possible. "We're both adults, and there's only one bed. It's not like this is some kind of rom-com or something." I laughed, but it was the weakest laugh in the history of humor. "We're in the middle of a haunting."

He stood so still, I wondered if I had turned him to stone. But then his throat bobbed, and it cracked the tension from his body. "Right," he clipped with a nod.

We didn't say much after that, as we went through similar motions to last night. We took separate candles to separate rooms to change. I was the first one back, so I quickly picked the side of the bed closest to the fireplace, blew out my candle, and slid underneath the covers.

Damn, this thing was comfortable.

I stared up at the ceiling, my heart keeping time with the seconds it took for him to return. I wasn't going to close my eyes or pretend to sleep—I wasn't going to give any appearance of wanting to hide from this situation. Because hiding meant I was afraid of it—afraid of what could happen. And I wasn't.

I was going to walk right through this fire to prove I wouldn't get burned.

Minutes later, the mattress groaned under the weight of him and all his weapons. His bare, toned chest. His gray sweatpants. His smoldering eyes. I didn't break from their stare for a single second as he climbed into the bed beside me.

If I was being honest, the mattress felt a whole heck of a lot smaller now that we were both on it compared to when it was empty in the center of the floor.

"You have enough blankets?"

"Plenty." And by morning, I'd probably hog all of them. *Lucky him.*

I was glad when he didn't reply. At least for a few minutes, I was, but then the silence started to feel less like a comfort and more like a chokehold. I was lying in bed next to the singular barrier between Lou and this inn.

We weren't touching, but that didn't matter. The flame never touched the wax of a candle, but that didn't stop it from melting.

"You know you can change your mind. Take Lou's offer and put an end to all this." My voice hitched inexplicably at the end.

I practically chewed a hole through my cheek waiting for him to respond, and when he did, it wasn't with a reply to what I'd said.

"Why did your grandmother know my name?"

Crap.

"She didn't."

"She absolutely looked at me and your cousin and said my name like it meant something."

"Because Chandler means candle maker, and I make candles, and now that my two older brothers are in relationships, I'm next on her chopping block," I rattled off, keeping my eyes locked on a string of cobwebs on the ceiling where the very faint streetlight caught the fragile strand. "If she knew who you were, she'd realize how wrong her thoughts were."

"So why didn't you tell her?"

My breath caught. *Why hadn't I?* Because I would've had to admit to this—being here with him. Except that was a lie—one I'd been content to live with until he asked me to face it.

"Because that would've been worse for you, trust me."

"So, you did something to spare me?"

I hated how I could hear the smile in his voice. "Don't let it go to your head."

"That you'd rather let your grandmother match-make us than explain that we're enemies?"

I tensed. "Not enemies. Adversaries."

"There's a difference?"

Twenty minutes ago, I would've said no. But right now, lying next to him, the difference was profound.

"Apparently," I murmured and turned on my side away from him, thinking the position would form some kind of mental block for all the things I shouldn't be thinking. Instead, my spine prickled to life from the heat of his proximity, warm electricity stretching to the far reaches of every nerve. Not being able to see him, even in my periphery, made me overanalyze every sensation, anticipating it as touch.

"Because you don't kiss enemies?"

My mouth went dry, and I fumbled for a reply. "I don't kiss anyone. What happened earlier was a mistake." *Famous last words.* I gave myself a mental eye roll. "All I care about is my candles—my business. Of all people, I think you'd agree that's most important, Mr. Business Not Pleasure."

He hummed, the sound creeping through all the cracks in my armor like a bug with a thousand legs.

"I do." He replied much more slowly than I'd antici-pated. "But maybe you don't want those muscles to atrophy."

Air sucked into my lungs, a tangle of heat and want and promise. Yes—*no.*

A thousand nos.

"Whatever I want, it can't be with you."

"Because we're adversaries?"

Because we're dangerous. The spark. The heat. *The burn.* I was rarely afraid of something. To try something. To test something. To tease or toy with someone. I was rarely afraid to put myself at risk because I did it so many times, I thought I'd numbed away the fear.

But I'd never felt at risk like this before. I could be silly or haphazard or even immature at times, but I knew real danger when I felt it. And all I felt when I was close to him—in his arms, locked in his kiss—was how unsafe every single second of that embrace could be.

"Because I'm here for my sister—for this inn." I huffed, like saying it enough times would make it the whole truth. "Good night, Chandler."

His silence belied how he didn't want to end the conversation, but ultimately, he didn't push.

"Good night, Frankie."

I hesitated and added, "Good night, ghosts."

We were adversaries. The match and the wick. If we weren't careful, it would be the both of us who would burn.

CHAPTER 13
FRANKIE

I was in trouble.

Strange, since usually I was the one responsible for the trouble, but it was no less the truth.

Kissing Chandler in my shop two days ago had been a grave mistake—a match that ignited an invisible fuse. And that night, when it came to backing down or sleeping in the same bed as him, I summoned every ounce of bravado and pretended like it wouldn't matter —like it didn't matter.

But god, did it matter.

The heat of the body next to me, my arm slung like a traitor over his chest.

For two days, I pretended that this didn't happen. That every morning, I didn't carefully extricate my body from where it had crept and curled around him like a vine. And that every night, I slid onto the air mattress, my mind ready to chase dreams that brought me close to him.

It was ridiculous. All of it. Every lingering stare.

Every caught breath. Every darkening of his gaze when it met mine for too long.

Every night, we fell asleep with a bomb in the bed, each of us waiting for the thing that would make it blow.

He made a low sound when I pulled my arm away and turned to my side. I waited for a split second, my stomach doing a little flip when I heard him turn and reach for me. Foolish Frankie waited for the approach of his heat like a flame she was dying to touch—and that was when I pulled away, rising from the mattress with such force and enough noise to make sure it woke him, too.

The last thing either of us needed was *both* of us knowing just how close we got each morning.

"Good morning," I said over my shoulder, quickly tying my hair back.

"Morning." His first words of the day were in a league of their own. Like salted caramel on my skin, they were sweet and smooth, with just enough coarseness to make me wonder how they'd feel against the shell of my ear or on the slope of my neck. "One more night spared from the ghosts."

Goose bumps took shelter along my spine.

I needed to do something drastic—something to put an end to this—before the idea of this ending began to ache a little too much.

"And the noises last night?" I shot over my shoulder.

Two nights ago, Nox moved all of our things.

Last night, we'd returned to the inn, fresh sets of batteries and lightbulbs for the lamps in hand, and just as we settled into our uncomfortable sleeping arrangement, there was banging coming from upstairs. The sound of footfalls on the floor.

Chandler had ordered me to stay downstairs while he rushed to investigate. As soon as he reached the second floor, the sounds stopped.

Or I thought they did.

I'd sat up on the mattress, a hint of triumph on my face waiting for him to return, when the banging on the windows started.

I jumped and cried out, diving under the covers as the old panes rattled and shook.

I knew it was Nox—not that we'd nailed down the details of this plan beyond *"I need you to haunt the inn. For Lou,"* because I couldn't risk it—but I still clutched the blanket to my chin, my heart pounding higher in my throat as my head whipped from one location to the next, trying to follow the path of the agitated rattle.

And then Chandler had barreled into the room, and the only thing I could focus on was him.

The hard edges of his expression. The thump in his jaw muscle. The ferocity bubbling under his typical veneer of calm.

"Are you all right?" Three little words made me melt.

Three little words spoken by a gorgeous man crouched beside the air mattress. Three little words quelling my racing heart as his gaze raked over me, the protectiveness in it as obvious as a lit match in the dark.

A nod hadn't been enough to assure him. Warm fingers gripped my chin, holding it firm for his demand. *"Say it."*

The words *"I'm all right"* trembled and fluttered

from my lips, my unsteady breath drawing him closer like a fishing line pulled taut.

Once again, we tiptoed at the edge of detonation. Destruction. *Desire*.

And then there was another rattle—one I wished I'd never asked for as it drew him away.

The second time Chandler returned, he was all business. He saw nothing upstairs. Nothing outside the windows. His gruff explanation last night was the same answer he gave this morning.

"The wind."

Was it the wind? Was it rocks against windows? Was it Nox running along the hall to the back staircase and then out the broken kitchen window?

"If you say so." I bit the corner of my lip and grabbed my bag. "I'm heading out."

Chandler moved on the mattress, and before I could catch myself, I found myself staring at his bare, muscled chest rising from the blankets.

"I'll see you soon."

I shouldn't want to hear those words. Shouldn't want to know he planned on spending another day babysitting my every move.

But as I left the inn, all I felt was relief, knowing he wasn't far behind me.

Every day the routine was the same.

I'd head home for a quick shower and change, then open up my shop. Within forty minutes of that open sign posted on my door, Chandler would stroll in, and I'd spend the rest of the day with my adversary. The one who helped me make candles. Who ordered food to the store when most days I would've forgotten to eat. And who talked to my customers like they were his own.

Like now.

I stood with my back to the wall, my head tipped to listen through the curtain as Chandler spoke with a young couple who'd wandered in. They were in Friendship on their honeymoon, headed further north from here to hike Acadia.

I'd been on my way out to introduce myself and my candles, but when I reached the curtain and saw how Chandler strode forward to greet them, I held back.

Some people had chocolate or wine or candy. But this was my guilty pleasure—listening to him market my candles. My business. *My dream.*

"Oh, is this cinnamon?" I heard the woman ask.

"Yes, that's our Cinnamon Swirl." *Our.* My breath caught. *Why was he so...him?* "But if you're here on your honeymoon, I'd recommend this." I bit my bottom lip, curious what he was going to suggest. "Our Blueberry Bomb."

Our.

It was a good choice even though the cinnamon was my favorite. He always seemed to turn people away from the cinnamon, I'd noticed. Maybe he didn't like the smell. Strange though, since it was the cinnamon candles I'd lit at the inn, and he hadn't said anything.

"Maine is famous for their blueberries, and the scent used in this comes from the blueberries grown by

Stonebar Farms. You can find their shop a few blocks down with some of their famous jam."

"Oh, yes! We stopped there yesterday and met the owner, Ailene. She's wonderful."

Minutes later, two more Blueberry Bombs were off the shelves and leaving with their new owners.

For over a decade, it had only been me. My dream. My candles. My store. But in a matter of days, he'd become a staple here.

A man I should hate because, in a few more days, he was going to break my sister's heart and sell her inn to someone else. *It's business* was always his response whenever we touched on the topic.

I knew it was business. I knew business. But this was my family.

And every time he sold a blueberry candle, more of my defenses seemed to melt away.

"Oh, Chandler!"

No.

The curtain smacked against the frame as I flung it to the side.

"Gigi—"

"Oh, perfect." My grandmother turned with a smile, her hands gripping a cardboard box. "Harper wanted me to give this to you."

The box landed presumptuously in my arms.

Of course, I knew what it was. Beeswax. My newest joint venture with my younger cousin. Beeswax candles made with wax from her honeybees.

"Great. Do you want to come in the back with me?"

"No. Actually, I came to talk to Chandler." She patted my arm and then shooed me away. *Shooed me.* And Chandler just stood there with a smile on his face.

I bit back a groan, deciding my next-best course of action was to set the box down and get back out here as quickly as possible.

The box landed with a thud, and I immediately pulled out my phone, searching until I found Nox's number.

> Last night was great. We need to step it up.

The dots appeared and then disappeared.

> Why were you at the inn last night, Frankie?

Shit. I swayed back, my hip bumping the counter. *Double shit.* After the noises scared the crap out of me, my next thought had been if Nox had seen anything—had seen me.

> Proving that it's haunted.

My cheeks were on fire as I sent the message and then instantly fired off another.

> If you tell anyone, Lou will lose the inn.

What was happening to me? Threatening Nox? It wasn't like I'd never threatened my cousins to assist in my schemes before, but this was different. I knew how it looked—like I was sleeping with the enemy.

> Please tell me you aren't...

> God no!!!

I shouldn't have sent three exclamation points. Three exclamation points was clearly a lie.

It was a challenge. We both had to stay at the inn. Me, to prove it's haunted. Him, to prove it's not.

And it'll be a massacre if Jamie finds out.

I huffed and rolled my eyes.

> It's only two more nights. One, if you can step up your game.

"Francesca!"

My head jerked in the direction of Gigi's voice, and I shoved my phone back into my pocket, sending up a silent prayer that Nox kept his mouth shut.

I didn't particularly like keeping things from my older brother, but he had this habit of still looking at me and Lou like we were seven instead of twenty-seven. A time when it was easy to convince us that boys had cooties.

Of course, there wasn't anything he could do about my decision...except blow up at Chandler and completely destroy any chance I had at salvaging Lou's offer.

"Here," I said, a little flushed and breathless when I returned to the front.

I caught Chandler's stare narrow curiously before his head dropped, distracted by the vibration of his phone.

His brow creased. "Excuse me." He spoke but didn't look up before stalking to the front of the store, his phone pressed to his ear.

My chest tightened. The call was important. Very important. For being who he was, I hadn't seen him take a single call in the last two days. It had to be Mr. Fairfax. What could be more important...and what other reason would he not want me to hear?

"So, we'll see you for dinner then, Francesca?" Gigi asked, the expression on her face indicating that my attention had been stuck on Chandler's retreat for a meaningful amount of time.

I exhaled. "I don't know. I have work—"

"Work isn't more important than family," she chided.

"I know—"

"Do you?" Her cloud of orange hair tipped to one side. "I don't think you've learned this lesson quite yet."

There was no point in arguing with her.

"I'll see—"

"Chandler is coming."

I choked on air. On nothing but the invisible boulder of fear that slammed into the front of my chest.

"You invited..."

"Well, of course, I did."

I groaned and covered my face. "No, Gigi. He's not coming to dinner. You don't know who he is—"

"He's Chandler."

My groan multiplied. "No, Gigi, you don't understand. He's—"

"The man who owns the inn."

My eyes bulged. "How..."

She cackled. "Who do you think I am, dear? Who do you think your mother gets her detective skills from?"

The color drained from my face. "Does Mom—"

"No, your mother doesn't know." She patted my arm again like that was supposed to comfort me. "Your sister told me."

My nostrils flared. "Lou—"

"Thought she was helping you by explaining why he couldn't be *that* Chandler."

Of course, she did.

"So then why are you inviting him to dinner?" I asked, my voice coming out in a hiss.

Her wide grin somehow spread wider. "Because this is exactly who *that* Chandler would be."

My heart did some kind of flutter inside my chest, traitor that it was. More excuses piled on my tongue, weighing it into silence for a second. *He's only here for business. We both only care about business. Neither of us want a relationship. He lives in Boston. He's going to sell the inn to some heartless developer, and I could never be with someone who cared so little about my family—*

"Oh, look at the time. I've got to run. See you both for dinner at the house." She moved with surprising speed out of range of further conversation.

The door didn't have a chance to shut behind her before Chandler slipped back through it, his eyes and head ducked.

I needed to get out of here. Get some space. Give us both an excuse to get out of dinner and prepare for another night in the same bed.

"I'm sorry about Gigi. Don't feel obligated to do anything she asked. I'm closing up for the day—"

"You're coming with me," he said, his voice like gravel.

Something was wrong. The tone of his voice. The tension on his face. His jaw was wrenched so tight, it looked about to snap.

"What?" I folded my apron in my arms. "Today's my half-day—"

"And we have to go." He took the fabric from my hands and stalked to the back to hang it up.

I bristled, blaming my irritation on his bold presumption and not on the unsettling idea that he was *that* Chandler. "I don't just go places with strangers when they tell me."

"You just share a bed with them for a whole week?" His brow arched as he stopped in front of me.

Five nights. "And if I have plans?"

"Do you?" he dared.

My throat bobbed as I forced myself to swallow. "No."

"Okay then." He angled toward the front door.

I grabbed my bag and followed, locking the door to my store behind us. "Do I get to know where I'm being kidnapped to?"

"You're not being kidnapped." He held the passenger door of his car open for me.

I paused. "I'm being taken against my will."

"You're being taken," he replied quietly. "But not against your will."

He wasn't wrong. Even with no answers, I was going to go with him because of the look in his eyes. It was broken and pained, and I wondered what in this world had the power to make this man weak.

"Where are we going?" I refused to get in without an answer.

His Adam's apple bobbed. "To see my mom."

CHAPTER 14
FRANKIE

We rode in silence, but if there was one thing I'd learned from Lou, it was how silence could speak volumes.

He pushed the speed limit, but it was the drum of his thumb on the wheel that shouted we couldn't get there fast enough. The pulse of his jaw screamed unrest.

I tried to focus on the blur of our surroundings—the thick of the trees growing denser as we drove inward from the coast and into the blanket of forest. Backroad after backroad until a discreet hand-carved sign labeled Edgewood Estate marked the entrance to a drive that tucked back through the trees to a large colonial manor house with several cars parked in the lot.

At first, I thought this was his mom's home. I guess, technically, it was, but it wasn't hers alone. We parked, and when we made it to the front porch, there was a young nurse in scrubs helping an older man up from one of the rocking chairs dotting the covered porch.

His mom lived in a nursing home.

Again, my questions would have to wait because the door opened, and we were greeted by a middle-aged woman wearing the same sage green scrubs as the other nurse. Her name, Cathy, was embroidered underneath the Edgewood Estate logo.

"I'm so sorry, Chandler." The woman ushered him inside. "I thought talking to you would help."

My head tipped and swiveled. A stone-crusted reception desk. A massive living room, couches and recliners, a large central fireplace holding a TV stationed on the Hallmark channel, and tables dotted with groups of elderly people.

By the time my gaze searched for Chandler, he was already halfway across the lounge with Cathy. I picked up my pace to catch theirs, smiling at everyone I passed. By the time I reached them, they were halfway up the staircase and knee-deep in a conversation that made Chandler's shoulders look like a thousand-pound weight rested on them.

"I have to warn you, Chandler, it's him she's been asking for..."

Chandler jerked. Not a lot. Maybe hardly noticeably. But it reminded me of those scenes in spy movies when two characters get close, then one stabs the other. That moment when the betrayal registers first before the life-threatening wound. And that was this moment for Chandler. The betrayal that startled him.

Who was Cathy talking about?

Curiosity got the better of me, and eager to hear his response, my foot caught on the carpet on the last step and sent me tumbling forward.

My small cry fizzled when Chandler's big hands gripped my shoulders and steadied me. How he'd heard

—realized what was happening when there was obviously a *situation* weighing on him—was crazy.

Or it was until my eyes connected with his. He didn't look like a collected businessman but like a man preparing for battle.

"I'm sorry—"

"Wait downstairs," he ordered, his voice vacant. "I'll be back."

He'd ordered me to come with him, only to leave me at the staircase? I didn't have an opportunity to protest before he was gone. His feet fell heavier with each step, and the way his spine stiffened...like he knew this was a battle he was going to lose.

"Come with me, Miss..." A hand touched my shoulder, and I faced the woman who'd welcomed us inside, noting the worried expression she tried to cover up with a warm smile.

"Just Frankie." I smiled back.

"It's nice to meet you, Frankie. I'm Miss Cathy. I'm sorry I didn't introduce myself earlier, it's just Miss Laura..."

"It's not a problem," I assured her with a smile, even as my eyes continued to dart in Chandler's direction. He stood talking with another woman who worked at the home based on her uniform, his hand resting on the doorknob of the very last door in the hallway, poised to enter.

"I'll bring you back downstairs." With gentle pressure, she guided me back down to the main floor. My head craned back until I could no longer see him, and when I looked back at Cathy, she gave me a sad smile and added, "I'm glad you came with him. I always hoped Chandler had someone other than Mr. Tom for support."

My well-honed skill in pretending came in handy. I pretended like I knew what was going on. I pretended like I knew more about Mr. Tom other than the familiar name of Chandler's business partner and the warm way Chandler had spoken of him. And I pretended like I was really...what she thought I was. *His support*.

"I'm glad, too." And because I couldn't help myself either, I asked, "Is she all right?"

"I haven't seen her get upset like this before." The woman's face fell. "There are days she doesn't remember who I am, but never like this." She shook her head and then seemed to recollect herself. "I'm sorry. I'm sure Chandler will make it okay."

I didn't have a response. Not to the revelation she'd left me with. It was a miracle I managed to keep a straight face.

I took another look around the room. The soft decor. The discreet-looking nurses. The small table of brochures by the desk.

The Edgewood Estate. Long-term care for those struggling with dementia and Alzheimer's.

"Would you like some water while you wait?"

"No, thank you." My throat constricted. "I'm fine."

"You let me know if there's anything you need," she said, and then left me to return to her post.

I stared at the brochures and then looked back to the staircase. *Wait downstairs* were my instructions, and I should obey them. God knew this was well outside the bounds of anything that was my business, and I shouldn't get involved. But...he'd brought me here. Some part of him wanted me here—wanted me to know the truth. And it was the part of me that had confessed the real history behind my candle business.

I couldn't wait here.

Maybe if I were someone else—someone wholly different from the person who injected herself in situations whether she was asked or not, welcome or not, and with her whole heart. I wore my best intentions like my finest dress even if it was a little too bold and a little too flashy for some. I couldn't *not* try to help.

My mom loved the candle.

I spun and beelined for the car. It wasn't my Beach Bum scent, but maybe cinnamon would do the trick.

I felt Miss Cathy stare as I darted out and back past the desk. The stairs rose and disappeared in front of me as I reached the second floor. I hadn't gotten much farther than that in my plan, but it didn't matter. When I reached the second floor, I froze at the sight.

I heard the hysteria all the way at the other end of the hall behind a closed door that had three medical personnel standing in front of it. Doctors and nurses, and they were ready with a cart that looked prepared with sedatives.

It seemed like I blinked, and I'd made it to the end of the hall with them, my candle clutched to my stomach.

"*Get out, Geoff. I want you out.*" The cry was forceful but feeble, and my heart lurched.

Who was Geoff?

The older woman, who I could see now was a doctor, reached her hand out. "Miss, if you could stay back—"

"I'm with Chandler," I blurted out, shelving for

later how natural the words sounded on my tongue. "I have to go in there."

"Mom, please."

The doctor and I returned our attention to the door, the sounds behind it becoming louder.

"Excuse me." The doctor inserted herself in front of me and knocked on the door. "Mr. Collins—"

"*Out!*" Something crashed, and before I realized what I was doing, I'd grabbed the handle to open the door, only to have it yank me forward when it was opened from the other side.

"Just give me another—" He stopped short when he saw me, and my heart broke when I saw him.

He was nothing like the cool, collected billionaire who'd walked into the coffeeshop two weeks ago. His shirt was wrinkled like someone had crushed the collar in their hands, and there was a gash on the side of his head, blood oozing from the open seam of his skin.

Minutes in this room had turned him ragged in a way I recognized—it was the same pain we'd all worn when Kit came home from the hospital. It was the pain of loving someone so much, and it not being enough to help them.

"Chandler..." I whispered his name, my racing heart climbing all the way into my throat.

His hardened gaze snapped to the doctor behind me. "I'm fine. Please, just one more minute."

"Who is it, Geoff?" A fractured voice approached.

My brows lifted. She was calling him Geoff.

"Who—"

He moved to the side when she tugged on his arm. In the second I had to glimpse between them, I saw what caused the cut on his face, the picture frame holding a butterfly shattered on the ground. And then his mom appeared.

"Who are you?" Laura asked, her brow furrowed and her gaze skeptical.

There were three things I noticed instantly about her. First, she couldn't be too much older than Mom, her hair was only starting to have natural gray. Second, she loved butterflies. It wasn't just the one on the ground, but her lavender sweater was embroidered with them and matched the color of her slacks, and she wore a butterfly necklace around her neck that matched her earrings. And third, she shared the same eyes as her son, except Laura's were foggy. Uncertain. Like the roadmap in her mind was only partially charted out.

"Hi, I'm Frankie. I make homemade candles, and I have one here as a gift for you." I smiled and shoved the cinnamon candle in her direction, praying she wouldn't throw it at Chandler's head.

Like the record previously playing in her head skipped, his mom's whole demeanor changed.

"A gift?" She blinked and took the candle. "From whom?"

"Your son."

Instantly, her expression filled with what I could only describe as a mother's love. "Oh, Chandler. He's such a sweet boy. So thoughtful." She sighed and took a deep breath of the scent, her eyes going wide. "Oh, my, that is wonderful. Come in. We should light this."

"I have a lighter," I offered, keeping my eyes away from Chandler's as I walked by him into the room.

I didn't know what I'd find if I looked at him. Anger

that I'd inserted myself? Relief that his mom was distracted from...whatever had upset her?

"You know, my son brought me another candle that I love. It's over there on my dresser."

"What does that one smell like?" I asked like I didn't know.

"Happiness." Her wrinkled cheeks creased even deeper with her smile.

"Well, wait until you smell this one." I ignored the broken frame on the floor just like she did, leading her to the small sitting area away from the scene of their argument. The lighter touched the wick, drawing it to life.

"This is my favorite candle," I told her, lifting the jar closer so she could smell.

"Cinnamon," she exhaled.

"Warmth and comfort," I countered with a smile.

"My Chandler got this for me?"

I nodded, desperately keeping my eyes from flicking to the man who commanded every room he entered except for this one. In this one, he hung back in the shadows.

"Yes, he did."

She smiled. "Oh, he's so good." Her eyes flicked to mine. "And handsome. He's going to be trouble for the ladies when he's older."

He certainly was. But I kept that to myself. It was obvious she was remembering Chandler as much younger than he currently was.

"Well, he certainly loves you."

"Oh, you're sweet." She nodded, and her eyes fluttered a little quicker. "He does everything for me. Everything. Too much."

Chandler didn't move. At some moments, I swore he didn't even breathe in case it might break her calm.

"He does too much," she repeated softly.

"It's never too much when it's for family." I leaned forward and took a deep inhale of the candle, and then added wryly, "Trust me, you should hear the things I've done for my family."

When I looked up at her, Laura had her head tipped to one side, an entertained smile on her face.

Crap.

"Well, now I think you have to tell me," she declared, linking her hands in her lap.

Nice, Frankie. I didn't plan on inserting myself into this situation, but I couldn't deny her. Especially when her emotional state was on the line.

I slowly set the candle on the coffee table, taking a beat to steady the erratic pace of my heart...and feel the warm weight of Chandler's gaze on my back. There were so many things I could say—so many stories—but for some reason, the only one I could manage was ours.

"Well, one time I pretended to be my twin sister so that she didn't have to go on a date with this guy she'd just met," I said, my head angling slightly because I swore I heard a low sound come from Chandler.

"Oh my." Laura chuckled. "Why didn't she want to go on the date?

"The guy...she wasn't sure of his intentions."

"Oh dear." She pressed a hand to her chest. "So, she asked you to go instead?"

"Oh no, I volunteered." I grinned.

"And what did you think of him?"

All my witty responses disappeared like dandelion seeds in the breeze.

"I thought he was...handsome. Charming. But a little too secretive."

"Oh, secretive? Sounds dangerous."

"Oh no." I waved my hand. "I'm pretty sure he's harmless."

That definitely elicited a soft growl from the muscled shadow clinging to the wall.

"So, how did it end?"

My mouth opened and shut. Was I really gossiping about my first fake date with the guy's mother?

Yes, I guess I was. If that was what it took to keep her calm.

"He kissed me good night."

"So, you determined his intentions were good, then?" she asked, and before I had to figure out an answer to that, she followed it with, "Was it a good kiss?"

I choked—again—on air, and I was pretty sure the fire department should be called for the flames licking at my cheeks. I didn't want to answer either of those questions. The first, because I shouldn't reveal that information to her. The second, because I shouldn't reveal that truth in front of Chandler.

"You can always tell by the kiss," Laura went on blithely, ignoring my near-death attempt to breathe and my lack of response.

"Tell what?" I probed—anything to get out of answering.

"If it's going to be something special." Her voice turned wistful, and her attention drifted to the frames of butterflies hanging on the far wall.

It gave me the second I needed to collect myself and gently put an end to the conversation.

"I don't think we're going to see each other again."

"Oh, that would be unfortunate." She reached out and gripped my hands, pulling them to her. "You should really try to see him again. If the kiss was good... if it was special." Her hold was surprisingly strong, and so was her earnestness. Later, I'd claim that was why I didn't correct her before she went on. "Take it from me. Don't let a chance at happiness and love slip through your fingers."

My jaw went slack, and I fumbled to reply, "No, I wouldn't want to do that." I gave her fingers a squeeze. "I have to get going back to my shop, and I think the doctor is here with your medications."

I glanced at the crowd in the doorway, the doctor who'd stopped me taking the invitation to enter the room.

"It was lovely talking with you," Laura said and stood with me. "Thank you again for the candle."

"Don't thank me. Thank your son." My gaze darted to Chandler for the first time since he'd opened the door, and I found his expression unreadable.

"Please," she begged. "Try to see him again."

My head snapped back, and I had to remind myself she didn't know that *he* was her son.

"Okay." I nodded and told myself I agreed only because the doctor was waiting.

But I also couldn't say no. Not when she looked at me like that. It was the same look Gigi had when she demanded I come to dinner. And it made me feel the same way. *Like I'd do anything for my family.*

I released her hands and moved back so the doctor could step in. When she did, Chandler moved from the shadows, his mouth in a firm line.

"Mom..."

Now, it was my turn to watch their interaction from a distance—from the doorway into the room, my hand pressed to the frame.

As soon as she saw him, the soft expression on her face soured.

"Don't come back, Geoff. I don't want you here," she said, her mind slipping again.

Her words flayed him alive, but like the powerful man he was, he didn't even flinch. He took every hit like he deserved it—like he'd withstand it all for her. *For the few moments when she was lucid and remembered him again.*

"Thank you," I heard him mutter to the doctor and two nurses, the one helping his mom and the other cleaning up the broken glass.

And then he was heading for me, his gaze like a bottomless well. The deeper I went, the more pain I found.

We didn't say a word as we left the building—not to each other, at least. Chandler led the way, exchanging pleasantries with Cathy, who gave me another warm smile on our way out. He held the door for me—both the one out of the building and the passenger door of his car.

This time, when he climbed in the seat beside me, the tension was different. The thread that had been pulled taut was now all tangled and loose.

"Chandler..."

"I'm sorry," he said, his voice strained.

Sorry? I bit into my tongue to stop a cry from leaking through my lips. He shouldn't be sorry. *Why would he think he should be sorry?*

"Who's Geoff?"

He exhaled slowly, like it was all the life leaving him in one single breath.

"My father."

CHAPTER 15
CHANDLER

T he band around my chest ratcheted tighter with every breath. She shouldn't be here, but if she hadn't been...my exhale hissed through my lips. *Fuck*.

"How long has your mom lived here?" Frankie asked, jarring me from the spiral of my thoughts. Her eyes followed the building as it disappeared in her side mirror.

I hesitated, but not out of embarrassment. There were only a handful of people who knew about Mom's condition—people who cared about her. People I trusted. I wouldn't risk someone trying to take advantage of her because of who I was—because of how much I was worth. And somehow, Frankie—*my adversary*—was about to become one of those people.

Because I'd brought her here with me.

"Five years," I rasped, the trees becoming a blur on either side of the road as I drove us back toward town.

Somehow, it was the afternoon already. The sky was void of color. The passing scenery was void of detail. My chest...was void of everything—pain and guilt and regret. Everything was hollow except the woman sitting next to me.

Frankie was full. Full of color from her cheeks to her clothes—a yellow tee and a pair of orange patterned pants that flowed so loosely, when she stood still, it looked like she had on a skirt. She was full of courage. To step in where my fear had locked her out. To put herself in the middle of everything to try and help. To expose her own feelings when Mom...

"Is it dementia or..."

"Alzheimer's." I couldn't remember the last time I'd spoken the diagnosis out loud to anyone other than Tom or Mom's care team. "The last year and a half it has gotten worse, especially with her recent memory. She gets more forgetful. More irritable." My jaw clenched. "They would've sedated her if..."

"You hadn't come."

My heart slammed against my chest. "No," I admitted hoarsely. "If you hadn't."

The truth fisted around my throat. When Cathy called earlier and told me Mom was hysterical, I ordered them not to sedate her unless they truly felt she was at risk of harming herself. I said I'd be there—that I would calm her. And then I'd hung up, and instead of just leaving, I'd gone back into the candle shop for Frankie.

Why? Because I didn't trust her out of my sight? *Bullshit.*

Sure, I'd aimed to spend every minute with her because I damn well knew the inn wasn't haunted. I wanted to prove I was right. And I wanted to see how resourceful she'd be to do the same. But that rationale—

that excuse—it disappeared days ago. It disappeared the second she told me why she started making candles in the first place.

And that was the reason I'd gone back—the reason I brought her with me.

Because underneath it all—underneath the woman who pretended to be her sister, who faked a séance on the sidewalk, and who slept next to a stranger every night—Francesca Kinkade was a woman who would do anything for her family. And maybe I was hoping she would do the same for mine.

"I'm sorry for telling her about our date...and after. I was just trying to distract her."

Mom wasn't the only one distracted by the story. Frankie could've told her anything—real, fake, it wouldn't have mattered. Mom would've been enrapt by whatever it was. But Frankie chose to tell her about us. About our first fake date...and that kiss. And the way she described it wasn't a lie. Not the pink in her cheeks or the flutter of her pulse against the side of her neck.

"Don't apologize," I ordered, a little more gruffly than intended. "Please. I can't thank you enough." I parked in front of her shop and killed the engine; the closed sign hanging askew on the door reminded me that she was off for the rest of the day. "Do you want me to drop you off somewhere else?"

Her head angled, and my hand on the wheel tightened as her brow creased.

"You're...dropping me off?"

"Yeah."

For what she'd just done for me—for Mom—the least I could do was leave her in peace. At least until tonight. She'd already helped me in a way she hadn't needed to, a way I wasn't sure I'd ever be able to repay. For the first time in a long time, I worried about what this would cost me. I worried about the price I would pay for needing Frankie Kinkade.

"What are you going to do?"

I had no idea. I couldn't go back to Edgewood. There was nothing more I could do there except stand around like a poster boy for pity. I should call Tom. Update him, even though Cathy probably already had. But to update him meant I had to explain Frankie...and I didn't have words to explain her right now.

Gorgeous. Defiant. Clever. Loyal. Generous. Persistent.

Okay, maybe I had plenty of words to describe her, but none to explain what she was doing to me.

"Work." My default. My shelter.

"Are you sure—"

"Just go, Frankie." My voice cracked.

She'd done enough. Too much. And if she stayed, she'd do more. Give more. And I wouldn't be strong enough to resist her.

"Okay." She opened the door and got out.

My head turned, following the sway of her hips toward her shop. That was too easy. My frown deepened, expecting her to turn around at any second and insist—demand something. To ask something. To say anything. But then she unlocked her shop and disappeared inside, and the weight on my chest that I'd hoped would lift only intensified.

"Dammit," I muttered and pounded my palm on the steering wheel.

What was I thinking, wanting her to stay? Wanting

her to fight for me? *Christ.* She'd already saved Mom today, who the hell was I to need saving, too?

I punched the start button, my hand landing on the shifter just as the dash beeped an alert.

Key not detected.

"What the..." My head whipped around, checking my pockets. I had it when we left Edgewood—obviously —or we wouldn't have made it back. My hand stilled, my fingers feeling in the cupholder where I remembered putting the keys, and then I slowly lifted my head, my gaze zeroing in on the door to the Candle Cabin.

Frankie.

My breath whooshed out. I should be angry, not relieved. I shouldn't be laughing that she'd stolen my damn keys so I couldn't leave. But I was. My insides felt like a tangled-up mess of emotions, and she managed to make me smile. Without even fucking being here.

I got out of my car and closed the door loudly, knowing she was listening. Waiting. *Knowing I wasn't going to get far.*

I tried the knob first. *Of course, she locked it.* I reeled in the smile that wanted to break free and rapped on the glass pane in the door. It opened almost instantly.

"Oh, you're still here," she said, blinking up at me.

God, I wanted to fuck that look of feigned innocence off her face. I wanted to the first time I saw it— standing on the damn sidewalk next to her fake séance. That was why I'd thrown down the challenge.

"Hard to go anywhere without car keys."

Her lashes fluttered again. "You don't have your car keys?"

"You know I don't."

She pressed her hand to her chest, incredulity masking everything but the dance in her eyes. "You think I have your keys?"

My head cocked. "I know you do."

The door swung wide. "You're welcome to come in and look for them."

I stepped inside, my arm brushing hers as she closed the door behind me.

"Frankie..."

"While you're here, let me clean up your face." She strolled ahead of me like there was no chance I'd protest.

Moving wordlessly through her shop, I felt the edge of my brow, wincing as my fingers brushed the slight swelling around the cut. *Damn.* I'd forgotten about that.

In the back, Frankie tugged out a stool from underneath the counter. It was the one she always sat on to review her orders. It was a simple wood piece that looked damn uncomfortable until I sat in it myself. The way the seat was carved forced my back straight.

"Jamie made it for me," she said, seeing me examining her chair. "He made all the shelves and furniture in here. He's incredible."

I slowly admired the craftsmanship of the work, my gaze sliding around the room until it landed on Frankie's ass. I stiffened. My cock stiffened. Hell, everything but my restraint stiffened.

She was bent under the sink, practically crawling completely inside the cupboard, leaving her ass up in the air. *Christ. Wasn't it bad enough I had to feel those curves pressed warm and soft against me every night?*

She made a sound of triumph and appeared with a smile on her face and a first-aid kit in her hand.

I cleared my throat and banded my arms over my chest, hoping she didn't look too far south of my waist.

"Doesn't seem like a great place for a first-aid kit."

"Says the first person I've had to use it for," she returned smartly, opening up the box and pulling out what she needed. She went to the sink next and wet a cloth with warm water.

"I'm going to wipe off the dried blood first and make sure there's no glass in there," she said and came to stand in front of me. Cinnamon burned into my nostrils, pulling my jaw tighter.

I winced at the first brush of her hand. Not because it hurt, but because it was her.

"I'm sorry." She dabbed gently, and her teeth clamped into her bottom lip.

"Don't..." I closed my eyes, unable to look at her—to know she was damn close and so fucking kissable.

Nothing existed outside the warm drag of the cloth over my skin. The uneven catch of her breath. The heat making the air between us buzz with electricity. It wasn't painful. It was torture. So, I kept my arms tight over my front, afraid if I loosened them an inch, the first thing they'd do was reach for her.

"It's a good gash you've got here," she murmured, attempting to add some lightness to her tone.

"Will I survive?"

She hummed, pretending to consider her answer. "Too soon to tell."

I let out a weak laugh. She wasn't wrong about that.

"If I don't, maybe I'll join the inn ghosts."

She stilled for a split second. "You'd have to expire there for that to happen."

My chest rumbled. "I didn't realize there were rules to haunting."

"Oh, many," she replied matter-of-factly, pulling the cloth away.

I opened my eyes, instantly finding hers. "So, if I expire here, then I guess I'd be stuck haunting you."

Her mouth parted, and I bit into my tongue to hold back a grunt of pain. My cock was so fucking hard, if skin had seams, mine would've split by now.

"You already do," she murmured, and the huskiness in her voice, the look in her eyes...she wasn't talking about the way I hovered around her all week.

My gaze dropped to her lips, and the hold I had on myself started to loosen. My fingers uncurled. The fire in my chest burned hotter.

"Frankie..."

Her head jerked to the side, and she plopped the cloth onto the counter, reaching for the alcohol wipe next. "I don't think there's any glass in the cut."

My throat tightened. "Good."

"I'm going to clean it with some alcohol and then put some tape over it for the night." She ripped open the packet and looked at me again with a warning. "This is going to sting."

I breathed out slowly, making sure I still had her eyes when I replied, "Maybe I enjoy the burn."

I'd never not enjoy surprising her. Ever. Her jaw went slack, her cheeks dusting a color of pink that made me want to heat the rest of her body to match. I imagined pouring hot cinnamon wax all over her tits to see if she'd enjoy the burn, too.

She didn't say anything, just pressed the pad to my forehead with more force than intended, the way she instantly let off the pressure.

"Sorry."

My breath hissed out, the alcohol disinfecting the exposed flesh. I no longer cared about the wound. Hell, I wasn't sure I ever had. I only cared about her. Her closeness. Her softness. Her warmth. I wanted to pull her to me—step right into her fucking flame and let it burn through me. Burn down the wall. Burn down the work. Burn down all the barriers I'd built to convince myself I was only made for business and let myself feel. Pain. Pleasure. Want. Hunger. I wanted to feel it all. Just once.

And then a burst of cool air rushed over the cut. My eyes snapped open, stunned by the sight of Frankie fucking blowing on my damn wound like I was a little kid. Her full lips puckered, and my cock started to weep. I couldn't move. Couldn't breathe. I couldn't do anything but watch this woman work her magic on me —healing me as surely as she destroyed me.

"What are you doing to me?" I growled deeply.

Frankie opened her eyes. There was no time—no way to hide how I watched her or how I wanted her.

She drew back, the color in her cheeks spreading to her neck. "I just want to put a little tape over it, so you don't get too big of a scar."

I tried to steady my breathing and curb my lust. I'd done it for how long, so why was I failing now? Why was it because of her? The stolen kisses were one thing, but to want more...I couldn't. If I fucked her, I couldn't sell the inn to her family. I could be cold. Ruthless. Callous. But I couldn't do that. How would it look?

How would it make her feel? *How the hell would I walk away?*

"Worried it will make me less handsome?"

"Maybe it will make you just the right amount of charming," she teased, tearing a few small strips and sticking them to the back of her hand.

I wanted the answer to the question that had come next—the one where Mom asked about our kiss and Frankie had gotten out of answering, but I didn't get the chance.

"What kind of butterfly was in that frame?" she asked quietly as she reached for my face again.

"A monarch." I forced my breath to stay steady again when she touched me. "They're her favorite. Tom brings them for her."

"That's sweet of him."

I tensed. I'd never thought of it like that. Of him—of them. *No.* I shoved the idea to the side along with the hundreds of memories that now suddenly begged to be revisited.

"It was the newest one in her collection, and she couldn't find it. That was what...set her off," I said in a low voice, closing my eyes as she put small pieces of tape over my wound and picturing Mom's frantic face. "It was my fault because I'd stuck it in a drawer last week where she'd put all her other picture frames, and she didn't know."

Mom was so upset. Hysterical. The nurse was trying to calm her, but it was only making it worse. She was frantic and unsteady, stumbling and banging into furniture to look for the frame and to avoid her nurse.

"As soon as I realized, I got it and gave it to her; I thought it would fix everything." *I was a fool.*

"She didn't remember you."

My jaw pulsed against her palm, a Morse code of my misery. "No," I croaked. Mom immediately thought I was Geoff. "She accused me of trying to take the picture—steal it." *Steal her happiness* were the words she'd used. "I reached for her. I don't know...I thought maybe if she looked right at me, I could make her see me. And when I did that..."

"She walloped you with it."

"Walloped?"

"Do you have a better word for it?" Her eyes flicked to mine.

I grunted.

After a beat of silence, she spoke again. "Does she always think you..."

My jaw flexed. "Are my father?"

"Yeah."

"Not always," I said, suddenly finding it hard to get the words out. "Some days, she thinks I'm a younger version of myself. Still in college. On her bad days, I'm my father." Something broke inside my chest, and the weight resting on it carried out on my heavy exhale. "Or maybe I'm the reason for her bad days because I remind her of him."

I could claim it was work that kept me from visiting or even the pain of being mistaken for my father, but this was the truth. What if seeing me worsened her condition? What if the way it upset her—made her angry—made everything worse? After today, what the hell was I supposed to think? She almost had to be sedated, and it was because of me—because of seeing me.

"I don't think that's how it works." Frankie lifted

her chin as she said it like she was a damn expert on the subject.

"How do you know?"

"Because of the way she talked about you and the way she looked when she did it," Frankie said, and the way she looked at me... "For so long, we tried to bring my brother, Kit, out of his darkness in ways that made sense to us. We'd do the same things we used to. We'd have the same meals. Watch the same movies. Visit the same places. We thought reminding him of all the good in his life before would help him."

"But it made it worse." Because that was how it fucking felt every time Mom looked at me and saw him. The man who hurt her. Used her. Left her. Abandoned us.

"No," she said with a little sigh. "It was like we were trying to open a locked door with the wrong key. We didn't make the door more...locked. We didn't make it worse. We just didn't have the right way to reach him. But it didn't change that we were there, waiting on the other side of the door for him to come through it."

"And if she never comes through it again?" I rasped, bitterness leaching into my tone from where it welled inside me. "Wouldn't it be better for me to stay away? To never see her, so she's never reminded of him? To not risk causing her pain?"

Her breath caught as though my pain had reached out and grabbed her by the throat. The color of her eyes darkened, but they also flickered with light. Twin flames that burned with emotion.

"How do you think she would feel on the days she does remember? On the days she is lucid and wonders where her son is? Why he doesn't come see her? What if she does peek through that door just a little bit?"

In an instant, all that bitterness transformed into something else. Something stronger but lighter. Something that filled my chest and fluttered, the cocooned bitterness transforming into something completely different.

"There's going to come a time when she has no memory, only moments," she continued, her voice turning breathless. "After that, a time when you will have no more moments, only memories...but only if you decide to keep making them."

The words landed like a pin in the cogs of time, stopping everything with the simplest, subtlest suggestion. To be there. To be present. My gaze caught like kindling in her stare. My pulse thumped heavily on the side of my neck up to where her palm rested on my cheek.

She was right. What she said was right. How she felt was right. But it was more than all of that. It was everything about her that was right...for me.

And there was going to come a time when I would have no more moments with her if I didn't do something about it now.

I cupped her face, the touch like a lever that parted her mouth, my thumb skimming the soft skin of her cheek. "Because a light isn't the only way out of the darkness."

Her breath hitched, her full lips parting like an invitation. "Exactly."

I wanted to kiss her again. Hell, I wanted to kiss her at every moment, and I wasn't going to waste any more of them.

My head dipped, a growl reaching from my chest—reaching for her. And then a boom of thunder reverberated so loudly it shook the entire cabin. Jars clanked and rattled. And it was only her quick lunge that stopped a precariously stacked beaker from toppling off the counter.

"Crap." She steadied it and said softly, "We should get going. If we leave now, we can probably pick up food and make it back to the inn before the rain hits."

"Okay."

Our eyes met. There was a powerful storm brewing. And it had nothing to do with thunder or rain or lightning and everything to do with my little candlemaker and the fire she'd started inside me.

CHAPTER 16
FRANKIE

I really needed to stop kissing Chandler. Or almost kissing him. Or thinking about kissing him. But the way I wanted to, was like a hold around my throat, siphoning off more and more oxygen the longer I was around him.

"Well, at least we're already prepared for the storm," I said loudly, rushing by Chandler as soon as he unlocked the inn's front door.

The weather had gone from ominous to torrential in the stretch between the taco shop where we'd quickly scarfed down dinner and the old building, the rain spilling from the sky like a broken faucet. I'd been the one who suggested we walk. After that moment in the shop, with his hands framing my face and the hungry tangle of his stare in mine, there was no way I could get back in the car with him. The closed space. The heavy silence. I couldn't do it. I needed space. A minute to breathe.

And it would be faster to walk than to drive and

find parking. *At least, that was what I told him.* But it wasn't fast enough to beat the storm.

The whole building seemed to shake when he shut the door, thunder rattling the frame.

"Are we?"

Our eyes met, and then mine slid over him. His shirt plastered to his broad chest. His dress pants molding to muscled thighs. We were both soaked to the bone.

"Hopefully it will pass through quickly," I offered, and as if Mother Nature wanted to laugh in my face, there was another flash of lightning and an even louder roll of thunder.

I folded my arms and forced my gaze anywhere else in the hall. If it weren't for the storm, it wouldn't be so dark in here yet, but the clouds were rapidly blanketing the sky in night.

"I'll start a fire, if you want to change first."

A fire sounded good. And so did a dry pair of clothes.

I followed him into the living room and crashed right into the wall of his back when he stopped short.

"Sorry." I practically jumped back, but his attention was elsewhere. His head whipped in every direction, scanning the room. "What is it?" I stepped beside him, squinting into the darkness when his phone flashlight came on.

Why didn't he just use one of—

"The lanterns are gone."

I stilled, following the source of his light as it roamed every corner of the room. The mattress was as we'd left it. The firewood was still by the hearth. But sure enough, it wasn't just the batteries and bulbs that had gone missing, but the entirety of the lanterns themselves.

"Stay here. I'm going to check the rest of the floor for them."

I opened my mouth, but he was already gone.

My heart thudded in time with the thunder as I moved deeper into the room, using the intermittent bursts of bright light through the windows to find my bag and the candles I'd brought over earlier. *Cinnamon.* Too bad for Chandler.

The wick sputtered to life and light, the familiar warmth instantly settling me. It didn't matter if the lanterns were missing, we were just going to go to bed anyway, just like we had the last two nights. Still, I found myself walking the perimeter of the room, searching for the missing lanterns.

This wasn't exactly what I was thinking when I told Nox we needed to take it up a notch.

It didn't matter, the storm would throw off anything else he had planned, and that would only leave one night left. One night to prove without a doubt the inn was haunted. *One night left to sleep beside the man who made me want things I'd never wanted before.*

The thunderstorm rioted outside, shaking the windows and quaking the ground. I stopped in front of the window, watching lightning streak electric tears through the sky to the edge of the horizon. It was so consuming, I didn't hear Chandler come back into the room, let alone come to stand behind me until he spoke.

"Frankie."

I jumped and spun. My cry of surprise turned into a whimper of pain when the sudden movement sent hot wax spilling from the candle onto my hand, burning me instantly.

"Shit," I muttered, my brain fritzing between adrenaline, pain, and *him*.

"Let me." Chandler took the candle with one hand and my hand with the other.

"I'm okay—" The words hitched at the end as he lifted my hand closer to his face, a gentle stream of air blowing through his lips to cool the wax.

But that was about the only thing it cooled.

Something hard and hot condensed in his eyes. Seeing the wax on my skin, it did something to him, and it was doing something to me. Something dangerous and exciting and one hundred percent trouble.

"I thought you liked the burn," he rasped quietly, his thumb making a slow pass over the lump of cooled wax.

My throat tightened. This wasn't the kind of burn I'd meant when I'd taunted him days ago...but it was the kind of burn I suddenly wanted to feel.

"I do," I heard myself mutter, enraptured by the way he was staring.

A deep sound rumbled from his chest as though an animal were caged inside it.

It didn't take much force from his finger to dislodge the solid wax, the sound of it falling to the floor disappearing in the booms of lust. The touch was silent. Like a hot, electric lightning bolt of lust. But it was the following thunder of ache that reverberated through me. It shook my bones and quaked through my blood. It wasn't just wanting him that was forbidden, it was the way I wanted him that felt dangerous, too.

He traced the perimeter of the red skin like the

patch was a sacred sight. "Do you know what temperature soy candles burn at?"

What temperature...my eyelids fluttered. Why was he trying to test my candle knowledge right now?

"One..." I paused and swallowed. "One hundred thirty-five to one hundred forty-five degrees."

He made that low sound again. The one that was hot and heavy the way it dripped down my spine and hardened the ache in my core.

"It's why soy wax is the safest. It has the lowest melting point, so it is less likely to burn the skin," he rumbled, and my brows slowly drew together, watching him bring my hand to his lips. The first brush was a lesson in tenderness. The press of his lips to the wound like a kiss could heal it. "I'd still hold it farther away, so it doesn't do this." His tongue slid out and licked my skin, but it was impossible to say which affected me more—the touch or what his words implied.

I'd been making and selling candles long enough to have a basic knowledge of what was involved in wax play. Which candles were good, which ones were better. Every so often, adventurous and unabashed honeymooners would wander into my shop and confirm that the soy wax used in my candles was safe for skin.

I'd wondered about the kink. I had at least a dozen scars from hot wax on my hands and arms, but every time it happened, there was only a flash of pain followed by a low, pulsing burn. A burn that made me wonder in those brief, unfiltered moments what drips of hot wax would feel like on other parts of my body. Pain mingled with pleasure. A burn on the outside to match the burn within.

His tongue flicked over the tender skin, sending a

shiver along my spine. A charge. A spark. I didn't want to wonder anymore.

"Show me."

Chandler stilled. His wet clothes reflected the ripple that went through his muscles at the words that weren't a plea but an order.

I wanted to know, and I wanted to know with him. Rules be damned. Situation be damned. Consequences be damned.

Frankie be damned.

His eyes lifted to mine, the dark pools molten with a kind of lust that made my nipples furl even tighter. Painfully tight.

"Show me," I repeated, just in case he doubted what he'd heard.

"Frankie—"

There was a loud bang from inside the house, and he whipped around, barricading me behind him.

"Stay here." His tone was hard. "Someone's in the kitchen."

The kitchen. He disappeared with my candle, and it only took a second for me to follow him. Nox wouldn't be here—shouldn't be here. Not in this storm. But if he was...

I was almost running by the time I reached the kitchen, and I instantly came to a halt. There was no sign of Nox. *Thank God.* But Chandler was standing on the counter in front of the window—*the one I told Nox to use to sneak into the building.* He wore a scowl when he looked at me, but it was no surprise that I hadn't listened to him.

"The latch on this window is broken." His gaze bored into mine, almost like he knew.

Crap.

"Oh?" I had plenty of excuses for my voice's higher pitch.

There was a pause. A long pause to see who would crack first.

"It was a gust of wind that must've caught it and caused it to bang," he said, shimmying the window and trying to force the lock to engage. "I saw a hammer and some nails in the hall closet. Can you grab them for me?"

My jaw went slack and then snapped shut. "Yeah."

I took the candle from where he'd set it on the counter and moved mindlessly into the hall. Sure enough, there was a hammer and a tattered box of nails in the closet left from when they'd started doing work to restore the inn.

"Here." I handed him the hammer, watching as he sealed shut my secret weapon. There was only one night left, and if Nox couldn't sneak in...I'd find another way. I'd have to.

"That should keep it closed." His shoes squelched when he hopped down from the counter, landing right in front of me.

"Chandler..."

"Let's start the fire before we both catch a chill," he said and maneuvered around me, his footsteps firm as he walked back to the living room.

He was trying to fight it, and maybe I should be, too. He was...who he was, after all.

But he was also the man who worked by my side without question. Who talked to my customers and sold my candles like they were his own. And he was also the man who was willing to do anything for the people he loved—even cutting himself out of his mom's life if it would spare her pain.

I could resist every other temptation the man possessed except the broken-hearted loyalty that had crushed him earlier.

I stood next to him as he crouched in front of the hearth, holding the candle steady as he unwrapped and lit a brand-new log. The wood crackled and popped to life, the flame slowly sinking its teeth through the worn, hard layers, not unlike desire, which had latched onto me. *Onto us.*

"You should change," he muttered, staying low by the fire.

My throat tightened.

"I don't want to change."

His shoulders jerked back, and then he straightened and turned in one swift movement to tower over me with an angry glare.

"What do you want, Frankie?" he dared, his husky voice making my core clench painfully.

I wasn't ashamed of who I was or what I wanted, and no matter the outside circumstances that brought us here, I wasn't going to share now.

I handed him the candle, holding his eyes. "I want you to show me."

His expression turned pained. "Frankie...I can't—we can't."

My chin lifted. "Because you don't want to?"

Something like a growl drifted between us. He moved so our chests were almost touching, his head dipping lower as he uttered, "I've never wanted anything more." He took the candle from my hand.

"But I won't do that to you, or to me, because we're adversaries."

My hand landed on his chest, stopping him from walking away again.

"Not in here, we're not," I murmured. "Not tonight." I felt him shudder against my palm. "Do what you promised."

His jaw tensed. "And what was that?"

"Don't mix business with pleasure."

His eyes flickered. Popped. Cracked. I shivered.

And then the flame erupted when his mouth claimed mine.

His kiss burned away the chill from my bones. He must have set the candle somewhere because his hands were on the sides of my face an instant later, tipping my head, angling it for the deep press of his tongue.

I wanted more. I wanted everything. I'd been so focused for so long—so single-minded about my own success—that I didn't leave room for distraction. But tonight, I wanted to be free. Tonight, I didn't want to care about anything except easing the ache that had been building from the second I'd met him.

Tonight, I wanted to be taken by my own trouble.

"Chandler..."

Water ran along my fingers and splattered onto the floor as I squeezed his shirt and pulled him tight. A groan rumbled from his chest, as unsteady as the ones that quaked from the sky, and he deepened the kiss. His tongue pierced every corner of my mouth, licking and stroking—*scorching* scars of pleasure with the same white-hot heat as the lightning outside.

I shook. The old building shook. The same rain that pelted the windows dripped from our clothes onto the floor. It was as though the fury outside was nothing more than a mirror for the tempest that consumed us. The tighter he held me, the louder the booms. The deeper the kiss, the heavier the rain.

My hands skated up to his nape, threading through the damp strands of his hair and wringing them dry. He was so hot, like molten stone pressed to my chest, and all I wanted was to be closer. All I wanted was to melt against him.

I didn't even realize when my hips began to rock, aching for the hard ridge of him wedged against my stomach.

"You're going to be the death of me," he rasped, his hands locking on my waist with a punishing grip as his mouth trailed a wet path along my jaw to the sensitive spot right below my ear.

I tipped my head back and panted. "I get that a lot."

"Not like this, you don't." He growled like a lion protecting his pride, and when I shivered, he ordered, "Take off your clothes."

I lifted an eyebrow. "So bossy. Do I call you Mr. Collins, or would you prefer sir?'"

A hint of a smile tugged at one corner of his mouth before it disappeared, and he gripped my chin, the intensity of his expression making my core clench.

"Such attitude." His thumb traced my lips. "I wonder how smart that mouth would be when it's stuffed full of my cock." My jaw dropped, and instantly his thumb dipped inside and pressed on my tongue as he bent forward and muttered, "To answer your question, call me whatever is going to be easier for you to scream."

And then his hand was gone. His heat. His proximity. He stepped back against the fireplace, his hands reaching for the buttons on his shirt as he stared expectantly for me to do the same.

Seconds passed, filled with the sopping slop of clothes peeling from skin and landing on the floor. The hearth hissed with the growing fire, or maybe that was just him—the breath leaking from his lungs as I stood in front of him, wet and bare and wanting.

I didn't hurry the moment because I needed to look my fill. He was gorgeous, and even though I expected it, I wasn't prepared. The raw beauty, all toned muscles and pulsing veins, and his thick cock standing heavy in front of him. *Good god, did the man have any physical flaws?* If he did, I was utterly blind to them. Like this, he wasn't put together or professional. He wasn't buttoned up, believing he was only good for business. Like this, he was exposed. Unfiltered. Unhindered.

And mine.

"Give me your hand," Chandler ordered, his voice sounding stripped, and my eyes snapped up from his waist.

Without hesitation, I extended my arm, and his grip locked firmly around my fingers. I watched him take the candle he'd set on the mantel and bring it close, the flame pulsing wildly like it was caught in our electric erotic storm.

Chandler held my eyes, swallowed them up in the dark pools of his. "I'm going to make you burn for me."

My nipples furled tight, and I taunted, "You can try." It was better than admitting I was already set aflame.

Again, his half-cocked smile appeared and sent a fresh rush of heat between my legs in anticipation. The candle tipped, and the liquid wax collecting around the wick shifted. Surged. *Spilled.* I shivered just before the first drops landed on the inside of my wrist and then gasped at the familiar but oh-so different sensation. It was hot. Scorching. But before I could process any pain, his mouth was there. He blew on the pool of wax, cooling it on my skin, and then he pressed his thumb firmly on top of it.

"Are you okay?"

My tongue slid along my bottom lip. "Yes."

But also no.

How many times had I burned myself with fire or wax in the last decade? Countless. It was a hazard of the job. But this was no hazard. This was intentional, illicit intimacy. This went beyond trusting him with my pleasure, I was trusting him with my pain—trusting him to wield both like the deadliest, double-edged sword.

"Good," he said gruffly. "Because I'm going to mark every inch of you." He lifted his thumb away, leaving behind a wax thumbprint like a seal over my pulse.

Instantly, I imagined those fingerprints burning all over me. My arms. My breasts. My stomach. Between my thighs.

"Chandler..." My throat strangled out his name.

In one quick movement, his thumb peeled off the hardened wax, the red skin underneath instantly covered by the heat of his mouth. The soothing kiss did nothing but make the ache inside me stronger.

I reached for his face, his expression angry like I'd ripped food right from his starving mouth. But I was starving, too. He was trying to go slow—to be tender. And while my chest squeezed at the notion, I knew what I was asking for. I knew exactly what I wanted.

"Burn me again," I begged throatily. *Mark me as yours.*

The kind of person who pleaded to play with fire didn't think twice about being consumed. That was how fire worked. There was no half-flame or partial light. There was only on fire or not. And tonight, I wanted to be on fire for him.

CHAPTER 17
CHANDLER

"Burn me again."

Using my hand around her wrist, I hauled her against me and kissed her like I'd been starved of her for the whole of my thirty-six years. Her plea ripped off the buttons of my restraint, and I bruised her smart, soft mouth with my own.

This was insane. I was insane. *The way I felt about her was driving me insane.* But I didn't care. I'd go mad if that was the price of one night with her. Or maybe that was the very definition of my madness.

"On the bed," I growled into her mouth. "Hands above your head."

I gave her a little push, watching her backpedal until her legs bumped the inflated mattress, and she lowered onto the blankets, her gaze never leaving mine as she tipped back.

Fuck.

Hot air hissed through my lips, and I couldn't help but stare. It wasn't restraint that paralyzed me, it was reverence. Frankie was fucking gorgeous. Her damp hair clung to her chest like hot honey, the ends sticking to the swells of her breasts. She looked like a damn siren captured straight from the sea, begging for a taste of my world.

I kneeled onto the bed next to her, watching her pink tongue dart out over her lips as her gaze shifted to my cock. The damn thing was right at mouth level for her, the end dripping with how fucking bad I wanted her. My jaw locked. It would be so easy to give it to her. To feed her my swollen length until she choked. But that would be the end of me. A tidal wave of accelerant onto an already uncontrolled wildfire.

"Eyes on me," I rasped, waiting for her stare to lift before I held the candle over her, high enough so it wouldn't truly burn her.

"Show me," she begged softly, her back bowing with how bad she wanted it.

A growl scratched its way from my chest as I slowly tipped the candle. Her breath hitched just as the wax fell, and time suspended just like the molten heat for a second as our eyes connected. There was no going back. No undoing. No unmelting the wax or unlighting the flame.

There was no undoing us.

The wax splattered on her sternum, and time galloped forward again, leading to her sharp gasp at the sensation. My eyes locked on my first mark, watching her skin redden around it, and the force of my groan shook my grip on the candle.

"Beautiful," I murmured, losing the last threads of my sanity at the sight of her. The dark honey of her hair. The cinnamon peaks of her nipples. The flush of goose bumps across her skin. Desire chewed through my veins like a starving beast. If I wasn't careful, the next thing that dripped on her would be cum from my painfully hard dick.

"Chandler..."

"Does it hurt?"

"Yes," she breathed out the word.

I lowered my head slowly, watching her stomach tremble as I got close and blew on the wax to temper it. "Do you like it?"

"Yes." She arched as she answered, and my body quaked at her responsiveness.

"I see it," I rumbled. "How flushed you are. How hard your nipples are." My eyes flicked to the bare skin of her pussy, and I started to salivate. "I wonder how wet it made you...how wet it will make you when I drip this on your tits."

"Stop wondering and find out," she dared, and my jaw locked tighter, so fucking tempted to obey.

"Soon," I promised, holding the candle above her again, but this time so the wax fell onto the slope of her left breast.

The sound she made—a gasp that melted into a moan—made my cock jerk. She was fucking perfect for this. All pale skin and unabashed desire. Her back bowed into the burn, her nipples pebbled so fucking tight, all I wanted was to sink my teeth into them.

"So fucking perfect," I muttered, letting the wax run closer to the peak before I lowered my head and stopped it with my breath.

With my lips hovering just above her skin, I saw every tremor and tremble of her flesh. Every goose bump and hungry beat of her pulse. And it was all for me. I pushed my fingers into the soft heat of the wax, dragging around the slope of her tit. I painted her skin with the warmth, watching it pebble and pinken— watching her tremble and come undone.

"Chandler, please," she whimpered, and, in my periphery, I caught how her thighs rubbed together. And that was how I missed her hand reaching for my head. I hissed when her fingers curled into my hair and pulled my head toward her.

I gritted my teeth for a fraction of a second, but I couldn't resist. Not anymore. I cupped the weight of her breast, feeling the wax mold it to my palm as I fed the tight bud of her nipple to my mouth.

"*Fuck*," I growled as my teeth hooked her soft flesh first, giving her that bite of pain before I pulled the soft bud between my lips. My deep groan came straight from the marrow of my bones. She tasted like cinnamon —or maybe it was the wax so close by that my brain conflated scent with taste. Whatever it was, I couldn't get enough.

"*Yes,*" she whimpered and writhed under me when I sucked hard, her hand clutching me tighter, not wanting me to stop.

Every stroke and flick of my tongue made her wild. I slid my hand to her other breast, pinching and teasing it with my fingers to mimic the movement of my mouth. She twisted underneath me, and there was part of me that knew I could make her come like this—knew I could come like this. Just from touching her—tasting her if I didn't stop now.

Her nipple popped from my lips, and I dragged myself away. "Another time I'll feast on every inch of you," I promised, like having more than this night— more than this inn—was even a possibility. I sat back on my heels, my palm grazing across the trembling softness of her stomach, resting there for a beat. "Arms above your head," I reminded her and sat still until her hand that had slid onto my forearm lifted and returned above her head.

"I want to touch you." Her eyes flicked down to my cock.

My jaw hardened, and I lifted the candle over her chest. "Not tonight." I dripped more wax onto her chest, the pain putting an end to that thought. I glanced down at my cock and let out a tight breath. *Fuck.* The swollen, red length confirmed that I wouldn't survive her touch.

My focus returned to Frankie, sinking two fingers into the hot pool of wax and dragging it in a spiral around her breast all the way to her nipple.

"God, I love the color this turns your skin," I rumbled, watching the heat char her skin to crimson.

"*Please.*" She writhed and twisted around the word like a fire stoked to life by my touch.

As much as I wanted to torture her, it was too much torture for me. I wanted her so damn bad.

"Let's see how wet you are, my little flame," I rasped and poured another stream of wax—the last of what was stored around the wick—from her sternum down to her stomach.

The sounds she made as she quivered went straight to my dick, the damn thing throbbing so fucking painfully I was starting to not see straight. But I ignored it as I wiped my fingers on the blanket and reached between her legs.

Our gazes locked. Hers was pulsing like twin golden embers. And mine, well, I was sure I looked like an animal. I wanted to see that look of surprise on her face when I made her come—the look no one else gave her. Fitting because I was going to give her an orgasm unlike anyone else either.

"Let's see how well you melted for me," I rasped and moved my hand higher up her thigh, watching the way her breath caught, and her eyes flitted a little wider, and then the way that perfect mouth of her parted with relief when I slid my fingers through the seam of her pussy.

"*Fuck...*" She was so damn wet. Molten and wet and mine.

"Chandler," she moaned and arched into my touch.

The heat of the wax was nothing compared to the heat of her cunt. I didn't even recognize the sound that escaped my lips as I pushed my fingers inside her, my thumb rolling over her clit.

"You burn so good for me, my little flame." I didn't know where the endearment kept coming from, but I wouldn't take it back even if I could. Not when she looked at me like she did—not when her body responded like it did.

I worked my fingers inside her, sliding in and out like her pussy was a damn instrument I was playing to hear the melody of her moans.

"*Yes.*" She bucked when I found her G-spot, her body becoming putty in my fingers. Before long, she was nothing more than trembling muscles and a frantic heartbeat, chasing the release my touch promised. "Please, Chandler..." Her head thrashed, her fists curling into the blanket above her head.

My breaths turned labored, watching how fucking

beautiful she looked as pleasure unraveled her tight control.

She could fool everyone else, but she couldn't fool me. Frankie was all fun and games for everyone but herself. When it came to her own life, it was business, business, and more business. When you spent almost ninety-six hours straight with a person, there wasn't a chance to hide faults—to hide much of anything. And I wasn't sure Frankie would've even tried to hide that she was married to her candles. It was admirable quality right up until my lips first tasted hers.

Then it became a challenge.

A challenge to bend my rules for the sole prize of breaking hers.

She started to tense, her body quivering around my fingers. She was so fucking close. One thrust of my cock would send her over the edge. But I wanted more. This woman didn't need anything from anyone, but so help me God, I wanted her to need me. Desperately. More than independence. More than oxygen. More than anything.

So, I stroked her inner wall, coaxed her orgasm right to the edge—right to where her jaw dropped and her eyes squeezed shut—and then I stilled my fingers and tipped the candle in my other hand, scorching the edge of her pleasure with another drip of hot wax low on her stomach.

"Chandler!" She bucked, her eyes snapping wide.

Her body jerked, the searing pain pulling her back from the edge of release. Her wide gaze swirled with shock and pleasure and pain, her chest heaving to try and catch her unsteady breaths.

A slow smile dragged at my lips. "Again."

Her mouth parted, and she choked out, "I can't—" She broke off with a moan as I rubbed her clit, the tight, aching bud so fucking desperate for release. "Chandler..."

"I thought you said you could handle the burn, my little flame," I growled, starting to pump my fingers inside her again. Now my cock was leaking steadily, knowing how fucking prepared she was going to be for me. How tight and desperate she would be.

She moaned and her thighs drifted apart, her body answering before her voice did, "I can."

"Good girl," I rasped, and I stroked her clit like I was fanning the most delicate flame. The sound of her slick heat taking the thrust of my fingers consumed me, my next words coming out raw and rough and absolutely fucking feral. "Because you only get my cock when you come through the pain."

Frankie shuddered, a rush of heat drenching my fingers.

"That's it," I growled, pumping my fingers faster and lifting the candle over her trembling stomach, watching and waiting for enough liquid wax to form.

The sounds she made started to blend together. Started to crack and fracture the way everything comes apart inside a fire. Her body tightened. Pleasure eating away everything but instinct.

"Please," she begged me—begged herself.

Gritting my teeth, I curled my fingers into her front wall at the same time as my thumb pressed the tight button of her clit. She bowed, her chest pinched in one last breath, teetering on the brink of release.

And I let the wax fall.

This time, the hot splash on her stomach didn't reel

her back from her orgasm but sent her shooting over the edge.

She screamed, coming so hard against my fingers she made my whole arm shake.

"Fuck." I blew out the candle and tossed it off the mattress. *She was going to be the death of me.* I grabbed her hips, replaced my fingers with the head of my cock, and buried myself inside her with one hard thrust.

There was no going slow. It was her muscles that pulled me deeper, her body that clutched me tighter. I watched my cock spread her tight pussy beautifully wide. Felt her legs wrap around my waist as she met me thrust for thrust.

My head tipped back, pleasure chewing through my veins like a beast with fangs.

I drove into her with hard, unyielding thrusts, and she took every thick inch of my cock like it was what she was made for.

"*Chandler.*" She panted. Begged. Choked and gasped. If she was new to wax play, it was a damn safe bet she was new to stacking orgasms. But not for long.

I drove into her with long, sure thrusts, watching pleasure fight pleasure until my own threatened to knock me out.

"Chandler..." Her hips bounced. Churned.

"Burn for me," I ordered roughly. "Burn for me, my little flame."

Her nails dug into my forearms, her pussy squeezing so fucking tight that I stopped breathing. Stopped thinking. Stopped everything except fucking her until she screamed my name again.

She came like wildfire around me. Hot and unstoppable, her orgasm absolutely destroyed me.

"Fuck," I swore. The ripple of her tight cunt was too fucking much, and I lost it.

I slammed into her hard and fast, the thrash of her climax igniting the pressure at the base of my spine. I knew nothing but the need to come, and I took it.

My cock swelled. Stretched. And then erupted. I came with a loud roar that shook everything from my bones to the bones of the old inn as I held myself buried inside her, filling her with jet after jet of thick release.

We clung to each other like neither of us had experienced anything like that before. *And neither of us were willing to admit it out loud.*

What happened after, I only processed in pieces. Kissing her gently. Cleaning us up. Pulling her close. Her slow, rhythmic breaths as she slept. And the words *"my little flame"* murmured as I pressed my lips to the top of her head, knowing I'd never be the same.

CHAPTER 18
CHANDLER

I'd never not wanted to get out of bed like I did at this moment—never wanted to not let go of a woman like this before.

I stared at the soft slope of Frankie's shoulder. She was tucked against me—had been all night. I rarely physically slept with women, and the handful of times I had in a very distant past, I'd never woken up still holding them. But Frankie...even my unconscious self didn't want to let her go.

I wanted the warmth of her beside me. Wanted the way she thawed parts of me I didn't know could still feel.

I tipped my head closer, taking another deep breath of the cinnamon that radiated from her. The scent would never be the same again. It belonged to her. It *was* her. *It was everything*. And when this was over, I'd have to figure out a way to avoid cinnamon for the rest of my life.

My phone buzzed, the pattern of the sound indicating who it was. *Tom*. And if it was Tom, it was about Mom.

I rolled to the side, carefully sliding my arm out from under Frankie's neck, and grabbed my cell from the floor, the screen lighting up instantly with the message.

> I'm at Edgewood now. She's asking for you.

"Shit," I muttered and did my best not to disturb Frankie as I stood.

My pants looked like shit, but at least they were dry. I shoved my legs into them, knowing I only needed to make it to the hotel with them, where I could change.

"One night was all it took to scare you away?" Frankie teased behind me, her voice warm and husky like a wick sputtering back to life.

I stilled and then grinned as I faced her. But my smile weakened at the sight of her. *My little flame*. Her hair spread over the pillow in waves of honeyed sunlight. The blanket covered just enough of her for me to resent it. The only thing I wanted draped over her was me. And the sultry upturn of her lips...

"I don't scare that easily." But maybe I should.

The way I looked at her. The way she was looking at me. *What happened last night*. This was the exact kind of thing I should be running from.

It had been a long time since I'd engaged in wax play. It required a level of trust that one didn't often get with one-night stands, even with partners who were into kink. But Frankie...she'd begged for it. Without fear and with implicit trust. For me. *Her adversary*.

I hadn't asked for it, and she'd just...given it to me.

Her vulnerability. Just like she'd given of herself yesterday with Mom.

"What's wrong?" Her brow creased as she sat up, and the blanket dropped, catching on the hard tips of her breasts and teasing me with her red-stained skin from the hot wax. Need slammed through me, and I gritted my teeth.

Frankie grabbed the blanket and pulled it higher—seeing the marks, too—before covering them up. A heavy exhale pushed through my lips when her eyes lifted to mine. The flame between us hadn't burned out. Not even close.

But that wasn't part of this agreement.

"I have to go," I said and grabbed my shirt off the floor, giving it a hard shake.

"To see your mom?"

*How did she...*I stilled. "Yeah."

"I'm coming with you." The blankets rustled behind me.

"Frankie—" I broke off when I turned just in time to watch her stand from the bed, rising like Venus from the waves, and the sight put me in a chokehold.

The dip of her waist. The swell of her ass. The full weight of her breasts...*god, I could spend a whole night worshipping her breasts*. Painting them with wax. Soothing them with my lips and tongue. She was wildly responsive. I'd make her come just from sucking her—*fuck*. My cock jammed against the front of my pants with more than enough pain to let me get my head on straight.

I spun away, pretending it was her privacy and not my own hunger I was trying to protect her from.

"It's fine," I managed curtly, shoving my arms through my shirt. "You don't have to—"

"I'm coming. My shop is closed."

I tensed. Yesterday, I'd brought her along in a fit of madness—let her through a door in my life I kept permanently closed and locked as a matter of principle and self-preservation. And now, I couldn't find the words to push her out of it.

"Going to be hard for you to go without me."

"And why's that?" I lifted one brow.

She bent and pulled something from her bag. "Because I still have these." She straightened, dangling my car keys from her fingers.

"THEY TOLD ME WHAT SHE DID YESTERDAY," Tom said and came to stand beside me, nodding in Frankie's direction where she sat at the edge of Mom's bed, smiling and showing her photos of the Candle Cabin.

Today, Mom remembered me. She was in bed, groggy and a little more sedated because they'd increased her meds after what happened yesterday, but at least she remembered me. I didn't know if this was how Alzheimer's worked or if it was how Mom worked, but the swings from highs to lows seemed more pronounced. What started as small missteps of memory turned into noticeable stumbles and then worrisome trips and then...yesterday. A fall.

"Yeah." I didn't realize how unprepared I was for this conversation. A reflection of how unprepared I was for how I felt about her...and what I was going to do about it.

"And it's her sister who's trying to buy the inn?" he asked, a glimmer of hope flickering in his tired eyes.

Mom wasn't the only one who was a little worse for the wear today. Tom looked just about as ragged. The creases on his face. The shadows under his eyes. I didn't need to ask if he'd slept at all yesterday because it was written all over his rumpled clothes and exhausted voice.

"Her twin sister." I had no idea why that was relevant to say, but I said it.

"And I take it you're now favoring their offer?"

My spine straightened. *Was I?* I should. *I couldn't.*

"No." I forced the denial out because it was our agreement. We weren't going to mix business with pleasure.

His head snapped to me, his expression more strained than before. "Chandler..."

"It's not the best deal." And that was all there was to it. I cleared my throat and took over the conversation before it continued any farther down this path. "The doctor said they'd return her meds to normal tomorrow?"

Tom hesitated and then nodded. "Yes. They wanted one day to let her rest, but they really did a number on her. She was very unsteady on her feet when I got here, that's why I suggested she relax in bed." A small smile worked its way onto his face as he added, "I told her we could have a picnic dinner in bed."

I made a low sound, and everything he said—everything he did—I saw differently after yesterday. "I didn't realize you got her all of these butterfly photos." My eyes slid to him, watching the subtle stillness that came over him.

"They're her favorite," he said simply, but it felt like there was more. The way he looked at Mom, it felt like there was something I was missing—something I'd been missing this entire time.

Him and Mom.

I didn't get a chance to turn the tables on him because Frankie came over to join us and said softly, "She's sleeping."

Tom gazed at her for a long moment and then said, "You're welcome to stay or sit downstairs and talk, but I don't—I can't leave her."

When I looked at him this time, it wasn't his feelings for Mom I saw in his eyes, but my own for Frankie I found reflected in his stare.

"No, that's all right," I murmured. "We should get going."

Yesterday had been a long day for Mom, and I didn't want to push my luck. I might not know everything that was between them, but I knew she was the calmest when she was with him.

I went to her bedside, her eyelids heavy as she turned to me. "Chandler..."

"I'm going to let you rest, Mom." I sat on the bed and took her hand in mine.

Her eyes glistened. "You and Frankie..."

Not her, too. "I'll be back tomorrow to see you," I said, ignoring her comment. "Tom will be here."

At the mention of his name, she looked to him and

then back to me, giving my fingers a small squeeze. "Don't do what I did, Chandler. Don't be too vulnerable."

I sucked in a breath, hoping she didn't notice the way I stiffened. Was she warning me away from a relationship? Did she realize what she was saying?

My head turned to Frankie, and my chest tightened.

Did I realize what I was doing?

"Where do you want me to take you?" I asked as we approached the center of Friendship, my thoughts in a tangle of topics.

My mother and Tom. Frankie. Last night. The inn. *Tomorrow morning*.

"Just keep going straight," she replied, her gaze toying with the sights out the window, looking but not really seeing them.

When we breached the far end of the town, I was about to ask again where I was taking her, but her next instruction came first.

"Turn right up here."

I followed her directions from there, making turns onto roads I was fairly certain had no name and a destination few people knew existed. I made one final right, and as soon as we passed through a thicket of trees, I saw how the drive unraveled in front of us, cascading through the large property all the way to a two-story, porch-wrapped farmhouse at the end.

"Your mom's house?" I asked like I was already sure of the answer.

"Yeah," she confirmed, pulling her plump bottom lip between her teeth.

My hand on the wheel tightened. *Dinner*. It felt like months had passed since Gigi's invitation yesterday morning. Her request was completely forgotten until now.

I parked in line with the three other cars out front but left the engine running. My eyes skated to the front of the house, and even though the shades were drawn and I couldn't hear a thing, I could feel the energy of her family pulsing inside it. The love they had for each other...for her...my teeth pressed tight. *Maybe this wasn't the best idea after last night.*

"Ready?" Frankie pulled her bag onto her lap.

She assumed I was coming. Well, at least that was what she wanted me to think. That was Frankie, boldly declaring her will and daring anyone to deny her. But after last night, I couldn't help but see the vulnerability there. It sounded like an assumption, but only to disguise the fact it was a plea.

"Frankie..."

The front door swung wide, a familiar head of bright orange hair popping through. "Francesca? Is that you out there?"

Frankie gave me a sheepish look. "No choice now," she said and opened the passenger door. "Hi, Gigi. We're coming."

"Are you? Because it looked to me like you were waiting for the red carpet to be rolled out."

My finger hesitated on the engine button. I could still leave. I could make an excuse and drive away. It wasn't like they had much cause to like me anyway. I was the person standing between Lou and her inn...and they'd invited me for dinner. I started to pull my hand away. It would be better for everyone if I didn't stay.

Frankie turned and looked at me, her mouth firming when she realized I was going to leave—that I was going to be the man I'd told her I was. And then, without thinking, my finger punched the engine button and shut off the car, earning me that look of surprise I craved.

Pink cheeks. Parted lips. For one more night, I didn't want to be that man. I wanted to be hers.

"Hello, Gigi," I greeted the older woman as I stepped onto the wrap-around porch.

"Chandler!" Wiry but strong arms enveloped me. "So good to see you again." Gigi pulled back and adjusted her massive glasses. "You look nervous. Why? I promise we don't bite." There was no question where certain parts of Frankie's personality came from. "Well...most of us." Her eyes flicked to Frankie, who faked a gasp.

"I don't bite."

Gigi made a sound of disbelief and then looked at me and winked. "I don't think Chandler would mind if you did."

"Gigi!"

I laughed. At this point, what else was there to do? *What else did I even want to do?*

"Let's not keep your mother waiting." She grinned and moseyed inside, Frankie mouthing an apology to me as we followed her.

The house was everything I didn't realize I was expecting. Warm and inviting, with sage wreaths and exposed wood. The open floor plan allowed me to see straight from the front door to the other end of the house and let the lively conversation reach us immediately. But it was the scent that overwhelmed me—it was the smell of the house that made me feel the way I did, welcomed and at home, not the cozy decor or the warm laughter.

And I'd bet a cool billion it was because of her.

I slowed by the photos on the wall, instantly picking out Frankie and Lou, Gigi, with varying shades of hair color, and then connecting the dots that the other woman must be Frankie's mom, Ailene, and the two large men, Frankie's older half brothers. Some photos even had her cousins. Well, at least the one I'd met, Nox. I just assumed the other guy and younger girl were family as well.

"Chandler..." Frankie paused, waiting for me.

"What's the scent?" I asked, stopping just in front of her. "One of yours, I'm assuming."

She caught her smile in her lower lip before it got too big. "Honeysuckle and mint. Mom's favorite. It's a limited-edition candle I make just for her."

I hummed. "Very homey."

Her mouth parted, and then she collected herself and said, "It's called Homey Honeysuckle."

Something buzzed through me, but just as quickly as it appeared, Frankie spun and led the way into the kitchen...and to meet the rest of her family.

In here, it smelled of barbecue and strawberries and oozed with laughter.

"Frankie's here, everyone. And she brought a... guest, Chandler." The pause before *guest* was painfully exaggerated, but aside from that, there was no awkward break in the conversation. No angry stare down or skeptical assessment. Even Lou was the first in the room to greet me, her shy smile unchanging from my first day in town when she'd given me a tour.

"Chandler, welcome. I'm Ailene, it's so nice to finally meet you." Frankie's mom wiped her hands, the small crowd of family around the island parting to let her through like she was a queen.

"Pleasure to meet you. Thank you for having me—oomph." I broke off when she pulled me in for a hug.

"We hug around here," she informed me with a friendly pat on the back. "Now, let me introduce you to everyone."

I received warm welcomes from Frankie's cousin, Harper—the one from the photo in the hall, Frankie's sister-in-law, Violet, her other cousin who owned the flower delivery service, Max, and her almost sister-in-law, Aurora. The other three men in the room greeted me a little more guardedly.

"Chandler." Nox extended his hand, and I shook it, but he looked much less thrilled to see me than the day we met at the Candle Cabin.

When he moved to the side, the last two stepped forward. Frankie's older brothers.

"Kit Kinkade." The one who inspired Frankie's candle business.

"Chandler," I said and gripped his hand, his stare hardening on me with dislike.

They had to know who I was—who I was to them. It would've been foolish to presume anything else.

Aurora came to his side and placed her hand on his

arm. When he looked at her, she smiled, and instantly, his whole demeanor changed. Like a knight shedding his armor, everything about him softened for her, and something in my chest twinged.

I looked away and came face-to-face with the last of the Kinkades.

"Jamie." *The oldest.* Her father figure.

He gripped my hand firmly, his gaze just like Frankie's when she measured me up. One look was all it took for the two of them to size up not just a man's character but his soul.

"Pleasure."

He drew back and folded his arms over his chest. "So, you're the one who won't sell the inn to Lou?"

"Jamie Kinkade, there is no business talk at family dinner," Gigi said curtly, giving the back of his leg a light whack with her cane, that I still had yet to see her use to walk.

Jaime grunted and mumbled an apology.

"Jamie, now that Frankie and Chandler are here, you and Kit should start grilling the chicken." Ailene handed them the full platter with a smile and shooed them from the kitchen. "Frankie, you're with Lou and Harper on table duty."

Frankie caught my eyes and then joined her sister and cousin in the dining room. Her other cousins didn't even need instruction before Max went to the bar, and Nox started taking drink orders. And that left me, Gigi, and Ailene.

Frankie's mom smiled at me. "So, Chandler, I hear you've been working at Frankie's store?"

"I have."

Her eyes sparkled. "Why don't you help me slice the vegetables and tell me all about it?"

Dinner passed in a blur of conversation. Between the twelve of us, there wasn't a moment open for silence before someone filled it, but never with discussion about the inn. Like she was the queen, everyone abided by Gigi's edict to keep business off the table. Well, except for Harper, who was allowed to discuss at length her new beekeeping venture.

Maybe it was because there were so many of them... or maybe it was because of who they were...but I didn't feel like an adversary here. Hell, I didn't even feel like an outsider.

But mostly, I watched how they interacted with Frankie. How they all instinctively looked to her to chime in at every turn. I didn't know if they realized it or not, how often they turned to her. Even when they teased her. Even when they shared stories about her pranks. They still anchored their conversation around her.

Maybe because it was so easy to find comfort in her warmth.

I would know...I had, too.

"Frankie, dear, can you help me and your mother in the kitchen?" Gigi asked as everyone stood to move the conversation to the couches in the living room.

Frankie flashed me an apologetic smile and followed Gigi, leaving me to follow the rest of her siblings and cousins into the living room. I settled on a spot next to the fireplace, standing with my shoulder propped against the hearth and my gaze anchored on Frankie. Sipping the last of my drink, I savored her infectious laughter that reached me all the way from the kitchen.

It was definitely a mistake to join them for dinner. A line that shouldn't have been crossed. But there was no going back now—I was afraid there never would be.

"Mr. Collins." Lou stepped in front of me, blocking my view of her sister. I should be seeing the same thing. The same honey hair. The same almond eyes. The same plump pink lips, perpetually pinned in a tempting smile.

But Lou looked nothing like her twin sister. Not to me.

"Please," I begged. "Call me Chandler."

Her shoulders rolled back, and she took a deep breath. Unlike her sister, Lou Kinkade had to physically prepare herself to stand up to me.

"I think I'd rather call you Mr. Collins for this conversation," she said simply, the words like a bucket of ice water over all the warmth in my chest.

It looked like the *no-business-at-family-dinner* rule was about to be broken.

"Of course." I nodded curtly. "I assume this is about the inn?"

"Yes," she hesitated. "And no."

"Interesting..."

Lou took a deep breath, glanced in the direction of the kitchen, and blurted out, "Mr. Collins, I'd like to match Mr. Fairfax's offer for the inn."

I swayed back. *Of all the things...*

"You want to offer the same amount?" I repeated, a little dumbstruck at the surprising direction of the conversation.

It wasn't that Lou's offer was unreasonably low. It

was pretty decent for someone who planned on revitalizing the property. But for someone like Fairfax, who was going to start from scratch and build modern condos, that return could justify a much higher bid.

"Yes."

My brow creased. "Are you sure?"

It wasn't my place to question her or any buyer's financial situation. If she was able to offer more, she could. But after all my conversations with Frankie, especially when she was pretending to be Lou, I'd gleaned that the woman in front of me was putting everything she had on the line to buy this place. And if that was the case, to offer more meant she...

"Yes, she's sure," a deeper voice chimed in. Kit Kinkade moved in behind his sister, his arms barreled over his chest.

He was the one chipping in.

"Kit." Lou shot her brother a look, one that reminded me of her sister's warning glare. Based on his response, it clearly wasn't a look he was used to receiving from Lou. "I'll handle this."

Kit grumbled quietly, his expression maintaining a distinct frown as he walked away.

"I'm sorry about that."

"Don't be. He clearly is very protective of the two of you."

"He tries to be." She laughed softly. "But only one of us usually lets him get away with it." *Her. Not Frankie.* At the allusion to her sister, she quieted, tucking her arms across her chest. "If I match Mr. Fairfax's offer, will you accept mine?"

My head tipped. "How do you know I wouldn't accept yours even if you didn't?"

The key to being a successful businessman—a successful anything, really—was understanding people's motives. I could offer three million for a property worth half that, but if the owner only cared about the preservation of the building, then the astronomical number wouldn't matter. In business, in life, you had to meet people where they were at.

"That's the problem, Mr. Collins. I'm afraid you would," she said softly. Surprisingly soft for how firmly she held my gaze.

"I don't understand."

"What's going on between you and my sister?" she demanded, her pulse rattling against the side of her neck.

Shit. I brought my glass to my lips and bought myself a few seconds to think with a long sip. *What was going on between Frankie and me?* We slept together. One night. The terms were clear—*only pleasure.* I didn't know the truth, let alone if I should be the one to break it to her family.

"Nothing," I clipped. "We have a business arrangement to assess certain...qualities of the inn."

She blushed, but not the way Frankie did. Lou's blush was instantaneous, like a firework of red exploding on her skin. Frankie's was slower. More subtle. Like the creeping stretch of a wildfire spreading across her face.

"But I know you already knew that," I added at the end. So why was she asking me? Because I was here for dinner? Because their grandmother kept looking at me as though she knew something I didn't?

"And what will you do when that arrangement ends, and you decide who gets the inn?"

"What do you mean?" I treaded cautiously.

"Will you leave? Go back to Boston?" she pressed insistently.

My jaw went slack. I hadn't gotten that far yet. Of course, that had been my plan—should still be my plan. But last night...Frankie...

"Don't do what I did, Chandler. Don't be too vulnerable."

"Yes." I cleared my throat and sank my chin into a firm nod. "Of course."

Mom's words earlier still gripped me—they hung over me like a kind of phantom I couldn't fully make out. The only thing I could think was she meant she was too vulnerable when she'd fallen for my father, and now she was warning me not to do the same.

Frankie and I had an agreement: to treat pleasure like business, and like any other arrangement, we'd walk away when the terms were done. Her, back to her business and her family. And me, back to Boston and the deal that would finally destroy all that remained of my father's legacy.

"Are you trying to pay me off? Get me to leave sooner?"

Tomorrow was the last day of the dare anyway, though I'd be lying if I hadn't spent a good portion of the day thinking about how to extend my time here. But I couldn't. I had to finish acquiring GC Holdings. I worked too long...too hard. I needed to be free of my father, and I couldn't let anything get in the way.

Lou gave a weak smile and then let her eyes wander in her sister's direction. "The thing about my sister, Mr. Collins, is that she puts on a good show. All my life, she's protected me. Stood up for me. Fought for me."

She cleared the emotion from her voice. "Did you know we've never traded places? In twenty-seven years, we've never pretended to be each other. Until you." Her gaze returned to mine. "My sister risked everything, including her identity, to help convince you to sell the inn."

"So, you want to offer me more money instead?"

"I was going to rescind my offer altogether, but after everything Frankie has done...I can't do that," she surprised me by admitting. "I was always the vulnerable one, so Frankie decided to always be strong. Tough. But staying with you at the inn...it's made her vulnerable in a way I'm not willing to risk," she declared, her chin notched high, and for a second, I wondered if she did know. *But how?* "So, I'm offering you more money, Mr. Collins, because I'm not willing to jeopardize her heart."

"You think her heart is at risk?" My own thudded unsteadily in my chest.

"I think I'm unwilling to find out." Her expression turned guarded. "My sister deserves something more than business in her life, so if you aren't going to stay, then I want you to go."

I stiffened, the invisible gauntlet glittering on the ground between us. Damn, these Kinkade women knew how to get you right where they wanted you.

"Does she know—"

"No." Lou shook her head. "She'd kill me if she did."

I grunted in agreement.

"I'll consider your offer and let you know in the morning." I tipped my head just as I felt her approach.

"What am I missing over here?" Frankie joined our

conversation with an easy smile—one she wouldn't have if she knew what she was walking into.

And then I watched something incredible happen.

Countless times, I'd listened to Frankie paint a picture of her twin sister. Of her personality. Of her honest personality and generous spirit. All throughout dinner, I heard tales of when the two of them were younger, Frankie finding trouble and dragging Lou into it with her.

If there was one thing I knew for certain about Elouise Kinkade, it was that she wasn't a liar.

Until now.

"Oh, nothing. I was just asking Chandler how he feels about the ghosts at the inn." Lou lied like her life depended on it—*like her sister's heart depended on it.*

And I realized everything I'd done, every time I'd let the magnetic draw to Frankie pull me closer, it was all a dangerous mistake. A dangerous vulnerability for the both of us.

I couldn't offer more, and Lou was right. Her sister deserved everything.

I smiled and blended into the lie like it was nothing, but the whole time, Frankie's eyes were on me. She sensed the change. Like a flame flickering from an invisible breeze.

The rest of the evening passed in a blur. Drinks. Family. Dessert. Countless times, I forgot why I was there—and why I wasn't staying. And that was why, by the time I held the door for Frankie and followed her out to the car, I'd already made my decision.

"Is everything okay?" she asked as soon as we were alone.

"Yeah." I started the engine and pulled out my phone. "Just worried about Mom."

It wasn't a lie, but it wasn't the reason I was texting Tom.

> We're taking the Kinkade offer. Please have Judy send everything over in the morning.

It would soften the blow of laving Frankie tonight.

CHAPTER 19
FRANKIE

"What did she say to you?"

"Who?" His hand flexed on the wheel as he started to park the car. This late, there was a spot right out front of the inn.

"Lou." Something was wrong with him, and it happened right after he talked to my sister.

Chandler got out of the car without responding, and I followed him to the entrance of the inn. I braced myself to argue—to demand answers—but the fight went out of me with a whoosh when he spoke.

"She's worried about you," he said low, unlocking the front door.

My throat tightened. Her and Kit and Nox. I saw the way the three of them looked at me tonight. Instinct told me they knew...something, but when it was only Lou who spoke to Chandler, I thought maybe I was being paranoid. Out of the three of them, Lou would be the last to be confrontational. *Or so I thought.*

"She's always worried about everyone." I waved off the concern and stepped through the open door. After a few steps, I stopped, realizing Chandler wasn't behind me. I turned and found him with his arms braced on the doorframe like he had to hold himself back from coming inside.

"What are you doing?"

His eyes flickered. "What are we doing?"

I walked back to him and said, "Staying one last night at the inn."

His body tensed. "I don't think we should."

A pit opened up in my chest. An impossible ache for a man I'd only known for a few weeks, most of which he'd spent being my adversary.

"What did she say?" I demanded, with an edge to my voice. I couldn't imagine what power Lou had wielded over Chandler when he wouldn't even sell his property to her.

"It wasn't what she said, Frankie, it was the reminder of why we're here."

My throat worked to try and swallow. "We had an agreement."

For someone who always had a plan, I sure was fighting hard for something that would be unknown come morning.

His eyes flicked up, their depths smoldering.

"No business. No relationship. No strings. Just a few nights of pleasure," I reminded him, the twinge in my chest matching the tic of his jaw.

I didn't want him to leave. I wanted one last night. Truthfully, I wanted more than one final night, but I was going to fight for the night I was promised.

I stepped closer, my hands finding purchase on the hard planes of his chest.

"Frankie..."

"What are you afraid of?" I murmured.

His hot stare roamed my face, marking it with goose bumps wherever it touched.

"Tell me."

Chandler let out a pained groan like he couldn't hold himself back any longer. And then his touch was there, his hands framing the sides of my face and holding it up to his as he murmured, "Having you haunt me for the rest of my life."

I sucked in a breath and shivered. It could be nothing. A joke. A tease. But what if it meant more? What if it meant everything?

I shouldn't have risked it. Shouldn't have inched closer to the deep end of vulnerability. But I didn't know how to be cautious. Not even when it risked my own heart.

"Then don't give me a reason to," I said softly. *Don't walk away. Don't leave. Don't let this be just one more night.*

His jaw muscles popped under my fingers, and then his mouth came for mine.

The spark of our lips connecting turned into an inferno in a nanosecond.

We kissed knowing the night had an expiration, like the fuse of a bomb drawing short or the wick of a candle melting low. Our time locked in this moment was going to end, but while we were here, we were going to burn and burn and burn until there was nothing left.

Our tongues tangled, the kiss scorching my mouth and then singing along every nerve to the ends of my fingers and the tips of my toes. I didn't just want one last night, I wanted one unforgettable night. One I could go back to when my business wasn't enough.

When I decided I wanted more from life. One that wouldn't haunt me but humble me for ever thinking a connection like this could be everlasting.

Chandler growled and pulled me closer, his teeth biting my lip and then my jaw and then my neck. The thud of my pulse fed the pull of his mouth, where he sucked on my skin until he bruised me.

I whimpered, wanting every possible mark he could leave on me.

"What are you doing to me, Frankie?" he rasped, rocking his hips—his erection against my stomach.

My breath caught. It wasn't what I was doing to him. It was what I *wanted* to do to him.

Two nights. One for my vulnerability. One for his.

I tugged on his hair, pulling his head away from my neck until our eyes locked.

"I want to burn you," I murmured, my voice sultry and hoarse.

His body jerked, and then I felt his hand slide up my side, along my arm, and then take my wrist in an imprisoning grip. With his jaw pulsing, he dragged my hand down his torso to his waist. My lips parted with a swift inhale when he pressed his cock into my fingers, the thick length hard and straining to my touch.

"You already do, my little flame," he rumbled, and my pulse tripped. *His* little flame. "Fuck," he breathed heavy when my fingers started to squeeze and massage him.

"You know what I mean," I murmured, licking my bottom lip. He hesitated for a beat, his stare tumultuous. "I want you to trust me."

The hot whoosh of his breath was the only warning

I had before his mouth crashed to mine. Once again, our flame went from kindling to wildfire in a blink.

The door banged as we shoved through it, then banged again when he kicked it hard to shut.

Tonight, our clothes fell into a trail of shadows behind us. Shoes kicked off. Clothes pulled from limbs. Everything disappeared into the darkness of the room as we stumbled toward the mattress.

His mouth was everywhere. A brand of lips and teeth and tongue on my jawline and then down my neck. I tipped my head back, gasping, and he lifted me into his arms, making my chest the target of his mouth.

He set his lips and tongue to one of my breasts, licking and sucking and swirling until my head spun and my limbs went weak. I clutched his head, holding tight as he lowered us to the bed, my wet core settling right on top of his hard length.

"You taste so damn good," he growled and sucked hard on my nipple, sparks of pleasure ricocheting through me.

Even though my limbs felt like Jell-O, somehow my hips managed to rock against him, grinding my slick pussy along his cock.

"Chandler," I groaned as he devoured me—marked me with the delicious bite of his mouth.

Everywhere he touched—everywhere he kissed— turned to fire. There was no other way to explain it. Nothing but scorching heat that physically altered me. It stripped away all my walls and changed my chemical makeup, and it was too late that I realized this night would destroy me. Irrevocably.

Because of him, I would never be the same.

The thought made me gasp. It made my eyes spring

open, and the sight of his mouth on me, melting me to his touch, made me desperate to return the favor.

"Frankie—" He started to protest when I moved lower, so I crushed my mouth to his.

He clasped my face, and our tongues sparred, hungry and wild, until I pulled back, panting.

"I want to taste you," I declared, watching his eyes darken.

He slid his hand from my jaw, his finger grazing my swollen lips, before he pushed two of them into my mouth.

"Do you?" he rumbled deeply.

Just because I couldn't speak didn't mean I couldn't answer. Holding his gaze, I sucked hard on his fingers, watching his lips twitch as he let out a groan.

Chandler slid his fingers free, wiping them over my lips to wet them. "You're going to need it."

I shivered, saliva pooling on my tongue as his cock thickened against me.

"Go ahead and taste me, my little flame."

I didn't need any further invitation, slinking down over hills and valleys of muscle, my lips grazing over his hot skin until I hovered over his cock. My eyes flicked back to his, a thrill running through me at the way he watched me. Like he was Prometheus chained to the rock for starting this fire, and I was responsible for his punishment.

I wrapped my fingers around his girth, unable to close them completely as I guided the swollen tip to my mouth.

The noise he made when I fit him between my lips sent heat dripping between my thighs.

I couldn't help my small moan as I took him deeper,

my hand feeding me more and more of his length until I started to gag. *And that was only half of it.*

"God, Frankie," he groaned. "You feel so good. So fucking..."

I reduced him to grunts and pants when I started to move. Up and down. Sucking him hard. Stroking him with my tongue. His hands worked their way into my hair, massaging my head as I tried to take him deeper.

"Fuck, Frankie..." he hissed, his cock swelling thicker between my lips. "Fuck, that mouth of yours..." he groaned when I took as much of him as I could, his tip butting against the back of my throat, and tried to swallow.

His fist curled tight and yanked my head back. "You want to burn me or blow me, my little flame? Because I won't survive both," he warned hotly.

I licked the saliva from my tingling lips, my gaze glancing hungrily at his cock. I wanted to blow him. I wanted to suck him so hard he'd swear I'd pulled his soul from his body. But not for our last night together.

Rising from between his legs, I picked up the candle we'd left on the floor last night. "I want to burn you." My tongue worked over the words as I lit the wick.

I trembled as I moved up to straddle him. His jaw pulsed wildly as I lit the wick and moved back on top to straddle him, his cock nestled against my core.

"I'm sorry. I only have cinnamon," I said, watching the wax start to melt around the flame.

"Why are you apologizing?"

"Because you don't like cinnamon."

"Why the hell do you think that?" he growled.

My throat bobbed. "Because...you always steer customers away from it at the store."

His eyes went wide, realizing just how closely I paid attention to him while he was there. And then he was moving—pushing himself up and hooking his thick arm around my back to hold me close so our faces were level.

"It's not because I don't like it," he rasped, his hand climbing to notch his fingers under my chin.

My brows creased. "Then why?"

His head came closer, his nose nuzzling mine for a second, before I felt him take a deep inhale.

"Because it's your scent, Frankie." His grip tightened possessively. "You smell like cinnamon, and...*fuck,* I don't want anyone else to have that." His eyes glittered. "I want it to be all mine."

My jaw dropped.

His cinnamon.

Something surged like a coil sprung in my chest, more powerful than anything I'd ever felt before. I felt the lightest graze of his lips over mine, and then he was gone—lying back on the bed, his eyes dark with desire.

"So burn me, my little flame. Make me yours."

My throat bobbed, my heart rioting in my chest at his words. They sounded like so much more than this— than just pleasure for one night.

My inhale was buried into the bottom of my belly as I lifted myself up, reaching down and notching his blunt tip at my entrance as I held the candle high over his chest.

Our eyes sparked together. Locked.

I tipped it to the side and let the wax fall, impaling myself on his cock at the exact same time.

My jaw dropped, but it was his roar that filled the room. He was so big—so thick. A moan escaped at the way he filled me.

"Fuck, Frankie, you feel so good. So tight." His hands roamed my waist and then gripped my hips like his body was a string about to snap.

I dipped my finger into the cooling pool of wax, tracing it out onto his skin like he'd done to me. He hissed.

"Is it too hot?" My voice sounded so sultry.

"Not as hot as your pussy." His hands tightened, and he pressed deeper inside me, making me gasp.

Biting my lip, I rose up on my knees and tilted the candle again, sinking down on his cock as fresh, hot wax splattered on his stomach. My jaw went slack when his cock rubbed against my G-spot, pleasure exploding through me.

I knew I was supposed to be the one in control. The one with the candle. The one on top and in charge. But desire scrambled my brain. The swell of him inside me. The friction. The heat.

I couldn't...I needed him.

One last night.

"Fuck me," I panted—*begged.* "*Please* fuck me."

A growl reverberated out of him, and then my hips were no longer my own.

"Anything you want, baby," he rasped and pressed himself deep. "I'm yours."

His hips angled back, and then he slammed up into me. I cried out at the assault of pleasure on my G-spot. He shackled me to the mercy of his thrusts, holding me as he drove up hard into my slick, welcoming body.

"*Yes,*" I moaned over and over, choking on the word

because he fucked me so hard my breaths couldn't keep up the pace.

Our bodies slapped together over and over. Between gasps, I tipped more wax onto his torso, relishing how each burst of pain made him drive faster. Harder. When my vision started to flicker and dim, I blew out the candle and let it roll out of my fingers and onto the floor.

"That's it, baby. Take all of my cock," he growled, and my vision wavered and then focused on him.

The flex of his forearms, the sheen of sweat on his skin. His core was tight, and his muscles lay like bricks below me. I rested my hands on his chest—in the soft wax I'd left there—feeling it mold under my fingers.

"Fuck, Frankie," he cursed, and pleasure coiled tighter inside me, every one of his thrusts rubbing that sweet spot buried deep inside me like it was made just for him to find. "Come for me." He drove deeper, the mattress groaning at every seam. "Burn me with your sweet cunt."

My core clenched, and I came apart with a scream.

My body spasmed around him, my muscles feeling out of control, and then he let out one last roar that shook my very bones. Holding my hips, Chandler thrust impossibly deep and held himself buried there, his big cock pulsing inside me. Filling me. *Consuming me.*

The pleasure. The pain. All of him consumed me.

"I've got you," he murmured, and only then did I realize I'd tipped forward onto him, and he held me to his chest, his fingers running a gentle path up and down my spine. "You okay?" he asked after a few minutes of silence.

My throat felt too tight to speak. Lying here with him, limbs and bodies entwined, my heart knocking against his...all of this—everything we've done, everything I felt—caught up to me and held me captive.

His fingers found my chin and lifted my head, and the tightness around my throat released, and with it, the words lodged inside.

"I'm yours," I heard myself say back to him, my heart stumbling around in my chest.

A low rumble escaped his mouth as it lowered to mine, the kiss gentle and deep at the same time. His mouth played with mine like some kind of interrogation, and only when my mind was sufficiently scrambled, did he pull back and murmur, "And if I want you for more than tonight?"

Hope burst in my chest like a fresh spring, my brain taking a moment to catch up to the rest of me before I could repeat myself.

"Then I'm yours."

SUNLIGHT BUZZED OVER MY BACK, SLOWLY warming me to the idea of waking up. I slept like the dead last night, utterly exhausted from...

Chandler.

My eyes opened, and without having to look, I already knew he wasn't in the bed.

All his things were gone, including his car keys.

I grabbed my phone from next to the mattress, my

heart lurching a second time when the only messages I had were cryptic and from Lou.

CALL ME.

It was sent two minutes ago.

One thing at a time, I told myself, staring at the spot where Chandler had been last night. And then my phone started to vibrate in my hand. *Lou.*

I let out a deep exhale and answered, "Hello?"

"Frankie, where are you?"

"At the inn. Where else would I be?" My voice cracked at the end.

The excitement in her voice deflated when she asked, "Is Chandler there?"

Her excitement wasn't the only thing that deflated when I looked at the spot where Chandler had slept last night. *And if I want you for more than tonight?*

A chill rattled along my spine. "No. Why?"

"Oh good." Lou sounded relieved. "I got the call from his office this morning. He's taking my offer."

My breath went out of me like it was a yo-yo she'd called back with her words. "What?"

"The inn is going to be mine. Your plan worked!"

My head turned slowly to the side, the empty space on the mattress staring up at me like a canyon. The inn. *Hers.* Chandler. *Gone.*

"Frankie, did you hear me?"

Hear—yes. I jerked out of whatever I was in because I had to be there for Lou right now. "Sorry, spotty reception. I heard you. I can't believe...that's incredible, Lou." I hoped my breathless voice came across as excitement that we'd won rather than the panic I truly felt wondering what I'd lost.

"I can't believe it, Frankie. I can't believe after everything...it's finally over. It's finally mine."

Twice I tried to swallow before the tightness in my throat would let anything pass, let alone the words to reply.

"Frankie..."

"Yeah?" I attempted a smile, and it only served to make the first tear fall.

"Thank you."

I stilled, her gratitude like the twist of a knife in my chest.

"If you hadn't done...everything...I know the inn wouldn't be mine. I know Chandler—"

I inhaled quickly, his name like a knife in my chest. "Lou, don't." I cut her off and haphazardly wiped my cheeks.

What was this—who was this? Not me. Not Frankie. And especially not for an arrangement with an expiration date, no matter what was said in the heat of the moment.

There could be a thousand explanations for where he'd gone. Why he disappeared. A hundred scenarios where he'd show up with coffee or breakfast or a good reason for disappearing without a note. But I'd be a fool to hope for any of them.

The note was the inn—the note was his agreement to sell to Lou.

If he planned on staying or even coming back, I wouldn't be hearing this news from my sister. No. The week was up. Our nights were up. His choice was to be made.

"I'll never be able to repay you, Frankie."

"I don't want you to repay me," I insisted. "I want you to promise me two things."

"Okay." Her tone became uncertain. Subdued.

"First, that whatever happens next, you'll do whatever it takes to make the inn everything you dreamed it would be," I said, swiping another tear from my cheek.

I heard her relieved exhale. Compared to the kinds of things I usually asked of people—of her—this was an easy oath to make. "I promise."

My tongue grew heavy, loading the next words into the chamber of my mouth. "And second," I began, ignoring the rattle in my voice. "Promise me that we'll never talk about Chandler Collins again."

Lou's inhale was swift and pointed like the prick of a pin, releasing softly with, "Frankie..."

"Promise me."

She didn't hesitate this time. "I promise."

I stapled a smile to my cheeks and replied, "Thanks. Now, why don't you have everyone meet at Mom's? I'll grab coffee and breakfast from the Maine Squeeze, and we'll celebrate."

"Oh, but it's not mine technically, yet—"

"It's yours, Lou, after all this time. We need to celebrate." And I needed to start building new memories on top of old ones.

Her resistance toppled, and she agreed within moments. *Perfect.* Better to rip the Band-Aid off Gigi's hopes now and make it clear in no uncertain terms that Chandler made his choice—concluded his business in town—and therefore was gone. *And that I was completely fine.*

The pain in my chest. The crippled thud of my

heart. I only had myself to blame. I'd mixed business with pleasure, thinking I could pull them apart like oil from water.

But they were inseparable, like fire from a wick. With him gone, so was the flame, but its destruction still lingered. The charred scars of how I wanted more...and how I felt more with him.

You should've kept to the plan like you insisted he did, my heart accused.

I exhaled and stood from the mattress, releasing the vent so it could deflate. Within a few minutes, I was dressed and had what was left of our ghost-hunting campsite collected in a pile by the door. Even though Lou knew the truth—or part of it—it would be better if she didn't see any evidence of what happened here.

My gaze swept one last time through the room, its emptiness mirroring the hollow inside my chest. Just like that, all traces of us were gone. *All traces of him were gone.* And that was the first moment I felt the inn was haunted. Not for everyone else, but for me. I'd never be able to walk through these doors and not remember the time I'd played with fire and ended up with the burn of a broken heart.

CHAPTER 20
CHANDLER

TWO MONTHS LATER...

"Chandler."

I lifted my head out of my hands, my thoughts and worries making the weight of it like a thousand pounds on my shoulders.

I hadn't slept well for two whole months. Some of that was because hospitals weren't known for their hospitality, even for a billionaire, but most was because worry and rest didn't make for good bedfellows. But when I did sleep, it was full of restless, regretful dreams of her. Her sun-spun hair. Her candy lips. Her cinnamon scent. And the fire she'd lit inside me wouldn't die, no matter how long and hard I tried to tamp it out.

Tom sank into the seat next to me, his face mirroring the ravage I felt on my own. We'd spent the better part of the last two months in these chairs. Waiting. Fearing. Hoping. And fearing again.

"She's going to be okay." He placed his hand on my knee. "We're going to be okay."

He stared at Mom lying peacefully in the bed as he spoke the words he'd said a thousand times over the last unending weeks. Sometimes they were for me. Sometimes they were for himself.

"Yeah," I agreed because there was no other option. Not for me. Not for her.

I slid my gaze to him, watching his jaw quiver as he nodded, and then a tear rolled down his cheek. He brushed it away with an apology. "I'm sorry—"

"Don't," I urged. Both of us had cried so many times in these seats. Separate. Together.

"No, Chandler." He shook his head, insisting as his hold on my leg tightened. "I'm sorry I let it go this long. I should've told you—we should've told you so long ago...I love her," he confessed brokenly.

I stilled, slowly releasing the breath in my chest when his watery gaze flicked to mine and then back to Mom.

"I've loved her for as long as you've been alive."

If I'd had my suspicions before, the last two months had without a doubt revealed the true depth of Tom and Mom's relationship.

"Tom..." I didn't know where to start.

"I'm sorry, Chandler." He wiped another tear away.

"Don't be sorry," I said, my voice hoarse. "I know you love her...knew..."

His head turned to me. "You did?" He swallowed. "Did Laura..."

"No." I shook my head. "I didn't know—didn't realize until Frankie—" I broke off with a groan, a sharp pain cracking through my chest like a wound being split back open.

I'd never realized the extent of Mom's feelings for Tom because I'd extended the blinders for my own life onto hers. Onto theirs. Until Frankie made me want more.

I'm yours.

God, how those words haunted me.

"Chandler."

Air hissed through my lips. "I'm fine."

This was the first time I'd said her name in months. I'd thought of her—dreamed of her—in every moment, in all the small spaces between all my massive worries, but I never brought her up.

There were so many reasons we shouldn't have been together before I left, and now that I had left, they'd only multiplied.

"You need to go back to her."

I flinched like he'd struck me. "I can't. I left."

"So—"

"When Mom's discharged, I have to go back to Boston. We secured that last property from GC Holdings, so it's finally time to make my play. After all this time, I'm on the brink of destroying his legacy."

"Oh, Chandler."

I hated the disappointment in his voice. Gritting my teeth together, I argued, "Mom is the one who told me not to be too vulnerable. She wouldn't want me to go back."

The morning I'd left, my only thought was Mom. For days—weeks, she was my only concern. And by the time I could even string two rational thoughts together about Frankie and how I'd disappeared...Mom's warning overshadowed everything, and I decided it was better this way. We—whatever we were—had been hours from expiring anyway.

It was an asshole move to disappear with no explanation. *Better to be an asshole than a fool.*

Tom looked at me, agape. "She wasn't talking about your father," he said brokenly. "She was talking about me."

My brow creased. "I don't understand."

"All these years, she thought she was showing you strength, taking care of you, supporting you as a single mom," he began, his jaw tightening. "She didn't want you to think she was vulnerable by being alone...or by needing someone."

I felt the tension soften in my muscles. "By needing you."

He nodded slowly. "That was our agreement. We could be together as long as no one else knew. Especially you."

"You agreed to be her secret?"

"Oh, Chandler." He sighed and gave me a small smile. "For her, I'd agree to be her anything."

My throat tightened. "I never would've thought her weak for loving someone else," I rasped. "For loving a good man."

Tom's smile tightened, and another tear fell. "I know." Clearing his throat, he went on. "She hadn't been too vulnerable to love again, She'd been too vulnerable to let you see it. To show it was just as important to take the risk as it was to show restraint."

I tried to swallow but couldn't. What he told me should've turned my world on end—upended the perspective I'd entrenched myself in since leaving

Friendship that morning. Instead, it was like everything that had been foggy came into focus.

"It wasn't a warning, Chandler. It was a plea. Don't be too vulnerable to not let Frankie see...to not take the risk."

"How can I go back now? It's been..." Too long. Too much silence. Too cruel the way I'd left.

My tongue felt heavy and thick in my mouth. I couldn't think about leaving the hospital right now, let alone going back to Friendship. Forget haunting me, Frankie would want my head on a pike. *And she deserved it for what I'd done.*

Tom placed his hand on my shoulder and looked me square in the eyes. "How can you afford to stay away?"

CHAPTER 21

FRANKIE

ONE MONTH LATER...

"This smells amazing!" Adele gushed, pulling the candle straight to her nose for a whiff before holding it out for Aria to smell, too. My stomach turned on itself.

"I like to think of it as pumpkin spice on steroids," I said through tight teeth, trying to hold it together. "If you'll excuse me a minute."

It was rude, but I couldn't wait for their reply. Thankfully, Adele Layton and her cousin, Aria, were friends of mine and Lou's from high school.

I darted for the back room, my hand pressed to my mouth. I should've just taken the pumpkin spice candles off the shelves and boxed them up far away so this didn't happen. But it was fall, and there was no scent more iconic for the season than pumpkin spice, and for the crowds of visitors coming to New England for the cool, colorful autumn, my pumpkin spice candle was by far my bestseller.

Anything for the business, I reminded myself as I shoved open the bathroom door and barely made it over the toilet before I heaved all of my stomach's contents into the bowl.

There wasn't much. I learned my lesson really quickly once I realized what was triggering the nausea and, instead, survived on saltines for most of the day until I closed up.

Why did it have to be the pumpkin spice? Why couldn't it be any other candle? Why couldn't it be *his* candle?

Taking a deep breath, I wiped my mouth with a paper towel from the roll I'd tucked next to the toilet for these exact moments, and then, when my stomach started to turn again, I reached for my last resort. The candle on the back of the toilet.

Chandler.

When I'd named the candle, I'd been angry. Not thinking clearly. I wasn't trying to commemorate him. I wanted to burn him from my memory. The man who'd dicked and ditched me. So, I distilled his scent, slapped his name on the jar, and lit a match. Unfortunately, by the time I realized it did nothing to help me forget, the sandalwood and cloves were the only things that settled my stomach—and his baby.

In and out. Breathe in and out. After a few deep inhales, my stomach settled, and I was about to put the candle back and straighten, my hand finding its way onto my stomach, always debating if I was starting to show yet or if it was just my imagination. *Or too many blueberry scones.*

I stitched a smile on my face and returned to the front of the shop. "Sorry about that, Adele."

"Don't worry about it—"

"We had you covered." Gigi appeared at my side with a grin, and behind her, Lou and Harper were admiring my fall display with Adele and Aria.

They knew. Mom knew. I'd told them first, needing an army when I sat down and told Jamie and Kit. Of course, they were furious. Not at me. I was a grown woman. Twenty-seven. I could bang and baby-make with whoever I wanted. But with Chandler...my growly, protective older brothers had watched my father leave our mother to be a single mom to not only her two boys but also her twin daughters. Jamie and Kit didn't like men who walked away, especially when the only thing those men seemed concerned about was money.

The scenarios were very different in my mind. My and Lou's father was a gold digger. Meanwhile, the only money Chandler was concerned about was his own. And to be fair, when Chandler walked away, he didn't know I was pregnant. Neither did I. I guess between sleeping at the inn and trying to resist him, I'd missed a few days of birth control.

But most importantly, I hadn't asked for more. Hadn't expected more. Hadn't even suggested more. Unfortunately, I'd wanted more. And those wants had bankrupted my expectations.

"Here you go, dear." Gigi patted my back and took the bag of candles Adele bought over to her.

I rested my elbow on the desk, my stomach making me wary of taking another step away from the bathroom.

"How are your parents doing? They must be so proud of you. Big-city lawyer..." Gigi gushed over my old friends, asking about their family and plans for the holidays back in Vermont, and in turn, Adele asked Harper how things were going with her beekeeping, and Aria asked about Harper's brothers. It was all a good distraction from how *unwell* I looked.

Lou came over to the desk, not-so-quiet concern in her gaze. "How are you feeling?"

I stiffened, changing hormones making me cling to anger that shouldn't be directed at her. Not really.

I'd told her first, the pregnancy test still sitting on my bathroom counter. I hadn't taken time to process—time to think. The first thing I did was call my sister and tell her she had to come to the cabin right away.

"I'm pregnant, Lou. With Chandler's baby."

Everything we'd been through, we'd been through together, and this would be no different.

Except I hadn't been the only one with a truth to share that night. And what she told me changed everything.

"I'm going to have to tell him, right?" For once, I wasn't sure what happened next.

"No, Frankie. You can't."

"Why not?"

She'd hesitated. Flushed. Lowered her eyes. She was hiding something from me.

"Why can't I tell him, Lou?"

"Because I paid him."

"What?" I remembered clearly how I thought I'd misheard her.

"Nox saw the two of you that night of the storm. He was worried. We both were."

"Worried? I'm an adult, Lou—"

"Who frequently gets in over her head!" She

couldn't help the way her eyes darted to my stomach. *"I'm sorry. I didn't know...I thought it was all for the inn —you told me it was all to get the inn, and I worried it was too much. So, I told Kit—not everything, but enough to explain why I needed to borrow money."*

At that point, it wasn't the baby that made me sick.

"At dinner that night, I saw the way you looked at Chandler, and I wanted to protect you. You were doing so much for me, and if he broke your heart in the process...so, I asked him what he planned on doing after he sold the inn, and when he said he was going back to Boston, I told him I was willing to match the offer from Mr. Fairfax."

All of a sudden, his behavior that night made sense. The way he'd turned guarded. The way he'd hesitated to stay the last night...it was because his business was concluded.

But why hesitate to stay for one last kinky fuck? Especially when there were no more strings attached.

I'd been angry for weeks. Hardly spoke to my sister or Kit. But in the end, when I finished Chandler's candle and let it burn, I realized my anger was misguided. It was her offer—hers to increase or rescind or change at will.

It was his choice to take the money and run.

And now, the prick of fury I felt was only at myself for wanting things to be different. *For believing Chandler that night when he made it seem like he wanted more.*

Like he wanted me.

"I'm fine." I started to smile, my stomach turning at that moment just to prove me a liar. I grabbed the *Chandler* on my desk and took a deep breath.

"That fine?" she murmured, her eyes probing.

I pressed my lips together. My twin had changed. Since she'd become the owner of the Lamplight Inn, there was a confidence that glowed from inside her that hadn't been as strong or as obvious before. There was more responsibility. More decisions to be made. *Higher stakes.* And I watched my sister's fortitude slowly but surely evolve and unfurl out of her former reserved cocoon.

It was a beautiful thing, but only until it was aimed at me.

"They say it shouldn't last much longer." Though I'd read plenty of accounts online of women who had morning sickness for the entire duration of their pregnancy.

"And how long is the secret going to last?"

My eyes darted to hers and then returned to the invoices I'd pretended to be examining. She didn't say anything, just stood there, elbows propped on the counter, chin resting on her hands, and her gaze steady behind her glasses.

After a few seconds, I couldn't take the silence any longer. "I don't know, Lou," I admitted painfully. "I don't know."

This wasn't part of my plan. Not him. Not my feelings. Not the baby. None of it. And maybe all my pranks and schemes over the years were wild and reckless and immature and careless...but they were all plans. Underneath all the chaos, there was a path to follow.

And suddenly, I didn't have one. I was adrift. Buoyed by the support of the strong women in my family, but still afloat on my own and wondering how I wanted to anchor my story.

Lou picked up the candle on my desk. *My safety net.* "Are you going to tell him?"

Him.

She never brought up his name like I'd made her promise, but that didn't stop her from asking. And she was the only one who asked.

From the night I told her to now, only Lou reminded me that I couldn't run from this. That I couldn't keep hiding in my shop, making candles, for nine months. I had to create a new plan.

Did I tell him? Yes, I should. It was his baby, after all. No, I couldn't. He would think I expected something from him, and the last thing I wanted was his obligation.

"I don't know, Lou. I really don't." Some days, I woke up having to re-convince myself that this was reality.

The first ultrasound photo helped with that. So did the nausea.

"You said after twelve weeks..."

An invisible checkpoint was what that was. An extension that I thought would buy me time. Instead, it passed by in what felt like a blink of an eye.

"I know." I sighed. "I just...ugh." I walked to the back, my fingers pressed to my lips, hoping she didn't follow.

Old Lou wouldn't, but this new Lou...

"I didn't expect more. I told him I didn't expect more." *Except for those few moments where I begged for it. But that was passion, not rational thinking.* "The last thing I want is a man in my life for the wrong reasons."

Lou adjusted her glasses and started to chew on her bottom lip.

"What is it?" I went to her.

"I'm sorry, Frankie."

I reached for her, pulling her tight to me. "Don't be sorry," I whispered, sighing when she hugged me back. If she hadn't apologized a hundred times since that first night... "You were trying to protect me—trying to do whatever you could to get the inn. I'm sorry I was upset. I never should've been upset with you."

We stayed hugging for what could've been seconds or several minutes, I wasn't sure.

"Lou? Where are—oh, there you are." Gigi appeared through the curtain, smiling when she saw the two of us embracing. "The bond between two sisters..." *Can never be broken.* She would say that all the time to us when we were younger.

"I'm ready when you are, Gigi." Lou pulled away first and then added, "We're on our way to the stair place to pick out banisters."

By the time reality sank in that Chandler had left and wasn't coming back, the inn was officially Lou's, and renovations had begun. Everyone in Friendship had celebrated the day she'd posted the brand new wrought-iron sign out front that read the *Lamplight Inn.* She'd even received donations—big ones—from people who were glad to see the inn restored to local ownership and in the care of someone who would diligently and dutifully preserve its history and heritage.

"Sounds like fun."

"They just finished all the floors. You have to stop by and see it."

I smiled and nodded, not trusting myself to speak. I hadn't been back inside the inn since the morning I left it. I kept busy or made excuses, but I couldn't bring myself to go back. Not yet. Not until everything looked so different that it would never make me recall what it had been before with bare rooms, an air mattress on top of the subfloor, and the man of my dreams.

"Yeah, maybe when they finish the stairs." And the painting and decorating and furnishing.

Gigi wrinkled her nose at me. "I've never known you to run from a challenge, Francesca."

"Gigi," I warned and lowered my hand to my stomach. "I'm not running."

She jutted her chin out. "You need to tell him."

Air deflated from my lungs. Gigi was the only one who argued with me. For some reason, she believed Chandler should know. She insisted on giving him the benefit of the doubt. Not some reason—the silly little label she'd given me a decade ago. Because she'd written *Chandler* on a stupid piece of paper, she believed that this tale had a happy ending, no matter how many times I insisted it was nothing more than a ghost story.

"It's not meant to be, Gigi."

"You'll see."

"See what?" Usually I didn't press her, but today I was feeling feisty.

She grinned and cupped my cheek. "That sometimes life doesn't go according to plan."

No crap, I wanted to retort. I was pregnant. From a two-night fling with a billionaire jerk who'd ghosted me in the morning. *Not part of my plan at all.*

"I know that, Gigi."

"Yes," she said with a sigh. "You will."

I bit into the side of my cheek, nodding at Lou's mouthed apology as she herded Gigi toward the front door. I didn't realize I was holding my breath until the door dinged close behind them and my chest caved in.

I was exhausted, and it wasn't even the baby. It was the not knowing.

Those who fail to plan, plan to fail.

A low, grumbly noise escaped my chest, recalling the little bit of wisdom Chandler had shared that first night and then beating myself up over it. I'd failed to plan. On him. On us. On this baby. And I was continuing to fail at planning with each day that passed.

Maybe the next step was talking to my brothers—to Jamie. Once I cleared his anger phase, I knew I could count on him to guide me, just like he always had.

But before I did that, I needed a nap.

I glanced at my phone. Tt was only a half-hour until close. I went to the back and sank onto the cushion chair I'd moved into the corner for my increasingly frequent power naps. I'd just close my eyes for a few minutes. I was sure I'd wake up if the door dinged.

IT WASN'T THE BELL AT THE ENTRANCE THAT WOKE me, it was voices.

"Thank you so much for all your help. This smells absolutely divine."

Help? My eyes fluttered open at the sound of people in the front of my shop. *Whose help? I was the only—*

"The cinnamon is my favorite."

My heart didn't trip or stumble. It fell flat on its face

hearing his voice again. Three months, three years... I'd never forget its smooth velvet or its confident tenor. *Nor the way it turned ragged with desire.*

I shoved up out of the lounge chair, speeding to the front of my shop like there were flames at my heels.

I had to be imagining. Hallucinating. He couldn't be—wouldn't be.

"Frankie."

If it wasn't my jaw that dropped, it was the sound of my stomach plummeting to the floor. *Chandler.*

He was here—right here in my shop. *Selling my candles.* I wanted to scream, sob, slap him, and have sex with him all at once. It was the most ridiculous pregnancy craving I'd had yet.

My eyes greedily clamored over him, still partially convinced I was afflicted with pregnancy apparitions as well as nausea. His long legs. Broad chest. Shirt sleeves rolled to his elbows. The first time I'd met him in slight disarray, it had been feigned. This time, it wasn't. The storm clouds in his gaze. The cobwebs of sleeplessness clinging under his eyes. Something had happened to him—something *that wasn't my business.*

I stiffened, the thought like a match to my fuse of fury. There were many things I wanted to do—wanted to say. Too many answers I wanted to know, but I was too smart now to risk something that might hurt in the end, no matter how good it felt in the moment.

"What are you doing here?" I asked, a dab of false sweetness in my tone.

Breathe, Frankie.

His gaze darkened. "What do you think I'm doing here?"

My lashes fluttered, and I asked innocently. "More business?"

I wasn't going to give him an inch. I couldn't. It was more than me—more than my heart—on the line. Twenty-eight years ago, my mother had been strong enough to do what she had to do to protect us, even if it meant becoming a single mom in the process, and now I'd do the same for my baby.

His growl made me shiver the way it imprisoned me still as he came closer. *God, I missed the heat of him... and the real taste of his scent.* My hands started to reach for my stomach, but I caught myself just in time and instead folded my arms over my chest.

"Frankie, we need to talk."

Everything about him was stronger because it was familiar. His warmth. His scent. The shoots of electricity up my spine and the gnawing pool of ache down in my stomach. That was the worst of it—the way I still wanted him.

"We do? I don't think so." I continued to play dumb because the alternative was to do something stupid, like listen.

The pain in his eyes wounded me. He didn't have a right to feel hurt. He was the one who left without a word. Disappeared. Never came back. He didn't get to decide almost three months after ghosting me that *now* he felt like talking.

"Frankie..." he rumbled and reached for me, and I jerked back like the touch of his fingers would've been the worst physical assault.

I banded my arms tighter and lifted my chin. "We had an arrangement, Chandler. A couple of nights sleeping at the inn to prove it was haunted. Those were the terms I agreed to, and now you've sold the inn to Lou, so there can't be anything more to discuss," I said, unable to stop myself from adding another barb. "Unless you're going to inform me of some *other* loophole in this sale that will take the building away from my sister *again*."

His jaw pulsed. He didn't like that. *Good*. I didn't much like him right now.

"Please, Frankie." His expression shuttered. "Let me explain."

No!

"There's nothing to explain—nothing to talk about," I said, frantically cutting him off before the barb of that temptation sank too deep and poisoned me with its ache. "It was a few nights and over. Nothing more than a ghost hunt."

He needed to go. He needed to not explain. If he had to explain, then so did I. And I had no idea how I was going to do that. No idea what to say. No idea how to approach this conversation. Jamie always taught us to *begin with the end in mind*. But I didn't know what end I wanted. I didn't know where I wanted this to go because, after three months of nothing, I never expected this.

"That's not true—"

"You're right. It's not," I rambled blithely, anything to stop him from talking. "It was never a ghost hunt because there were no ghosts. You were right. I made the whole thing up to try and get you to sell Lou the inn."

"I know, Frankie." He let out a sound that could've been a chuckle in a different conversation.

"Oh, good. Well, then there's nothing else to

discuss. Business concluded." My heart rattled like a marble in a tin can.

His jaw fired again. "This isn't business, Frankie. *We* were never business."

I whipped around, causing him to almost run into me. "So that's why you disappeared in the middle of the night? Hours after my sister matched Mr. Fairfax's offer?" My brow raised so high it was a miracle I didn't pull a muscle.

He swore under his breath, eyes flashing like he hadn't expected me to know about that. *Of course not. If it hadn't been for the baby, Lou probably never would've told me.*

"If you'd let me explain—"

"I don't want you to explain, Chandler. Explaining is the kind of thing you do the morning after. Or a day later. Or even over a phone call or text after disappearing on someone—" I stopped myself and shuddered. "Explaining isn't something you get to do after three months of silence."

He wrapped his arms over his chest, looking as though he wanted nothing more than to reach out and pull me to him. To hold me tight and force me to listen to...whatever kind of confession he had.

"I'm sorry, Frankie." His broken apology rasped from his lips like embers from a fire, sparking and smoldering and begging for my forgiveness to blow them back to life.

And, goddammit, the troublemaker in me wanted to give it.

"I want you to leave right now," I declared, tacking on the barb at the end. "I know you're familiar with the concept."

He grimaced but didn't make a move to comply. And me...stupid, irrational parts of me were too busy savoring the sight of him to continue to press the demand.

I couldn't believe he was here—couldn't believe he'd come back. He had to know I'd be angry. That this would be the reception he'd get. And still he came. I lifted my chin and swallowed down the bout of weakness that almost asked for an explanation.

"Fine, I'll go," Chandler relented. At least those days spent together had taught him one thing. I was formidable. "But I'm not leaving town. Not until we talk."

"Then I hope you're prepared to stay for a very long time, Mr. Collins," I warned, thinking that being stranded in this small town, away from his city and his big business, was the worst punishment I could inflict.

He stepped close to me so fast there was no chance for me to avoid him. Even if I did, I risked getting too close to the pumpkin spice scent in the back, and as angry as I was, vomiting all over him wasn't part of the punishment I wanted to extend or part of the conversation I wanted to have.

I sucked in a breath as his heat enveloped me. His scent invaded every receptor in my brain, bringing me back to that night in his arms. That night I thought everything had changed for me. For us.

"I'm prepared to stay forever, Frankie, if you'll let me." His words were the perfect brand of promise that made my resolve start to melt.

Bullshit, my racing heart chided. *Bullshit sweet words. Bullshit promises. Bullshit torture for a broken heart.*

"Please go." My voice cracked.

"I'll be back tomorrow."

I didn't have it in me to protest. Not when it took every ounce of my strength to stop myself from calling out and begging him to stay.

If it was only me, I'd risk my heart for answers. For that explanation. But like my mother, I was going to protect my baby from a man who wasn't worthy, even if that man was the father.

CHAPTER 22
CHANDLER

I bent over the sink and splashed water on my face, hoping it would wash some of the raggedness from my expression.

I'd fucked everything up. I knew that. I knew I was returning to scorched earth—whatever had started to grow between us was charred by how I'd left. But I was here to make it right. *To take the risk.*

I'd expected Frankie's anger. Her barbed words and firm resistance. And I'd gotten them that first day. But after...I hadn't expected her avoidance. Her silence. Her utter lack of curiosity. I'd banked on Frankie's eagerness for answers. The bold lengths she went to outsmart and be on top of every situation was the first thing I'd learned about her that morning at the Maine Squeeze. I'd counted on her to at least want to know why I'd up and left, even if she still wanted to punish me for it.

But she didn't. She ran from the conversation like it was a loaded gun, and I couldn't fucking understand why.

I grabbed my phone and tapped on Tom's name.

"Hello?" he answered after two rings.

"How is she?"

"Fine. Good. Doctor checked her again last night and said she's in the clear."

I let out an unsteady breath. Lately, all my breaths seemed unsteady. Like they were just waiting for the next thing to catch them off guard.

"Good." At least one thing was going in the right direction.

"How are things going with Frankie?"

I wiped a towel over my face and grunted. "They aren't."

"Still won't talk to you?"

I frowned. "No." If it were easy, it wouldn't be Frankie.

He made a noise.

"Are you laughing?"

"No." He paused. "Maybe a little—oh, hold on." There was a rustle, and then I heard his muffled voice say to someone else, "I'm laughing because Chandler has found someone who's just as stubborn as he is."

My shoulders sagged.

The line rustled again. "Your mom wanted to know why I was laughing."

"Great."

"She wants to see you, Chandler," he said, his voice lower so she wouldn't hear.

I hadn't seen Mom since we'd brought her back to Edgewood a week and a half ago—a whole four weeks after my conversation with Tom at the hospital. After what happened, I couldn't help but think it was my fault she'd ended up in the hospital in the first place. I was the one who'd made her so upset the day before. I was the one who caused the first domino to fall. And now that she was finally healed and home...I couldn't live with myself if I was the one to make things worse again.

"Maybe," I croaked. "Maybe after I talk to Frankie... if I ever talk to her."

For a week, I'd showed up at the Candle Cabin with a blueberry scone and a coffee from the Maine Squeeze the way I knew she liked it. Every day, I walked in the front door, and she walked to the back. So, I left the breakfast on her desk with scribbled notes on the napkin.

I'm not leaving, Frankie.

Please talk to me.

I'm not going anywhere.

At first, I thought it was a good sign that it was gone the following day until I stuck around on Wednesday to see if she'd break down and talk to me and instead watched her take the coffee cup to the back, only to hear liquid poured down the drain a minute later.

"What would Frankie do?" Tom asked.

I gritted my teeth. If our roles were reversed, who the hell knew what she would do. Kidnap me and tie me to a chair and force me to listen to her. Get her brother or her cousin or some other conspirator to drive her around behind me with a megaphone so there was no ignoring her. Fly a plane and write her confession in smoke signals in the sky.

"She wouldn't play fair."

"So then don't play fair back."

Maybe that was the answer. She would do whatever it took, and maybe it was time I did, too.

"And if she calls the police on me?" I wondered, only partially teasing.

Tom chuckled again. "I guess it's a good thing you have me to bail you out."

I STOOD AT THE GATE IN FRONT OF THE INN—THE rust removed, and the iron repainted since the last time I'd walked through it three months ago. If I was going to get through to Frankie, I wasn't going to do it alone, and the one person—the first person I knew I needed on my side—was Lou.

I looked up at the façade of the building, already so much of it having changed—improved from before. Even the heavy bronze sign, the Lamplight Inn, embossed into the metal, heralded the historic weight of the landmark to the community.

I'd long resigned myself to the fact that I'd decided to sell Lou the inn from the moment Frankie had impersonated her on our date...and we'd kissed. I was used to all kinds of bribes and bets and blackmail to make business deals happen, but I'd never had someone fight for something quite the way she had. And it sold me— unknowingly at the time—on them. *On her*.

I stepped onto the property, noting the clean-cut grass cleared of sunset-soaked leaves that had just started to fall from the trees. The steps didn't creak when I approached the front door, and I would've knocked if the door hadn't been open. The tool bags on the front porch and the low rumble of conversations from inside suggested there was a crew busy inside working.

The new hardwood floors gleamed even under a coat of dust from the continuing renovations. Gone were the tattered wallpaper and the torn-up walls, and in their place was crisp new drywall ready for paint. Sunlight streamed through clean glass, the windows repaired or replaced, and the frames refurbished.

I ran my finger along the doorframe into the living room, my gaze skimming the fireplace on the far wall. They'd done a phenomenal job on the restoration, and it wasn't even finished yet. Honestly, I didn't expect anything less. Not from Lou. Not from the Kinkades.

I took a deep breath, and beneath the scent of sawdust and stain, I swore there was a trace of cinnamon. A tiny thread that wrapped around all my memories like a bow. No matter what changed here—the floors, the walls, the layout, the decoration—I'd always see that mattress in the center of the floor, the fire in the fireplace dancing shadows across Frankie's bare skin, the soft canvas a masterpiece of wax and bite marks.

"Can I help you?"

I turned and boxed up those thoughts as a burly man descended the steps. Salt sprinkled his short beard, and the pencil tucked behind his ear introduced him as a carpenter without him saying a word.

"I'm looking for Lou."

"Think she's in the kitchen with Hank. Let me grab her for you. What did you say your name was?"

I let out a breath. "Chandler."

Hopefully she came out and didn't call the police.

Not even thirty seconds later and her familiar braids and glasses appeared at the end of the hall, stopping for a second as though she didn't believe it could be me. *Like there were so many men named Chandler*.

Her shoulders rolled back, and then she came toward me, her steps carrying a kind of commanding weight that hadn't been there before.

"Mr. Collins. I didn't expect to see you again. What can I do for you?" The politeness to her tone was thin.

"This place looks incredible, Lou," I said sincerely. It couldn't hurt to start this conversation with a well-deserved compliment. "Really, you've done an amazing job already. You should be proud."

Red splotched into her cheeks, and she adjusted her glasses. "Thank you," she stammered, and then collected herself. "But I don't think you came all the way back to the middle of nowhere to check on a property you never wanted."

Touché.

"No." I gave her a tight smile, shifting my weight. "I came back for your sister."

She made a sound that fell somewhere between a laugh and a choke—neither of which were particularly hopeful.

"I need to talk to her, Lou," I went on. "I need to explain...what happened. I know she's angry, and I understand. I just need her to listen, but she won't. Even before when she hated me, she didn't avoid me."

"Why would I help you?"

My jaw locked. "Because it wasn't supposed to happen like this."

"Like what? Where I offered you more money, and you left without a word?" The color in her cheeks deepened. "I thought my offer would fix things before they went too far, but I was too late. I didn't...I didn't know about the two of you. If I did, if I knew you were just going to take the money and run—"

"I didn't take the money, Lou."

She jerked, her jaw going slack before it snapped closed, and she collected herself. "What do you mean? Of course, you did. I know you did. I paid you. I borrowed money from my brother to pay you."

"Yes," I croaked. "And who do you think donated that exact difference back to you?"

There were a few things I'd managed to do in the hospital once things with Mom settled down, and the very first was to figure out how to give Lou back the difference that she'd paid for the inn. I'd never planned on taking more than her original offer, but I hadn't had a chance.

The color drained from her face, her eyes going wide. "No." Her head started to shake. "That's from Ms. Laura Todd."

"Laura Todd is my mother," I rasped quietly. "She stayed at the inn a long time ago and had a lot of good memories there. I donated the money in her name—for her." I cleared my throat. "And because I doubted you'd take it from me."

Her eyes batted, and she pressed her hand to her mouth. "I don't...I don't understand."

"I wasn't going to leave, Lou. That's what I'm trying to tell you." I exhaled raggedly. "I lied when I told you I was going back to Boston. Not lied—" I broke off with a curse. "I told you what I wanted to believe, but it wasn't the truth."

"Then why did you take the money in the first place?" Her brow creased.

My chest tightened. "Because I didn't want your

sister to ever doubt why I was staying," I rasped. "And afterward, I knew you wouldn't accept a donation from me—or if you would, Frankie wouldn't. So, I gave it back to you this way."

"I want to believe you." Her throat bobbed. "But you left...you left her."

"I had to. You have to believe me. I need to explain what happened to Frankie, but she won't listen to me," I said, watching her chew on her bottom lip, still debating whether or not to believe me. "It was beyond my control, Lou. I swear. I'm not like your father."

Her head snapped up. "She told you about our father?"

I nodded slowly, watching her expression relax. "My father left my mom and me, too. It's why I didn't want this inn."

Understanding filtered into her eyes, not only about me and my actions but also how Frankie and I had connected.

"You tried to talk to her?"

"Every day for the last week. I bring her breakfast. I order lunch or dinner for her, depending on how long she's working. But she won't—" I broke off with a huff and dragged my hand along my jaw. "She won't let me explain."

"What happened? What did she say?"

My fists balled, pain shooting through me to recall the pained look on Frankie's face.

"Everything," I croaked. *Everything she could to make it clear what we had was over.* "And then she told me to leave. That there was nothing to talk about. That it was a fling, and it's over, but that's not true. You know it's as far as hell from true."

Her eyes widened. "Frankie told you...everything?"

"Yes, of course." Frustration coursed through my words. Like it mattered that she faked the haunting and the ghosts. Like I'd really believed it was spirits that kept moving and stealing our stuff. So why did Lou seem so surprised? I gritted my teeth and added, "What would be the point in keeping it from me now? It's not like I didn't realize it immediately anyway. I might be a lot of things, but I'm not an idiot."

She still looked shocked. I didn't get it. The color was gone from her face. Her mouth opened and shut several times like she'd lost the ability to speak. And all because Frankie had told me about her prank? Was she afraid I'd try to take the inn back or something?

"Lou." I shoved my hand through my hair. "How do I get Frankie to listen to me?"

Her eyes fluttered like the gears in her mind were finally clicking back in sync.

"Well, I think the first thing she needs to hear isn't why you left, but why you're here to stay."

I inhaled sharply, a fresh burst of understanding flooding my brain. "Got it. Easy," I said. "What else?"

"If you came back for her..." She hesitated, but only for a split second. "If you came back for her, Chandler, she needs to know you're not staying out of obligation to the baby."

My heart stopped. *Baby.* Everything stopped. Not everything. Lou's mouth kept moving, but I heard nothing except the crash of my world coming down around me.

I checked the floor like it had opened up beneath me. I looked at the walls, sure that a wrecking ball had come straight through the building. But no, everything was stable. Intact. Everything but me.

Baby.

"Chandler? Are you okay?"

"What baby?"

I COULDN'T RECALL THE LAST TIME IN MY LIFE when I'd run. Lifting. Rowing. The occasional bike. Sure. But running—full-on sprinting. At least two decades. Until now.

I didn't trust myself not to break every speeding law and jeopardize any pedestrian who got in my way. Not to mention my fucking car—I couldn't even remember where I parked it. my brain was on fire. Ablaze with a single, scorching fact.

Frankie was pregnant.

Later, I'd remember the stares I got sprinting down Maine Street in dress pants and shoes. A full-on fool to get to the Candle Cabin and talk to her. Because we were definitely fucking talking now.

I pushed through the door, grateful for small mercies that no one was in the store at that particular moment.

"Frankie!" I boomed, my chest heaving.

There was a commotion in the back room. "Go away, Chandler!" she shouted, but something in her voice was wrong.

"We need to talk," I said between deep breaths.

"There's nothing to talk about."

Growling, I spun and flipped the sign on the door so it showed *Closed* and then slid the dead bolt closed with a loud *thwack*. I whipped the curtain back with one arm, stopping short when I didn't immediately see her.

"Frankie?"

"Go away."

My head turned to the right, her voice slipping out from under the bathroom door.

I took another scan of the back room. Her jars were out. Scale set on the counter. Wax was already cooling in a batch of jars on the center island. *She was in the middle of making a batch.* From the smell of it, it was the fall pumpkin candles she had on the main display.

"I'm not leaving until you come out." I rested back against the counter and stared at the door like I could see through it.

Pregnant.

She was pregnant.

I should be shocked. I *was* shocked. But at the same time, I wasn't feeling any of the things I thought I'd feel if this moment ever came. Instead, the only thing on my mind was her. Making sure she was okay. Getting through to her. *Letting her know I wasn't going anywhere.*

"I told you. I don't want to hear your explanation right now..." She trailed off, and I swore I heard a noise that sounded almost like she was in pain.

"And I've waited a week for you to change your mind."

"Oh, my goodness. The big bad Mr. Collins doesn't get his way in a whole week and loses his mind?" she mocked from inside the bathroom.

"I lost my mind the moment I left you," I said without hesitation. Without thinking.

The door swung open, her expression pained. "Stop," she insisted, and suddenly, a switch flipped on her face. Her eyes went wide. The color evaporated from her cheeks. And she turned and would've shut the door in my face except my foot was there waiting.

"No—" She broke off with a groan and then crashed to her knees in front of the toilet.

"Shit," I muttered and dropped with her, grabbing her hair just before she vomited...onto my shoes.

She groaned. "I'm sor—" This time, she made it into the bowl, not that there was much in her stomach to heave up.

Gritting my teeth, I continued to gather strands of her hair in my fingers, holding them safe until her stomach settled.

"I'm sorry." Her voice was raw. She'd clearly been at this for a little bit before I'd arrived.

Dammit.

I should've been here sooner. Earlier. All day. *Every damn day.*

"I don't give a fuck about my shoes, baby," I rasped, the endearment slipping out without thinking. "Stop apologizing."

"I'm pregnant," she groaned, unceremoniously clutching the porcelain bowl.

"I know."

She whimpered, and I thought it was from what I said, but then she jerked forward and puked again.

"What can I do?"

"Shut the door," she said between gasps.

Locking my jaw, I wedged myself inside the tiny-ass bathroom with her and closed the door. For long seconds, I didn't say anything—do anything, except hold her hair and let my fingers trace slow circles on her back, watching as eventually the tension in her body finally relaxed with a deep exhale.

"It's the stupid pumpkin spice. Makes me sick." She moaned again, and I tensed, preparing for another bout of sickness, but it never came.

"Then why are you using it?" I said, trying to hold back my growl.

"It's my most popular..." She pulled the lid over the toilet and flushed it, her shoulders sagging with the effort.

Anything for her business. My jaw tightened. Well, not this. Not while I was here.

"Hold your breath," I ordered.

"What—" She stopped and filled her cheeks with air when she saw me reach for the door handle.

I slipped back into her workroom and firmly shut the door. From there, it only took me a couple of minutes to give my shoes a quick wipe, clean up the jars, and seal closed the wax, but even then, the scent still clung to the air.

I went back to the bathroom door and asked through it, "Is there a scent that makes it better?" *Because, knowing Frankie, she would've found it.*

"Yeah," she answered and paused for so long I really thought she was going to make me ask what it was. "The candle on my desk."

With a few steps, I found the one she was talking about. *The candle with no label.* I grabbed a lighter from her drawer and lit the wick. I couldn't help but bring my nose to it as I carried it to the back.

It smelled like...sandalwood and cloves. I wasn't that good with scents, but I knew what was written on the bottle of cologne I used every morning.

My chest tightened. *Did this candle...did she really make one?*

"Frankie." I knocked gently on the door.

"Yeah." Her voice was weak.

"I cleaned up all the pumpkin spice from the back, and I've got your anti-nausea candle right outside the door."

There was soft shuffling, and then the door opened, her head hesitantly poking through. She snatched the candle from me like it was an oxygen mask in a burning building and took a deep inhale, holding it close to her face as she stepped out of the room.

"Thank you."

She looked pained and exhausted—defeated—and the sight killed me.

"Does salt air help?"

Her head tipped. "I...it doesn't hurt."

"Good." I nodded and held back the curtain. "Let's go for a walk."

She stilled. "And if I don't want to?"

"You puked on my shoes. You owe me."

She winced and then grumbled, "Okay."

Even like this—drained and nauseous—she still wouldn't let someone try to take care of her without some kind of threat or bet in place. I admired her independence as much as I hated it. But what I hated more was that I'd contributed to it. That I'd made her feel like she couldn't trust me.

But no more. I didn't care what it took or how long...
Frankie Kinkade was going to learn I was here to stay.

For her.

And for our baby.

CHAPTER 23

CHANDLER

"I'm sorry about your shoes."

My toes sank into the cold sand. I'd dropped my shoes in the trash can at the edge of the beach. The only thing worse than shoes with puke all over them was shoes with sand-crusted puke all over them.

"Just shoes, Frankie. I can get another pair." I took a deep breath and glanced at her. She wobbled a little on the uneven terrain, but I shoved my hands into my pockets instead of reaching for her. She was fine. A little shaken, but fine. And if I reached for her, she'd only pull farther away.

We reached the flat stretch of sand that was just short of where the waves crashed and broke. Here, the beach was bereft of people. Lou had pointed out this part to me the morning she'd taken me on a tour. We'd been on the larger, more public rim of coastline, and when she'd pointed out the lighthouse where Kit lived, she'd also mentioned a smaller, more private section of the beach that only the locals knew about.

"I'm pregnant," she repeated, the words still sounding like they were foreign on her tongue.

"I gathered."

"Who told you?" She bundled her arms in front of her as another breeze swept through.

I shook off my jacket and handed it to her. "It was an accident."

The horror on Lou's face when she realized I didn't know about the baby and that she'd just revealed her sister's secret was branded into my mind. It wasn't her fault. It was mine. If I hadn't left—hadn't disappeared the way I had—it wouldn't have been a secret at all.

"Lou." She stared at me, hesitating a beat before another whip of wind made her grab my coat.

"She thought I already knew." *I should've already known,* the thought punched to the front of my mind, but I reined it back, keeping silent as she put on my jacket, and we continued our slow stroll toward the tower of the lighthouse.

"So you're..." I lifted my fingers to count, not trusting my mind with even the simplest of mental math.

"Almost thirteen weeks. I...I had my twelve-week check-up last week."

Checkup. That meant at a doctor. A doctor with tests and scans and imaging. A checkup with pictures and ultrasounds and a beating heart. My throat felt like it closed up, but somehow, I still kept breathing.

"Frankie..."

"Just say it." She huffed, suddenly annoyed. "You have to be angry I didn't tell you. Didn't reach out. You can say it. You can be angry. It's fine—I'm fine." The flippancy in her tone was anything but fine.

"I was going to ask if you had a picture."

She stopped walking, her head lowering for a second before she fished underneath my jacket and pulled out her phone. The waves crashed and roared, louder and louder in my ears, until I realized it wasn't the sound of breaking waves at all but the thundering churn of my heart.

She handed me her phone and everything stopped. Stilled.

I turned away from her, staring at the black and white speck on the ultrasound image. *My baby*.

I was going to be a father.

My pulse trampled through my veins, the word never having any kind of positional connotation in my life until this moment. Until it became me.

"Chandler..."

I looked up and blinked. I didn't even realize I'd sunk down to sit on the sand, my arms propped on my knees, holding the phone as I stared.

Shit.

"Can I...have this? The picture," I stammered like an idiot. "Not your phone."

She nodded, and I swore there was the tiniest of smiles on her face.

My finger shook as I entered my information into a contact card in her phone, changed some of the settings, and then sent the image to myself. "Thank you."

She took her phone back and sat down beside me, the two of us watching the spin of the tide. *Pregnant*. It changed things, but not everything. Not why I'd come back. Now how I felt.

There were a million things I could say—even more that I wanted to say—but this moment was hers. She'd given me the photo. She'd sat right beside me. She wasn't pushing me away for the first time in a week even though I probably still deserved it, so that was why I stayed silent. Because this conversation was going to be on her terms.

I lost count of how many times the waves rose and broke on the shore before she spoke over them.

"When I realized about the baby, I was in shock. I guess I must've forgotten to take my birth control one of those mornings, or who knows, maybe it just didn't work," she began and sighed. "I took the test, and the first thing I did was call Lou. She...well, I think she was more shocked than I was."

A ghost of a smile tugged at my lips and then disappeared at her next words.

"My first thought was that I had to tell you. I was still upset, but I had to tell you. And then Lou told me she'd offered you more money for the inn...and you'd accepted."

My heart beat like the walls of my chest were closing in—violent and feral and desperate to exonerate itself to escape. But I didn't want this to turn into a conversation about me and why I left. My reason didn't matter if she didn't believe I wasn't going to do it again.

"I did," was all I said when I felt her looking at me, waiting for my confirmation or denial.

She looked away quickly, but not before I saw how her face blanched, and she clutched her legs tighter to her.

"After that, I was pissed. I was angry, and it was still early. Anything could've—"

"Don't," I interrupted. The thought was already

clear in my mind, I didn't need to hear her say it. If she'd miscarried and been alone...if I never knew...

She exhaled slowly and admitted, "I don't know that I was ever going to tell you, Chandler. Honestly, I don't. Especially if you hadn't..."

"Come back?"

Frankie made only a soft sound as a reply and then drifted into silence again.

"This wasn't what either of us planned...what either of us wanted," she said and crossed her legs. "And I want to be clear that I don't need anything from you. I'm not asking for anything. You don't have to have any part in this—"

"Don't do that, Frankie."

"Do what?"

"The thing where you push people away to prove you're independent."

She blustered and stood. "I'm not pushing—"

I rose with a growl and grabbed her arm, hauling her back to me. Her gasp was soft and fractured when she landed against my chest, her palm gripping my shirt but lacking any kind of pressure to push me away.

"I get that you've been the strong one, Frankie. I get that no one asked you to do it, but everyone admired you when you did. When you became the strong sister for Lou when she was timid. For Kit when he was broken. For Jamie and the rest of your family so they didn't need to worry. But let me tell you something, baby, I'm not here to tell you you can't be strong, I'm here—will be here—to show you that you don't have to be alone."

Her lips parted, her pulse fluttering like a wild bird trapped in her throat.

I shouldn't have reached for her—shouldn't have pulled her close. It was a selfish thing after months of fantasizing about her. And now that I held her—felt her warmth and softness fitted right to me—I didn't want to let her go.

"Chandler..."

My hand slid up her neck to cup her cheek, my thumb stroking her cheek like I could wipe the blush from her skin. The breeze tangled around us, and cinnamon swept into my nostrils, my head dipping lower to feed on her scent.

Her gaze drifted to my mouth, her tongue sliding out and wetting her lips. An invitation. A dare. The flame inside me surged and turned every inch of me hard in a second. I wanted her so fucking bad. For months, I'd wanted her like this. And it was more than desire. More than passion. It was the whole of her warmth. The heat of her boldness. The strength of her compassion. She'd set me on fire, and now all I wanted was to burn and burn and burn.

"Frankie," I groaned, my fingers sliding to her chin and lifting her mouth to mine.

Her breath caught, and she stepped back. I didn't want to, but I released her.

"You left," she said, doing her best to hide the way she panted. "Without a word."

My jaw locked. Again, I felt the truth knocking at my lips. I could tell her everything—lay the reasoning bare at her feet right now. But I wouldn't enter through that door until she trusted that I wouldn't walk right back out of it again when she needed me most.

"And now, I'm here to stay."

She let out a laugh of disbelief. It hurt, but it was deserved.

"All week you've wanted this, and now you're hesitating to tell me why?"

Now I saw it. The curious light flickering in her honey eyes. The need to know. To figure it out.

"Not yet."

"Why not?"

I stepped close to her again, feeling a small surge of victory when she didn't back away. "Because I want to show you that you can count on me first. Because when I tell you what happened, I don't want there to be any doubt in your mind that I'd never leave you like that again."

Her throat bobbed. She was so used to banter, so used to a fight...I loved the look on her face when she saw someone fighting for her.

"And how do you plan on doing that?"

"Well, for starters, I'm going to let you stalk me."

Her jaw dropped. "What? How? Wait—what if I don't want to stalk you?"

Flustered Frankie was adorable. "You don't have to, but you can."

"I don't understand." Her brows bunched together.

"You sent me that photo, and I enabled the 'share my location' on my contact. So now, you can always look and see where I am," I told her, watching her eyes widen. "Or not look. It's up to you."

"I probably won't look," she said defiantly.

"You probably won't have to," I agreed. "Because I plan on spending all my time with you."

"So really, you're the one who's going to stalk me," she countered but didn't sound upset by the idea.

My head tipped, and I flashed her a grin. "I prefer to think of it as haunting."

CHAPTER 24
FRANKIE

"Where is he?"

My head snapped up at my brother's voice, my heart rocketing into my throat. "Jamie—"

"Absolutely not, Frankie. He's not welcome here. Not after what he did. How he left—how he left you..." His eyes picked up where his words left off—at my stomach.

I rolled my shoulders back. "I can handle this—"

"I'm back here," Chandler's voice boomed.

Jamie whipped toward the back, too quick for me to grab him. *Crap.* I really needed to start telling people things, but this...I wasn't ready to share that Chandler was back because I was afraid. Even after he'd continued to show up after a week of the cold shoulder, bringing me coffee that I couldn't drink and blueberry scones that I devoured only to throw up later, he still showed up.

And after he learned about the baby, well, he wasn't a stalker like I'd teased. He was my shadow. From dawn to dusk, he was by my side at the shop. At the store. Grabbing dinner. We didn't talk about us or that kiss, only candles and the baby.

The very first thing he'd done was declare that he'd make the pumpkin spice batches in the back while I manned the store out front. Of course, I wanted to argue. No one else made my candles. No one else had ever made my candles. Okay, maybe my family and friends had made one or two here and there for fun, but not like this. Not for my business.

But the alternative was that this season, I'd be selling the scent of pumpkin spice puke. So, I caved. *For the business*, I reminded myself every time I heard him utter a curse from the back, adding another wax burn to his hands. Or every time he carried out a fresh batch of capped candles in nothing more than a T-shirt stretched full of muscles.

And that was another problem.

The way I wanted him was now on steroids.

Every day I drooled over his tipped smile, his broad shoulders, and the tight curves of his ass. I considered offering him another *pleasure* arrangement at least a dozen times a day, always remembering just in time what trouble that kind of decision-making ended up in the last time.

It wouldn't be just pleasure. Not this time. Not the way he fed my pregnancy cravings nor the way he put pregnancy audiobooks on full blast so both of us could listen. Not the way he rubbed my lower back at the end of a busy day when I started to hunch over my desk. And not the way I saw the ultrasound photo was now the background on his phone.

It was a mess. *I* was a mess. I was afraid of all the

things he made me feel—all the things he promised to give me—and that was why I hadn't told the rest of my family that he was back. And after her slip about my pregnancy, Lou buried herself in the renovations at the inn and excused herself from the entire narrative.

But the secret could only last so long. I guess I was hoping it could last just a little longer. Like a kid who'd stolen a bag of cookies, I wanted to hide and devour all these moments myself without sharing them with anyone, afraid the second I did, he'd be taken away.

"Collins, I want you gone. What you did—"

"Stop, Jamie—"

"Frankie, stay back," Chandler warned, and I halted just at the curtain. The pumpkin spice fragrance stretched the very tips of its fingertips under my nose, and my stomach started to churn. *No.* I squeezed my eyes shut and tried to will it away.

"No, she can be here. She should hear this." My brother stalked toward Chandler, whose eyes were only on me. "She doesn't need you in her life, let alone controlling—"

"I'm not leaving."

Jamie grabbed him by the collar. "The hell you aren't."

"Jamie!" I didn't think. I pushed into the room to stop my brother from being crazy and gasped a huge lungful of pumpkin spice.

Oh no.

It was like a wave. An instant tsunami of nausea that crashed over me.

I groaned and grabbed the counter as I started to double over, catching the panic on my brother's face as he let go of Chandler.

"Dammit." Chandler's curse reached me a second before his strong arms did. The next thing I knew, Jamie was shouting, and my feet were lifted off the ground, Chandler carrying me with surprising speed to the front of the shop.

I heard the bell at the door.

I felt the fresh, clean breeze swipe over me.

"Breathe, baby. Just breathe." Chandler's voice soothed me even as my brother threatened him.

"I don't know what the hell you think you're doing, Collins, but I swear to God, if you don't put her down—"

"What I'm doing is getting her away from the smell that makes her sick—that makes her vomit the very soul from her body," Chandler growled over his shoulder and then lowered me onto the wood bench in front of my store. Ignoring my brother for a second, he asked me, "You okay? Do you need my shoes?"

That made me laugh.

"No," I murmured. "Just need a minute."

His face tensed, and he nodded. If I would've known he was going to then stand and face my brother on his own, I would've told him I needed something else.

"I don't understand," Jamie said in a low grumble, his fist balling at his side. "What's going on?"

"The pumpkin spice makes her sick. That's why I'm in the back making the candles because she can't stand the smell."

Jamie growled. "My sister can speak for herself."

"Yes, she can," Chandler growled back. "She can also stand up for herself and protect herself and make decisions for herself, and yet, you're still here acting like she can't."

Oh boy.

My brother winced at that, the barb instantly deflating some of the vengeance from his expression. Only then did it seem like Jamie realized what Chandler was wearing—a wax-splattered apron over his jeans and T-shirt—and what it meant. *A billionaire burning his hands to make candles for my business. For me.*

His protective bluster cracked and crumbled as his gaze shifted to me. "Frankie..."

"I'm fine, Jamie," I said. *Promised.*

He would always protect Lou and I like this. It was who he was. More father than brother. But what Chandler said hit him hard.

I could stand up for myself. Defend myself. Just like I could take care of myself and manage this pregnancy on my own. But that didn't stop either of them from showing up, because they cared. Because they love—*no.*

I pulled in a deep breath and sat up tall. *I couldn't go there.* That was way off the deep end.

Jamie looked back at Chandler and muttered grimly, "Hurt her, and I don't care how much money or where you disappear to..."

"Your sister has my location on her phone at all times. If I hurt her again, you have my permission to hunt me down, take all my money, and do your worst."

Jamie tried to hide how pleased he was with that answer with a grunt and a grumble, stepping around Chandler to bend forward and kiss the top of my head.

"I'm here if you need me," he said quietly.

"I know." I smiled at him.

He made some kind of noise directed at Chandler

before walking away, and I could only assume it belonged to that mysterious man language of grunts and groans and growls because Chandler just nodded at him like he understood what it meant.

Once Jamie was gone, Chandler knelt next to me and dragged a hand through his hair, the dark strands now more often troubled than tamed.

"Are you all right?"

"Yeah." I took another deep breath to be sure and then stood. "I'm sorry about my brother."

"Don't be," he said sincerely. "If I were him, I'd want to kill me, too."

My breath hitched, and suddenly, the need to know overwhelmed me. All week, it slinked through my mind like a beast in the shadows. I thought the longer I held out, the more it proved that I could coexist—I could co-parent—with him and not need anything more.

But today, now... I didn't need him. But I wanted him. The truth hit me like a wrecking ball, and I felt tears prick at the corners of my eyes. I wanted to know what happened because I wanted him to stay.

I wanted what he kept promising to give.

"Chandler." I reached out and laid my hand on his chest, my throat tightening around the words.

"What is it?" He pressed his hand over my own.

I released all the air from my lungs and let out the question I'd held inside for far too long. "I want to know," I murmured softly, watching his eyes widen and flicker with surprise. "Tell me why you left that morning. Please."

"Okay." He took my hand and brought it to his lips. "Let me clean up inside first."

CHAPTER 25
FRANKIE

It was almost an hour later before Chandler appeared back through the curtain, the lines on his face heavier than before.

While he cleaned up, I sat out front finishing up my inventory with the unnamed candle burning on my desk. *His candle.* The one that soothed my stomach... and other parts of me I didn't want to talk about.

"I'm done," he said, his stare flickering as if to ask, *are you sure? Are you ready?*

"Not here," I blurted out, my heart thumping. I didn't know why I felt like this—like my skin carried an electric current and my insides were made of butter-flies. "I don't want to talk here."

I wanted a fresh slate. Somewhere private, but a place that hadn't been tainted by all the memories my mind wanted to focus on. The way he cared for me. Held my hair back in the bathroom. Didn't care when I puked on his shoes. Made my candles when I couldn't. Stood up to my brother, not on his behalf, but on mine.

"Where?"

I lifted my chin. "Your hotel."

He stiffened but agreed, waiting as I collected my things and then locked the door behind us. The next twenty minutes passed in a blink. Walking to his car. Picking up dinner from my favorite Mexican place. Driving out of town to the small hotel he'd stayed at the last time. Next thing I knew, I stepped into the small suite that overlooked the ocean. It had to be the nicest room in the hotel. *Of course.*

"You should eat," he murmured, setting the takeout bag on the small table near the windows. "Just a little," he pleaded, catching my wary gaze. "I'm going to shower so I don't smell."

It was faint—the offending scent and the way it clung to his clothes and skin—but all it would take was one too-deep breath from a little too close.

"Thank you," I blurted out for what felt like the hundredth time today and then tried to lighten it with, "I wouldn't want to puke everywhere and have you lose your security deposit on the room."

Chandler reached out and trailed his finger along my cheek, a half-grin toying with the corner of his perfect mouth. "Puke wherever you want, baby. I'll buy the whole damn hotel if I have to," he declared, leaving me wide-eyed and gaping as he disappeared into the bathroom.

I didn't stand a chance against him. Not then. Not now.

I took a seat in one of the chairs and opened the bag, taking a hesitant inhale of the warm tacos and then a deeper one when it didn't immediately send my stomach into somersaults. And my memory flashed back to the last time I'd had tacos; it was the night of the storm.

While I ate, my eyes scanned the room. The colors were light—coastal, but the decor was modern. Not the typical vomit of seashells and lighthouse paraphernalia that places around here usually had. The space felt cool and comfortable. Relaxing with the stretch of ocean right outside the large windows. It could use a candle, though. A good scent to tie everything together.

"You okay?"

My head turned, and my jaw went slack. I was okay...until he came out of the bathroom wearing those sweatpants.

"Yeah." I snapped my mouth shut. "Just taking in the view." Of course, I was looking at him when I said it. I meant to turn toward the window, but I just couldn't. I couldn't tear my eyes from the broad stretch of his shoulders, remembering how it felt to hold them, or the hard expanse of his chest, or the way the steel of his muscles rippled under the hot wax.

Wanting him was the worst pregnancy craving I'd experienced yet.

My tongue swiped out, wetting my bottom lip as my gaze sank to the taper of his waist and then lower, where the gray sweatpants hugged...*enough*.

"What happened, Chandler?" I pulled my legs up onto the chair, holding my knees to my chest.

This time, the question looked like it wounded him.

He walked to the window and bundled his arms over his chest. Here, like this, he didn't look like an all-powerful billionaire who'd just promised to buy an entire hotel if my not-confined-to-morning sickness made me destroy a hotel room. He looked like a broken soldier. One who'd given everything to his final battle and still lost.

"My mom fell."

Only three words, and my gasp through the room was audible. *Was she okay? Was she...*my throat was too tight to let any question through it, my tongue too weighted from all the heartbreaking possibilities.

"My phone started going off at five thirty that morning. She'd fallen on her way to the bathroom. It was bad. I didn't even think, Frankie. I just left." His jaw pulsed, the muscles working up the courage to continue. "I got there, and they'd already flown her to the hospital. There was so much blood...she'd shattered her whole leg."

"Oh my god."

"I went to the hospital. She was in surgery after surgery after surgery. I didn't sleep. Eat. I didn't..."

"Exist," I said softly, the small word breaking his trance. His head turned slowly, his ragged gaze finding mine as he fought to swallow.

"Yeah," he croaked.

I felt the pain in his soul like it reached right out of him and wrapped its hand around my throat, so I offered him a piece of mine in return. It had been a long time since I'd felt that kind of pain. A long time since that wound had healed. But I'd never forget the memory or the pain.

"When Kit was injured at the marathon, we got the call and nothing else mattered. He had a lot of burns. Needed so many surgeries. We thought he was safe because he was home, and he almost died," I murmured. "The weeks he was in the hospital, it was like everything stopped. Like nothing could go on until we knew if he..."

"Would make it," he finished for me this time, his mouth pulling into a tight line before letting loose a heavy exhale. "The next time I could think about... anything, it was almost three weeks later. And then I remembered how I left...how you had no idea..." He paused and cleared his throat again. "I remembered about Lou's offer... about how I'd agreed to it the night before and pushed it through...and then I realized how much worse it must've looked...felt...when I disappeared."

My insides felt like a tornado trapped in a washer. A storm on the spin cycle. Everything I thought—my entire perception of that morning, of what transpired, of why he left—was all wrong.

"You agreed before you left?"

He nodded slowly. "That's what I was texting Tom about in the car as we left your mom's house. I told him I was going to sell to your sister and to get the paper-work moving."

"So, you didn't take the money and leave?" I murmured, my heart fluttering like a caffeinated butterfly in my chest.

"Technically, yes I did." His voice cracked on the single syllable, like even the idea of it was too painful to sustain. "But I never meant to. It wasn't my plan, Frankie. And that's why I gave it back."

My brows pulled tight. "I don't understand."

His mouth opened and shut on a muttered curse, and then he drove his hand through his hair. "I never wanted to take the money, but I never got the chance to fix it. When I realized—remembered everything that happened

—it was too late. The sale was done. Lou paid what she paid. So, I donated it back to her...in my mom's name."

My eyes went round, all the pieces clicking into place. Lou's excitement over the massive donation had been contagious. We'd all celebrated with her for days—for everything she'd be able to do now for the inn that had previously been on a five-year plan. I could still feel the buzz of her happiness and excitement, maybe because it was that strong, but also because it had come just a few days before I took that pregnancy test.

I lowered my chin, feeling the weight of betrayal start to suffocate out the breath of hope that filled my chest. So, he hadn't taken the money and disappeared. Not intentionally. *But why...*

"That was two months ago, Chandler." Two whole months that I'd believed the worst. That I'd been angered and hurt and forced a show of bravado unlike anything I'd ever felt before. "Two months..."

"I was going to bring Mom home. Get her settled. And then come...explain," he rasped slowly, weeding through the words. "And the night before she was going to be discharged, she had a pulmonary embolism. A blood clot in her leg traveled up..." I pressed my hand to my mouth to stifle a sob. "And it was everything all over again, except worse. She was already so frail from the fall. They weren't sure..."

He couldn't finish. Couldn't say the words. I remembered those moments—those days in the hospital with Kit. I remembered holding myself together for Mom. For Lou. I remembered being so broken inside it was only the pain clinging to every fiber of me that acted like glue to hold me together.

"She's back at Edgewood now. Stable," he said after a few seconds of being unable to finish his last sentence. "In a wheelchair and on a bunch of medication, but she's stable."

"Good," I choked out and swiped away a tear before it blazed a trail down my cheek, my lashes fluttering quickly to clear the rest away.

When I looked back at him, his gaze was waiting for mine. Dark and warm and containing the ashes of a hundred hardships he'd held contained, letting them burn down to his very soul to protect everyone else around him.

"Frankie..." he rumbled, and my lips parted. "I'm sorry."

A cry bubbled through my lips as I shoved out of the chair and went to him. I launched my arms around his neck, his arms instantly holding me close. The thud of his heart was heavy against my chest. Or maybe it was mine against his.

"I'm sorry," he murmured against my neck. "I should've...I should've done so many things."

My throat swelled tight as I tipped my head back, my hand finding the side of his face and lifting it until I found his eyes. "Me, too," I said quietly, my voice husky with a hundred emotions, only one of them winning out as my focus lowered to his lips.

"I came back to tell you I'm not going anywhere. I don't want to go anywhere. I want you," he rasped deeply, the words, their weight making me shiver.

"What does that mean?"

"Whatever you'll let it mean, baby."

It wasn't fair the way that word had become a

weapon—the smallest, softest sword against my independence.

My whole life I'd planned on being alone. And then I met Chandler, and I wanted something...else. And then I got pregnant, and now everything was off course. *Or maybe it was on course.*

"I don't know what I want it to mean," I admitted. The temptation was strong, but so was the fear.

As a general rule, I wasn't afraid of much. Even realizing I was pregnant...I was shocked, but I wasn't afraid. I loved kids. I was in a good place in my life. I had a good support system. I wasn't afraid of being pregnant or having a baby or even the change it would bring to my life. But Chandler...I was afraid of him. Afraid of how I felt about him and how easy it was to feel more.

"Well, I'll be right here waiting until you do."

I didn't want to think about the future. I didn't want to think about how one week of taking care of me and one heartbroken apology seemed to be all it took for me to want to hand my heart back over on a silver platter.

It wasn't characteristic Frankie...or was it? *To leap heart first into a situation without concern for the consequences?*

I swayed into his heat, relishing the hum it sent through my veins. "Chandler..."

I didn't know what I wanted for the future, but I knew what I wanted in this moment. *Him.* His mouth. His hands. His cock. I wanted to feel again—to be on fire. I wanted to let go of all my tightly clutched strings of control and be the only puppet of his pleasure. And he felt it, too, this magnetic pull that neither of us could escape.

I wasn't afraid of being alone. I was afraid of being without him.

"Tell me," he muttered, his nose nuzzling mine. "Tell me what you want."

"You," I breathed instantly. I wanted him. I wanted him here. In our baby's life. In my life.

"I'm yours, Frankie. For however you'll have me."

My throat tightened, panic seizing its familiar hold. "I want you," I repeated. "But I want to go slow."

"I'm not going anywhere, Frankie," he murmured like he could read my thoughts.

But when Chandler started to step back, I tightened my arms. "Not slow for this part."

"No?" He lifted a brow.

"No." I framed his face and pulled his mouth down to mine.

The kiss was everything. From the sweep of his tongue to the growl from his chest to the way it wasn't just my body that sighed into his embrace but my heart, too. It was nourishment after months of starvation. It was fire after weeks upon weeks in the cold.

His kiss felt like coming home, and it sprouted the seed I'd tried to keep buried. I was falling in love with Chandler Collins.

My head swam, and my body swayed, the whole of me on fire with ache. It ate at my cells. It devoured my breath. It feasted on my racing heart. And it was ravenous for more.

"Please, Chandler," I whimpered, afraid I'd go up in smoke if he didn't do more than kiss me.

"I've got you, baby," he rumbled, kissing along my jaw and neck.

His hands went to my top first, lifting the soft long-sleeve tee over my head, and then he lowered to one knee. I tried to stop the cartwheels my heart rounded in my chest. He looked up at me as he hooked his fingers in the elastic waist of my linen pants and brought them along with my underwear to the ground.

I didn't know what I expected next, but it wasn't for his hands to sink into my ass and haul me to his face, his tongue spearing straight for the nub of my clit.

"Chandler!" I gasped, and my eyes rolled back as I grabbed for his head, clutching his sinful mouth tight to me.

And then, on his knees, he backed me up to the bed, his lips and tongue latched onto my pussy as he pushed me back.

"Yes, Chandler," I whimpered, melting onto his tongue as he hooked my legs over his shoulders.

"You taste so good, my little flame. So fucking good."

I almost came at the endearment I thought I'd never hear again. And then he growled and doubled down between my thighs, licking and sucking until I couldn't catch my breath.

"Don't stop," I begged. Cried. Pleasure constricting around me until my hips bucked. I didn't know how starved I was for this—for him—until now. Until I was right on the edge of orgasm, his tongue sliding and sawing over my clit.

"More," I whimpered, grinding my hips up toward his mouth.

And then the world went upside down. Or I went right-side up and right on top of him.

Chandler flipped us so I was sitting on him, my legs framing his face that was buried between them. Gasping, I tried to lift up on my knees, but his hands on my waist stopped me. Held me. And then, holding my gaze, he let out a growl and set his tongue back on its path of complete clit destruction.

Between licks and sucks, I melted onto his tongue. I'd never felt pleasure like this before. So consumed. So powerful. My head tipped back, and my hips began to grind against his mouth, hard and demanding. Air scissored out of my lungs as I moved faster and faster, needing more. Needing it all.

"*Chandler!*" I exploded, my body trembling and almost tipping over as pleasure whipped like a hurricane through me.

I didn't know how long it took for my breath to finally catch, but he held me the entire time, his mouth gently coaxing every drop of my release onto his tongue like a man who'd never get enough of the taste.

I looked down at him, his dark eyes tangling with mine from between my legs. His face was wet with my want, and heat warmed my cheeks. I carefully slid off to the side of him, and he reluctantly let me go.

"Sorry," I murmured, fairly certain I almost suffocated him there for a minute.

"You're carrying my baby, Frankie," he growled. "You can fuck my tongue any time you need." And to prove his point, his tongue dragged over his sinful lips to make sure to claim every last drop.

I slid my gaze down his torso to where his sweats were massively tented around his arousal, and a fresh wash of want flooded through me.

Should I? Should we? Was it too fast when I said I wanted slow—

"I don't just want to fuck your tongue."

Instantly, the ease of his expression was gone, replaced by raw hunger. "Frankie..."

I reached for the stiff ridge, and his deep groan was melodic as I palmed his arousal.

I lowered his sweats just enough to free his cock, trailing my finger along the thick vein that stretched up his massive length. I shuddered as a wave of need went through me. *Damn, this pregnancy made me horny.*

"Frankie," he groaned.

"And what about this?" I asked huskily, rising back up on my unsteady knees and straddling him. "Can I fuck this any time I need?"

"God yes," he swore on an exhale as I dragged the head of his cock along my slick seam.

I felt like a goddess as I tipped my head back and let myself sink down onto his length. Inch after inch, I went slowly, letting my tight muscles adjust to him.

"I forgot how big you are," I murmured, and then let out a small sigh when he was fully seated.

Chandler was quiet for a second, his jaw ticking, before he muttered, "Don't worry, I won't let you forget again."

I bit into my lip, but my moan escaped anyway as I began to ride him. Like this, the tip of his cock bumped against my womb every time I bounced. It hurt and felt so good at the same time. *Just like the wax.*

Before long, the grip of pleasure had me in a choke-hold again. I lifted and rocked my hips, the friction heightening on my clit as he somehow sank deeper.

"That's it, baby. Take all of me," he growled, his hands tightening on my legs, or maybe he was helping them because I didn't feel steady enough to know how I kept moving. "I'm yours, Frankie. Yours."

At that, I gasped and faltered.

Without warning, he flipped us over, his hand tangling in my hair as he found my gaze. "I'm not going anywhere, Frankie," he swore with such bone-deep sincerity it made my breath catch.

And then he started to move. Long, punishing thrusts all the way to the center of me.

I was so stretched, so full, but I whimpered unintelligibly for more. And Chandler understood. He thrust deep and hard, hitting some buried pleasure point that either only he could reach or that only existed for him. I couldn't breathe. Couldn't think. Couldn't move.

"That's it, baby. Come again for me."

I couldn't do anything until he begged, and then my body orgasmed again so hard, this time I saw stars.

His ragged curse followed me over the edge as he drove himself through my release once—twice—and then came, his cock jerking roughly inside me, filling me with his cum.

"You okay?" he rumbled, placing soft kisses along my neck to my ear.

"Oh my god," was all I could say. "That was..."

"Incredible?" he suggested.

I moaned. "Dangerous."

He chuckled and pressed his lips to mine. I whispered, "I don't...I can't move."

"Don't worry. I'll take care of everything."

He would. I knew he would. *He always did.* Not because he had the money to or because I needed him to, but because I wanted him to. Because I trusted him. Because I...*no, Frankie.*

Too fast.

Too reckless.

Too real.

I curled under the covers, eagerly wading along the shores of sleep as Chandler cleaned us, then cleaned up from the takeout. I was almost out—maybe I was out when a low buzzing woke me, and I turned, searching for the source.

"It's mine," he said, striding quickly to the nightstand where his phone vibrated. "Dammit."

"Is it your mom?" Alertness sprung like ice water into my veins.

"No." His head shook. "Just the GC Holdings acquisition. It's coming to a head." His jaw flexed. "I'll take it in the hall. I'll be right back."

I sagged back into the pillow, listening as the door opened and shut. I didn't know how long it was that I slept or that he was on the phone, but when his weight dipped the mattress next to me and his arm reached over to rest protectively over my stomach, I opened my eyes long enough to think he had to have been on the call for a while because it was completely dark outside. But then he pulled me close, and the thought didn't matter anymore.

CHAPTER 26
CHANDLER

"All right, I think these should last you until... tomorrow."

Frankie shot me a glare that turned into a smile, admiring the towers of pumpkin spice candles I'd set out on the display. She wasn't kidding that these were her bestsellers. I couldn't make the damn things fast enough. It seemed like as soon as I filled the center table and then the second placement on the side shelf, I'd take one phone call from my secretary, Judy, and at least half of them would be gone.

"Am I making you work too hard, Mr. Collins?" she teased as I came up behind her, sliding my hand over her stomach and pressing a kiss to the crook of her neck.

"Never." I trailed my mouth up the soft column of skin, savoring the way she moaned.

"Is this a new one?" She lifted my hand and examined my thumb, a patch of peeled red skin signaling a fresh burn.

I grunted.

I turned her to me, capturing her chin in my fingers. "You know how much I love to burn for you."

Her breath caught, and I dipped my head to claim her lips, but her hand on my chest stopped me.

"Chandler."

"Yeah?" I pressed my hips against hers so she could feel how hard I was.

"Can we go visit your mom?"

I stilled, the question like ice water through my veins.

Mom was doing well—really well according to Tom, and I checked with him multiple times a day. But if I were being honest, the longer it went, the more I convinced myself he was the best person for her. The more I rationalized that it was my fault for what had happened and the risk I'd be taking by going to see her.

"Frankie..." I clenched my jaw.

"It's not your fault, Chandler," she said softly, and for some reason, I could believe it coming from her.

"I don't want to make it worse."

She made a soft sound. "What if you make it better?"

My chest squeezed. "How?"

"By telling her about the baby."

I took a measured breath. Mom would be thrilled. I could see her face now. No matter what tangle her memories were in, knowing she was going to be a grand-mother would bring her out of them. But it wasn't just the baby, it was Frankie I wanted to tell her about, too. And I didn't know if she was ready for that.

When it came to Frankie Kinkade, I was a beggar, not a billionaire, and I was willing to take whatever pieces of her, however meager, she'd give me. But every day that passed was one more bit of evidence to the notion that I wanted everything. I wanted her schemes and her smiles. I wanted her laugh and her body. I wanted this baby, and I wanted her forever.

And the moment I shared that with Mom was the moment Frankie had to know I wasn't going to let her go.

"Is that what you want?" I stroked her cheek with my thumb.

"I want her to know," she murmured, meeting my gaze. "Don't you?"

"I do," I said hoarsely, my throat bobbing as I swallowed. "But I don't want her to just tell her about the baby... I didn't come back here for the baby, Frankie. I came for you. So, if we go, it's not to tell her this baby is mine. It's to tell her you're mine, too."

Her lips parted, and I took the invitation rather than risk her protest.

It took only a second before her mouth opened to mine and a handful more before her arms wrapped around my neck and her body melted to mine.

"Chandler..."

"I want you, Frankie. I want us."

She drew a shuddered breath and then, in the softest voice, said, "Me too."

"Frankie—"

She framed my face with her hands. "I want us, too."

I kissed her again until we were both panting. Until I had her sitting on the edge of her desk, until her flowy fall dress was hiked up around her waist and my fingers were priming her slick pussy for my cock.

"Tell me you're mine," I rasped, stroking her G-spot until she drenched my palm.

She moaned and reached for the waist of my pants. "I'm yours," she said only once she had my cock in her hand.

I shuddered as she stroked me. Drew me to her. "Say it again."

She pulled my hand away and replaced my fingers with the head of my cock, finding my eyes as she tipped back onto her hands and murmured, "I'm yours."

I let out a low growl and drove my cock home.

"*Yes*," she moaned and wrapped her legs around me, my hips working slow, deep thrusts all the way to her womb.

This was always my favorite way to end the day, my hand resting on her growing stomach and my cock nestled deep inside her. But today, hearing those words...

"Again," I grunted, steadily picking up my pace.

"I'm yours," she repeated over and over, and each time I rewarded her with deeper, faster drives.

When I felt her muscles start to contract and her arms tremble to support her, I snaked my hand around her neck and hauled her lips to mine, sinking my tongue deep into her mouth and tasting her cry as she came.

I fucked her through the peak of her orgasm, torturing myself just so I could savor the way she melted for me, and only then did I finally let the pressure building at the base of my spine go.

I thrust as deep as I could go and let my release take me.

Minutes later, when our breathing steadied, I

pressed a kiss to her forehead and murmured, "We can go visit my mom tomorrow."

She tipped her head back, finding my eyes. "Good. Because I want to tell her you're mine, too."

My jaw clenched, and then I kissed her again...and we didn't leave her store for another hour.

"Tom," I greeted, and he hugged me.

It hit me that he'd only hugged me since he'd met me at the hospital that day. In all the years I'd known him—all the years we'd worked together—it was always a handshake and a nod. A professional veneer that he'd maintained for me.

"Frankie." He smiled and pulled her in for a hug. "It's good to see you again."

"It's good to see you, too." When she pulled back, Tom's gaze met mine, something unspoken passing between us.

Being around Frankie was like lighting my soul on fire. There was no only letting some of me burn.

"How is she?" I asked as he led the way into Edgewood's lobby. It was cozier with more people inside because of the cooler, fall weather, and a fire in the fireplace.

"Good." He nodded and smiled, the wrinkles and strain I'd last seen on his face at the hospital much less pronounced now. "Today's a good day."

Surprisingly, the shock and trauma from her fall

and then the embolism, or maybe just all the medications she'd been on, seemed to reconnect some of the wiring in her brain. At least, according to Tom, it had. I guess seeing me would put it to the test.

"I brought a cinnamon candle for her. I know she loved this one."

Not as much as she'd love her grandchild.

My heart was racing by the time we made it upstairs. Every step down the hall was another crank that made it beat faster. Harder. *What if she forgot? What if she got upset again? Hurt herself—*

I sucked in a breath, small, warm fingers sliding in between mine and giving them a squeeze.

"Frankie, we shouldn't." I tried to disentangle my hand, but she wouldn't let me.

Her eyes met mine, and her grip firmed. "You held my hair. Now it's my turn."

I didn't even get a chance to pick my jaw up from the ground before Tom opened the door. "Laura? Look who's here to see you."

My heart stopped, seeing Mom sitting there in her wheelchair. It was hard to see her like this, but not as hard as seeing her in that damn hospital bed.

She stared at me for a second that seemed to span forever and then smiled. "Chandler." I didn't realize I was holding my breath until she said my name.

"Mom," I rasped and went to her, bending down to pull her into a tight hug. "How are you?" I made sure I pulled back enough to see her face when she answered.

"Oh, I'm good, honey. Too good the way Tom takes care of me." Up close, I could see the fullness that had left her face and the purpling under her eyes and all the places where she bruised easily now because of her medications, but the way she smiled was all that mattered.

"Good. He knows I'll give him hell if he did anything less." I heard Tom chuckle with me, but my eyes only turned for Frankie. "I brought someone with me...to see you."

As soon as she could see Frankie, her smile went wider. "And who is this?"

She didn't remember Frankie, but it was probably better that she didn't remember much about that day.

"I'm Frankie." Frankie took it all in stride. "So, I brought you one of the candles that I made."

Frankie held onto the candle even when Mom's hands wrapped over hers to make sure it wasn't dropped.

Mom took a deep breath and blinked a few times. "Oh, Frankie. You know I love this one."

My chest squeezed, forcing me to clear my throat. *She remembered.* The scent made her remember Frankie, just like the ocean made her remember me and Friendship.

"I know you do."

"It's my favorite, too," I rumbled, catching Frankie's eyes when she looked at me knowingly. *My favorite because it was her scent.*

"I'm so happy you're both here," Mom said softly, looking between Frankie and me like there were some things she hadn't forgotten, like the look two people share when there is an invisible string tethering them together.

"Chandler," Tom chimed in. "I'm going to pop downstairs and check on dinner. Will you both stay?"

"Yes," Frankie answered before I had a chance, and

it was a good thing she did. I probably would've talked myself out of it, worrying it would be too much for Mom. And too much for Frankie.

Tom let himself out of the room, and when the door closed, Frankie looked to me. She waited for my lead even though her hand floated to her stomach. A movement I bet she didn't even realize she made.

"Oh, Chandler, I'm so happy you're here," Mom repeated, her memory flickering. "Come look at the new butterfly Tom brought me."

Frankie moved to the side, setting the candle on the small table, while I crouched next to her chair so I could take a look at the frame. It was a photograph. The orange and black butterfly perched on the edge of an equally orange flower.

"Beautiful."

"He took it."

My head turned. "Tom took this?"

She nodded. "He took all of the monarch photographs that were at the house and all the ones here for me."

My throat tightened. It wasn't until we'd moved Mom here that I realized how much she loved butterflies. Her bedroom in the brownstone I'd bought her in Boston was covered in these photographs, and when we moved her things, I remembered thinking it was strange that she hadn't put the butterfly photos elsewhere in the house if she loved them so much, but now I realized why. Because it wasn't just the butterflies in the photos that she loved, it was also the man who'd taken them.

There was so much I didn't know about their relationship—so much I'd missed. Overlooked because I didn't want to see it. But now, I saw it everywhere. All the things Tom had done for her over the years. The way he'd been there—steadfast and patient, loyal and loving. All this time, I hadn't been able to recognize it until I'd met Frankie.

"I didn't know that," I managed to say.

"He doesn't like people knowing how talented he is." She stared at the photograph with a look that made my heart thud, and then she looked at me and smiled. "Do you remember the one time we went to the beach in Maine?"

"Yeah," I rumbled, keeping to myself that she'd told me this story before.

"Well, there was an inn we stayed at. I don't remember the name, but the room I'd stayed in was decorated with butterflies, but there was one photograph over the nightstand of a monarch. I told him how much I loved it..." She trailed off, seeming to lose herself in the memory for long enough that I wasn't sure she was going to come back, but then she finished. "One comment when we were in be—there—and two months later, he gave me the first photo as a birthday present. So thoughtful." She lifted her hand to her cheek, wiping away the single tear I'd almost missed.

"Mom." I took her hand in mine and squeezed, my tongue growing heavier with the words that formed on it. "I have something to tell you."

"Oh, my. It must be something good." Her eyes twinkled. "You only worry about good things."

I swore Frankie made a little noise behind me, but I ignored it. "It is something good." More than good. It was everything. "Mom," I started again, taking a big breath before I exhaled the most precious part of my soul. "Frankie and I are having a baby."

Again, it took a second for the dots to connect. For her eyes to widen. Her jaw to drop. "A baby?" she whispered.

I nodded. "Yeah."

Mom let out a happy sob and pulled me to her chest. My arms shot out to steady her, her hold surprisingly strong for a woman in a wheelchair.

"I can't believe it, Chandler. I can't...I'm so happy," she said right as she promptly shoved me aside and motioned to Frankie. "Come here and give me a hug. Oh, I can't believe this. I'm so happy."

I sat back on the floor, resting my arms on my knees, and watched Mom gush and moon over Frankie. *My Frankie*. And she took it all in stride. Every tear, every hug, every laugh. She took it and gave it all right back at two hundred percent.

It was the first thing I'd admired about her. The first thing that drew me to her. The first thing of myself that I recognized in her. When we went into something, we went all in. Whether it was pretending to be her twin or haunting an old inn or having a baby together.

Now, I just had to convince her to go all in with me.

I listened as Frankie gave her every detail—weeks, due date, our baby's fruit size—all things I knew but couldn't help but be mesmerized as she spoke them. *I was going to be a father*.

The word—the concept—was still a sore spot. Not the gaping wound it was before but still tender to the touch. I was going to be better, the thought bolted through me like lightning. A better businessman. A better father. A better man. Whatever it took, I was going to show them all I was better.

"Excuse me a minute," Frankie murmured and stood. "I shouldn't have drunk that whole water bottle so fast."

My gaze followed her as she disappeared into the bathroom.

"What's wrong, Chandler?"

I turned back to Mom. "I love her." It might be a revelation to the world, but it wasn't to me. I'd fallen for Francesca Kinkade a long time ago, but like any good businessman, I'd kept my weakness to myself.

Mom's smile softened, and her gaze dropped back to the photograph of the butterfly before lifting back to mine. "You'll never get as many chances as you want to tell someone you love them, so you better start using all the ones you've got, honey."

Regret tainted the well of happiness in her tone. I could've told her that Tom always knew. That even if she hadn't said the words, he knew how she felt about him, just like she knew his feelings for her. But knowing and saying are two different things. Like seeing the sun through the window versus standing in its warmth.

One side of my mouth lifted. "Yeah, I guess I should." *And what would Frankie say to that?* "I just want to show her I'll be there—be better," I added, a prick of pain tainting my words. "I'm going to be better than him, Mom. I promise. And everyone is going to know it."

Instead of looking happy or relieved or proud, the only thing I saw on her face was concern. "You already are, honey. You have nothing to prove."

I tensed. She'd said those words to me countless

times in the few years before the dementia set in. So many times, it was one of the recurring arguments we'd had. That I was too focused on proving myself to the world, to *him*, and she worried.

I didn't want to argue with her now. I wouldn't. So, I swallowed down the bitter pill of disagreement and simply said, "I love you, Mom." The times I'd have left to say this to her, where she was this lucid, were dwindling.

"I love you, too, honey." The concern in her eyes deepened. She pulled her hand from mine and reached for the butterfly photo again. "Do you know why I love the monarchs?" She handed it to me.

I knew why she loved these photographs, but the butterflies themselves... "Because they're pretty?" I guessed.

"Well, they are." She nodded and rested her hand on my arm. "That was what drew me to them, but monarchs in particular are an incredible story of what is passed on."

I turned to her.

"Monarchs can't survive the North American winter, so every year, they migrate south all the way to Mexico. Four thousand eight hundred some miles." Her finger traveled along my arm like she was tracing their path. "But the incredible part is the ones that fly south aren't the butterflies that return north the following spring. It's their children's grandchildren that make the journey back north, back to the very same milkweed plants their great-grandparents left the fall before." Her hand steadied on my heart. "They come back. To a place they never knew. Only the future revisits the past."

"Mom..." I placed my hand over hers, my throat tightening.

"How do they do it? How do those great-grandchildren find their way back to a place they've never been?"

I swallowed over the lump in my throat and teased hoarsely, "Breadcrumbs?"

Mom gave me a gentle swat and then a soft smile. "There's always something that ties us to what's important. To what has been. Even when the people and the memories we thought anchored us there are gone."

I couldn't speak. My tongue felt like a thousand pounds, and my eyes burned with unshed tears. Even when she was gone—when the part of her that remembered me, remembered this, and remembered herself was gone—there would still be something greater that tied us together.

"This is your future, Chandler. She's your future." There were tears in her eyes, and I could tell this was one of those increasingly rare moments, not only when she was lucid enough to remember me and the past, but also to be aware of what was happening to her. Of what she was losing. Of what I was losing with her. And of what she was worried I'd lose without her. "Don't make the same mistake I did."

She looked to the door, and I realized she was speaking about Tom. "He deserved all of me, and I was too stubborn to give it until it was too late."

"Mom." I squeezed her hand, watching her lip quivered. "Tom loves you—"

"And I should've loved him better. Should've loved you better—"

"No—"

"Instead, all I showed you was that proving your

father made a mistake—proving that I didn't need anyone else—was the most important thing."

"Tom knows you love him." I couldn't argue anything else. I couldn't turn off that drive inside me. I couldn't.

"Now." She nodded. "Don't make her wait that long."

I handed the framed butterfly back to her, the symbolism making me understand why she loved them the way that she did. A reminder of the strength of the things that bound us together even when they couldn't be spoken or seen.

The bathroom door opened, and Frankie appeared, our eyes meeting.

Sometimes light isn't the only way out of the darkness.

"Is everything okay?"

I glanced at Frankie, realizing I'd been silent since we'd left Edgewood.

"Yeah." I nodded.

"You just seem distracted since your phone call."

I exhaled slowly. It wasn't the phone call that distracted me. It was the way Mom looked defeated when I'd left the table at dinner to take it.

"It was just an update on an acquisition. Confirmation really."

"So, it was good news?"

My half brother and his partner at GC Holdings

were reviewing my offer and would be in touch within the week to finalize the details. The last three years of my work had been for this moment, but for some reason, the news didn't feel as good as I expected.

But I didn't want Frankie to worry, so I reached for her hand over the console, pulled it to my lips, and murmured, "Yeah."

CHAPTER 27
FRANKIE

"I'd like to make an accusation."

Everyone turned to Chandler, his narrowed eyes moving around each person seated on the living room floor.

"Be careful, Chandler. This group is very clever," Gigi warned from her perch on the couch, excluded from the game during the last round because of a wrong guess.

"I think it was Mrs. Peacock in the dining room with the lead pipe," Chandler forged on, his tipped smile confident as he reached for the *Top Secret* folder in the center of the Clue board.

I knew he was wrong before he slid the cards out. I had the lead pipe card in my hand.

"Shit," he muttered a second later and shoved the cards back in the small envelope while Lou and Harper high-fived, Max and Violet shook their heads, and Jamie and Mom just stared each other down, their competitiveness almost as comical as the way Gigi was always the first one out. "I was so sure..."

I bit into the side of my cheek to keep from smiling. Failure looked adorable on him. Everything looked adorable on him. I swallowed a groan, wishing I could blame these thoughts on pregnancy. I did—I would, but I had a feeling in another five months, I'd look at him, the big, bad billionaire sitting on the floor of my mom's living room, agonizing over a game of Clue with my family, and still think the same.

I was in love with him.

The man who didn't believe in my ghosts. The man whose touch gave me an out-of-body experience. The man who made candles for me when the scents made me sick. *And the father of my baby.*

"All right, Frankie, you're up." Jamie kept order during game nights.

"It was Mrs. Peacock in the dining room with the candlestick," I declared and reached for the envelope, Chandler's gaze pinned hotly to me. A second later, I smiled and laid out the three cards in the center of the board. "I win."

"Of course you do," Chandler muttered, a small smile toying with his lips. "With the candlestick, no less."

I stuck my tongue out at him playfully, but the look in his eyes when I did it made my skin feel like tinder, catching aflame with the heat of his want. Nothing like feeling as though I were on fire in the middle of the living room, burning in front of my entire family.

For him.

Because I loved him.

"Winner cleans up," Harper said and pointed to the large charcuterie board next to her. It was one of three that had been passed around during game night, everyone picking as we played.

"Yeah, yeah." I grabbed it with a winning smile on my face, but before I could make it to the other two, Chandler had already grabbed them.

My pulse fluttered. Like my cards, I'd kept my emotions close to my chest. I'd let them swell and strengthen over the last two weeks since he'd said the words to me, but every time they felt about to burst, something held me back.

We went into the kitchen, followed by Gigi, who'd asked Lou to help her with some jam in the basement.

I went to grab Ziploc baggies from the drawer when Lou came rushing up the stairs and darted through the kitchen, her distress as explosive as a firework.

"Lou, wait!" Next thing I knew, I was following her into the hall and grabbing her arm. "What is it?"

She shook her head and tried to tug her arm away. "Nothing." She wouldn't meet my eyes.

"Not nothing. Tell me."

Her lips pulled together, the flutter of her eyelids exaggerated underneath her glasses. It took a few seconds, but finally, her shoulders dropped, and she said quietly, "Now I know how you feel." Before I could ask, she lifted her arm and unclenched her fist, a crumpled paper in the center.

No, not a paper. I took the label from her hand, my chest tightening as I unfolded it and read Gigi's handwriting, the single word stained with a tear.

Cheated.

My swift gasp punctured the air, and Lou let out a small cry.

"It doesn't have to mean that," I blurted out, shaking my head vigorously. It couldn't mean *that*. My shy, thoughtful sister deserved a better destiny than *that*. "It could mean anything. Just look at me—at mine. How long did I think that Chandler meant candlemaker?"

The question was meant for her—meant to strike a different thought in her mind than the worst-case scenario—but instead, it struck me.

He'd always been my destiny.

"I don't think there is anything it could mean that is good," Lou said and took a trembling breath, her eyes slowly going vacant. "It's fine. I have the inn now, and that's all that matters to me."

"Lou—"

"I think you're right, Frankie," she interrupted, a spark glittering in her gaze. "Maybe it does mean something different for me. Maybe it means I've cheated my way out of needing love to be happy."

Oh, no.

"You thought you were the one who got to escape matchmaking, but maybe this is proof it's been me all along. That I get to just be satisfied and focus on my dream."

"It...could." What else did I say? It could mean anything. It could mean nothing. *I didn't want it to mean this.* Not for Lou.

"Thank you." She pulled me in for a tight hug and then released me, saying, "I'm just going to get some fresh air," before disappearing outside.

I stared at the front door for a long second, wondering how I was going to fix this for her. *Wondering if I even could.*

"Is everything okay?" Chandler rumbled when I returned to the kitchen.

I nodded slowly, about to explain, when Gigi appeared at the top of the steps. "Francesca, where is your sister?" Gigi looked upset, too.

"I think she stepped outside."

"All right." The brightness in her eyes had dimmed. It was the first time I'd ever known Gigi's premonitions to be painful. "I have this for you, Chandler." She set a label face down on the kitchen counter. "Francesca can explain. I have to talk to Lou."

When she left, Chandler looked at me, then to the label, and then back at me again.

I placed my fingers on top of the rectangular slip.

"Gigi has...a thing. A gift, she likes to say," I began, my own curiosity itching to know what she'd written for him. "Sometimes, when she gets to know someone, she'll get a vision, usually a word or two, that generally reveals something or someone in their future."

"And this is mine?" His brow lifted.

"I know it sounds crazy, but I promise, it's the truth—"

"I believe you," he broke in and added with a tipped smile, "I know what you look like when you try to lie about the supernatural."

I pursed my lips and pushed the label toward him, my heart thudding louder. He reached for it and then paused, his gaze lifting to mine again.

"What did yours say?"

My jaw went slack, heat dousing my cheeks. My tongue took a minute to work before I could wet my lips and then trace out the syllables of his name.

"Chandler."

At first, he didn't realize I was answering him. His eyes narrowed in that probing way, but something on my face made him realize because then everything softened.

"Your...fortune was my name?"

My chin dipped, and it felt like him knowing this somehow connected the last of the dots inside me. All the pieces of my life—my past, my dreams, my future—all circled back to him.

"It was so long ago. When she gave it to me, I thought it meant my business because *chandler* means candlemaker."

His eyes went wide. "This was why she was so excited when she met me..."

Again, I nodded.

"So, all this time, I've been your destiny, and you're only telling me now?" he rumbled and stepped closer.

"I like to keep my cards close," I murmured softly.

He cupped my cheek and tilted my head up. "No, you don't like being told what to do."

A whisper of a smile teased my lips. Months ago, I would've hated the idea of someone knowing me this well, but now I ached for it—for him—like a drug.

I swayed toward him, my gaze drifting toward his mouth. "No one told me I had to fall in love with you."

I watched the rush of air pull through his perfect lips. Watched a different kind of fire ignite in his gaze. He reached for me, his intent clear.

"Wait, your label—"

He balled it in his fist. "You're it for me, Frankie. I never needed it written down," he growled and kissed me.

My curiosity melted under his caress. The hard

press of his lips. The deep swipe of his tongue. And then he drew back with a curse.

At first, I thought it was because he realized we were in the middle of my mom's kitchen and not the most private place for us to...but a second later, the real reason appeared.

He dropped the crumpled label on the counter and pulled out his phone, the screen lit up with an incoming call. "I have to take this. I'm sorry."

I started to catch my breath as soon as he left the room, but my heart I was afraid was too far gone.

"Frankie?"

I smiled at my mom. "What's up?" I went to the sink before she could get a good look at my face. "Lou and Gigi are outside," I offered up as a distraction.

"I'll talk to your sister later. I don't want to overwhelm her." Mom sighed, always aware of what was going on.

"I told her it could mean anything. It doesn't have to mean *that*."

Mom hummed, not taking the bait. "Is everything okay with Chandler? I saw him rush out of the room."

I swallowed through the tightness in my throat. "Yeah. Just a work call."

"This late on a Saturday?"

I breathed out slowly. "It's a big acquisition."

She hummed again and waited. Unfortunately for me, I could only scrub a cutting board for so long, and when I turned, she was waiting for me. Mom stood on the opposite side of the counter, her arms crossed and her expression firm. She looked regal.

"I'm going to tell you what I plan on telling your sister," she said and rounded the counter until she was in front of me. "Neither of you are going to settle for anything less than you deserve."

A cry bubbled from my chest, and she pulled me to her in a tight hug. I wanted to ignore it—the doubt itching in the center of my chest—but now, her words wouldn't let me. As much as Chandler had made me a priority. As much as he'd melted away all my anger and distrust and fear, there was still this—his dedication to his business. The common ground we'd had when we met. A thing I'd once admired was now the thing that could harm me.

But I didn't deserve to come in second place in the life of a man I loved. And neither did our baby.

Mom squeezed, and then, with a murmured, "I love you," went back to the living room, leaving me with nothing but those last words.

And Chandler's label.

I couldn't stop myself, my emotions were like a tangled, thorny knot in my chest. I grabbed the slip like it would inflate into a lifesaver. Instead, the word gutted me.

Freedom.

"I'm sorry about that."

My head snapped up as Chandler strode back into the kitchen, a different kind of hunger on his face.

"What happened?" I wanted to talk about anything except the elephant in my chest.

"The deal's done—or will be done," he said, a tentative smile breaching his face. "GC Holdings has nothing left. My acquisition of the company will be finalized this week."

Done.

Relief spread through me. *Why was I worried?* It was over—or would be soon.

"That's great." I went to him, knowing how hard he'd worked to finally erase this last piece of his father's legacy.

"I have to go back to Boston this week," he interrupted, the single sentence spearing straight through my chest. "I have to meet with them. Review the terms. Signed papers. This is only the first step. Once I take control of the company, I'll have to split up all the pieces. Sell what's failing and revitalize what's left. By the time I'm done with it, no one will be able to recognize any of the pieces that belonged to him. Like a butterfly from a caterpillar."

Pain speared through my chest. *By the time he was done with it, I wouldn't recognize him.*

"My doctor's appointment is this week. Another ultrasound," I croaked, only able to cling to concrete things at the moment.

His jaw tightened and released. Twice. Like two gunshots to my heart. "I'll try and make it back—"

"No." I shook my head and stepped out of his hold, something wild breaking loose inside me. "Don't."

"Frankie, please—"

I ignored his pained voice and moved around him, beelining for the front door and hoping Gigi and Lou had finished their conversation or taken it elsewhere.

"Frankie, please." He caught up to me on the porch. Before I turned, I noticed how the sky was devoid of stars tonight, like even they didn't want to risk my wish being made on them.

"I can't do this, Chandler. I'm sorry," I said, lifting my chin.

"I'll be there. I'll be at the appointment."

"Even if it's the same day as your meeting?"

"I—yes." His hesitation was his downfall.

"I'm sorry, Chandler." I forced myself to be strong. "You can be a part of our baby's life. A part of my life. But not...not like this." *Not where he had the ability to hurt me like this.*

"Please, Frankie. You don't understand," he protested, taking my balled fist in his. "I have to do this. After what he did, I have to."

"I do understand," I said softly. I remembered the anger that gnawed inside me, waiting for the moment I turned eighteen so I could change my name. I remembered the need to destroy anything and everything that tied me to the idea of my father after how he'd hurt Mom.

And that was why I couldn't be angry at him. I knew his hurt. I knew why he needed to do this. No one deserved to be chained to the past like that, especially by someone they loved—by someone who loved them.

I just wished his own happiness was the key to unlocking that chain and not his vengeance.

"I love you, Frankie." His hands tightened around mine as he repeated the words against my fingers. "I love you."

"I love you, too," I said, tears leaking down my cheeks. "But it's not enough."

It wasn't until I went to pull my hand from his that I realized there was something in it. *His label.* I uncurled my fingers and held it out for him to take.

"This is yours," I said softly, watching as he took the crumbled paper like I was giving him the remains of my heart—my heart that had the word freedom etched into its very beat.

It was what I was giving him. *Freedom*. Because I loved him too much to take it away.

"I hope you get everything you want, Chandler. I really do," I said and walked back into the house, leaving him to read his label alone. And free.

CHAPTER 28
CHANDLER

Tick tock.

I watched the clock like it was a bomb strapped to the boardroom wall. Ten minutes until the event that would change my future.

My attention slipped to my phone, opening my message to Frankie for the hundredth time that morning.

> I love you.

It was the first text I sent her every morning since I'd returned to the city earlier this week, and every night, I typed out a book on how the day went. I didn't want to leave things like this. I wanted her to know it would be okay if I had to be here, okay if I had to focus on this for a little.

Or maybe I was only trying to prove to myself that it would be okay when every minute that passed was evidence stacked that it wouldn't.

I swiped back and opened up my chat with Tom,

catching him just as he was typing out an answer to the message I sent him every morning.

> How is she?

His response appeared.

> Good today. She says you're being a stubborn fool.

My jaw locked.

> She knows why I have to do this.

> No, she doesn't. You've always been a better man than your father.

"Fuck." With a groan, I reached for the knot in my tie and loosened its strangle around my neck. Even with that, I couldn't inhale deeply.

I'd been after this company for almost three years now, carefully moving the chess pieces on the board. Closing in and cornering GC Holdings until I'd finally forced them here. *Checkmate.*

Now, all that was left was to deliver the final blow. Watch as they were forced to take my offer, signing over everything that was left of my father. Watch as they gave me the power to absorb it. Destroy it. To wipe him from its history and legacy and prove that I was the better man. *Prove to a dead man that he never should've left me.*

But instead of feeling energized—instead of the buzz I normally felt in the moments before I closed a huge deal—I felt a pit. A hollowness inside my chest that was eating me alive, its teeth sinking through my heart and soul.

Everything about this felt wrong. I felt nothing like the better man, instead, the thought of going through with this deal seemed more and more like a sign of our similarities. It wouldn't prove that I was better. It would prove that I was exactly like him, a man with no time for the woman who'd loved him and his unborn child.

A soft knock jolted my attention to the door. "Mr. Collins. Mr. Thomas and Mr. Mark Collins are downstairs. Should I send them up?" my secretary, Judy, asked. She knew something was wrong with me. She never would've needed to ask this before.

"Yes," I clipped.

As soon as she closed the door, I reached for my glass of water, only to realize I'd already drunk all of it. *Empty*. Just like me. Just like I was—would be without her.

I couldn't do this.

I didn't want to do this.

The door opened, Judy introducing the three grim-faced suits who followed her in. "Mr. Collins, Mr. Thomas, and...Mr. Collins and their lawyer, Mr. Masters."

I stood, watching the two majority shareholders of the GC Holdings and their lawyer approach me. My heart beat too hard against my chest, and I swore buttons were going to start flying from my shirt.

You can't be all business and be here, Chandler. I'm sorry.

It hit me. I wasn't all business. I was bitter and broken. I wanted to prove I was enough to someone who wasn't even around to see it—who didn't deserve to see it. And I wanted to prove I didn't need anyone, just like my father hadn't needed me.

And I was wrong about it all.

I thought I admired Frankie's independence and her strength. Her ingenuity and her determination. And I did. But I fell in love with her confidence. Her self-worth. She never needed to prove who she was or what she deserved—never questioned it, even when it made her break her own heart.

Mom was right. *I was a fucking fool.*

"Mr. Collins..."

I blinked and realized I was still standing and staring vacantly at the words swimming on the paper in front of me. The deal. The death of my father's company.

Mr. Thomas glanced at my half brother and their lawyer and then looked back at me. "Is everything okay?"

"No." I shook my head slowly. "Everything's not okay."

Their eyes went round. "Mr. Collins, we've reviewed the deal—"

"The deal is off." I picked up the packet of papers and tore it in half.

"Chandler, please." Mark rose, addressing me out of desperation, his knuckles white at his sides, and I froze. His body trembled. "So, you'll ruin us because of our father?"

That was the corner I'd backed them into—the choice either bankruptcy or being bought. And I no longer recognized the man who'd done that. I didn't want to recognize him. And I didn't want this to be part of the legacy my child would inherit.

"No." I shook my head. "I have to go, but someone will reach out in the next day or two with the details and the deeds to the five properties I outbid you on. I'm signing them over to you, no strings attached."

"What—"

"They're yours. They should be enough to turn the company around." I yanked my tie loose, grabbed my jacket, and headed for the door.

"Chandler—"

I turned at Mark's voice and met his gaze. "Let's do better," I said, and as soon as I recognized the unspoken agreement in his eyes, I walked out of the room, shouting to Judy to call for my car as I jogged for the elevator.

I didn't even take a second glance at my office—the room where I'd practically lived for a decade. I wasn't coming back, and for the first time in days, I took a full breath.

"Chandler, what happened to the deal?" Tom answered on the first ring. I wasn't surprised he already knew. I had a feeling he would be Judy's second call after the valet.

"Fuck the deal," I said, a crazed smile spreading over my face. "I don't want his business, Tom, and I don't want to ruin it either."

"Chandler..."

"All this time, I thought to be better than him meant I had to be better at business. That I had to do more.

Own more. Be worth more." It sounded so stupid now. "But it's none of that. None of that matters. I told Mark I was transferring over the deeds for the last five properties we took over. It should get them above water again."

The tires squealed as I pulled out onto the street, heading straight for the highway.

"Are you there?"

"Yes." He sniffed. "I'm sorry. I'm just..."

"Proud?"

"I've always been proud of you, Chandler. I wouldn't have worked with you otherwise," he said, his voice worn soft. "I've always been proud of you, but today...today, I get to be happy for you."

My pulse galloped. For the first time in days, I felt alive. Hopeful. Filled with purpose.

"Tom..." I took a deep breath, one last knot still remaining in my chest. "Why do you think my father willed me the inn?"

I always saw the inn as a burden. A random, decrepit piece of real estate that he'd willed to me like a slap in the face—a reminder in death of how little I'd meant to him in life. But maybe it wasn't that at all. Maybe he saw what I was willing to sacrifice to the grim shadows of success. Maybe he saw what I was becoming—that I was becoming like him. And maybe the inn was meant to make me reconsider.

"I think Geoff had a lot of regrets at the end, not unlike many of us do, but was smart enough to know what happened...what he'd done...it went beyond an apology," Tom said, carefully parsing every word. "He knew what the inn meant to your mother. I think he hoped it could mean something more for you."

Sometimes a light isn't the only way out of the dark-

ness, and sometimes words aren't the only way of an apology.

"Thanks, Tom," I said over the lump in my throat.

"Don't thank me. Just go get your girl."

My foot settled harder on the gas pedal. "That's my plan."

I hung up with Tom as I pulled onto the highway north, the invisible string tugging stronger toward Frankie. *Toward home.* I went to set my phone in the cupholder, and something crunched underneath it. Muttering a curse, I fished out what was jammed in there, and my heart stumbled when I realized what it was.

The label.

I'd shoved it in there the night I'd left Frankie's mom's house five days ago, too upset and frustrated to care about a stupid jam label that was supposed to dictate my future—a future it seemed to be indicating would be free of Frankie.

But this time, when I looked at the scrawled word, I read it differently. *Freedom* wasn't freedom from Frankie or a relationship. It was freedom from the weight I'd been carrying all these years. The burden to prove I was better. The expectation that I didn't just have to be the best, but I had to destroy what was left of my father in the process.

And that was all because of Frankie.

She wasn't just my heart or my soul or the mother of my child or my future, she was my freedom. She made me free to feel. Free to live. Free to love. And I'd almost fucked it all up. *Again.*

I reached for my phone once more, my thumb

hovering over her name, itching to call her now and beg. For forgiveness. For her future. For mine.

But it wasn't enough.

I scrolled down and tapped on another contact instead, my jaw locked tight until the line picked up.

"Hello?"

"Lou, it's Chandler. I need your help," I said and didn't want her to agree before telling her exactly what I was thinking. "I need to borrow the inn."

"Is this another one of Frankie's schemes? Because I don't want to be involved in any more plans. And I don't want my inn involved—"

"No, it's not," I cut her off. "This is all me. Frankie has no idea. And it's not a plan. It's a proposal."

CHAPTER 29
FRANKIE

"Lou, pick up your phone. You can just cryptically text me like this. You're worrying me," I scolded into my sister's voicemail, locking the door to my shop with shaking hands and then opening up her text message again.

> You need to come to the inn right away. It's an emergency. Don't tell anyone else.

I tried not to think of how many times I'd made my sister or my brothers or my cousins feel the exact same way I did now with my many dramatic requests over the years. But this was different. Lou always tried to solve problems on her own, and if she couldn't, she was very discerning when she decided to ask me for help because she knew, well, she knew me.

My pace picked up as I got closer to the inn, reaching a jog when it came into sight.

From a distance, I saw the gate was ajar, and my stomach turned. And then I saw it—the flickering in the front windows like there was a fire inside. *And not a good kind.* It was too dark to look for smoke, and all I could think was that Lou was inside—in danger. I started to run. The front door was left open, too, requiring no effort to push through it.

"Lou?" I called into the space, panicked. "Lou, where are you? What's going on? Lou—"

The swivel of my head stopped at the living room. I hadn't been inside since the day Chandler left, but it wasn't the beautiful remodeling and careful restoration of the space that caught my breath. Nor was the inn on fire like I'd feared.

It was Chandler standing in the center of the room where the air mattress had been, surrounded by dozens and dozens of candles. *His and mine.* Sweet cinnamon and spiced masculine. A combination I hadn't considered. *Ours.*

"Chandler." I found my voice, and even though my heart hurt to see him, especially in this place, I managed to step just over the threshold of the room. "What... what are you doing here?"

"I'm here for you, Frankie. I love you."

I bit into my tongue to stop the cry my heart wanted me to make. "Chandler, I told you, this isn't going to work." I scrambled onto the excuses I'd given before like a life raft in the middle of a storm. "I'm not saying you can't be here or be a part of our baby's life, but I can't...I won't let us come in second."

He took a step toward me, and I tensed like a deer in headlights, prepared to bolt the second he got too close. I'd walked away from him once, and in the last five days, being alone with all the reminders and memories and messages from him, I knew I wasn't strong enough to walk away a second time if he touched me.

I thought I was strong. Determined. Resolute. But so help me, I missed his embrace. I missed waking up next to his warmth and spice. I missed working all day in the comfort of his presence and spending all night exposed to the heat of his touch. I loved him, and I hated that I had to break my own heart because I loved him too much.

"I won't either, Frankie."

I shook my head like my emotions were dust I could shiver off. "No. You can't say that. You left again. For your business—because of your father—"

"I walked away from it, Frankie. I gave...I restructured the arrangement with my half brother. I'm giving them back the properties I acquired so they can stay in business."

"What..." My head was swimming. I couldn't believe what I was hearing.

"Taking over it wouldn't make me better, Frankie. It would make me the same as him. A man who destroyed things," he rasped. "And I don't want that to be my legacy."

"But your business..." I was rapidly losing my foothold in resistance.

"I'm walking away from all of it. I should've walked away a long time ago when Mom got sick. I don't need the money. Haven't for a long time."

My heart pounded like a jackhammer on cocaine, blood humming in my ears. "What?" I shook my head. "No. You can't. It's your business, you can't walk away from it. I would never ask you to. I have my own business, I know how important—"

"No, Frankie. Your business is your passion. My business was a weapon. A tool to gain wealth and power to prove I was better than my father. You started your business to remind people of the pieces of the world they love. I started mine to prove why the world should love me," he insisted, and even though I was shaking from the sincerity in his words, I was frozen in place as he moved toward me. "But I don't need the world to love me, Frankie. I just need you to."

My finger buttoned over my lips as soon as a cry escaped them. I didn't even feel the tears in my eyes until blinking sent them racing down my cheeks.

"Chandler..."

He unfolded something in his hand. It took longer than it should've to recognize his label from Gigi because my eyes swam with tears.

"You're my freedom, Frankie. The reason I have a future. A life. The reason I have to smile," he said quietly, and I couldn't stop myself from sobbing. "You're the reason I have to love."

"Chandler, please." I begged for mercy as he came to stand in front of me, his big hands framing my face.

"I love you, Frankie. And if you'll at least hear me out, I have a new deal I'd like to offer you."

I only had to breathe him in to know I would say yes to whatever it was.

"A new deal?" I managed to rasp. My mind was so scrambled by his presence—his proximity, *his scent.*

"The last time we were here, we agreed to one week to prove the inn was haunted." His hand cupped the side of my face. "This time, I'd like to propose something a little more permanent."

I should've seen it in the bright embers in his eyes or

heard it in the husk of his voice when he said the word *propose*, but Chandler Collins had always been an expert in surprising me.

My jaw lowered along with him until he was on one knee in front of me.

"Francesca Kinkade, I'd like to propose a new deal," he said and materialized a ring box from his pocket, drawing the lid open. "Forever with me so I can prove how much I love you."

The sight of him swam in front of me, tears obscuring everything except the unimaginable swell of happiness in my heart.

"And if I say no?" Even my tone betrayed that impossibility.

A small smile tugged at his lips. "Then I have a lot of candles here to help convince you to say yes."

I shivered and laughed. "Resorting to threats to get me to marry you?"

"It could be worse. I could be resorting to ghosts." His grin softened and then disappeared. "Will you marry me, Frankie?"

I bent forward and brought my face to his, the flicker of the candles turning into a glowing haze around us. "Yes, Chandler. I will marry you."

His mouth claimed mine, firm and demanding, and the instant explosion of electric heat made my knees tremble.

"I love you," he drew back and repeated, sliding the delicate diamond flower ring onto my finger.

"I love you, too."

And then he was standing, and I was in his arms, my toes barely scraping the ground as he held and kissed me.

"How did you do all of this? I can't believe Lou..." My sister was fanatical about the inn and keeping everything under wraps and untouched until it was ready to open...but she'd let Chandler use it for this.

"I'm not the only one who thought you deserved some of the magic you give to everyone else."

A fresh round of tears washed over my cheeks. "And you knew I'd say yes."

He grinned and lowered his mouth to mine. "I only make deals I know I'll win."

I tipped back, evading his searching lips a moment longer. "You didn't win our first deal. The inn is haunted."

"I guess we'll just have to stay the night for you to prove it."

"Really? Lou said—"

"Your sister said I had free rein of the inn for one night."

"What did you have to promise her?"

He brushed a strand of hair back from my face. "To make you happy."

I cried and smiled at the same time as I said, "She let you off easy. I guess I'll have to make you work for it."

He growled and came for my mouth again, pulling me tight to where I could feel his thick length pressing against my stomach. "Oh, I plan on working for it all night, my little flame."

CHANDLER
EPILOGUE

"A wedding and a baby shower was a genius idea. Pure genius." Gigi pulled me in for a strong hug.

"It was all your granddaughter," I confessed, my gaze sliding over to my wife.

My wife.

More than any sale or acquisition or any number of zeros in my bank account, making Frankie mine was the most rewarding thing I'd ever accomplished. Every day since I'd asked her to marry me right here at the inn, I'd felt lighter. *Free.*

"She is something, isn't she?" Gigi looked at her granddaughter with the kind of pride that couldn't help but fill me, too.

Heat thrummed through my veins, my gaze traveling back to the woman who held my heart...and carried my baby.

Frankie had holly woven into her hair and a fur

shawl draped over her shoulders. A winter goddess in a flowing white dress that fit just a little too damn snug over her chest, her breasts so full now that we were in the last trimester. *And sensitive.* My new favorite pastime was worshipping them until she came.

"Yeah."

"They both are." Her gaze softened—saddened—a little when she looked at Lou.

Frankie's twin was in a deep emerald dress standing by her side. She looked happy, there was no question. But as someone who'd seen her that night at the house after she'd read her own label, there was a weight about her. Frankie still wouldn't tell me what was on it, and I wouldn't ask. It was obviously something a whole lot more than the responsibility of the inn that she'd shouldered so effortlessly.

"She'll figure it out. Whatever it is," I assured her quietly, knowing it weighed on Gigi to have given her the message.

Four months with the Kinkades were plenty to appreciate Lou's understated resilience.

"Congratulations, son." Tom appeared, pushing Mom in her wheelchair over to me, and drew me into a hug.

The last three months hadn't been a walk in the park. Dozens upon dozens of video conference calls not only to get GC Holdings back on its feet, but to finally hand over the reins of the Collins Corporation to the capable people who'd watched me bury myself in the quest for its success for too long. But thanks to Tom, it all got worked out, and when it did, he officially retired.

"Thanks." I held him close. I didn't call him dad because at this point in our lives, it didn't seem right, but out of all the words I could use to describe him—friend, mentor, business partner, love of Mom's life—it was the qualities of a father he most represented.

I pulled back and looked down at Mom, feeling the familiar pang in my chest.

"What a beautiful wedding. The two of you look so in love." As she said it, her head tipped back to Tom. "Thank you for inviting us..."

"Chandler." I smiled, even though it hurt.

"Oh, how wonderful. My son is named Chandler..." She trailed off, her gaze turning foggy like it did every time the present tangled with the past.

She rarely remembered me now. The regression of her memory happened quickly after we'd told her about the baby. I knew it was going to happen—thought I was prepared for it, but I wasn't sure it was something one could ever prepare for. The first time she looked at me like a stranger, I thought I would break, but Frankie was there, holding me together.

Sometimes light isn't the only way out of the darkness.

She might not remember, but she was still here. She still smiled every time we brought her candles. She still celebrated every time Frankie told her about the baby and showed her ultrasound photos. And she still loved to tell her stories about Friendship, and the inn, and the monarchs.

Her memories might not be there, just like that first generation of butterflies that migrated south in the fall, but there was an instinct that drew her back to me. Instinct that made her always share memories of when I was a kid. At the park. At the beach. Instinct that brought her back to a place she knew without knowing. A place where I still felt her love.

Only the future revisits the past.

"I'm glad you're here," I murmured and bent down and hugged her.

She didn't remember me, but she hugged me like she had all my life, especially in the moments when she was happy for me. "Me too, Chandler. Me too."

I straightened, and Gigi, seeing that I needed a moment to collect myself, stepped forward. "Laura, I'm Gigi, it's a pleasure to meet you."

They'd met a dozen times before, but Mom was always meeting new people nowadays. Except Tom. And for that—for him—I was grateful.

I turned instinctively to Frankie, her gaze tangling with mine.

"Go," Gigi murmured, shooing me in the direction of my wife, and then gleefully diving into how *she* and her *premonition preserves* were responsible for today's wedding. It was a story she'd told Mom a dozen times, but Gigi loved to tell it, and Mom never remembered it, so it worked out for the both of them.

I wove through the crowd, following the string that brought me to her.

"Chan—"

I cut her off with a kiss. One that was heavy and slow like an anchor mooring me to her.

Nox cleared his throat. "You want us to cut the party shorter?"

I looked at Frankie and smiled, drinking in the sight of her flushed cheeks and hooded eyes.

"I think Lou would be pretty mad if you pulled the fire alarm."

"Who said anything about a fire alarm?" Nox laughed. "I have a better idea." When I looked at him, he smirked and added, "A little ghosting goes a long way."

When I looked at Frankie, she drew her fingers across her lips like she was zipping them closed, effectively revealing who had been her accomplice when we'd stayed here all those months ago.

My eyes widened, and then I laughed. "You know," I said, "we never got Frankie's sleeping bag back from when you took it."

His head cocked, and he grinned. "I never took a sleeping bag." With that, he winked and walked away.

"Seriously?" I turned to Frankie.

She shrugged. "He insists it wasn't him."

"Interesting," I murmured and pressed my lips to her forehead, wishing I could carry her upstairs right now and finally get her alone, but I wouldn't.

"Thank you for everything, Lou. You too, Max." I smiled at my sister-in-law and her cousin, who'd supplied all of the flowers for the celebration. "This is incredible."

Today—our wedding was the soft opening for the Lamplight Inn. Lou had spent two weeks of sleepless nights and endless preparation to open its doors for tonight and welcome friends and family for our wedding celebration, and when the weekend was over, it would be the public's turn.

"Of course." Lou smiled back.

"Anything for family," Max added, and then tipped his head to Lou. "You've got a good setup here. I really think you should add wedding services to your business plan."

Lou blushed. "Let's just get it open to the public first and see where it goes."

"Speaking of opening day. How many arrangements did you say you needed?" Max was supplying fresh flowers for the lobby on Monday.

"I'll show you." Lou hooked her arm in his and led him away, leaving Frankie and me alone in the sea of people.

And I wasn't going to waste a second of it. I pressed my mouth back to hers, my tongue sliding along the seam of her lips that instantly melted open for me. The preparation...the ceremony...the whole day had flown by, and having to share her with other people for most of it wasn't something that I was used to anymore.

"Chandler..." She sighed and pulled back, catching her breath in small bursts. "We can't."

"It's our wedding. We can do whatever we want," I said, wrapping my arms around her and pulling her to my front.

"No, we can't," she murmured, her face glowing.

I lowered my head and rasped next to her ear, "I never hear you complaining when I do whatever I want to you."

She shivered and reached for my hand. "You're right. I'm convinced," she said, pulling me toward the hall. "Let's go upstairs."

"Are you sure? You're supposed to be the resilient one."

"I don't want to wait." Her head tipped up, her eyes smoldering. "You're my husband, and I want you now."

Fuck. Well, there was no staying now—not without every wedding guest getting a front-row show to how fucking hard I was for my wife.

She took my hand and started to lead me toward the stairs.

"Francesca!" Gigi called, her swath of freshly dyed red hair appearing in front of us.

I stepped behind Frankie, using her and our baby as a shield for my arousal.

"Where are you two off to?"

My and Frankie's eyes collided, and then she had an answer. *She always had an answer.*

Frankie leaned forward and said in a loud whisper, "We're making sure there are no ghosts left upstairs." *That was my wife.* "Don't tell anyone. We don't want them to worry."

Gigi's eyes went round, and then a slow smile spread across her face. "Your secret is safe with me."

I caught the old woman wink before Frankie pulled me up the stairs. We made it to the first landing before Gigi's voice rang out once more.

"Oh, Francesca!"

I bit back a groan and watched Frankie look back.

"That reminds me. I have your sleeping bag."

My and Frankie's eyes crashed together. *Gigi had been the one to take Frankie's sleeping bag that first day?* By the time we looked back, Gigi's bright red perm was bobbing through the crowd.

"The whole time..."

Frankie threw back her head and laughed as she pulled me the rest of the way to the second floor. We made it without any other interference, but we didn't make it into our room before my mouth was back on hers.

We bumped and banged into walls and doors, our hands too busy unraveling our clothes to pay enough attention to our surroundings. I was panting by the time I closed our door, and Frankie's dress had fallen so low on her shoulders, the edges of her nipples peeked out from the fabric.

"You're incredible," I rasped, drinking in the sight of her, my very own flushed Greek goddess.

"Chandler..."

I pulled her back into my arms, my mouth branding hers. Desire burned away space and clothes. It charred sounds and surroundings. It engulfed everything until there was nothing left but the way our bodies melted together. The way Frankie rose up over me, my hands roaming her stomach and breasts as she rode my cock hard, chasing the release we both needed.

Hopefully the music below hid the way she screamed.

"I love you, Mrs. Collins," I said a little while later, the two of us lying in bed, listening—feeling—the happiness surrounding us.

"I love you, too, Mr. Collins," she murmured, giving her ass a little wiggle where it was pressed against my cock.

I let out a low groan, feeling my body start to stiffen. "Frankie..."

"Do you think they're wondering where we went?"

"Gigi has our excuse," I grunted and pressed my lips to the crook of her neck. "We're ghost hunting before the grand opening."

"And if no one down there believes in ghosts?" She shivered and turned toward me.

I lowered my mouth to hers. "Then I guess I should make you scream again to prove that there are."

A LOOK AT BOOK FOUR:
THE INNKEEPER

Elouise 'Lou' Kinkade doesn't do love stories.

She runs an inn, manages a mile-long to-do list, and dodges her siblings' matchmaking efforts like a pro. But when a drunk Hollywood actor takes a dive down her stairs, Lou's quiet life turns into tabloid bait.

Desperate to avoid a scandal, Lou does everything she can to help her unconscious guest, and somewhere between the ambulance and his hospital bedside, she's mistaken by nurses and then parents for his girlfriend. And correcting the lie? Not exactly convenient.

But not everyone's convinced.

Wade Stevens has spent his life building up the reputation and success of his family's law firm, while his brother has been content to break every rule in the book. He's not surprised that his younger brother ended up in a coma, but he's shocked by the beautiful woman at his bedside. Lou might be smart, successful, and maddeningly charming—but Wade's not falling for an act. Or her. Probably.

One lie. One inn. One unexpected complication neither of them saw coming.

AVAILABLE NOVEMBER 2025

Rebecca Sharp is a contemporary romance author of over thirty published novels and dentist living in Pennsylvania with her amazing husband, affectionately referred to as Mr. GQ.

She writes a wide variety of contemporary romance. From new adult to extreme sports and forbidden romance to romantic comedies, her books will always give you strong heroines, hot alphas, unique love stories, and guaranteed happily ever after. When she's not writing or seeing patients, she loves to travel with her husband, snowboard, and cook.

www.drrebeccasharp.com
Rebecca Sharp's Sexy Little Sharpies